THE BLACK GOD'S WAR

SPLENDOR AND RUIN

BOOK I

MOSES SIREGAR III

THE BLACK GOD'S WAR

"... A tale spun with a degree of elegance I did not fully expect. The Black God's War is a great example of how there are extremely talented indies."
—Ron C. Nieto's Stories of my Life Blog

"If you want to read a talented new author with a flair for storytelling, you should definitely pick up this story."
—Two Ends of the Pen Blog

"Siregar's debut is an excellent example of the quality the indie author scene is capable of ... More like this, please."
—Signal dot Noise Blog

MOSES SIREGAR III

"Moses is a fine writer deserving of success and I think that it will follow. I really enjoyed Moses's work."

—NY Times Bestseller David Farland

"The Black God's War is, to date, the finest example of quality independent fantasy I've seen … This is what indie publishing is all about and I have no qualms about recommending this great novel."

—Indie Fantasy Review

"I don't give many 5 star reviews … I find I really can't stop thinking about this story. Unforgettable story, intriguing characters, compelling journey with unexpected twists—in short, a very satisfying and engaging read."

—(5/5 stars) MotherLode Review Blog

"… a rather brilliant climax that left me grinning from ear to ear …By the time you flip to the last few pages, I hope you have the shivers just as I did …"

—Journal of Always Reviews

"An inventive tale with high command of craft."

—Scott Nicholson, Bestselling Ebook Author

"For such a short piece of work, it is surprising just how much complexity Siregar managed to fit into this novella … [The] novella is an introduction to what I think will be a great novel." (Review: 8.5/10)

—FantasyBookReview.co.uk

"The writing is tight, the characters well-drawn and deep, and the world feels alive and many-layered … this is no one- or two-dimensional and predictable plot/conflict, but rife with undercurrents and tensions that just spread out like so many strands of a spider's web."

—W. Brondtkamffer's Blog

"Siregar's strongest suit may be the character development on display, as the royal siblings and a few other characters exude their personalities and frailties in a believable fashion."

—Skull Salad Reviews

For Molly, Athens, and Mom.

Thanks to Homer and Carl Macek (Robotech).

"Every old poem is sacred."
-Horace

Chapter 1:
Sing Muse, of Hades and Light

IN THE KINGDOM OF REZZIA, inside the highest chamber of the grand minaret, ten-year-old Lucia looked out to see her father, King Vieri, on the balcony. He lifted her newborn brother high above his head, and the masses, hundreds of feet below, roared with devotion.

Father, what are you doing! she thought. *Be more careful with our savior.*

Lucia glanced down at her mother resting in the birthing pool. The queen's black hair clung to her neck, all of it soaked by the holy waters.

"You did it, Mother!"

Kindness brightened her mother's face. "Thank the gods, dear. You have a brother now. A very special brother. Go, join your father and wave to the crowd."

"You stay here and rest. I'll wave to them on your behalf."

Her mother laughed. "Thank you, Lucia. That sounds perfect."

Lucia crept toward the archway leading to the balcony, which wrapped around the circular chamber. She squinted, fighting the midday sun. Tears soaked her father's cheeks as he presented the pink baby to the faithful. Nature had tattooed thorny red and black vines on little Caio's hands and forearms: the holy markings of the Haizzem.

As she gazed at Caio, a spiritual energy filled her body with peace and warmth. Her spirit soared. *The teachings are coming true!* A Haizzem had come again, to rescue all the world. Her brother would conquer Rezzia's foes and bring the gods' light to everyone.

Lucia skipped forward to participate in the royal scene. She looked down at tens of thousands of pilgrims in their cream robes and felt dizzy. The clay-white acropolis of the holy city sprawled across the desert plateau: massive domed structures, spiraling minarets, and temples of the ten gods supported by grand columns.

She clutched her father's ceremonial *cremos* robe to steady herself. The fabric was bloodied; he had obeyed the scriptural commandment for Rezzia's king to oversee the birth of his own Haizzem son. She felt so lucky, knowing every Rezzian alive would love to be in her place, touching the king's garments and the words of divine power stitched into them.

Her father pressed the baby against his chest, and pushed Lucia backward with his free hand. He raised up baby Caio and beamed his joy again.

The rejection shattered Lucia's bliss.

Her father's face, with his heavy brown eyes and his perfectly trimmed beard, always showed his serious nature. But as he admired the baby—so high above the masses—he transformed, positively euphoric. He looked at Caio with such true love, a look Lucia had never, ever seen before.

Lucia's vision darted from her father to her brother and back again. *Your love for me is a lie.* She dropped her head and long vermilion hair fell around her face. She wouldn't cry. Not then. Not in front of him.

The crowd's chanting grew louder and louder. They cried out in the old tongue, we love and adore him!

"Havah ilz avah Haizzem!"

"Havah ilz avah Haizzem!"

"Havah ilz avah Haizzem!"

Hearing their hypnotic praying, her pummeled heart found direction and clarity. The truth struck her as she watched the red-faced babe glowing against the sky: Her brother was divine. According to the warpriests' teachings, it had been hundreds of years since a Haizzem graced the kingdom with his holy presence. They said Caio would possess spiritual gifts beyond compare, including the ultimate proof of his godliness: He would be able to resurrect one person from death during his lifetime.

I don't matter anymore. Her royal duty would be pure devotion to him. As his only sibling, she would always be there to provide whatever he needed. All of her divinely given powers from the goddess Ysa would serve him alone.

A deep voice rumbled from inside the chamber, startling her: "My dearest Lucia."

The man's tone upset her stomach. "Sweet Lucia, come see your mother."

She turned, tugged on her father's robe and pointed into the sacred chamber. "There's a man in there!"

The chanting of the crowd grew louder. Her father pushed her away, harder this time.

"There's a man in there!" Lucia stomped one foot and swung her fists through the air.

Her father ignored her again. She crept closer and peeked inside. A colossal man stood behind the now much bloodier waters of the birthing pool, looming above her mother. The black of his bald head and muscular arms was as dark as the leather he wore from his shoulders to his thighs. A single orange teardrop decorated the skin beneath his left eye. She recognized the face from scriptural stories: The Black One, the god Lord Danato.

"Your mother is going away forever." Danato crossed one arm over his chest and put his other hand to his jutting chin. "Come, be with her while you can."

Lucia breathed heavily with her mouth open. Her mother's face had looked peaceful before—now it was tortured.

"Father, come quickly!"

King Vieri continued to hold Caio in the air, but turned his head to look at his daughter. "Everything is fine, Lucia."

"No! There's a man in here. Muh—Muh—Mother needs you!"

He lowered the newborn to his chest and waved to the crowd.

"Father, listen to me!"

As her father strolled into the chamber, all joy drained from his face. He ran straight to Lucia's mother, never looking at the black god. The queen's blood was reddening the holy pool.

"Don't you see him?" Lucia asked.

Her father laid the baby on the stone floor.

Her mother opened her pained, bloodshot eyes.

Lord Danato sauntered toward the stairs that led to the attendants below.

With his hands on his wife's sweating brow, her father prayed to his god.

"Lord Danato did this to her!"

"Get help, Lucia!" Her father wouldn't take his eyes off his queen's face.

Danato stood in the archway between Lucia and the stairs, gazing at her with stony eyes.

"Lord Danato is there! Don't you see him?"

"Stop your nonsense. Get help!"

Her mother screamed, a harrowing sound Lucia knew she'd never forget.

The baby cried.

8

Her father kept yelling at her.

Lucia froze. She watched her mother, feeling helpless and mute.

Danato's voice boomed, "I am sorry, Lucia. There is a reason for all things."

She looked down to avoid the god's stare and squeezed her eyelids shut. She found the courage to look up again.

The Black One was gone.

Vieri pulled the queen's lifeless body from the pool and squeezed it against his trembling chest. His wailing drowned the holy chamber in woe.

Lucia's dreams of an idyllic life flew away from her, sucked into the black god's tempest of dust.

Chapter 2: The Ten

Three years later.

"COME HERE, CAIO. Let me dress you." Lucia lifted Caio's infant *cremos* so he could see it. He looked up, but kept playing with his toys in the center of his room. She scanned the walls of her brother's spacious chamber as she waited. The earthen white surfaces would be painted later this day, after Caio chose his patron god or goddess.

As Lucia approached him with the silky robe in hand, he scurried away with his toy horse gripped in his tiny fingers. "Come back here, silly boy."

Caio dropped to his knees in the corner near his bed and let out his adorable laughter. Lucia stood over him and felt her heart warming as she savored the innocent sound.

"Come now. You need to wear this."

"Aw."

"No more joking. Father will be upset if you aren't ready."

Caio stood still and let Lucia pull the robe over his head. So excited for this day, Lucia had put on her own *cremos* robe earlier that morning.

Caio ran back to the rug. She followed and sat beside him.

"We're going to the atrium and there will be lots of people there. Remember what I told you. A man with silver hair is going to ask you to pick your favorite statue of the gods. Whoever you choose will be your special deity for the rest of your life."

"Can you help me?"

"You need to choose on your own. This is very important. Just choose whoever you like the most. Any god you pick is good—except for the one with no hair. He is very mean, Caio. Do you understand me? Don't pick the man with no hair."

"Yes, Lucie."

"Good. It will be very easy. Very, very easy."

10

Lucia played with Caio as they waited for their father. They pretended his toy animals were being fed by the goddess Jacopa, the mother of nature's abundance.

The arched, wooden door creaked as it opened and her father entered the room with a satisfied gleam in his eyes. Lucia smiled at seeing him happy, a rare sight since her mother's death.

"There's my special son!" Her father squatted as Caio ran to him squealing with joy. "On his special day." Vieri pressed the side of Caio's face against his chest and hugged his tiny body. "Ready?" he asked her.

"Yes. Can I hold Caio's hand and lead him? He'll be more comfortable—"

"No." He shook his head as if she'd asked an ignorant question. "Our people will want to see him with me."

I'm the one who takes care of him, she wanted to say. *You should let me do it.*

"Caio, has Lucia explained what is going to happen?"

"Yes." Caio nodded his head vigorously.

"Good. Put your hands together like this and pray with me. Good."

Lucia knelt and did the same, thinking it's what her father would want her to do.

"We pray to you, The Ten of Lux Lucis, to lead Caio to his ideal patron today. My Lord Galleazzo, we pray thy will be done." He prayed to his chosen deity, the god of most Rezzian kings.

King Vieri stood, lifted Caio into his arms, and carried him out of the room. Lucia followed behind them so her father wouldn't see any disappointment on her face. Her father's heavy footsteps echoed through the wide clay halls, while Caio talked to himself in his tiny voice.

Muscled soldiers guarded each corner, standing with stately posture. Lucia tried not to stare at them, but she found their sculpted bodies too tempting to ignore. As usual, the soldiers did not look back.

As they wound through the holy palace toward the atrium, the chanting and commotion of the pilgrims grew louder, as if they were coming upon a great waterfall of human voices.

The king stopped at the twisting stairs leading down to the cavernous hall. Lucia peered through the cloud of sweet incense. Directly beneath the circular opening in the clay roof, dim sunlight reflected off the clear pool. On the other side of the stone path around the water, the ten alabaster statues of the gods towered over thousands of devotees.

11

Religious ceremonies typically required worshipers to wear their sacred cream *cremos* robes to honor the unity of The Gods of Light. But on this day, the people celebrated the diversity of the gods with dress unique to each divinity.

From below, a powerful voice shouted the prayer, "Havah ilz avah Haizzem!" The crowd of hundreds repeated after him before they observed silence.

Lucia followed her father down the wide steps. A gathering of dignitaries received them at the landing. She recognized some of the most senior warpriests, bald men in loose, white tunics that covered all but their hands and feet. She recognized the three highest-ranking Strategoi, military commanders in tasseled red uniforms; one of them, a cheerful man with curly hair, winked at her. Tiberio, the highest warpriest, The Exalted, stepped forward muttering prayers and sprinkled holy water on Caio's forehead.

Tiberio took Caio and carried the young Haizzem through the crowd. Lucia followed beside her father. They walked past worshipers of the goddess Vani. The men and women jumped in place with their hands in the air, wearing colorful jewelry and crowns made of lavender flowers. One of them caressed Lucia's hair as she walked past.

Silver-haired Tiberio led them toward the pool and statues, to the front of the crowd, between the statues of Lord Galleazzo and his wife, the goddess Jacopa. By the statue of Galleazzo, the stately followers of her father's patron god wore golden sashes across one shoulder, over their short white tunics and leather girdles. They bowed to their king and then kept their heads low.

The barefoot devotees of the goddess Jacopa mostly wore primitive dress, earthy, non-dyed clothing. Each of them held either a pomegranate or an orange. Lucia assumed they brought the fruits to give to Caio if he chose their goddess.

The statues of Lord Danato and his sister the goddess Ysa stood across the circle. Lucia gave a quick glance at the bald, black-clothed devotees of Lord Danato. Many of them had a tattoo of an orange tear beneath their left eyes. Seeing them, Lucia felt unclean beneath her skin.

She focused on the devotees of the goddess Ysa, her patron goddess, The Protector of Man. The men and women who worshiped Ysa wore red metal circles in their earlobes and clean yellow dresses or tunics. The metal symbolized the goddess's holy shield, a relic Lucia knew she would be entrusted with some day.

Tiberio placed Caio on the ground before the statue of Lord Galleazzo, the traditional choice for a future king. "Choose your god, young Haizzem." Tiberio sprinkled more holy water over Caio and stepped back, still muttering prayers.

Good luck, Caio! Lucia felt so excited she wanted to squeal.

Caio looked up at Lord Galleazzo's statue and smiled, but turned to his left and continued along the ancient stone path around the sunken pool. King Vieri's eyes drooped in disappointment.

Her brother looked up at the joyful goddess Orazia and giggled, leading to contagious laughter erupting around the atrium. Behind the statue, Orazia's worshipers cheered. The beloved of Orazia stood out with their bright, parti-colored clothing.

Caio continued to the statue of broad Lord Sansone, The Servant of Man. Miniature black anvils hung from the corded necklaces of the god's worshipers. They wore common, coarse wool and looked sturdier than the other devotees, many of them powerfully built. Little Caio turned his head and studied the statue with a mischievous smile.

The crowd held its breath.

The boy lifted his head and walked on, his stubby legs carrying him to the statue of the goddess Vani, The Bringer of Love. He left a tiny red object at the goddess's feet and kept moving around the circle. Lucia realized he'd dropped a toy pig he must have carried with him.

Caio approached the statue of powerful Lord Danato, The Black One, and stopped directly under the god's frowning glare. The boy looked around the circle for Lucia. She waved to him and barely shook her head 'no.'

Her brother walked to the goddess Ysa. Caio turned his head from one side to the other as he studied the goddess's armor, rounded shield, and sword. He sat and put one of his little hands to his cheeks, as if contemplating. Ysa's devotees lowered themselves to their knees and prostrated to the young Haizzem. He turned back to Lucia and smiled his dimpled smile, picked himself up, and moved on to the next god.

Behind the statue of Lord Cosimo, the god's male followers wore only loincloths, while Cosimo's female devotees covered their bodies in loose, purple robes. Caio raised his red and black hands and clapped them for The Lord of Miracles before continuing on.

He skipped to the goddess Mya. Vines covered her statue as well as the next statue, her brother Lord Oderigo. Vine circlets wrapped around the foreheads of

Mya's worshipers. Vine-wrapped cloth belts decorated the followers of Lord Oderigo. Their devotees shared in common sea green and royal blue tunics running down to their ankles.

Caio skipped on toward Lord Oderigo. He stopped, chuckling unselfconsciously for some time as the crowd laughed with him. He walked between the statues of Oderigo and Mya, off the stone path, then sat on the hard clay and stared at the pool.

A ray of sunshine burst through the smoky air and landed on Caio and the two statues beside him. The vines adorning Mya and Oderigo miraculously grew down the statues, onto the floor, and crept toward the boy. The vine from Mya wrapped around his left forearm; the vine from Lord Oderigo wrapped around his right.

"Havah ilz avah Haizzem!" The Exalted shouted, and the crowd repeated the chant ten times.

Lucia realized that either Caio had just chosen two deities or they had chosen him. Mya and Oderigo, brother and sister, like the goddess Ysa and Lord Danato. The vine-blessed followers of Mya and Oderigo rose to their feet and cheered as Caio stood, many of them weeping and wailing with joy.

"My dearest Lucia."

That sick voice again.

From behind the statue of Lord Danato, the black god himself appeared, tall as his likeness. His coal eyes froze her with terror. She couldn't feel her body.

Lord Danato walked in front of Ysa's statue.

Stop him, my goddess! Ysa!

The vines trailing from the statues of Mya and Oderigo seemed to be holding Caio's tiny body in place. He giggled, playing to the crowd, and the people filled the atrium with their laughter again. Their chuckling sounded like mockery in Lucia's ears.

Danato walked in front of The Lord of Miracles.

You're jealous he didn't choose you!

Lucia came to her senses and ran past her father, past Tiberio, past the statue of the goddess Jacopa. "Stop him!" she screamed. "Lord Danato's going to kill Caio!"

Caio looked at her with his mouth wide open.

She ran in front of Lord Oderigo's statue just as Danato stepped behind the vine-covered goddess.

14

A hand gripped one of her upper arms. "Lucia!" her father said through clenched teeth. "This is no time for jealousy."

Lucia struggled to breathe. *I'm not*, she wanted to say.

"Warpriests, take her away. This is the Haizzem's day."

Lord Danato stepped behind Caio. "Sweet Lucia, do not fear your Lord."

"Get away from him!" she yelled back.

Two bald warpriests lifted her from under her arms. She struggled at first, but it was no use fighting them.

Goddess, please save my brother. Please save him!

The men carried her back through the crowd. She swallowed her voice and strained to see Caio through the throng. Once they lifted her to the top of the stairs, she saw Lord Danato again, staring up at her with his hand resting on top of Caio's skull. Caio didn't seem to notice. The warpriests carried her into a hallway, out of the public's view.

She squirmed. "Let me down. Let me walk."

They released their grips and one said, "Then go on to your room. We'll follow you there."

The military Strategos with curly hair entered the hallway. His eyes shone with concern above his rosy cheeks. "Is everything all right, Lucia?"

"No! Caio isn't safe."

"He's absolutely fine," the man said. "Perfectly all right. Can I walk with you?"

Lucia clenched her jaw and stared at him.

The Strategos put his hands on the shoulders of the two warpriests. "Let me handle this."

They bowed to the older man and stepped back toward the stairs, watching her as they exited.

The Strategos put his hands together near his solar plexus. "My name is Duilio. I'm sorry you're upset."

"Lord Danato intends to kill my brother. If you want to help me, go now and protect him."

"Your father and the warpriests won't let that happen. I promise you, everything will be fine. I will walk with you, Lucia. Let's talk."

She squeezed her fists, wondering if she could run past him to get another look.

"Lucia, don't make your father angry again. Let's walk together please."

15

She spun around in defeat and began walking toward her chamber. They passed two statuesque soldiers. Lucia kept her gaze down.

Outrage and embarrassment boiled inside her.

She erupted, turning and pounding her fists against the hardened clay wall.

Duilio held her arms. She screamed through gritted teeth like a trapped animal.

"It's all right, Lucia. It's all right. I know you've been through a lot."

"Let me go!"

"Tell me, do you know about The Lord of Miracles?"

"Of course I do." She relaxed a little.

Duilio released her. "Will you join me in praying to him?"

Lucia slumped down onto the floor and leaned her back against the wall. "No. I only pray to Ysa. I don't even know if she hears me."

"Of course she does, dear. You once chose her on a day just like this, on your special day, and now she watches over you."

Just like the goddess Jacopa looked after my mother?

"If you don't want to pray with me, I would still like to pray for you."

"Do what you like."

"My Lord Cosimo, I humbly beseech you to grant Lucia your miracle. She worries about Lord Danato harming her brother. Please intercede on Lucia's behalf. Please heal the source of her fear. Will you please? She is our royal daughter. Her brother needs her. Her father needs her. Rezzia needs her. Look after her. She more than deserves your grace."

Lucia felt a little calmer as she heard Duilio praying.

"I saw," she said before stopping herself. *You won't understand.*

"What did you see?"

"Nothing. I'm going to my room."

Lucia stood and turned her back to the Strategos. She ran to her room and heard Duilio following her at a distance.

'*'

The Black One shadowed Lucia as well, invisible to the eyes of men. The black god visited Lucia again that night, after she drifted off to sleep. It was the first of many more nightly visits from the god, and the onset of Lucia's transformation.

16

"The descent to Hades is the same from every place."
-Anaxagoras

THE FIRST STANZA

TO BRAVE THE DIVINE

Chapter 3: A Sacrifice for Apollo

Caio's nineteenth birthday. The day of the Dux Spiritus ceremony in Remaes.

JURG FORCED HIS WAY across the white, stone plaza, plowing ahead on his good leg while dragging the aching, lame one. At the end of his long journey, he held just one target in mind: the Haizzem boy.

The exotic, curving architecture of the Rezzian holy palace loomed over the crowd with its religious gravity. Behind it, the vanishing sun fell onto the desert horizon.

You're an ugly people with an uglier religion, he thought, *but you've made one beautiful thing—this white city. I'm glad to see it before I crumble to dust.*

The pilgrims pressed in on Jurg from all directions, muttering prayers in their guttural language and shouting exultations. Their saccharine incense filled his nostrils, making his stomach sick. Jurg smashed his way through the crowd with his thick forearms, his bloodied Andaran garb staining their immaculate *cremos* robes. The Rezzians just swayed in worship, lost in ecstasy.

In a sea of white, Jurg was a haggard red stain.

Good thing most of the freaks are gone. Those who'd left had already gotten what they wanted; their holy savior had touched them. Now Jurg was one amongst a crowd of only a few thousand. His chances of intercepting the Haizzem might still be good.

Walk faster, you damned, useless legs. You're not that old, are you?

Bashing his way through the crowd gave him little guilt, but leaving his people and family still weighed on his mind. He'd left the forests of Andars weeks ago, knowing he would probably never breathe in their crisp sweetness again. He'd yet to stop worrying about what would become of young Sky, Dag, and Idonea.

Amazing, how easy it is to approach this Caio. After the day's Dux Spiritus ceremony, the Rezzians' passion now focused on just one man, no longer two. The king retained his political throne, but the military power now belonged to his son; the religious savior was the new Dux Spiritus of Rezzia's armies. Ironically, the young man was also believed to be a great healer.

The hypnotized crowd faced the palace, the Haizzem, and the setting sun. All at once, the people dropped to their knees in prayer, giving Jurg a clear view of the man he'd come for.

The Haizzem was like the brightest star on a hazy full moon night, the only one shining in the fog. Something about his kind face was so captivating that Jurg stopped to stare. Like most Rezzian men, the Haizzem's thick, dark mane fell around his shoulders; but Jurg found the boy charming, even beautiful.

The young man had touched and supposedly blessed more than a hundred thousand Rezzians on this day. His filthy robe must have been grabbed by nearly everyone who'd approached him—yet the boy radiated remarkable warmth and energy.

Jurg experienced a rare moment of joy. At last, the long journey felt worthwhile. As he saw the guards around the new Dux Spiritus, he began to question his plan.

The Haizzem stood three levels up, on the giant steps that curved around and led up to the holy palace. More than a hundred soldiers formed a wide semi-circle around him. An enormous warden stayed close beside the new Dux Spiritus, scanning the crowd with hawk-like eyes set in a gentle face; his short blond hair stood out in the sea of dark Rezzian features. Jurg's blond hair did, too. The Haizzem's protector would see him soon.

A shame my body isn't what it used to be, he thought, tasting more blood in his mouth.

Many of the guards closed their eyes in prayer. Others had already turned toward the massive archway of the white palace. It must have been a welcome sight to them after the long ceremony and parade. Unfortunately, because the steps were so wide, Jurg was not nearly as close as he'd hoped to be when he approached the Haizzem. Jurg could burst past the soldiers' line, but the blond would be ready to intercept him.

So be it.

As the flock prayed in silence, the savior looked up and locked eyes with Jurg. If the stories about the Haizzem's spiritual powers were true, the boy might already know why he had come.

'*'

Caio gave the sun a melancholy glance. *I'm not ready for this day to end.*

He turned to face an elderly woman and felt the gods' love coursing through his heart.

"My knees," she pleaded as she grabbed his *cremos* robe.

"I know, love."

He quickly kissed his red and black fingers and touched her knees. *Your miracle please, Mya.* Caio sensed that she would be healed of her arthritis within days. The woman stumbled back with an empty look and a young man pushed his way ahead of the devotees, into her place.

After Caio blessed a few more, his protector and friend Ilario whispered in his ear the words he'd been dreading.

"It's time to go, my Haizzem. The sun is setting."

Caio would have to leave the holy city tomorrow. To join his father's war.

Ilario wasted no time, organizing the soldiers in a wide arc and putting them between the people and their Haizzem. Caio ran forward and pushed against the soldiers' line, reaching with outstretched fingers to the crowd. They rushed toward him, grabbing at his hands and sleeves. The soldiers stood their ground, and Ilario pulled back on Caio's robe.

Caio held his ground. "You'll have to pull me away if you want me to go."

Ilario's powerful arms wrapped around Caio's waist. Caio decided not to fight him. His friend pulled him backward, up two more steps.

"Stop." Caio raised his left hand. "I'll pray with them once more."

Ilario stood aside.

Caio turned to the crowd. He kissed the fingers of his left hand, then his right. He raised his hands high, and the crowd dropped to its knees. Most of them put their heads to the ground in prostration. Caio scanned not only the crowd, but also their hearts and minds. "In my absence, keep faith and devotion to the gods of Lux Lucis in your hearts."

The crowd responded in unison: "Havah ilz avah Haizzem!"

During the moment of silence that followed, a ragged figure emerged from the crowd and looked up at Caio. Aggression gleamed from his reddened eyes, though Caio sensed that the poor man felt only sorrow. They looked at each other fearfully and Caio tried to impart his grace to the foreigner through his glance. The man shook his head violently, and Caio's heart felt stabbed by what was about to transpire. He knew if the man had focused on his gaze a moment longer, he would have received all he came for; instead the blond Andaran man began barreling toward him.

The foreigner slammed into a praying soldier with his bear-like shoulders and arms, knocking the Rezzian onto his back. The next closest soldier threw himself at the man's legs, but the Andaran jumped over him with a hoarse yell. The foreigner sprung onto the step below Ilario and Caio.

The crowd looked up at the scene and pressed backward with shock as Ilario drew his sword, stepped forward, and yelled at the onrushing man, "Stop!"

The Andaran kept coming. He released a tormented cry and drove straight for Ilario.

No, Lord! Caio beseeched his vine-covered patron, The Lord of The Book of Time. All movement, save his own, slowed to a crawl. Caio surged forward and pulled back on Ilario's shoulder.

"He doesn't intend to hurt me!" Caio slipped between the two, and the normal flow of time resumed.

The Andaran fell down on his knees, grabbed Caio's revered feet, and began to wail.

Caio yelled to his protectors as they sped toward him, "Let him be! He means me no harm." He held the man's head and caressed his matted hair.

The crowd continued scattering away. Someone screamed that the foreigner carried the new plague.

Ilario held his sword high, ready to strike. "You don't need to help him."

"His disease cannot harm me," Caio said.

Ilario took three steps back and sheathed his blade. He closed his lips and looked around at the crowd while Caio consoled the sobbing foreigner.

Caio searched the man's emotions and felt his concern for his family. He spoke in the man's native tongue, "Feel the goddess Mya's cool grace, my brother. Receive her healing warmth in your heart." He squatted and leaned over to kiss the back of the man's head and his cheeks. He tasted the man's sweat and tears.

Then she appeared.

The goddess Mya revealed herself to Caio alone. Her short dress made of lush vines left her shoulders and knees bare and elegant. Her soft brown hair gathered behind her head, tied loosely enough for some to hang neatly around the sides of her face. She sat down on the other side of the sick man and stroked his back to comfort him, looking down with a countenance like a calm lake.

The man's body writhed with spasms. He cried and pleaded in Andaran, "Help me. Heal me or make the suffering go away. I've come so far."

"I know you have." Caio leaned closer and whispered in the man's ear, with an arm around his shoulder, "She will help you, if you rest in her grace. Everything else will take care of itself."

The man stopped shaking. His entire body surrendered and relaxed on the pale clay. He rolled onto his side and showed Caio his blissful face. His arm beneath his body reached up to the sky with palm upturned, then fell flat against the ground.

Mya, why?

The goddess's eyes flashed toward her beloved before returning to their downward gaze.

Caio cradled the dying man's head in his hands and looked into his faraway eyes. "She blesses you. She wants your suffering to end. She will protect you in the afterlife."

Though I wish she would save you, and return you to your family.

The attention of the hushed crowd focused on Caio as he held the dying man.

The peeling skin on the man's face glowed as his pale lips stretched gleefully. He whispered, "I never believed in your gods ... Not once in my life."

The foreigner's eyelids closed.

Ilario stepped forward and rested his strong hands on Caio's shoulders. "Let's go. You need to rest."

Caio stood up and looked at the crowd with sadness. He raised his hands as the guards reassembled in their formation. Those nearest to him prostrated again and the rest followed, all of them moving downward in a gentle wave.

The dead man's body lay abandoned on the wide step. Caio struggled to put the man's family out of his mind.

"I will return soon, after our victory. The gods of Lux Lucis watch over you." Caio put his hands together prayerfully and a warm tranquility took root amongst the faithful. They chanted in unison:

"Havah ilz avah Haizzem!"

"Havah ilz avah Haizzem!"

"Havah ilz avah Haizzem!"

22

Chapter 4:
The Remonstrations of Achilles

Two days later.

ILARIO'S HORSE CRESTED THE DRY HILL with Caio beside him, giving them their best view of the reinforcements since they had set off from Remaes the day after the Dux Spiritus ceremony. Elite spear throwers from Satrina and light cavalry from Lympia marched with the legions of heavy infantry from the holy city. The organized procession stretched westward past the distant horizon, ten soldiers wide and thousands of soldiers long.

"Isn't your army impressive?" Ilario asked.

Caio glanced in Ilario's direction with a grin. "You're still trying to get me used to the 'my army' concept?"

"As usual, my Haizzem, you've read my mind." Ilario put his heel to his stallion and they started down the hill. Below, the Neda River ambled across the road, flanked by desert trees.

Caio leaned toward Ilario. "It will be a long time before my father's boots fit me, if they ever do."

"You should keep an open mind. Maybe they will soon."

"Only in my nightmares." Caio winked. "At least I'm blessed to have good company with me."

"We need to have a talk." Ilario pointed to the river. "Let's have a rest by that cluster of trees?"

Caio glanced up at the red sun. "Even Lord Galleazzo would welcome the shade."

They dismounted on the soft earth by the riverbank, under the cover of long-limbed trees. Ilario grabbed two waterskins off his dark chestnut steed and waited for the warpriests to lead their mounts to drink. The percussive chirping of the insects came as a welcome change from the clamor of the marching army. Ilario inhaled deep breaths to savor the refreshing, moist air.

23

More than a dozen horse-pulled water wagons rolled up to the river. The servants and slaves rushed around, refilling the urns. Hundreds of soldiers milled about, many of them heading to the river to drink and bathe. Many more gathered around their Haizzem to receive his blessing.

Ilario stood beside Caio and scrutinized each man who approached him. At least they were quick about walking up to him, bowing, and moving on after Caio touched their foreheads. One man held up the line to ask Caio to pray for his family, but no one lingered too long. Eventually, the crowd dispersed.

"Shall we?" Ilario started for the grove he'd spotted earlier.

"What is it you want to talk to me about, brother?"

"Can you tell? What do you sense from me?" Ilario asked.

"I can feel your sense of responsibility, not only to me, but also to our kingdom. You probably want me to embrace my duty as Dux Spiritus."

Right again. "I've watched you for nearly ten years now. It's strange to see you like this. You're not a pessimist."

Caio rubbed his forehead. "This campaign has gone on for more than nine years, and we've made little progress. I don't even believe in this—"

"Then that's a big problem. You are our Haizzem. You are our Dux Spiritus. *You* must lead us to victory."

"And I'd rather be in Remaes, healing the sick and comforting the bereaved, leading worship in The Reveria, not praying over the funeral pyres of soldiers who didn't have to die."

"These men left their homes to fight for your father. Now they look to you. You must show them they haven't fought in vain, that their brothers haven't died for nothing. If you don't dedicate yourself to winning this war, many more will fall."

"I have to take lives to save lives."

"Unfortunately, yes. That's the way it is. That is your duty and you need to accept it."

Caio exhaled a loud breath. "You're right." He frowned. "I don't have a choice, except between killing Pawelons or letting our men be killed. That's not much of a choice, is it?"

"No one ever said war is the most noble thing a man can do, but once this is done you can do better things."

"Maybe afterward I'll finally have time to heal the world? All those I could help if I weren't going to this gods-forsaken canyon?"

"Your father nearly defeated Pawelon on his own. With you and Lucia beside him, we'll have the power of four gods, Caio!"

"Yes, I know. I only have to ask my goddess to kill for me. I'm sure The Compassionate One will want to do that."

"Put your trust in history. Haizzem win wars. You were born to do this."

Caio looked away and kept quiet for some time. "It doesn't feel like it. Maybe I'm not like the other Haizzem."

"But how would you know? You've never had to do anything you didn't want to do."

Caio continued walking, giving no answer.

"I apologize, my Haizzem. I shouldn't have spoken to you like that. I beg your forgiveness."

"You could never offend me, Ilario. It's only that ... until this I've always enjoyed doing the things that were expected of me."

"Your father's put a lot of faith in you. You cannot disappoint him."

They entered the grove and came upon a unit of ten soldiers resting. Ilario commanded them to rise. The men stood and bowed, muttering, "Havah ilz avah Haizzem."

Ilario waved his hands. "Clear out."

"Yes, sir." They hurried away. One of them walked up to Caio and bowed his head to receive the Haizzem's blessing before continuing on.

Ilario and Caio sat against the trees, and Ilario threw Caio a waterskin. Ilario lifted his and filled his dry mouth with hot water. He took another sip and spat it back out. "We should've refilled at the river first." Ilario said. He met Caio's eyes.

Caio's voice was kind, as ever. "My friend, I know there's something else weighing on you."

Ilario looked down and mashed his lips together. *I hope you don't–*

"You're worried about someone you love," Caio said.

Please don't.

"You know," Caio continued, "I've been thinking a lot about Lucia. She's certainly brave, supporting our army without my father's help—or mine. What does she know about war?"

"Lucia's trained for this. She carries Ysa's sword and shield. Her goddess will keep her safe until we arrive."

Caio looked at Ilario with understanding eyes. "Are you worried about her?"

25

Gods! It's so hard to hide anything from you.

Caio continued, "Let's continue to speak freely. Do you have feelings for her? You know you can tell me the truth, and I wish you would before we reach the canyon."

The truth was that Ilario couldn't wait to see her again. Ironically, the war could give him the chance to finally spend meaningful time with her. Lucia had spent most of the last nine years visiting the provinces, maintaining her father's alliances. Every time she returned to Remaes, Ilario had been involved with other women. Now he was determined to tell her how he felt—even though he knew it wouldn't make any difference in the end. She deserved someone better than him, someone with status, someone who could devote the time to her she deserved.

"Ilario, I wouldn't judge you. Believe me, I'd much rather see Lucia with you than with someone I barely know."

Impossible. "I can't talk about this, my Haizzem." *She's your sister.*

"Know that you would have my blessing."

It would be an insult to your father after all he's done for me.

"And my father loves you like a son," Caio said.

"Please. I can't."

Caio nodded in defeat.

Ilario wiped his brow with the hard muscles of his arms. Despite his marjoram and cardamom scented oils, he still reeked of sweat. "Shall we go back?"

"Give me a little more time. I like it here. This reminds me of when we went to Gallikos."

With Lucia.

Ilario heard voices approaching from the river and surged to his feet. He gripped the pommel of his sword at his hip as he searched through the trees. "Caio, it's your father."

Caio put one hand on Ilario's shoulder and leaned against him. "Just remember I wouldn't judge you."

Ilario's heart filled with relief and guilt at the same time.

The king approached with two warpriests and two soldiers at his side. He wore a long, loose tunic, maroon with yellow stitching at his shoulders and down the center of his chest.

Ilario knelt and bowed his head.

"Ilario, I take it my son came here to rest?"

"Yes, my King."

"Then I hope you don't mind my presence. Soon enough, we won't have opportunities like this."

Caio clasped his father's forearm, as his father clasped his. "Of course you're welcome here, Father. I'm glad you've come."

"Please stand, Ilario." The king motioned the soldiers and warpriests away. He glanced up at the canopy of trees. "Such a pleasant oasis."

Vieri removed a sealed parchment from his belt and handed it to Caio. "It's from your sister. The messenger told me she wrote it yesterday, first thing in the morning. She asked him to ride as fast as he could. It's addressed strictly to you."

"Thank you." Caio broke the red wax seal, unfolded Lucia's letter, and scanned it. "It's a bit long. I'll read it soon." He folded the paper and tucked it into his belt.

"There's something I need to tell you both, something I am going to need your help with," the king said. "When I was in Remeas, Tiberio told me something disturbing." His eyes turned glassy as he diverted his gaze. "He sensed some sort of darkness around Lucia. He told me I should search out the cause of her suffering."

Ilario felt his blood surging with anger. He clutched the black anvil hanging off his necklace, and asked his family's god Sansone to protect her.

"Tiberio's words were cryptic, but he suggested that I am partly to blame for her affliction." Vieri's unfocused eyes rolled around, gazing at the landscape. "It seems absurd. But I will need you to look out for her, Son. And you, Ilario."

"Certainly, my King," Ilario said with his jaw tight.

Caio's wide eyes looked devastated. "Of course I will. I'll also pray to Mya to give Lucia comfort, and ask Lord Oderigo for insight."

"Very good," his father answered quickly. "You'll let me know whatever you discover."

"Do you know anything else about her condition, my King?" Ilario asked.

"The Exalted told me three days ago that he believed Lucia had not been harmed in battle. He described the dark force as something of a mystery, even to his profound sight. I have put my trust in the goddess Ysa to protect my daughter, and I have faith that she will. Let's speak of this no more. Worrying will do us no good."

Neither will ignoring this, Ilario thought.

King Vieri put his hands behind his back and stepped around the clearing, looking up at the greenery. "Now tell me something, Dux Spiritus, how does it feel to finally have a hundred thousand warriors at your disposal?"

Ilario heard a hint of jealousy in the king's voice. Only two days before, Vieri had relinquished his position as Dux Spiritus to his son, after being Rezzia's military leader for nearly thirty years.

"It's different, Father ... It's entirely new."

"I should hope it's more thrilling than that."

"I mean no disrespect," Caio said. "You know I am honored that you've put so much faith in me."

Vieri looked down at his son with his sad, brown eyes. "My decision required no faith at all." He walked to Caio and held up his son's red and black hands. "These are the hands of a Haizzem. The gods promise us you will succeed where I have not."

"Pawelon is a worthy foe."

Vieri dropped Caio's hands and intensified his stare. "They shouldn't be. Pawelon is where your legacy begins."

"And where yours will continue," Caio said.

The king kept his eyes on his son. "Ilario, you know Caio so much better than I. Do you truly feel he is ready for this glory?"

"Our Haizzem will not disappoint you, my King. He amazes me more every day. He will surely make you proud."

"I am sure of it, too." Vieri turned his eyes to Ilario. "Thank you again for being like a brother to him while I was at war. I'll never be able to thank you enough."

"Of course. It has always been the highest honor and a joy."

The king stepped to Ilario and they grabbed each other's forearms. "I chose well. You were the right man. Never hesitate to ask me for anything you need."

"You honor me again. I will never be able to thank you enough for all you've given me."

"Do this for me, then. Make sure my son is ready for this war. My legacy depends on it."

Chapter 5: The Furies

The day after the Dux Spiritus ceremony.

EXHAUSTED FROM THE DAY'S CARNAGE, Lucia wrapped herself in white sheets and prayed to the goddess Ysa before resigning herself to another unbearable night. After a long, somber quiet she was not yet aware the cloth had become soaked in red; she would need time to understand why.

'*'

As Lucia lay in sheer darkness, the voice of the god Danato rumbled all around her: "Don't you hear me, my daughter?"

Why do you even ask?

"Why do you not answer your Lord?"

Because you've invaded my bed and my dreams? Damn you for making me feel ill again!

"Only one god dwells in the dark. Do you believe I wished to be him?"

More gods-damned theology.

"I did not. I chose the lot I had to choose. This is the nature of free will, for both gods and men. Choosing and wishing are not the same. Soon you and your brother will know this, too."

How long can a narcissistic god talk to himself?

"If none of us had chosen to live in the underworld, you would have no gods or goddesses. My sister Ysa could not exist without me. Remember, you are called to worship us all."

And I neither wished for that, nor chose it.

"We chose Rezzia and made your people special. We gave you religion and noble purpose. We watch over you. Yet you reject me, Lucia."

You traumatized an innocent girl and want to be worshiped? Perhaps it's forgiveness you're after? I still remember the sensation of my own flesh burning, even though it was only a dream.

29

"The truth is that I love you, now and forever. Sleep deeper, my daughter. Sleep deeper."

Lucia awoke to eerie sunlight shining through the canopy of her royal yurt, and was appalled to find a crowd waiting for her. Ten Rezzian guards stood in their cream tunics, with their backs turned to her bed. With their identical wide belts and sheathed swords, it was impossible to tell them apart.

She bolted upright and tightened her robe. "What is this?" As she ran her fingers through her long hair, she found all of it soaked with sweat. A rotten, sweet odor filled the air.

The guards moved to either side of the yurt, giving her a view of a tattered family of four—more sufferers of the new plague. They sat with their legs folded and stared down shamefully at the palatial rug. The little boy and girl leaned against their mother, their bare feet twitching.

"We couldn't leave them outside," a soldier said.

The father lifted his head slightly but kept his gaze downward. "Your Grace, we are dying. We need a miracle from our Haizzem. Can *you* grant us the gods' mercy? At least heal our children, if nothing more. Please!"

"He will be here soon. My brother will surely heal you." Lucia stood up and itched to do it herself.

"We can't wait days. Last night my son stopped breathing. We were sure he had died. He's still with us, but for how long? His episodes come at all times. Please!"

"Our only son," the mother said with a whimper.

"I can pray for you," Lucia said, "but you may still need to wait. Our Haizzem is leaving Remaes this morning. He should arrive in no more than six days." She took a few steps toward them.

The nearest soldier partially blocked her path. "It is not safe, Your Grace. Please stay where you are."

The boy, no older than four, fell forward onto his stomach. He choked, fighting to suck in air, but his lungs wouldn't expand. His arms flailed as his parents dropped to their knees and put their hands on his body.

Lucia ran to the boy and lifted him into her arms. His tiny face flushed with pain and begged her to save him.

Ysa, this child is innocent. Whatever the reason for this plague, it had nothing to do with him. Grant him your grace.

The boy went limp, his little head hanging off her elbow.

Lucia's blood pulsed with indignation as she heard Lord Danato's voice again.

"They are dying, Lucia. Children, parents, grandparents, and soldiers. Sadly, this boy will die soon, too. But there is a reason for all things."

Lucia turned and thought she saw a blur of black skin. No one was there. No one else seemed to hear the voice. She relaxed and shook her head, realizing she was experiencing yet another nightmare from Lord Danato.

The girl grabbed Lucia's leg. The parents began to wrestle the boy from her, almost fighting over the corpse.

"Gian, it's your father. Wake up, boy. Breathe for me!"

The mother wailed. She yanked her son away and pressed his body to her breast. The boy's arms and legs dangled like a doll's.

Lucia knew she would never forget Gian's dying eyes. Her muscles shuddered with rage, knowing the boy would eventually die from this plague.

"Arrows, arrows, arrows. So many burning arrows, Lucia. Thousands of your soldiers dying with each battle, as if the gods of Lux Lucis have forgotten Rezzia. Yet your men feel they honor us. You will watch them fall for a decade more."

Lord Danato had been telling her this every night since she arrived at the canyon. It still made no sense. The long record of history was clear: Once a Haizzem commands Rezzia's armies, historic victories come swiftly.

Pawelon's ancient citadel would have to fall soon. Even though Caio wasn't mentally ready to assume the role of Dux Spiritus and kill the Pawelon pigs, her father's strategy was still sound.

Once Caio enters the valley, the gods-damned war should be won within a year, if not a moon. Not ten.

Lucia awoke in a panic, finding her sheets drenched in blood.

She squirmed and tossed the sticky linens to the floor. She stood on the opposite side of the bed, threw her robe down, and examined her body.

I haven't bled. This isn't my blood.

Her fingers feverishly scratched down her arms and legs, trying to erase the foul stains. Failing, she grabbed a pair of long black gloves off the table beside her bed and stretched them from her hands up to her muscled upper arms. From her great-grandmother's antique chest, she removed a brown cloak. She quickly tied it around herself, then ran to the double doors and pushed them open.

31

Outside, ten soldiers stood tall and disciplined. The brisk air felt cruel against her face. In a few hours the desert would feel like a dry sauna again.

"Have any of you been here the entire night?"

"Yes, Your Grace."

"Did anyone enter my yurt?"

"No, Your Grace, is something troubling you?"

Lucia stepped inside and slammed the doors. Disgust stirred in her belly. She looked across the room at the bloody sheets and felt her face twitching. Her mind raced, wondering if The Black One had spilled the blood himself.

A warpriest's voice rang out over the camp, calling the men to morning prayer.

"Bring me warm water and washcloths," she said through the door.

'*'

Lucia scrubbed at the obstinate stains. Once certain she'd washed the blood away, she dragged the sopping cloth along the firm contours of her beige skin and recalled a bitter montage of recent dreams. She ran her dripping fingers down her accursed arms—now forced to bear even greater burdens.

I have to tell Caio. There's no other option.

She stood with sudden conviction and dressed herself, looking to the goddess Ysa's martial relics for courage. Ysa's sword, shield, and silver armor rested on their decorated black walnut stand. She reminded herself how many royal men and women throughout more than a thousand years of history had carried these objects, and of all the miracles they'd invoked with the blessed metal to protect Rezzia.

Her round shield scintillated with hundreds of tiny crimson and amber gemstones forming ten concentric circles, a geometrical work of art. Ysa's white sword was immaculately symmetrical, made of an inscrutable metal that still had not been re-created anywhere on the planet of Gallea. Bright yellow and white stripes curled around the sword's grip ten times until they met a golden, crystalline pommel.

Lucia closed her eyes and asked Ysa for firm resolve, then sat at her small desk littered with correspondence. She stared at a blank parchment, breathed deeply, and picked up the quill. She labored to compose the first half of the letter, then reached a burning pitch as long-withheld truths erupted onto the page.

32

Beloved Caio, my Haizzem,

It is the beginning of my eighth day in the valley. It is another world, this war, like the tales of Lord Danato's underworld hell. By Ysa's grace, I have not been injured, though the battles have been fierce.

Finally, yesterday, something occurred to encourage my sanity. I celebrated your ascent to Dux Spiritus with our soldiers and warpriests. We remained in our camp and worshiped together before we saw the great flash when the sun reached its zenith. Such a deep silence took root in us, a hundred thousand praying together. I will always regret not having been there for the ceremony, but my abilities have been needed during father's absence.

I do not wish to put any more weight on your shoulders, but the fighting has been gruesome, and our Strategos Duilio, who is remarkable even in his old age, says Pawelon's archers have become even more deadly over the last year. It is as if we have been cursed by the dark spirits they command. With you here, I know this will change. Everyone I have talked to believes in you, and will rejoice in seeing you.

I must tell you something else now, Caio, a grave thing. I have never wanted to burden you with my troubles, and until now I never felt I had to. I did not come to this decision lightly, for you will see it has the greatest implications. Please trust I have not gone insane.

The Black One hounds me, brother. He has ever since you were born. Lord Danato comes to me in dreams and visions and tries to speak to me, though I have rarely given him the pleasure of an answer. I have never before seen a reason to burden you with any knowledge of this, but now he comes to me with matters involving you and all of Rezzia.

In the past, he would come on occasion, but recently he has been relentless. He has visited me every night for at least a moon, burdening my soul with so many things I will never be able to speak of.

I must tell you, his dark prophecies have always proven true, and now he terrifies me about this war. He connects it with the new plague. He shows the fighting raging for another ten years, even after you join it. The record of history makes it very hard for me to take this seriously, but he is an insistent god. We both know that ten more years of fighting is not an option, assuming it is even possible.

Please pray to Oderigo and Mya. Perhaps channel a scripture directly from Lord Oderigo. Find out if Danato's vision is to be taken seriously, and if it is, how we can alter it. I have always felt powerless before him and his demands on me. In his presence, I feel like a little girl, awkward and angry and unable to speak my voice.

33

I must go. Our armies are leaving for the day. Please give Ilario my best and tell him I look forward to seeing him. I am sure you are growing even closer now. I hope to be the first to welcome you both to our camp. Together, we will watch a golden history unfold.

The light will come.

By Ysa's Grace,
Lucia

She exhaled a heavy sigh and lowered her chin to her chest. The sense of defilement still plagued her body.

The clamor of soldiers came from all directions. A guard said through the doors, "Your Grace, the army is gathering."

Lucia glanced again at Ysa's sword and shield. "Tell the Strategos I'll be there soon."

Chapter 6: An Apple for the Fairest

Kannauj, Pawelon. The day of the Dux Spiritus ceremony.

NARAYANI LAY SUPINE, nude on the mattress made for a prince. Her mind wandered the maze of the high eggshell ceiling with its curving olive, grey, and purple flourishes. With one hand beneath her head, her other fingers slowly traced patterns over her brown chest and thighs, occasionally touching her lips and long neck. She imagined it was Rao's mouth and tongue circling sweetly, so that by his mysterious powers each pattern he etched tied their hearts and souls together for all eternity.

She rolled onto her side and squeezed her knees to her chest, staring longingly out the window at the cloudy sky.

At least I can feel at home in your world.

The walls, built from the rich, dark wood of the southern Pawelon forests, helped the enormous chamber feel warm. Bookshelves filled with rare and costly treatises lined the room and, though she had no interest in the philosophy, history, or religion in Rao's prized collection, the books and scrolls gave the room a comforting touch. They reminded her of him.

When she finally heard the sound of the countless soldiers outside the room coming to attention, she sat up, making sure her hair was still pulled back neatly. She crossed one shaven leg over the other while pointing her lightly oiled chest at the door.

Rao stopped as soon as he saw her. His new saffron-colored sage uniform showed off his tall shoulders and athletic build. He looked over her body with an amorous smile. His dark hair had been neatly combed, but she'd have it tousled again soon enough.

She patted the bed. "I have something for Pawelon's *youngest ever* sage. His initiation ceremony lasted all morning. It's been so hard for me to wait."

"I should inspect this present for him to be sure it's safe. It could be a Rezzian trick. An assassin!"

"Right. They would do anything to get to him."

Rao slipped off his tailored leather shoes and glided to the bed. He sat, still and quiet, gazing into Narayani's eyes.

"All the girls have been saying our prince is *ravishing* in uniform. I couldn't agree more."

"Your beauty shines, as always, like a Sravasti diamond."

She smiled. "I hope you're happy because of what you see in front of you, not because of your accomplishment."

Rao's chest rumbled as he laughed. "Well ... it's only due to you, my love."

"That's what I want to hear." Narayani came forward on all fours and stopped with her lips in front of his, waiting. She received his hungry kiss, and her world disappeared.

Rao stood and removed his tight uniform. Narayani stretched out on her side. Rao pressed his warm body to hers.

"You know I would do anything for you," she said.

"Then let me hold you."

But I don't want to wait.

Their bodies were more than ready. She flicked her tongue at his neck. He held her close, kissing her sweetly around her face. She ran her nails down his back and grabbed his tight buttocks.

"I want to bear your child, Rao. Your father would be thrilled to have another heir, wouldn't he?"

His voice lost its swagger as he said, "That's probably true."

"What's wrong?"

"Nothing. Everything's fine."

"How was the ceremony? I know your father would've liked to have been there."

His warm, brown eyes focused on her again. "It went a little long. I'm glad it's over. Now all that's left is for Aayu and I to decide what we want to do."

You'd better not even think about joining the war. "It's almost over, isn't it? Almost ten years now, and they still haven't taken the citadel. Your father wants you to stay in Kannuaj."

"I know, but we're sages now. My father needs all the help he can get."

"They don't need you or Aayu. They're doing fine without you. Your father will be angry if you go. My father isn't an easy man to get along with, either." Her father, the supreme general of Pawelon's army.

36

He took in a deep breath, then expelled it all at once. "Probably right again."

Narayani kissed Rao's neck, then his chest, and on down below his firm stomach. She looked up and batted her painted eyelashes, biting one side of her lower lip. He stared back, breathless. She savored feeling in control of her lover, the Prince of Pawelon.

"There isn't anything I wouldn't do for you."

Rao swallowed and nodded.

Without warning, a blinding light poured through the enormous windows overlooking the fertile lands of Pawelon. A wave of heat flushed through the room. Rao jumped out of the bed and pulled up his long pants. He ran to the window and stared down at the rows of crowded streets surrounding the palace.

Narayani covered herself with the sheet and sat up. "*What* was that?"

"The storied solar flash. It means ... their Haizzem is the leader of their army. He's their Dux Spiritus now."

"I thought he was too young?"

"Exactly. I'm only a year older than him." Rao's head moved from side to side as he collected his thoughts. "They—they're not doing what they were supposed to."

"You said the Haizzem wasn't going to fight until he's older."

"That's always been their history. They've abandoned their tradition." Rao rubbed his forehead. "This changes everything."

"Then maybe peace is coming. Maybe he doesn't want to fight."

Rao turned his eyes to her again. "There's no chance of that. Retreat isn't a word in the dogs' vocabulary."

Narayani threw off the sheet covering her body. "Come back. I'm not done with you."

"Narayani, I'm sorry. I have to talk"—someone knocked upon the heavy door—"to Aayu."

"Rao ... Narayani ... stop kissing and let me in."

The worst possible time for my cousin to show up, she thought.

"Hold on there, *bhai*," Rao answered his great friend.

Narayani whispered, "Tell him to go away."

"I have to talk to him. Please get dressed."

"I've been waiting all day for you, Rao."

"Please. I need to do this."

37

After giving Rao an annoyed look, Narayani stood up and wrapped herself in her favorite silk sari, the one she wore the first time she met Rao and danced with him at the palace's Navariti festival. Green with yellow patterns, it exposed her navel and one shoulder and fit tightly around her breasts. But she knew she had nothing more to offer Rao. She wasn't going to be able to change his mind. No matter what she said or did, she knew he was going to leave her.

Chapter 7: Trojan Gods

RAO MANAGED TO SMILE, in spite of the sun's ominous portent, when two hundred fifty fleshy pounds of Aayu entered his chamber wearing a skintight saffron sage's uniform.

Aayu's face still somehow showed his usual mirth. "What on Gallea is going on?"

"This changes everything," Rao said.

"We're definitely going now," Aayu said.

"What?" Narayani's voice raised an octave and then came back down. "Rao, be rational."

"Narayani, if their Haizzem defeats our army, it will be the end of everything we love. They'll burn this city. They'll definitely kill me, and they'd take you and—"

Narayani froze Rao with her glare. "Then let's go somewhere else and wait until things calm down."

Rao reached out to hold her. He knew she wouldn't understand.

Aayu threw up his hands. "Cousin, there won't be anything to come back to if we don't go. The army's going to need our help."

Narayani broke free of Rao's arms and snapped her head at Aayu. "What are you going to do? Meditate with the soldiers? Neither of you know anything about combat. I'd be more useful to the army than either of you. I've done actual healing work."

Aayu smiled at Rao with raised eyebrows, and Rao overcame the urge to grin. Narayani, like nearly all Pawelon women, knew very little about what sages actually did. "My love, he's right. Aayu and I have abilities we can use to help our troops."

Aayu sat in the chair in front of Rao's desk and leaned back. "Cousin, listen to me. Rao completed his training with one of the best assessments in our history. They're going to need our help."

"Why? You've always said there are a lot of sages at the citadel."

39

Rao reached out his hand to her. "I wish I could explain, but you know I can't."

Narayani crossed her arms.

Rao extended both of his hands, but she refused him. "My father and your father will be glad to have Aayu and me when they see what we can do to help them."

Aayu laughed. "Are you serious?"

Rao's cheeks tightened as he smiled. Granted, his father, the very rajah of Pawelon, would probably need some time to warm up to their presence. Rao's father had forbidden him from joining the war. And General Indrajit, who was Narayani's father and Aayu's uncle, made a stern impression on Narayani and Aayu when they were children.

"Why are you joking?" Narayani asked. "We're talking about your lives. Rao, what about the things we want to create? The arts programs? The meditation center? The projects for the poor?"

"Those things will have to wait." Rao lowered his hands to his sides.

"You expect me to wait here all by myself?"

"No, Cousin," Aayu said, "we decided you should pick up a long spear and fight. Doesn't that sound good? Come right along."

"I can't wait here. I hardly know anyone in this city. You can't go, Rao. I swear it here and now. This is my *sankalpa*: I will not be separated from you."

Rao stared at Aayu, but his *bhai* also had no answer to her solemn resolve.

Narayani pointed her index finger forcefully as she talked. "And *if* you're going, I'm coming with you."

"No, that's not possible. It wouldn't be safe."

"But I can help. Don't they need healers? If you're ever hurt, I can help you."

"Cousin, you're insane. No. I promised your father I'd watch out for you. That means you're staying in this palace, where you'll be safe."

"You're not in charge of me. If you go, you can either take me or I'm going to follow you." Narayani let out her frustration with a scream. She grabbed a pillow off the bed and threw it against a wall.

Rao found Aayu sticking out his tongue at him.

I really wish this was funny. "If I could convince you we're going to be safe, would you agree to stay here?"

Narayani sat on the bed. Her eyes darted between the two of them. "Probably not. You can try."

Rao sat beside her and held one of her hands. Her long eyelashes brought out the sparkle in her brown eyes, even when she was angry. "Promise me, my love. Please."

"Only if you can absolutely convince me."

Rao looked over at his even darker-skinned friend. "I want to tell her about our abilities."

With an inflection both joking and serious, Aayu said, "Oh. Really?"

Rao shrugged his shoulders. "Do you have a better idea?"

Aayu scrunched his lips to one side of his face.

"I'm sure everyone tells their wives anyway," Rao said.

Aayu's round belly shook as he nodded. "I still wouldn't do it, though."

"Are you two done keeping secrets from me? It's rude."

Rao looked in Narayani's eyes again. "Could you promise to keep everything I tell you a secret?"

"You sure about this, bhai?" Aayu asked.

"I solemnly promise that I will not tell a soul," Narayani said.

Rao looked down at the intricate dark patterns on his sheets. *I may regret this, but somehow this decision feels right.* "Aayu, feel free to interrupt me at any point."

"I think I can manage that."

Rao let out a deep breath. "Early in our training, each of us is tasked with mastering a state of awareness, something unique. This is called your *sadhana*, and our gurus choose this focus for us early on. The hope is that someday you can teach other sages how to achieve your *sadhana*, too. Later, we develop a secondary *sadhana*."

Rao took both of Narayani's hands in his own. "Aayu's *sadhana* allows him to become transparent to the physical senses. When he focuses his mind with the aid of certain mantras that came to him after years of meditation, his consciousness changes enough so that no one can see, hear, touch, smell, or—"

"Don't say it, bhai."

"Or taste him."

"Disgusting," Narayani said.

"Forget that part. Since he and I have always been partners, I know something about his *sadhana*. I'm not as good at it as he is, but I can do it. He

41

can make others invisible too, and sometimes I have been able to do that, as well."

"Hopefully I can do this for a lot of people someday, like an entire army," Aayu said. "I've already taught some of our gurus how to do it on their own. It's really not that difficult."

"Then let me see you use your ability now," Narayani said.

Aayu stood and closed his eyes. One breath later, his physical form vanished. Narayani jumped off the bed and ran to where Aayu had been standing. She waved her arms around, finding nothing. "Amazing!"

"We haven't figured out yet how to influence the physical world while in this state—we call it *shunyata*. Right now he's aware of us much like he was before, but he can't *do* anything to us." Rao leaned back against the large pillows and the wall. "Occasionally other people can see through our *shunyata*. We believe this has something to do with the other person's state of mind and their own spiritual awareness. Some of our teachers can see us in *shunyata* if they reach a deep enough state of meditation."

"Then that's a problem." Narayani kept walking around the room, swinging her arms around and looking for Aayu. "Can you do this as often as you want to?"

"For the most part, but it requires concentration initially. It also requires a certain amount of *ojas*, subtle energy that can only be gained through spiritual practices."

Rao cleared his throat as he thought about how to explain more. "The mind is the master of the physical world. The physical isn't observed by the mind—it's actually dependent on the mind. It's more correct to say that the physical world is also mind. Remove or transform the mind, and the physical world has no independent existence. When you know the truth about reality, you don't have to fear anything in the physical world. As sages, we are trained in this understanding, and we use this awareness to protect ourselves."

"But if Aayu's *sadhana* doesn't work on everyone, what if their Haizzem can see through it?" She was still looking carefully for Aayu.

Rao stood and followed her around his chamber. "These aren't our only powers. Like most sages, we also learn things that allow us to support our soldiers or to fight when needed."

"Rao's *sadhana* is really strange." Aayu appeared on the bed, lying on his side with one hand propping up his head, looking up at the ceiling.

Narayani walked over to her cousin and pinched his full cheeks.

"It's really me," he said.

Rao pulled over the chair from his desk and sat down, leaning forward. "With enough training and awareness, it's possible to attune ourselves to vastly different worlds and travel between them. Our bodies condition us to believe we are finite beings that exist in only one time and place. But other planes intersect our own world at all times. Distance is an illusion, and we can move between different vibrational states of being because at the heart of everything is a single, unified consciousness. My *sadhana* has been to contemplate the interconnectedness of all things. Because of this, I can travel to other planes of consciousness."

Narayani stared with her mouth open. Her body shook as she chuckled. "This is a lot to take in, Rao."

"I understand. You're right."

"He can do more than he's saying, too." Aayu lay flat on the bed, his hands beneath his head, staring at the ceiling.

"But that should give you an idea. Aayu can also use my *sadhana*. We can do more, plus we each have a secondary *sadhana*. Aayu can make a person appear exactly as someone else, while he takes on their appearance. Mine is more philosophical. It's about instantly enforcing the principle of karma."

"I know that one," she said with a proud grin. "It means the fruits of actions return to their sender."

"Right. These abilities will allow us to protect ourselves and fight for Pawelon. Remember, their entire religion and its magic is based on mythology. None of it is real, unless we allow ourselves to believe it is."

"Narayani, Rao is very humble but the things he can do—they're so far beyond what our gurus ever expected. They say he's the most naturally talented sage they've ever trained. He's worked hard at his *sadhana*, too. Once Rao gains your father's trust, I promise you, he'll be able to defeat their Haizzem all on his own."

Rao focused on his breathing to keep his mind off Aayu's praise.

Aayu continued, "They think his ability has unlimited potential. And I'm really good at what I do, too. Rao and I have taught each other things over the years."

"I wouldn't go down to the citadel without Aayu, Narayani. He and I are more powerful when we work together. I'm confident we can help our army. If

43

this Haizzem chooses to fight us, I'll fight him on a plane of existence he doesn't even know exists. They brought this war to us, and we have to defend ourselves."

Narayani seemed to be weighing her options. She walked behind Rao, put her hands on his shoulders, and remained quiet for a long time. "I'm sorry for what I said ... I was being immature." She paused again. "But I have one request. I want you to come back and see me once every moon."

"My love, it takes five days to travel between the citadel and Kannauj in good weather. Maybe I can come every three moons."

"Every two moons."

I'm going to regret saying this. "All right. If I can, I promise I will. We agree that you can never go down to the valley?"

"Fine."

Aayu sat up and looked at his cousin. "You're doing the right thing. Rao and I would be distracted, worrying about you the whole time. And your father would *hate* me and Rao for bringing you there. We're going to be taking orders from him."

"I can accept all of that. And ..." Narayani rubbed her chin and exhaled a long breath. "I'm really proud of you for all you've accomplished—even you, Aayu. I'm sure there's a lot more I don't know."

Rao reached up to his right shoulder and held her hand there. Narayani's skin was flushed and her jaw tight. "We have to leave tomorrow. Their Haizzem must still be in Ramaes. That's where they do all their official religious ceremonies. He could join their army in six or seven days. If he's traveling by horse, he could be there much sooner. We'll try to arrive before he does."

"Get out of here, Aayu," she said. "Rao and I need some time alone."

"All right. We'll leave at dawn tomorrow, Rao. I'll make sure we have enough soldiers and servants for the journey." Aayu moved toward the door, then turned to Rao again. "I don't know how you feel about this, bhai, but I'm excited to see more of the world." Aayu's face bloomed with a childlike grin.

"Me too, bhai. Thank you. I owe you for arranging the details."

"Make sure you can still walk tomorrow. I'm not carrying you down there."

"Get out of here," she pointed to the door.

As Aayu turned to the door, he swung his arm with dramatic flair.

Once the door closed, Narayani grabbed Rao, squeezed him with all her strength, and released the first flood of her tears.

Chapter 8:
Interlude: The Journey to Ilium

RAO AND AAYU WALKED EASTWARD through lush country on their way to the mountains and the high desert beyond. Women carrying wicker baskets, farm workers, livestock, and beggars crowded the muddy thoroughfare as always, but on this day after the solar flash, streams of would-be warriors merged with the human river.

Some fighters arrived in groups, representing their tribes and villages. Others showed up two or three at a time, including many fathers with their sons. A great number looked too old, too young, or too skinny to fight, but they came raising their improvised spears and simple bows, shouting for the death of the Haizzem and the expulsion of the Rezzians back to their eastern lands.

On the brink of subjugation, Pawelon had been shocked into action.

Rao and Aayu traveled with an impenetrable wall of men around them. The full regiment of soldiers protected the rajah's only son at all hours.

The procession grew as the day went on, with newcomers flocking around the professional fighters. Behind them, dozens of servants in soiled clothes carried supplies and directed water buffalo pulling overloaded carts.

The miniature army camped at the base of the green peaks of the Mahayana Mountains. In the morning, they marched again. A ravine cut through the towering landmass, with a river, fed by trickling streams and thin waterfalls, running through its center. The water flowed west to the farmlands and forests where the masses of Pawelon struggled in poverty.

The caravan journeyed deep into the mountains. Two days in, the riverbed transformed into a swath of dry, smooth stones. Once they advanced beyond the range, modest hills took over the land from gorges. The greenery gave way to shrubs. Cliff walls surrendered the sky to desert panoramas.

After the earth flattened out and only bare-branched trees stood taller than men, the troop caught sight of its destination. They spied Pawelon's great fortress as a square speck on the horizon. The citadel's majestic size was increasingly realized over the next two days. By the fifth nightfall, only a short march remained between them and the ancient structure that had kept the invaders at bay for nearly ten years.

They pitched camp for the last time under the light of the bright, waxing moon. Rao and Aayu found themselves too anxious for sleep. They lay beside their campfire, enjoying the enchanted desert and speaking of their dreams for themselves and their people after the war's end. Rao envisioned a more educated and enlightened Pawelon society. Aayu dreamt of traveling the lands beyond Pawelon.

The next morning, excitement, pride, dread, and awe hushed the men as they bent back their necks and beheld the mountainous fortification. Throughout Pawelon, parents told their children stories of the great desert canyon dividing the lands of Rezzia from Pawelon, and of the mammoth fortress on the western rim which rivaled the valley's grandeur. Scholars still debated whether men built the citadel in a long gone era, or whether the fabled race of giants constructed the monument. Enough heavy stone to bury a small city thickened the curtain walls, so much that men felt as small next to the structure as they did against the backdrop of the stars.

As the elephantine gates opened, the vibrations of creaking metal shook the air like a belching whale. Pawelon's two great leaders awaited Rao and Aayu in the courtyard: Devak, Rao's father, the giant rajah of Pawelon, and his steel-eyed general, Indrajit, Aayu's uncle. The young sages feared what their reunions might bring.

A woman in the guise of a servant hurried forward for a better view of Pawelon's titanic leaders. A ragged brown robe covered her completely, just as it had for the last five days. Narayani peeked out from behind the hood and stared at her father—a man she barely knew—and Rao's father beside him.

Chapter 9: Fury of Priam

AAYU LOOKED UP AT RAO'S FATHER and tried not to stare at the rajah's pockmarked face. The man hulked over Aayu and Rao in the shadowed courtyard. Aayu tried to shake a disturbing image from his mind. *I'm going to try not to think about how many harlots you've crushed with that big body of yours, Devak.*

"Why are you here?" The rajah demanded an answer from his son in his deep, rumbling voice.

I'll let you handle this, bhai, Aayu thought.

"Aayu and I finished our assessments. After we saw the solar flash, we had to come. We want to help."

Devak and General Indrajit had waited to receive them at the gate. A third man, a high-ranking sage, stood beside Indrajit looking annoyed; he too wore a saffron uniform, but with seven green stripes at his collar. Thousands of clamoring troops marched out of the fortress through the opposite gate in the east, to the sound of deep-bellowing horns.

A brisk morning wind swept through the courtyard. The sun would not rise over the citadel's curtain walls for some time. Devak stared expressionlessly at his son.

Aayu pulled at his uniform's collar. *I wish I could thank the tailor who decided to constrict the blood flow to our hands, feet, and neck all at the same time.* He decided that Uncle Indrajit's stern face made Rajah Devak look, in contrast, like a whimsical seven-foot boy. Indrajit's aquiline stare reminded Aayu how intimidating his uncle could be; if he were half as good at waging war as he used to be at scaring children, Pawelon's military was in expert hands.

Indrajit made a fist and held it up in the air. Rao quickly matched his salute. Aayu clenched his right fist too, after recovering from the awkwardness of the greeting. *So wonderful to see you again after all these years, Uncle Indrajit.*

The third man, whom Aayu decided must be the world's most sullen and ugliest sage, stepped forward. He might have been forty, or thirty with ten years of constant stress. The sage's dark eyes quivered as he pronounced his judgment on Rao: "You're not ready for this."

"Who are you?" Aayu shot back.

"He is your superior," his uncle said. "He has been defending your freedom since you were a boy, and you will address him with respect." He turned to the sage, "My nephew still has not made the acquaintance of the virtue of discipline."

You old flatterer.

Indrajit continued, "Prince Rao, Master Aayu, this is Briraji. Watch and learn from him. I recommend you observe his conduct and model yourselves after his subservience to his duty."

Briraji's eyes wouldn't stay still; the black orbs seemed more attuned to another plane than the here and now. "*Neither of you* is prepared for this."

Rao's father sounded detached as he said, "Briraji may be right."

"We have earned the chance to fight for Pawelon, have we not, Father?"

"My Rajah, if I may." Aayu bowed his head. "Rao finished his training with the best assessment since you've ruled Pawelon."

The rajah's deathlike eyes yielded no ground.

Briraji's voice broke to a higher pitch. "Is that right?"

"As I said." Aayu stared unflinchingly into the high-ranking sage's dark eyes.

General Indrajit and Briraji shared a skeptical glance. Rajah Devak's stony face held steady.

"Congratulations," Briraji reached out to shake Rao's hand. The sage stood almost a foot shorter than Rao.

"Briraji, I have so much to learn." Rao sounded sincere, but Briraji's heavy staring made Aayu want to smash an elbow into the sage's gloomy face.

A voice called out behind them amid sudden whistling and shouting. "Rao! Aayu!"

Aayu knew that woman's voice.

"Wait for me."

He knew that woman's voice.

"I'm coming."

He knew ... Narayani's voice.

She walked toward them in that revealing green sari she loved. Every soldier around, thousands of them, ogled her.

I'll kill every one of you if I have to, Aayu thought. *Nice choice of dress, Narayani. The stone walls are probably staring at your breasts too.*

Indrajit asked, "Is that ... my daughter, Master Aayu?"

48

"Yes, sir."

Indrajit's tone betrayed his rising anger. "Why in death's name is she here?" *Think fast.*

Aayu scanned Rao's face. Both were trying not to look surprised. Narayani walked up to them with a smile that said nothing could possibly be wrong, as if butterflies fluttered all around her and pink flowers bloomed at her feet.

"You should have waited for me. I told you I was right behind you." Narayani knelt and touched Indrajit's feet. "I'm honored to be in your presence, Father." She stood again and turned to Devak. "My Rajah, I am Rao's lady, Narayani. I've come to help, too. I am a healer." She put her hands together in front of her heart and bowed before him, looking up at the giant with her long eyelashes.

Devak squinted and tightened his face even more.

"Uncle Indrajit, you told me to make sure she stayed safe. I couldn't leave her alone in that city." *Now I'm just hoping you won't notice these thousands of soldiers drooling over her.*

"You bloody fool, are you insane?" Indrajit asked. Aayu remembered that Indrajit almost always managed to keep his voice cool and controlled. Here was an exception: "This is no place for a young woman, especially not her!" Meaning, the most beautiful woman most of these men had ever laid eyes on, a perfect fantasy at seventeen.

Aayu tried to respond, but Rao spoke over his words. "I fully agree with Aayu. General Indrajit, you must have loyal men you can trust to guard her. She can stay with me in the tower, so you won't have to allocate more resources, except when I'm in the field. That is, assuming Aayu and I can stay."

As Devak stomped toward Rao, the full power of the giant's voice exploded. "You've insulted our general!"

Rao flinched and looked down and aside.

Aayu took a step toward Devak. "I must stand by my idea to bring Narayani here, my Rajah. I had to convince Rao, but I'm glad he's come around. I know she will be safer here." *Now will anyone believe this?*

Briraji smirked at all of them. Aayu decided the sage needed a heavy fist to correct his lopsided face.

"You are an idiot. A born idiot," Indrajit said.

Narayani was nearly in tears. "I didn't mean to cause any problems. My Rajah, I can help the wounded—"

49

"She's right." Aayu nodded. "She knows her medicines."

Narayani wiped her nose. "If anything should happen to Rao or Aayu, I can give them the best possible care."

Aayu was staring at Narayani's blameless portrayal of herself, and shaking his head inwardly, when he heard the back of Devak's hand smash against Rao's jaw. Rao stumbled backward and fell.

Aayu instinctively stepped between Rao and his father, but had no time to defend himself against Briraji's conjured force that slammed his shoulder into the compacted ground.

Before Aayu could think, he lunged at the little sage and pinned Briraji's arms to the desert floor. Briraji's eyes trembled as he began invoking another power.

Devak wrapped his arms under Aayu's and pulled him off the sage and onto his feet. Aayu knew Rao's father was holding back most of his strength.

Briraji stood and spit flew from his mouth. "You have no self-control. How can you be a sage?"

"Don't question whether I am worthy of this uniform," Aayu said. "I look out for those worth protecting." Aayu glanced around at the many soldiers staring at them.

"I was protecting our Rajah. How dare you assault him?" Briraji asked.

"I wasn't going to touch him! I was only—"

Indrajit's stare froze Aayu. "You are an utter disgrace."

Devak's deep voice growled, "He was defending my son. You will not punish him for that, Indrajit." Devak released Aayu from his hold. The Rajah's face seemed inflexible as rock. "Aayu, apologize to Briraji."

Aayu swallowed, trying to down his pride. It was so hard—almost impossible—to say it. "I apologize, Briraji."

Rao was out of breath and on his feet again, rubbing his jaw. He tried to sound strong, but his pain came through in his voice. "I'm sorry to have upset you, Father. I understand your anger."

Narayani stood beside Rao, her lips trembling.

If Indrajit was bothered by Rajah Devak's rebuttal, it didn't show. "Our warriors are leaving. We have wasted enough time. Briraji, take my daughter to the chambers below the rajah's. For now, she will share the space with Prince Rao. Assign enough men to guard her. Be quick, then join me on the northern trail."

Devak spoke in the same commanding voice as ever, as if nothing had happened. "You'll need another sage to protect you in the meantime. Rao, go with General Indrajit. Indrajit, explain the recent developments to my son."

The general hesitated, creating an uncomfortable silence. "My Rajah, he ... I need a proven sage at my side." Indrajit stood with the posture of a proud commander, even as he pleaded.

Devak stood even taller. "According to what your nephew said, Rao is ready. You can also take Aayu with you."

Aayu glanced at Narayani. *I'm not leaving her with Briraji.* "My Rajah, I would like to stay here with Narayani, to make sure she is comfortable and safe." Aayu looked at the little sage as he finished.

Devak nodded. Rao nodded too, giving Aayu an understanding look.

Briraji brushed more dirt off his uniform. "I will join you soon, Prince Rao. I'm sure you'll find a live engagement a stirring experience. We're taking the fight to our enemy."

"We're doing *what?*" Rao asked. "That's not in keeping with our tactics, is it?"

Briraji dismissed Rao with a brief laugh and a smirk. "It is until the Haizzem comes. We've decided to meet their full army with our own. Our arrows, spears, and sages will show the dogs the full fury of Pawelon."

"You're emptying the citadel? This isn't how we fight them," Rao said.

Devak spoke over Rao's last few words. "It is for now." He looked at Aayu. "Aayu and Briraji, I expect you to get along from now on."

"Yes, my Rajah," Aayu said, and Briraji echoed his words.

Devak stepped in front of Rao again. "Protect General Indrajit and support my army. Impress me."

Rao clenched his fist in salute. "I will."

Indrajit saluted before hurrying toward the columns of spearmen and archers.

Rao hugged Narayani, kissed her cheek, and whispered something in her ear. He slapped Aayu on the back and said, "Watch her," then ran after Indrajit.

After saluting, Aayu grabbed Narayani's hand and pulled her along as the two followed Briraji to the legendary tower at the center of the courtyard. It loomed as the only structure inside the citadel higher than the curtain walls. The tower's heavy stone construction rivaled the thick masonry of the fortifications,

51

but unlike the outer walls, parts of the tower's walls had crumbled and now functioned as windows.

"I am sorry." Narayani's sad eyes tried to sell her innocence as they walked. "I didn't mean to get you into trouble."

Aayu bit back his words and could only shake his head as he looked away from her. *Your safety is my responsibility now, even more than before. What on Gallea am I going to do?*

Halfway to the tower, Aayu turned his head. Rajah Devak stood in the same spot, watching Rao chase after Indrajit and the army. The old man stood still with perfect posture, his face a pockmarked mystery.

At least he's on our side.

Aayu looked at Rao once more, frustrated that Rao would soon be fighting without him. *Good luck, bhai.*

Chapter 10: Cranes in a Cloudy Sky, Obscured by Dust

RAO STRUGGLED TO REMAIN CENTERED in the midst of Pawelon's forces as they marched into the valley. A well of emotional pain gushed within, aftershocks of his father's blow. He breathed in and out in specific ratios, attempting to assert control over his feelings. *In: one ... two ... three. Out: one ... two ... three ... four ... five ... six.*

In his current condition, he knew he'd be useless if General Indrajit, who walked beside him, needed him to access his powers. Effectiveness as a sage depended on acute presence of mind, detached observation of all internal and external phenomena. Both the inner and outer worlds were pummeling his awareness.

Their troop created a menacing spectacle: fanged long spears and great bows raised high above thundering footsteps, death-lust in the warriors' eyes. Hatred and fear blanketed the atmosphere, palpable to Rao's keen senses. His years of training rescued him from being totally overwhelmed. He concentrated on breathing.

The desert felt increasingly oppressive as the sun climbed and they descended the sloping path. As Rao trod the baked earth, after five days of hiking from Kannauj, his sandals chafed his sore feet. Red cliffs enclosing the winding passage blocked most of the sky. Heavy clouds flew at a bizarre speed above them. Rao wiped the moisture from his face.

It's too humid. This weather isn't natural.

As he watched the scene around him, an image flashed in his mind. The army's legs swung forward—right leg, left leg, right leg, left leg—kicking boulders down the path with each stride. His mind intuited the symbolism: The war's momentum could not be reversed, stopped, or even slowed. Every person was merely a spectator of the unfolding drama.

No, he corrected his initial thoughts, *this is as transient as anything else. It's a fiction that will collapse if but one man can see it for what it is and speak the truth.*

53

Rao's emotions were still jagged. He'd held naive expectations for his reunion with his father, believing he'd be proud of him and thrilled to see a son he barely knew. So many uncontrolled emotions were completely inappropriate for a sage—and they indicated he was in real danger.

General Indrajit finally broke the silence. "There are only two ways down to the canyon, two ways for the dogs to climb to the citadel. Each day, we defend both routes with bowmen hidden in the cliffs, infantry at the base of the trails, and, further up, tight spear formations blocking the trails at their narrowest points. The Rezzians carry one throwing spear each, believing it is dishonorable to use more than one ranged weapon in any battle. They believe only cowards use bows. So determined to die, they keep coming in droves, year after year, and we keep killing them."

If the general was still bitter about the confrontations from earlier that morning, Rao couldn't detect any sign of it on Indrajit's hard face.

The general spoke with professional detachment and kept his cold eyes trained far ahead. "The dogs have a grotesque pride that drives them directly into our defenses. They are always aggressive, even when it least serves them. Their blind faith renders them imbeciles. They believe their gods protect those who should live, and that men who die in battle are glorified in the afterlife. If they had any sense—"

"But we're the aggressors today, General." As Rao spoke, he felt his inner turmoil fueling his tone. He knew he was out of line.

Indrajit stared forward like an eagle, no reaction at all. "Prince Rao, we *want* them to come and battle us in the open field today. They have neither king nor Haizzem in the valley, men who command great powers. We must break their army's spirit, perhaps even destroy their camp, before the king returns with his son. Striking them now gives us our greatest chance for victory."

Rao couldn't stop his words. "General, the Rezzians made the mistake of initiating this conflict. Aren't we acting like them now, recklessly provoking such a large battle? This doesn't seem like Pawelon's way. It puts our survival at risk. All actions return to their sender. Karma is immutable"

"Once they began this war, it became ours to finish. The principle of reaction states they must face the repercussions of what they have done. We are *enforcing* the principle of karma."

"I say this with respect, sir, but men cannot administer karma themselves. Karma is a natural law, beyond our ability to enforce. When we try to do that, we are entangled in the same sticky web, pulled into the same mire. The fruits of their actions will return to them inevitably. The natural balancing in the universe is far more powerful than any worldly army." As he spoke, Rao saw a dour curling of Indrajit's lips, but he continued, "They will meet the consequences of their actions if we refuse to become like them. If we adopt their principles, we could become lost in a perpetual cycle of violence."

Indrajit's voice grew louder. "Aren't we already? Within days, a Rezzian with the power to rule the world will be here. And you would have us wait for him and let their forces rest? Did you come here to be passive, or to fight for Pawelon, my Prince? What karma would come to you for standing aside and watching your own nation fall?"

Rao's pride burned within. He knew his ego was too attached to the debate. "If we attack them in the open field, we'd be just as much at risk as they would be. Haven't we kept them at bay all these years with proven tactics? Why expose our whole army to them?"

"Our gamble is wise given the circumstances. Their decision to meet us is not. They should wait for their king and Haizzem, but since the king left they've been too proud for that."

This debate has its own momentum. I can't stop it now. "I find it strange that one reckless strategy can be so right, and the other so wrong."

"Because you are not seeing anything in context. We are seizing our best chance to send the dogs home." Indrajit tightened his jaw, and a few teeth showed through his snarl.

"We've held them off for nearly a decade. We've perfected our defenses. Why take such a risk? We could throw everything away guessing about a new development we don't understand yet. Patience is a valid tactic in war, isn't it? And observation? Who knows what the Haizzem will do?"

Indrajit's cutting eyes shot toward Rao. "War doesn't always afford us the luxury of contemplation, sage."

"Should we become just like them?" Rao heard his voice wavering with insecurity. "Change ourselves because they pushed us? Haven't we lost already then?" *I sound like a starry-eyed juvenile.*

"The arrogant cannot be defeated with flowers or meditation. Only force can stop fanatics." Indrajit pointed a finger at Rao. The general's arm shook as he paused. "My Prince, you have no experience to back up your platitudes, but you mouth your tripe as if you're wiser than a man three times your age. Join me in the real world if you have the stomach for it. Your father does."

Rao's gut turned over, but his convictions spewed out. "I can help you today, General. I'm sure of that. But I didn't come here to be the aggressor. I came here to defend our people and our territory, not to bring the fight to our enemy. I'll do my part to ensure our soldiers return safely today. If their Haizzem leads them into battle, I will adjust. But I will never throw the first spear."

"They have thrown the first spear for nine long years. Now, while they are without their spiritual leaders, we can push them back. If we don't stop them here, our way of life may soon be over. Your royal line could be snuffed out. Our people could be their slaves. Could you live with that karma?"

"A man must act on his conscience. I would rather die than live by no greater principle than my own survival."

Indrajit glared sideways. "Be careful what you ask for. A spiritual prodigy should understand the power of his own words."

They rounded the edge of a red cliff wall, and the great valley opened up before them. "Look, Prince Rao. The dogs are coming to meet us."

Spanning across most of the horizon, the Rezzian army advanced from the east. Behind them, their dust cloud turned the blue sky ochre.

"We are going to fight them. If you're determined to be gutless, then don't help us drive them back to the hells." The general looked up at the suddenly brooding sky. "No wonder your father thinks so little of you. You are weak. Less than his shadow."

"You're right, General." The voice of the sage Briraji came as a surprise.

"Welcome, Briraji," Rao said, "we were just—"

"Engaging in an adolescent's debate," Briraji quipped. "General, I can relieve Rao from his duty and protect you now."

"Then do so, master sage," Indrajit said. "Prince Rao, I have no use for you on this day." Indrajit's eyes bored into Rao once more. "Officers!" The general strode ahead and began giving his men directions for the coming battle.

Rao slowed and stayed behind the commotion, but remained close enough to observe the general.

Briraji kept pace with Rao. "You will see us using some truly amazing powers today. I have a deadly surprise for their leadership. Watch for it. It will come from the heavens." Briraji recoiled as crackling lightning illuminated swift, dark clouds over the valley.

The goddess Ysa, Rao realized. *This storm means the royal daughter is here.*

Rao maintained a respectful tone, as his training dictated with a high-ranking sage. "I will observe your powers, Briraji, and hope to learn of them from you, when you deem me worthy enough to teach."

Brijaji only narrowed his eyes.

Indrajit yelled at Rao from a dozen paces away, "I go now to defend Pawelon."

Rao yelled back, "I can't sanction your aggression, but I will protect our men. This storm is from their goddess Ysa. The royal daughter must be here. She will have her own powers."

"Then she will be my target," Briraji said, beside him.

A clap of thunder shocked the air.

"We will handle them with or without you." A rare smile appeared on Indrajit's face, and he yelled louder so that more men could hear him. "It's a shame the rajah's only living son is afraid to fight a girl. If your brothers had lived, perhaps your father could have been proud of one of them. Our enemies killed the wrong ones."

Indrajit's taunting felt like an icy blade cutting Rao's heart. The general obviously knew more about what happened to Rao's brothers than he did.

Rao moved outside the formation and let the waves of soldiers march past him. He scanned the determined faces of the rows of men marching toward the battle.

You won't die if I can do anything about it.

He followed the troops into the valley, and climbed atop the highest rise overlooking what was to be the battlefield. Only parched shrubs, noisy insects, and black birds seemed to live at the valley floor. Hills and ditches made much of the canyon land uneven, but the armies were converging on a plain. Another great mass of Pawelon troops approached from the southern trail, but they wouldn't be able to join the battle for some time. Because of this, the Pawelon troops near Rao were outnumbered by at least two to one.

The Pawelon and Rezzian armies marched closer together. Closer and closer until Pawelon's forces were commanded to stop. Their infantry extended long spears and held great round shields along the front lines, weaving a tapestry of muscle and iron to punish any Rezzian charge. On a hill near to Rao, a score of sages stood with their arms held rigidly overhead like the branches of tall trees, humming a complex scale of mystical tones.

The enemy's legions charged as expected, running ahead in great rectangular formations with their long, curling rectangular shields held in front of their bodies and over their heads. Pawelon's archers pulled back on their bows, a sinewy and screeching racket, and unleashed their volley.

Pawelon's missiles took flight in a black swarm. The sages' toning deepened. As their humming grew louder and reached a stirring pitch, the arrow swarm expanded before raining down in a supernatural torrent, the density of arrows multiplied by the sages' powers. Rezzian screams filled the air. Rao observed the horrible noise with detachment, not allowing himself to feel or contemplate its full meaning.

He breathed deliberately, pulling his consciousness inward, seeking his calm center.

A high-pitched whine blared from the darkening heavens. A blazing object burned through the sky, aiming at the rear of the Rezzian army. The celestial fireball arced down and exploded with an ear-splitting boom, creating an eruption of high-flying sparks near the center of the Rezzian forces. The valley floor shook, rumbled, and cracked.

As if responding, the clouds swirled faster, turned pitch-black, and hovered above Pawelon's forces. A vicious, freezing wind blew down on them.

And terror filled their veins.

Chapter 11: To Dream of Battle

BY THE TIME LUCIA SET OFF on horseback to meet Strategos Duilio, the Rezzian army had already begun its trek through the valley. The formations inched forward like an army of ants in the basin of Gallea's most impressive canyon, long-haired infantry clattering with tall shields on their left arms, held throwing spears poking up above right shoulders, fat double-edged stabbing swords still sheathed, wrought iron cuirasses over maroon tunics, and bronze helms with long cheek guards and colorful horsehair plumes.

Pawelon's citadel peered mockingly over the edge of the high western rim. The Rezzians anticipated the usual skirmishes with their enemy on the trails leading up to the fortress. Early battles each day typically took place around the mouth of the northern or southern trail, sometimes at both locations. Pawelon would either fortify the wide trailheads with countless rows of long spears, and archers stationed on ledges in the cliffs, or they would spread out their forces with long spearmen placed, at least seven rows deep, at the most narrow points along the two routes to the citadel.

Whenever the Pawelons left thin resistance below, the Rezzians climbed in tight formations like tortoises, carrying their curved shields at their front, sides, rear, and over their heads to defend against any Pawelon archers able to find purchase among the tall cliffs.

Throughout the Rezzian army, it was widely believed that the apathy of Lord Galleazzo, King Vieri's patron god, had blocked them from reaching the citadel over the previous year. The soldiers also noted that the new plague began soon after their martial luck turned sour. But by divine will—whether miraculous or ironic—the plague had spared the army itself; the sickness only afflicted the common people of Rezzia and their neighbors.

'*'

Lucia rode toward the troops on her white mare, flanked by her bald warpriest guards. She'd been told the canyon floor had been beautiful before so many soldiers trampled its vegetation over the course of the war. Still, the desert smelled clean and fresh, noisy insects and birds lived among the land, and the red dirt held a hint of magic, despite its bloody history.

To distract her thoughts from the impending carnage, she mused on Ilario's arrival. There would be no other women around the camp besides the harlots, so he would have no more excuses. If he loved her, this would be his chance to say it. She'd waited long enough.

Up ahead, a standard-bearer held the round, tasseled, crimson and gold imperial flag, a proud rendering of the sun. Normally the standard would follow the king in battle, but for now it signaled the Strategos's position at the rear of the army's dust cloud. After a pull on Albina's reins and a firm kick, Lucia soon approached the old man whom her father had entrusted with his legions.

The Strategos was nearly seventy now, with curly white hair hanging down to his shoulders. Duilio's kind disposition shone from his rosy face, a countenance Lucia found amusingly ill-fitting on the commander of Rezzia's feared army.

"Tell me, how does Your Grace fare on this glorious day?"

Lucia surprised herself with a smile brought on by Duilio's charm. She wondered how he managed to remain so cheerful in this soul-crushing place.

"It's the most recent worst day of my life," she said. "Thank you for asking."

"I hope you will continue to let me know every way I can make you feel more comfortable. Your father and brother come closer to us every day now—we expect them in merely two days."

"I don't suppose we could call all of this off then? Take a holiday to celebrate our new Dux Spiritus?"

"If you would prefer it, Your Grace."

So very tempting, she thought. "It hardly seems practical, Strategos."

They rode on in silence. She knew Duilio was giving her the chance to agree to his offer, but her father's instructions were clear: Engage the enemy at every opportunity, just as he would. Maintain pressure and do not let the Pawelons rest, so that victory will follow soon after Caio's arrival.

"Your Grace, do you know much about Lord Cosimo?"

"Strategos, you asked me the same question when I was a girl."

Duilio reached behind his breastplate and gathered his ragged necklace, pulling up the hanging symbol of his god, a curved letter in the ancient script indicating the vast totality of all possibilities. "Few understand The Lord of

Miracles. Most take miracles to be gifts that come freely to the lucky. If you would like to join me in praying to him today, pray not for powerful wonders to rescue us, but for the dedication to noble values and endeavors which make us worthy of receiving such grace—"

"Duilio, why are our soldiers stopping?" Odd, because they were far from the trails that climbed to Pawelon's citadel.

"A very good question, Your Grace."

Soon every soldier stopped and looked around for an answer. A messenger on horseback brought shocking news. The Pawelons had marched, early in the morning, perhaps all of their forces into the valley, half of them down the northern passage, half down the southern one. Two rectangular formations approached, one from the northwest and one from the southwest, so that in the worst event Rezzia's army could be outflanked by a monstrous pincer.

From Danato's nightmare hell to this one, Lucia thought.

She waited with Duilio for Rezzia's commanders to join them to discuss their strategy. The rest of the army sat and chattered in hushed but excited voices.

Lucia watched the sky filling with dark clouds and felt humidity moistening her face. *What madness is this?*

I'm dreaming. She looked high and low for signs of Lord Danato. *No, I woke up this morning. But these black clouds! And this unbelievable challenge from Pawelon. This cannot be reality. They wouldn't change their tactics and throw their entire army at us.*

"What now, Danato?" she mumbled without intending to. *You want me to experience all of our soldiers dying this time?* "Wake me up now, bastard." She meant to speak the second time.

"What is that, Your Grace?"

"Duilio, they wouldn't leave their citadel, would they?"

"I apologize. I did not foresee this possibility."

"The bulk of their forces have remained close to their citadel the entire war." Lucia pointed up to the west. "Isn't this absurd?"

"It is indeed a drastic departure for General Indrajit."

"And the clouds. How often do you see clouds like these in the valley?"

"Never before, Your Grace." Duilio searched the sky, contemplating. "We must hope it is not an omen for us. Perhaps it is an unfortunate omen for Pawelon. They are acting out of character."

Show your foul face to me, Black One.

Lord Danato did not appear. Instead, a veteran council of long-haired Rezzians quickly formed around Duilio and Lucia.

First came young Tirso, from the far eastern coastal villages, believed by his men to be the son of the god Sansone. Heavy Manto, from the sparse forests south of Remaes, rode to them on a fat, dull horse. Fair Raf, long-bearded and moustached, from the wide nomadic plains, carried the historic great sword of his tribe across his back. Noble Alimene, known throughout the army for his captivating tales of the sea, represented the great port city of Peraece.

The brothers Fulvio and Forese, sons of the wealthiest family in Rezzia, from the Lympia province made fertile by the goddess Jacopa. Giunto, the protector of windy Petrus's walled cities, so feared by the scavenging clans who were Petrus's enemies. Wandering Belincion, leader of a mysterious order of men and women devoted to the goddess Vani. And from the empty, lifeless region of Satrina came Pexaro, slovenly cousin to Lucia's father, who brought with him a constant stream of deadly spear throwers.

"Is it possible they outnumber us?" said a voice from the chorus.

"It is possible. Yes," Duilio answered. "Their numbers are a mystery, but our scouts estimate their forces to be relatively equal to our own."

Mighty Tirso barked from beneath his red-plumed helm, "It wouldn't matter if they outnumbered us three to one. Once we close with them, their spearmen will be no match for our swords."

Giunto slammed the butt of his throwing spear into the ground. "Our Haizzem ascends to Dux Spiritus and, look, our prayers have been answered. We have a chance to fight the pigs on a real battlefield, as if they were not cowards for just one day."

"But our position is a disadvantage," Belincion said in placid tones. "They come from the north and the south."

"No," Giunto answered, "we still have strategic options if we act quickly."

Tirso explained, "Move the bulk of our troops either directly north or south, being sure to keep the Pawelons in front of us. They will not dance with us all day. When they close in, we will not find ourselves caught between them."

"And that would be suicide for our camp," Vani countered. "Our food and water. Our tents and supplies. The wounded and the servants could all be killed."

Tirso stepped toward Belincion and leaned his spear forward. "Only if they keep their forces split, giving us an overwhelming advantage against whatever they send against us. We still have reserve men and warpriests at the camp."

"And that could mean total victory for Rezzia." Giunto's expressive face shone with courage. "Praises to the gods of Lux Lucis!"

Bearded Raf raised one hand. "Be cautious, brothers! The pigs' sages must have surprises in store for us. We have an obligation to our Haizzem not to risk his army."

"Indeed." Fulvio looked like a king in his exquisite, brightly polished armor. "We may not be ready for their dark trickery. And the gods only seem to ignore us. Soon our Haizzem will come. We should behave guardedly until he arrives."

"Your Grace," The old Strategos turned his soft eyes to Lucia, "I regret that you are in the middle of this predicament, in which we find ourselves unprepared. Is there anything you wish to say?"

Lucia dismounted and stood amongst the men. She removed Ysa's helm and tossed her dark red hair behind her shoulders. "I find all of this hard to believe." She looked around and behind them, finding nothing of Danato. *Fine, I'll play your awful game.* "Their sudden desperation could be to our advantage, but it seems they're looking for a wild melee. Why play into their hands? There is still time to fall back and protect our camp."

"We are not cowards." Tirso did not move as he spoke.

"We did not come to retreat from an inferior enemy," Giunto said.

Alimene bowed before he spoke. "Your Grace, my men left their families to join your father. They came to glorify their souls, their gods, and their king in battle. Now they can finally prove their worth as warriors on even ground."

Lucia held Ysa's helm to one side and placed her other hand on her opposite shoulder. "I admit if my father were here, he would engage them. But now this army belongs to my brother. We cannot be reckless. We'll be stronger once my brother is here."

Tirso crossed his spear in front of his shield as he leaned his head back. "Duilio, will you see my warriors commanded to flee by a woman?"

Lucia fired back. "I do not command this army, Tirso, the Strategos does, and he will decide our course. I am only here to carry the relics of Ysa to protect our warriors." Lucia unsheathed Ysa's white sword, pointed its tip at Tirso's feet, and rotated the blade. Duilio bowed while astride his horse and the others bowed from their standing positions. She lifted Ysa's bejeweled shield, miraculously light on her gloved arm, and slammed the flat of her blade against it, producing a rousing hum that silenced the assembly.

I dare you, Danato, to torture me with your sister's relics in my hands.

'*'

Unseen by all, the petite, blond goddess Ysa rode her enormous bone-white horse around the council. The beast stepped around the assembly with godlike patience, a perfect reflection of its rider. Ysa's stoical face pointed away, to the Pawelons in the west, as she absorbed their words.

'*'

"Do you believe Ysa will protect our men this day?" Alimene asked.

"How long have our ancestors fought under the spiritual protection of Ysa's sword and shield? For centuries. Yet I can only pray to my goddess with her instruments in my hands. I can't make any promises about what gods will do." *Because I don't understand their logic at all.*

"My brothers," said a voice from the chorus, "look at the coming storm! Perhaps the goddess Ysa is with us already."

Lucia hadn't considered that. It might be true, although the sky was also dark enough to indicate another deceit from Lord Danato.

"He is right!" Giunto said. "Look, how swiftly they move. They must be from Ysa!"

"Brothers, it is time for a decision," Duilio said in his easy voice, astride his decorated horse. "I can only believe what Tirso and Giunto have suggested. Look at how the clouds come from the west, casting a dark shadow over Pawelon's army. I believe Ysa is with us today—all praises to The Protector of Man—and that she is prepared to defend us with her storm and fury. I feel this in my heart, men, do you not? Are we not in the right?"

Fulvio and Forese nodded vehemently. Their nodding grew contagious and a consensus formed with cheering followed by raised throwing spears.

"Then we shall do as our king has instructed us," Duilio continued. "We must engage and pressure our enemy, and weaken them for his return and for the coming of our Haizzem. We will grant our royal daughter her wishes, as well. Manto, I must send you and your men back to our camp. Remain there, no matter what occurs in the valley, and ready our defenses in case they are needed.

The rest of us will immediately march north. Raf, lead your cavalry quickly ahead and prepare to slip around their right flank when we rush forward.

"Should they move their entire force toward our camp as we move aside, we will allow it, block their retreat, and trap them in the valley. We will defeat all they send against us, and with the gods' good fortune we may win this war today. I ask you humbly to pray with me to Lord Cosimo, not for an easy victory, nor for anything we do not deserve. Pray for the miracle of utter devotion to our chosen path, so that we may attract the gods' aid, like a determined flower calling to the sun from a rocky field."

Lucia mounted her mare again and listened to the proliferating commands directing the bulk of the Rezzian army to move north and leave their camp exposed to their enemy. She looked about for signs of Danato's presence but found none. Whether dreaming or awake, she was perfectly confused.

'*'

Ysa rode directly in front of Lucia, anticipating her devotee's every movement. The goddess kept her cool gaze upon the distant Pawelon army, and willed the sky to fill with darkness.

Chapter 12: The Wrath of Athena

THE REZZIANS gave rise to a percussive din: rhythmic crunching of boots, hearts pounding against metal, out-breaths exploding in unison, tens of thousands racing as one, muscling to live another hour beneath the goddess's baleful sky.

Lucia watched as Duilio ensured the legions advanced in ideal formations. His corps of commanders rode on horseback, giving commands and receiving information, relaying to the Strategos detailed accounts of their movements.

Soon after the council had ended, the legions held their shields and spears close to their bodies, each man turned in place to his right, and they ran north in formation to avoid becoming surrounded by Pawelon's two armies. Running hard, they advanced farther north than Pawelon's northern troop, which had been slow to respond to their sudden change in direction. That Raf's cavalry were well ahead suggested their northern flank would remain protected.

Duilio smiled above his caparisoned steed. "Our men are fit. The pigs are slow, physically and mentally. They won't outmaneuver us today."

Lucia watched the Pawelon armies falling behind their own. "I hope our men won't be too exhausted to fight."

"Oh no, Your Grace. These men yearn to push against impossible odds. They are heroes."

Swift, grey clouds overshadowed them all, flaunting a supernatural origin. Lucia knew that had the legions not been rushing to save their lives, each and every man would have stopped and stood in awe of the waves of lightning streaking around the dark sky.

Confusion still clouded her mind. Was this the obvious stuff of Danato's dreams, or a harsh reality that looked like a fantasy? She prayed to Ysa to protect them.

'*'

Unseen by men, the goddess Ysa's beast of a horse walked confidently through the Rezzian ranks, its thin rider demonstrating unshakeable poise. Her pointed nose, tight cheeks, and thin lips—and around her face a silver helm framing her jaw—made her fair-skinned face appear sharp with deadly calm.

Ysa willed her horse to gallop and soon halted in the narrowing space between the two armies. A cool breeze swept through the desert plain. She studied the Pawelon army, her blond hair stirring in a full-bodied mass near the center of her back. She looked to Lucia, far in the distance, and raised a fist covered in a bright gauntlet.

'*'

Lucia spotted a searing burst of light near Pawelon's army. Once it dimmed she focused on the enemy's changing positions. She yelled to Duilio, "They're widening their front line."

The old man looked intently with an air of disbelief, his vision aided by the fingers of lightning glowing above. Pawelon was creating a wide front line from north to south and stretching its northern flank farther back to the west, toward the nearest canyon wall. They were digging in for a fight and trying to keep the Rezzians from encircling them.

Why aren't they delaying to bring their armies together? Lucia wondered. By stopping and lengthening their formation, they were cutting off Raf's attempt to outflank them, but they would soon be engaging Rezzia with only half their strength.

"They're daring us to engage them," Lucia said.

"They can dig their graves if they want to," Duilio said as his horse moved about nervously. "Now pray for glory."

Duilio unsheathed his short blade and raised it as he screamed, "Advance! For Lux Lucis!"

'*'

At the front of the Rezzian line, Atius heard the fierce pounding of drums ordering the onset of the charge. Across the desolate battlefield, distant rows of round enemy shields waited motionlessly. Behind them, Pawelon's archers hid like cowards.

He set his feet for the charge, pointing at the heart of the enemy.

Gods, grant that I may gut ten pigs before I fall. And take me before you take my brothers.

Atius banged his throwing spear against his shield. His brothers did the same. Their clangor rolled across the desert and rose to the dark heavens.

"March!" he bellowed.

He made long strides into the open field, his men following in ranks beside him. The muscles in his arms clenched with excitement, yearning for the slaughter to come. With his body protected behind his shield, he'd rush past Pawelon's outstretched spears, ram his own shield against his enemy's, and surprise the first pig with a violent stab to his gut. He'd push further into the wall of spears, lashing out with his sword like a snake's tongue whenever his enemies least expected it.

They drove onward, silent and focused, within range of Pawelon's bows.

The first volley of Pawelon's black arrows took flight, soaring up against the backdrop of the red cliff walls.

Atius issued the command, "Tortoise!"

He raised his curved rectangular shield in front of him, covering himself from knees to nose. His brothers along the front and the flanks raised their shields with him, overlapping as a bulwark against the falling arrows. The remaining shields formed a tight ceiling above them. The soldier to his rear rested the forward edge of his shield on Atius's head, restricting and focusing Atius's vision forward.

"For Lux Lucis!" he yelled as they pushed on.

The hissing of arrows filled the air. The shield above Atius blocked his view of the projectiles above him, but across the field more volleys were loosed.

Atius's heart jumped. Arrows cracked against the shield over his head and at his front.

"My shield!" a man shouted.

A sudden pain ripped through Atius's left leg and he screamed. Ripples of agony arrested his mind and vision.

An arrow stuck out from his calf. His broken greave fell to the ground.

He drove on in agony, unable to do anything but march alongside his brothers. He yearned to grab at his wound, but his mind held strong and he refused to lower his shield.

The shafts rained in front of them as a black blur. Some lodged into the earth, some skidded along the ground, others shattered upon impact.

He gritted his teeth and forced his wounded leg to swing forward.

More arrows crashed, like a swift explosion of hail on a rooftop. Men screamed in horror.

How is this happening? On other occasions, he'd witnessed the volleys loosed by ten thousand Pawelon archers. Now ten times more arrows were falling. The ground became a sea of black wooden shafts.

Their sages ...

He saw his wife before his eyes, her long, thick hair and full lips above soft breasts and shoulders. She'd wear black for him when he died, and pray to Lord Danato to guard his soul.

"Aaargh!"

A second arrow pierced his wounded leg. He reached down reflexively, lowering his shield and leaning forward for just a moment.

An arrow whizzed past his ear and the soldier behind him screamed and crumpled. The soldier behind the fallen one tripped and fell forward, knocking against Atius's legs as the man's shield rattled against the ground.

Atius turned to look at the fallen warriors. An arrow ripped into his left shoulder. An uncontrollable scream escaped his lungs.

In horrific pain, he tossed his spear as far forward as his muscles allowed. He tried to raise his shield to protect himself, but his arm refused, trembling.

More screams.

More arrows falling around them.

He stumbled and collapsed, choking as blood filled his mouth.

A final pain shot through his heart.

'*'

Frowning creases appeared on Duilio's dry face as his mouth pursed closed. "It's some sort of trick by their sages. They've multiplied their arrows."

Lucia watched the chaos around her, faintly hearing terrible screams in the distance. Would this prove to be a nightmare, or her end? She knew if she died today, her father and brother would bring such a fury against Pawelon that nothing would remain of their fortress and army.

Then, as she contemplated the worst, a distant whining turned into a terrifying howl. A fiery light burned its way across the sky, from the west above the Pawelon citadel and all their distant lands. The object arced its way downward, flying toward her and the Strategos.

"Think of Lord Cosimo now, Your Grace." Duilio spurred his horse toward the conflict.

Lucia followed. "We are too late now. Stop!" She caught up with Duilio as he halted and looked to her.

"I believe in you, Lucia. Do what you can."

Lightning exploded and etched its way across the sky like a drunken spider's web, then disappeared in an instant. As the sky grew dark again, the incandescent object plummeted at an ungodly speed.

Lucia prayed to Ysa and thrust her shield over their heads as if trying to block a hurricane with a hat. A long fork of lightning lit the sky.

A wave of force emanated from the shield. The celestial object exploded well above Lucia, blasting shards of smoldering rock all about and knocking every man within a hundred paces to the ground.

Duilio's horse reared up as the blast drove it backward, and the old Strategos fell hard. Lucia's mare went straight down with its legs bent. The earth rippled and split as crevasses erupted across the desert floor.

She threw an arm around Albina's neck and rolled to the ground once the rumbling calmed, many breaths later. Soldiers slowly came to their feet, grimacing and holding their wounds.

Lucia and many others rushed to Duilio's aid. The Strategos lay on his back mumbling. He tried to stand but fell sideways.

She knelt beside him and touched her black-gloved hand to his forehead. "Cosimo and Ysa saved us, Strategos." She could barely hear herself speaking; her ears were nearly deaf from the explosion. More aftershocks jostled them and for a moment she lost her balance.

Duilio smiled. The right side of his head was a mass of blood. "Lucia, go. We need your goddess."

She kissed Duilio's forehead. "Keep thinking of Lord Cosimo."

She left the soldiers and warpriests to tend to the Strategos and mounted Albina again. Arrows continued knifing her soldiers. Pawelon's front line held strong. Though the enemy forces were greatly outnumbered, because of their trickery they were on the verge of routing her army.

Ysa, I beg you, protect us now, before we all perish. I want to see my brother again. And if this is a dream, let me know now. She drew the sword from its scabbard and

70

held it at her mare's right side. She pulled her shield closer to her body, squeezing the leather-covered metal grip. *Ysa, please ...*

Every warrior in the valley cowered as the goddess's thunder detonated and assaulted their ears. The boom rolled around them, like a coiling sonic snake. It tumbled, turned in all directions, rose and fell wildly.

Yet to Lucia's traumatized ears, the thunder sounded muffled. She turned her head sideways and observed her kingdom's frightened warriors.

Go to them, she heard an inner voice, a firm-sounding woman. *Then give yourself to me.*

She yelled and spurred Albina into motion, then headed toward the violence at what felt like an impossible speed. Many soldiers and warpriests tried to keep up with her, but their horses fell behind. Everything blurred before her eyes and her head throbbed with dizziness.

Without warning, her mare stopped and Lucia pitched onto the compacted ground, her shoulders and head scraping along the desert floor. As she lay recovering for a moment, a burst of intuition told her Ysa's armor and helm had prevented serious injuries. She willed herself to stand without knowing where she was and raised Ysa's sword and shield in self-defense.

The sword vibrated powerfully enough to nearly make her arm numb.

Nearby, a band of Pawelons marched forward, using their spears to drive a group of Rezzian soldiers back. The Pawelons' uniforms were dark blue, their skin deep shades of brown. She hadn't intended to come this close to the fighting. A tall Pawelon surged forward and thrust his spear through a Rezzian's shield, into his chest.

The rangy Pawelon spotted her.

His snarl deepened as he raced toward her.

With gusty winds eddying around them, she raised her shield arm barely in time to deflect the spear. As his momentum carried him off balance, she stabbed the blade across her body and into his chest.

They both screamed, and the Pawelon fell and grabbed her legs. She jumped backward and watched the man clutch his wound. The blade still sent tremors through her body.

She looked down. The white metal dripped with his blood.

She had no time to grasp what she had done before the clouds literally fell down like a sagging belly over Pawelon's forces. The midday shadows were like

71

night, and the temperature plummeted to freezing. Gusting winds swept waves of hail toward the Pawelon troops, overtaking their arrows for command of the air.

She heard the woman's voice again in her ear: *Surrender to the ancient implements to control the storm.*

Some buried instinct took over as Lucia began to let go of control. Her musculature softened and her heart warmed. Every hair on her body stood straight up as she felt an awesome power flow through her. She began to *feel* the storm so profoundly that the boundary between her spirit and the sky dissolved. Was she directing the weather, or was it directing her?

She felt the tempest responding to her, and the more she allowed herself to welcome it, the more aggressively it pounded the Pawelon forces with deluges of ice. Her instincts led her inward to even greater exultation. As she went deeper all capacity for rational thought disappeared.

A column of lightning erupted. It streaked down and startled her with its thickness, as it pulsed and rolled all around Pawelon's forces. Moving by sheer instinct, Lucia squeezed Ysa's sword and her body tingled with divine power from head to toe. She felt flushed with heat, feeling the storm ravaging the Pawelon men with savage power.

Another column of electricity came down. Another. And another.

And then, without warning, the sensations subsided. The lightning columns shrank and then disappeared. Her mind returned to a normal state of awareness, and her profound connection with the natural elements dried up. The clouds turned from black to grey, then chestnut to white, rising into the heavens. She felt a sense of loss, of abandonment, as the sky no longer embraced her.

Looking down at the blood coating Ysa's white blade, she remembered what she had done.

Lucia sensed an evil presence, and nausea overcame her.

Chapter 13:
A Burial Truce Offering

THE CLOUDS SWIRLED faster above Pawelon's forces and turned pitch-black. A vicious, freezing wind blew down on them. The deafening thunder drubbed Rao's ears and seized his heart. He cowered as the boom froze his mind.

The storm goddess's rage weakened his muscles, his concentration, his resolve. *Did Briraji kill the royal daughter?*

It doesn't matter.

With those words, Rao withdrew his attention from his body and physical senses, resting for a moment in the spacious emptiness underlying existence.

He returned his awareness to his body: muscles relaxing, blood flowing, breath arising and falling.

He adopted a wide, solid stance and detached again from his thoughts, body, and senses. A single point of light appeared in the black emptiness and it became the focus of his meditation. His attention remained on the tiny light for seven long breaths, until the light expanded and washed over him, giving him glimpses of nonmaterial realities intersecting his world.

Focus on the battlefield.

The chaotic flood of information fell away from his awareness, like light retreating into a tunnel. His physical being transformed into a lighter, subtler body, and he saw the battlefield anew.

The storming sky appeared as a complex mass of blinding light and shadow, unified as a single field by some greater intelligence. The sky breathed with wild contractions, moving lower and lower to the ground, until it hovered just above Pawelon's troops.

Rao steeled himself with conviction. *You will not engulf my people.*

He pushed his awareness into the body of a random Pawelon soldier to witness his experience, finding panic amid the darkness, bitter cold, and biting hail. A moment later, a pillar of electrical force ripped through the man, slamming him like a thousand bricks.

73

Rao drew his consciousness away and observed the scene. More columns of lightning arose between the ground and sky, moving around like puppets under strings. The deadly clouds sank lower and the Rezzians began racing toward the Pawelons and throwing their spears. If they kept coming, close combat would favor the invaders.

He meditated: *How can I stop their goddess?*

He noticed then, despite all the dazzling flashes of light, the glowing of a single human soul where the two armies were colliding. The subtle bodies of most men appeared a dull red, but here was a gigantic, swirling field of yellow and white surrounding an intense red and black pulse. Trails of light stretched up from this being to the sky.

The royal daughter is alive!

Each vibrant line between her and the sky was a gossamer trace of psychic influence. Rao poured his awareness into one of the trails of light.

Such a glorious sensation! Expanding light and power, ecstasy and interconnection.

He tried to focus his attention, to sever this connection between the royal daughter and the storm. The light swung around wildly, battling his will, shocking his mind. He recognized the royal daughter's talent for defense and control.

Rao settled deeper within himself, calling on deep reservoirs of spiritual energy, and visualized the stream of psychic energy vanishing to nothing.

It exploded outward with an electrical burst and scattered his consciousness with it. An unknown length of time passed before his awareness coalesced again on the ground near the royal daughter. Her unique aura revealed a strange blend of spiritual light, potent aggression, and fear.

Rao focused his attention to stop her before she could conjure another miracle. He could attack her subtle body directly, leaving her spirit fragmented. Or, he could take a very different approach, one full of risk and hope.

Rao studied the shimmering light and pulsing darkness around her aura. He decided to address the light. He sent toward her a great thought form, an idea that would go deeply into her subconscious mind.

Peace ...

He watched her aura ripple and flux.

Her consciousness became still, then inactive like someone beginning to sleep.

A flash of light washed over him.

Rao opened his eyes to a blue sky, lying on his back on an empty patch of land not far from General Indrajit.

My spiritual energy is gone.

Indrajit was in the midst of an intense discussion with Briraji and four other high-ranking sages. Rao formulated his argument, stood, and ran toward them.

He tried to appear full of breath and vitality as he approached them. "General Indrajit, Briraji, I've stopped the royal daughter from connecting with the elements. She controlled the storm. Her power could return, and I may not be able to stop her again. We should leave now, before she acts again."

Briraji only scowled, while Indrajit's gaze seemed to be searching Rao's soul. Indrajit turned to Briraji, but the sage had no words.

What other choice do you have now, general?

The general yelled to his messengers, "Call for our full retreat."

His instructions commanded the archers and sages to work together to create enough arrow fire to deter the Rezzians from following them. Pawelon could not engage Rezzia's forces directly without risking being overrun, nor could they afford to wait for the rest of their forces with the desperate Rezzian army so close and the royal daughter still among them.

The Rezzians apparently did not wish to see the multiplying of Pawelon's arrows again. They stood their ground and yelled insults as the Pawelons backed away and retreated toward their citadel.

And so the armies returned, Rezzia to their camp and Pawelon to their fortress, dragging their dead and supporting their wounded.

Chapter 14:
The Unseen One in Prophecy

Lucia dreamed ...

CAIO SLIPPED OUT OF BED after midnight wearing a plain white robe. He quietly removed Lucia's letter from under his pillow and tiptoed out of the yurt, relieved that Ilario remained asleep. Once outside, he quickly covered his mouth to ask the guards to remain quiet. As Caio walked away, ten soldiers silently followed.

He turned away from the winding road packed with sleeping reinforcements and walked into the desert, heading for a distant hill. The night was nurtured by soft moonlight, smelling of sage, filled with the chirping of insects. The soldiers followed at a respectful distance.

Caio asked them to remain at the base of the slope, and began to climb. Lucia's curling parchment crinkled as he pressed it into his palm. After reaching the peak, he gathered ten large stones and set them in a circle as an altar to the gods of Lux Lucis.

He prayed out with passion, "Lord Oderigo, God of Prophecy," and then placed the letter at the heart of the makeshift shrine. "I seek your light and beg you for rays of truth. Why does Lord Danato stalk my sister in the quiet of night?" Caio prostrated, lowering the crown of his skull to the earth.

Many heartbeats passed as no response came ...

Rocks stirred in the distance.

Heavy footsteps walked toward him.

A loud pop shattered the quiet—the sudden closing of a heavy book.

The figure approached, kicking dusty stones at Caio.

"Look to your Lord."

Caio lifted his head to see majestic Lord Oderigo covered in vines and lowering the heavy Book of Time to him. The god's luminous skin smelled of holy *myrrha*, so much that it transported Caio to boyhood memories of ecstatic worship at the Reveria. Oderigo's eyes were vacant black portals stretching into the future and past, into all that had been and all that would come to be.

"Stand and read."

The Book of Time rested on Oderigo's enormous hands, its pages edged with gold. Caio bowed his head, held out two fingers on each hand to thank his lord, and opened The Book. He read accounts of Lucia's long suffering, of the fervent interest The Black One held for her since the death of their mother. Caio grimaced as he read on under the radiant light of the moon, all the way through to a prophecy of the present day:

And so a choice lay before the daughter and son of King Vieri. Lord Danato's terrible vision was certain: the war with Pawelon would not end for another ten years. That is, unless the pair journeyed to Lord Danato's fabled underworld, that harrowed place which confronts men with their shadows and promises tragedy in compensation for His mercy.

Caio closed the book, looked down and shut his eyes.

The wind howled a deep, echoing tone.

He looked up and found Oderigo gone. Lord Danato towered over Caio, his black skin reflecting the bright moonlight.

Caio fell to his knees and spread his arms forward in prostration to The Black One.

Lord Danato picked up Caio with both hands, his pointed nails cutting into the Haizzem's chest.

He wrapped his pitch-black fingers around Caio's neck and squeezed so tightly that Caio's choking failed to produce a sound.

Caio's eyes trembled with sorrow as they closed. Danato released his corpse onto the stony altar.

'*'

Peace to you ... Caio prayed for Lucia and looked down on her distressed, sleeping face.

Lucia woke with a gasp.

Caio sat in a chair beside her bed, feeling all the love he possessed for her. He had lit the candles on her dresser after he entered her yurt. Shadows danced around the room.

77

I was so afraid I'd never see you again, he thought. *Father was right. Ysa kept you safe.*

"Caio!" She left her mouth open and blinked repeatedly, as if she thought her eyes were deceiving her. Only her face peeked out from beneath the cream wool blanket.

"I had to see you as soon as I arrived. We were too close to stop again overnight."

"Is it really you?"

He leaned down to hug her through the blanket, and she squeezed his chest so hard he stopped breathing.

"Are you well?" she asked. Lucia let go and let Caio sit up again.

"Yes. I am only tired. I haven't been able to stop thinking of you."

She frowned, seeming at a loss for words.

"I'm so sorry," he said. "I've never been able to know what you are feeling—I don't know why. I wish you had told me before now."

"You didn't need to know. Did you consult with Lord Oderigo?"

"Yes. I couldn't sleep after I got your letter. I went out alone into the desert, and he came to me—"

"Lord Oderigo did? What did he say?"

"He showed me The Book of Time. I saw many things. And," Caio considered his words carefully, "he showed me that Danato's message is indeed very serious. But there may still be another way." *I hope and pray this is true.*

"What did you see? What other option do we have?"

Caio had already decided not to tell her what he read about visiting Lord Danato's underworld. Scripture promised that such a journey might cause more problems than it would solve. "It is up to us to find another way."

"Caio, I dreamt about all of this. Just now, just before I woke up. I was there. I saw you." Lucia's brow tightened with concern. "At first I saw Lord Oderigo with you, but then, after you read from The Book, in my dream Lord Danato himself stood over you."

Then Lord Danato entered your dreams again. "No, it was only Lord Oderigo."

"And I read ... did you read what Danato has done to me?"

Caio hadn't planned on letting her know. "Yes." He wondered if in the dream she read the same thing he did about visiting Danato's underworld, but he was not going to bring it up. They stared at each other in silence, too afraid to say any more about what was written in The Book.

"Ilario is outside. If you want to see him—"

Her eyes sparkled. "He's right out there? I just need a little time to get dressed."

"Of course. We both want to hear about what you've been through."

"I'm sure that would do me some good."

Caio leaned down and kissed her cheek. She smelled of jasmine and perspiration.

"I couldn't have waited another day for you," she said. "I've thought up a plan."

Chapter 15: The Lovers' Respite

ILARIO WAS CHATTING WITH LUCIA'S GUARDS, recounting the glorious Dux Spiritus ceremony, when Caio exited the yurt. The soldiers dropped to their knees and prostrated again. Caio thanked them for their service and walked among them, touching the backs of their heads to bless them.

As Ilario hunted for movement in the darkness, with his ears keen to every rustling noise, anxiety still vexed him. "Is she ... ?"

"She's all right. She wants to see you. She's getting dressed."

Ilario nodded and tried not to look too eager to see the most arresting woman he'd ever laid eyes on. Over the years, he'd hid from his feelings for her with countless pretty faces and fleshy bodies that meant nothing to him. All the while, Lucia rejected every suitor who proposed to her. If she was actually waiting for him, she wouldn't be able to wait much longer.

Lucia opened the doors of her yurt, rivaling the beauty of the moonlight. She wore a flowing, brown, long-sleeved dress. The fabric clung tightly around her hips and ruffled near her shoulders and feet. Her breasts were fully covered, but prominent enough. "It's good to see you, Ilario. Come in." She touched his shoulder with one of her gloved hands and met his gaze with her guarded eyes.

Already you give me more than I deserve, he thought.

Candles glowed atop a dresser and from two tables on opposite sides of her bed. Against the fabric wall to the left, the armor and sword of Ysa glinted in the wavering light. Ilario bowed his head to pay respect to the goddess's relics. Amber resin incense burned and smoked atop an antique chest.

Lucia sat at the edge of her cream bed, facing the doors, and Caio and Ilario sat down in wooden chairs before her.

"Are you all right?" Ilario asked.

Lucia glanced down and narrowed her eyes, blinking.

Caio rested his elbows on his thighs and leaned forward. "Dear sister, you are safe now. The messengers told us the goddess Ysa saved you?"

Lucia looked away and wiped a tear from her cheek. "Yes, Ysa saved me."

"They only told us you were found unconscious," Ilario said.

Lucia seized him with her obsidian eyes. "After we survived the object from the heavens—truly a miracle—Ysa channeled a great storm through me, through her implements, and then ..." She stopped and struggled to swallow. "I felt a great evil around me. Dark Pawelon magic. I felt a presence. I am certain someone was there, close to me. I thought I was going to die. That's the last thing I remember."

Ilario jumped to his feet and pounded the floor as he paced the side of the room opposite Ysa's ancient metal. "We are going to find whoever did this to you." He finished each thought with a swing of his fist. "We are going to find him. And I am going to bloody kill him. I swear to you, I am going to kill the pig that did this to you."

"I wouldn't mind that," she said, "but I need to tell you, I've had a change of heart about the war. I never liked the idea of it, but after seeing its worst, Ilario, we've got to end it."

Ilario stopped his pacing and stared at her. *First Caio, now you?*

"I agree," Caio said. He knelt on one knee at Lucia's feet. "We almost lost you. We've lost so many. Palla and Nese are gone forever. How many more?"

"I'm not really important here," Ilario began, "but isn't it your duty to win the war? We could put an end to all this at any time by fleeing, but then Pawelon would actually win. And all this effort, all these lives, would be for nothing."

"Ilario is right." Lucia's steady voice put Ilario's mind at ease. "Our people have sacrificed too much for this to end without our victory. My hope is that we can force Pawelon to surrender. I have a proposal, if I may, Dux Spiritus."

"Of course, Lucia. I always trust your counsel."

"I believe if you can deal a quick, decisive blow, we may be able to shock them into surrender. They're desperate. They're clearly afraid of you. If you can overwhelm them in your first engagement, we could send a shocking message."

"We haven't engaged them since you were hurt?" Caio asked.

"No. Duilio and I decided to wait for you. Since the battle, they've remained close to their fortress. We don't really know if their tactics will be different when we next face them, so we may have the chance to meet another sizable force. Caio, if you pray to Mya and I to Ysa, we can ask that our advance be concealed with a great rain until we come upon them. If our goddesses are with us, they'll grant our request."

Lucia sat on the floor and used her fingers to paint a crude map, illustrating the situation. "They have two sentry outposts in the valley, one to the north and one to the south. If we could overrun one of them without being noticed and then conceal our advance, their defenses would have no warning. We could go out together, with just a small number of warpriests, and use our prayers to overcome these sentries."

If Ilario didn't already respect Lucia's competence, he would have thought her idea reckless and mad.

She leaned back against her bed and continued to hold their attention. "I've already discussed this with Duilio. He would go out as a distraction to the southern sentry. With luck, they might divert too many of their forces toward him. Behind us, in the north, our strongest units can march behind whatever weather we can conjure and surprise their forces on the northern trail, allowing us to march straight to their citadel."

"About these sentry outposts, what would we be up against?" Ilario asked.

"The garrisons are in remarkable defensive positions. They sit atop two of the highest peaks inside the canyon, stocked with archers and sages. Duilio tells me we have overtaken the outposts before, but always at a great loss of life, losing many thousands in exchange for the few hundred men they station there. They've taken them back from us each time, somehow much more easily. Because of this, for years now we've left the outposts alone. It's not as if we keep great secrets from them. But in this case, if our goddesses conceal our advance, surprising their main defenses could be a great advantage. It would add to their fear of our Haizzem." Her eyes narrowed as she finished.

"And you feel that if we achieve a great victory—" Caio started to say.

"Yes, I think they might realize what they're up against. If you can punish them soundly and impress them with your power, perhaps they would be willing to discuss terms for surrender."

"Your father won't accept their surrender," Ilario said. "He'll want to destroy them completely."

"Ilario, you're right. But this is your army now, Caio. You can decide our strategy. If you want this war to end without a great slaughter, we have to try something different. But if our father questions you, you'll have to stand firm."

"He's got so much invested in this war." Caio walked over to the smoking incense and took in a deep breath. "But I can't allow tens of thousands more to die. If I can stop this fighting, I must. How can I let so much blood be spilled under my command?"

"You don't have to, Caio," Lucia said, still leaning against her bed. "You command our forces now. You must accept and embrace your role, because you will have to live with the consequences, as will many others."

Now this is a surprise, Ilario thought. After all that Lucia had been through, to hope for mere surrender? What about the men who gave up their peaceful lives for the chance to defeat Pawelon completely and gloriously? Casting them aside and allowing diplomats to deal the final blow would be an insult to their honor. *But I've already said too much.*

"I agree with you. If we can enact your strategy, we will," Caio said.

"We should act before they even realize you are here," she said. "It's good you've come early. It might give us another surprising element if we can leave in the morning."

"Very well. We will need to get some sleep then," Caio said. "I'm going to step outside for some air, Ilario. The guards there are protection enough. I'll let you get caught up."

"My Haizzem, I cannot leave your side."

"But you aren't leaving me. I'll be right outside, with ten of Rezzia's most capable men. They protect my sister. I'm sure they can watch over me."

Lucia watched them silently.

"Just for a little while then," Ilario said.

Caio embraced his sister before he left. Lucia sat at the edge of her bed. Ilario stopped pacing and returned to his chair.

Ilario told himself, *Don't mess this up. Don't offend her. Just be yourself.* "It's really good to see you again."

"I've prayed every day that you and Caio would arrive early. My prayers were answered. How is he doing?" Lucia sounded just as awkwardly formal as he did.

"He really struggles with the concept of warfare. He's still accepting his role."

"If we succeed tomorrow, he may not have to fight again."

Until the next war. "Let's hope so." *Come on, this is your chance.* "I really ... I can't wait to hear about all you've been doing. Everywhere you've been. And, what you've done here."

"Ilario, I feel like I've been tasked with one thankless burden after another, year after year." Lucia stared at the fragrant smoke and let out a deep breath. "I'm tired of the traveling," she paused again, "and I've seen enough death and gore now to last me the rest of my life." She turned her attention back to Ilario with a sober look. "I don't have any more time to waste. I feel like I'm still looking for something greater."

"And you deserve that. You ... deserve the very best." *Why does everything coming out of my mouth sound stiff?* "What else *are* you looking for?"

Lucia stared at him even more intently, yielding the next move.

"You probably want to marry," Ilario said. "I know your father's pressured you."

"I've had offers. The problem is that I would like to be happy, above all else. I haven't found that anywhere yet."

"I think you will find it. I'm sure you will. And you will make one lucky man very, very happy."

Lucia looked away and ran her fingers along her face.

"The journey from Remeas—" Ilario began to say.

"What do you want for yourself, Ilario? You've had romances with a good number of ladies, haven't you? Maybe you're not cut out to be with just one woman."

Gods, this is my chance.

"No, I think I am—I know I am. I would like to be with just one woman. She would have to be very special. But it seems my duty doesn't really allow me the time."

Lucia looked away again, not quite hiding her disappointment.

"But maybe," he said.

"Why maybe?"

"I'm not sure. If the right woman came along. I don't know. It doesn't really make sense."

Lucia stared at him with a sharp, tender look in her eyes. A smile tugged at one corner of her mouth.

"I've been thinking about you a lot," he said. Her smile widened, but she obviously wasn't going to make this any easier for him. Ilario cleared his throat. "I really enjoyed being with you the last time we saw each other. I felt like I was finally beginning to know you."

She cupped one side of her face, from chin to ear, and waited for more.

You want me to say it. All right.

"I absolutely loved that time with you, Lucia. I would say I care for you, but that wouldn't be proper for me to talk about, would it?"

"Why not?"

"Who am I to think about you? I'm the furthest thing from royal stock—I'm not even a native Rezzian. And your father employs me. I've thought about this more than you'll ever know, but I'm already lucky to be so close to your family."

"You're where you are because my father admires you. He knows your heart is good. My life is mine to live. Whatever I decide, my father will need to accept it. And he *likes* you."

Ilario lowered his shoulders along with his glance. "I respect your father. He's given me so much. I could never do something to upset him. You couldn't be with me, anyway."

"I can do whatever I want." She patted the bed. "Come sit by me."

Ilario's heart raced with excitement. *All right. If that's how you feel about it ... I won't be afraid either. Who knows? Maybe your father would approve. He already trusts me with his son's life.*

He sat next to her and stared at her soft skin and proud face. Lucia looked as receptive to him as he'd ever seen, though her eyes were fearless. Ilario could barely breathe. *No man could be worthy of you. But if you give me the chance, I would try.*

He leaned forward and kissed her. She met him without hesitation. Her lips were soft and confident; his lips tingled against her flesh. She responded to his forceful movements, answering with even greater passion.

Ilario felt whole, reunited with some part of himself Lucia seemed to possess. He pulled her closer.

She pulled away and squeezed his knee, looking deeply into his eyes.

I want nothing more than to know the depths of your heart, Lucia.

"We'd just have to start somewhere and then find out where things go," she said.

"That's what I want. We need to defeat Pawelon and get out of this valley. Get back to Remaes, discuss this with your father, and"—he tried to win her over with his wide smile—"keep both you *and* Caio in the holy city."

After Lucia stood up, Ilario followed her lead. She embraced him, and he wrapped his arms tightly around her waist. "I'm very sorry," she said. "We don't have time now. We need to rest and wake early."

Right. If I can even get to sleep after this.

"Pray that all goes well tomorrow," she said.

"I will pray to Lord Sansone for a swift victory. Lucia, I want to know you. I want to know things about you that no one else has ever known."

She kissed him again, with her sweet tongue exploring his mouth. He wrapped her up and pressed her full chest against his. Feeling her feminine strength against his body filled him with yearning. *It's been so long.* She pushed him back with one hand, flashing her seductive smile.

"Until the morning, beloved of Sansone. Help Caio. Give him confidence."

"I will." Ilario glanced at Ysa's armor with an enormous grin. "I can't wait to see you wearing all of that."

She only winked and pushed him toward the doors.

This is really happening.

The doors shut behind him, and Ilario rejoined Caio. The young Haizzem had all of the guards laughing about something, but he turned right away and gleamed at Ilario with the purest acceptance.

I love her, Caio.

Chapter 16: The Long Wait

The previous night.

RAO'S STEPS ECHOED as he passed his father's guards and walked under the archway to the rajah's quarters. Burning lamps flickered and gave the place an oily scent. Dim, orange light flitted around the cavernous space like a somber ghost. The dilapidated stonework provided nearly all the decor.

Five paces to Rao's left, his father sat behind a massive desk upon which rested a metal goblet and a plate of crumbs from his dinner. An open passage behind the rajah led to his bedchamber. One other large object furnished the room, a dark hand-carved table and eight matching chairs.

The only item with any real color hung behind the desk. The painting stole Rao's awareness and breath, fixing his vision inside its solid frame. He'd last seen it when he was a child, before the war, when his father still lived in Kannauj. He wanted to run to it, to study the likeness of his mother and his brothers.

Instead, he strode to the desk and raised a fist in salute to the unresponsive man before him. "Hello, Father."

The rajah's silent stare felt especially cold in the emptiness of his hall.

What have I done to deserve your scorn? Before I came here, I've done all you've ever asked of me.

"I spoke with Indrajit." His father stood and returned the salute with a giant fist. He placed his hands on the desk and leaned forward. "He told me you refused to fight."

Really? "Is that all he said?"

"He told me you helped him once things looked grim. He said you stopped the storm."

"Well, yes, I—"

"Is it true?" Devak narrowed and focused his black eyes.

"It was a terrible situation, I—"

"I don't want your modesty. I need facts."

"Yes, I used my *sadhana* to stop the storm. I think the royal daughter caused it. If I'm right, she's extremely powerful. She was actively controlling the sky. It was—"

"I know. Too many of our men died." His father straightened up. "Why didn't you fight when the battle started?"

You're about to lose whatever respect you might've had for me.

"I believe it was reckless to risk our entire army, and wrong in principle to be the aggressors. Our defenses have been successful. Why—?"

"I think you're half-right." The rajah crossed his arms over his thick chest. "It was reckless. I don't care about your principles, but I had my reservations about Indrajit's strategy."

Rao stared at the swaying flame of the lamp nearest to the painting, letting his father's words sink in. "I didn't expect to hear this."

"Indrajit has yet to disappoint me. But it sounds like we were fortunate you were there."

"Thank you, sir." Rao felt his chest expanding with his next exhalation. His shoulders relaxed.

"You've done well for yourself. Narayani's stunning. How is she adjusting?"

"She seems in good spirits. I wonder if you have any trusted men who could watch over her when I'm away?"

"My best men guard me alone. If she wants to stay in my chamber during the day, she's welcome to. It is always well guarded."

"Thank you. I will tell her."

"Don't worry about Indrajit's men. He'll make sure his daughter is taken care of." Devak walked around to the front of the heavy desk, and crossed his arms again before he spoke. "Rao, when I hit you I was protecting Indrajit's honor. And I was angry at you for coming here."

Rao looked at the stone floor, hardly believing that Rajah Devak was explaining his actions—not with an apology, but maybe with some degree of remorse?

"You're a grown man," he continued. "Your actions and accomplishments make that clear. I didn't want you here, but you've earned the right."

"I want to fight for you," Rao said. "If I am ever to be rajah, I should be willing to do the same things that I ask of our soldiers."

"That's debatable, but I'll leave that decision to you."

"Thank you. Father, I'm only here to help you."

"This isn't about me. It's about our way of life. Our freedom and our culture. And punching the dogs right back in the mouth."

"I agree."

"Rao, I'm going to put you in charge of your own unit." His father spoke in the same rumbling monotone as always. "You and Indrajit aren't working well together. You'll take the men you brought from Kannauj and direct them independently from Indrajit's commands. You'll choose their orders. So far, your instincts have been ..." He stopped for a long breath. "Very good."

"Thank you, sir." Rao had expected to be punched again, sent back, berated, punished, or worse. "I won't let you down. Aayu and I will work together and we *will* impress you."

"Good, then. When their Haizzem comes, we're going to have to find ways to counter his powers. Either that or we're going to need other creative solutions."

"I agree. I've been thinking on this ever since I saw the solar flash. I'm going to do my best to come up with some way to stop him."

Rao's attention returned to the painting. "Father, I haven't seen this portrait since I was a boy. May I have a look?"

His father raised his arm and waved his hand at the cracked but vivid canvas.

Rao stepped slowly toward the scene.

His mother—Kunti was her name—stood beside his father twenty years ago, holding two toddlers who clung to the sides of her body. She had light skin for a Pawelon. Her face was proud, with the same high cheekbones Rao possessed. Her stare penetrated, but there was an undeniable sweetness to her eyes. His father actually had hair then, long and thick. His mother's black hair ran past her waist where the painting ended.

Devak looked at him occasionally, stroking his chin.

"Can you tell me more about what happened to them?" Rao had long assumed his father had ordered everyone silent on the matter. Throughout his life, no one answered his questions about his family. They only said what he'd already heard many times, that they died in a tragic accident while traveling.

"No. We have more important things to think about."

Listening to the cool wind blowing outside, Rao stared again at his mother's face, noticing her strong smile and athletic build.

I have not one memory of you, not a single one.

His father walked to the other side of the room. He stared through a hole in the stone wall that functioned as a window.

Rao forced himself away from the painting and walked back to the archway. "I should go. Thank you for having faith in me."

Devak gazed into the night, with his back turned to his son. He stayed silent as Rao started down the stairs.

Chapter 17: An Innocent Plot

NARAYANI LAY ON A OPULENT BED of pillows, staring at the crumbling ceiling and listening to the wind howling through the eroded holes in the stone tower. The quarters she shared with Rao were just high enough to give a view beyond the fortress's outer walls during the day. At night, the darkness was undone by seven rustic oil lamps.

"Do you think this tower is safe?" she asked Aayu. "What if it collapses?"

"Yes, it's well supported." Aayu stopped pacing and jumped up and down on the ancient floor. "It's stood here for longer than anyone knows."

"Stop, you're scaring me. I believe you." She sat up and noticed Aayu's tight lips and tense forehead. He was still angry with her.

"You want something." He resumed pacing. "I can tell because you're looking at me."

She let out a frustrated sigh. "I don't just look at you when I want something."

"Yes, you do."

"I don't *want* something from you—I want to make things *easier* for you. What if you taught me the mantras for your *sadhana*, then I could protect myself better. You wouldn't have to worry so much—stop laughing!" He didn't. "You don't know this, but I meditate." *I mean, I tried a couple times.* "I don't tell anyone that."

"That's funny. What's even worse is the thought of you hiding all over this fortress, spying on everything and everyone. I *like* being able to keep track of where you are."

"Oh sure, you'd rather I be defenseless and get assaulted by some brute that hasn't seen a woman in ten years."

Aayu stood still and glared. "Oh sure, Cousin. That's it."

She didn't see Rao until he'd taken a few steps into their chamber. His head hung low and his shoulders drooped with exhaustion.

"You're just in time," Aayu said, "to hear her arguments for why I should train her to be a sage."

Narayani shot him a sour look. "You need to stop making things up."

She hurried to Rao and kissed his lips, feeling a warm rush of passion through her body. Her fingers pressed into the fleshy palm of his hand and she pulled him deeper into the room. "Look, my father collected all of these pillows for me. Wasn't that nice of him? Lie down. You look terrible."

Rao collapsed just as she thought he would.

"How did it go with the old man?" Aayu sat, leaning back against the stone wall closest to Rao.

"Altogether, much better than I expected."

"So he's fine with us being here?" Aayu asked.

"Maybe more than fine. He's given me command of the soldiers who came with us from Kannauj. We're to act as an independent unit."

"That's incredible. Ha!" Aayu smiled his giant smile and looked at Narayani before turning back to Rao. "Congratulations."

"He even agreed that Indrajit's strategy was reckless."

"Rao," Narayani interrupted, "you look exhausted, mentally and physically."

"And then some more. My spirit feels like it's been bled dry."

"I have something I want you to take. I'll hear no argument about it."

Narayani slipped around the musty old linen she'd hung over the entrance to their bed chamber as a curtain. She knelt beside the feather bed she would share with Rao and rummaged through her belongings. She had carried all of her medicinal herbs and tinctures in the same sack as her clothes and jewelry, which was why she was only able to bring eight changes of dress. The glass vials clinked together as she dug through them looking for the *ashwa*.

She hurried back to Rao and put the dry root in his hand. "Suck on it and chew it very slowly. It will restore you completely and give you more energy than you thought possible. But eat it all the way through. *Ashwa* is very rare, so don't waste any of it."

Rao puckered his face as he sucked on the root. He coughed. "Thanks," he joked in a high-pitched voice.

"No complaining. You're going to feel so alive when you wake up tomorrow."

Rao nodded and labored to smile as he chewed the bitter root.

That's it. Just do whatever I tell you and you'll be fine, she thought.

"Good," Aayu said, "because I think they're going to need us. Rao, you didn't finish telling me what happened."

Rao continued the story he'd started before his father called for him. "So, somehow I was able to negate the connection between her and the storm. I wasn't sure what to do after that. I could have been more aggressive, but ... I decided to offer her a way out first."

Rao looked at Narayani and Aayu, hesitating. "I sent her a thought-form of peace, one that went deeply into her being. By that time, I couldn't remain in my subtle body any longer. When I talked to Indrajit, he agreed to pull back—reluctantly—and the Rezzians watched us go."

Narayani looked at Rao for some time, trying to imagine the scene.

"That's absolutely incredible, bhai. I'm so sorry I wasn't there." Aayu looked down, kneading his hands. "I should've been with you. It could've gone so much worse."

"We lost a lot of men, but it ended as well as it could have. I'm going to need you tomorrow with our unit. We're going to be acting on our own. My father told me we don't have to follow any of Indrajit's orders if we don't want to."

Over the next few hours, they talked about every topic on their minds: the horrible taste of ashwa, how Narayani disguised herself and hid among the servants, the mountains and the desert they traveled through, the invading army, the family portrait in Devak's quarters, Indrajit's attitude about the war, and Briraji's abilities as a sage.

Narayani was able to feel comfortable and safe that night, because Rao and Aayu seemed to let go of their resentment and accept her being there.

In the back of her mind one thought still distracted her. She had no idea how long her father would allow her to stay in the citadel with Rao.

If I could convince Aayu to teach me his sadhana, I wouldn't have to worry about my father telling me to go—and then if I wanted to, I could even witness the fighting up close. I could be there to help Rao ...

Chapter 18: Preparations for War

AFTER A BRIEF AND RESTLESS SLEEP, Caio journeyed out from the camp along with Lucia, Ilario, and ten warpriests selected by his father. The king declared the ten to be the most perfect spiritual warriors in the Rezzian army and gave them the task of protecting his children, no matter the cost.

It hadn't been easy for Caio to convince his father that he and Lucia should go out on such a dangerous mission, but appeals to faith and the appeal of Lucia's strategy won the king over. Lucia reminded their father that Caio, as Dux Spiritus, had the right to pursue any tactics he chose, and that his son's will was divine. Caio didn't want to force his father to do anything.

Caio sensed that his father couldn't pass up the chance to have his Haizzem clear the way for his army; it was too great a tactical opportunity, and he was excited to see what his son could do. Vieri consented only after making them promise that if they encountered trouble, they would flee and let the warpriests sacrifice themselves to protect them.

Duilio agreed to do his part as well, to lead a significant diversion to the south. He also shared some news: "We have received an incredible report from our spies. The rajah's son, Rao, joined the conflict on the same day as their bold attack. We assume he had something to do with their more aggressive tactics. I am told that the tales of his powers are already becoming legendary amongst their soldiers. In fact, they say it was he alone who stopped the goddess Ysa's rage."

Lucia reminded them that an evil force had violated her with some overpowering magic. Her father and Ilario agreed that Pawelon's prince would be their target if they could find him on the battlefield. With Rao dead, they would have an even greater chance to intimidate their enemy into surrender.

The king gave the expected response, an unequivocal desire for a total victory that would allow them to bring significant changes to Pawelon politically and spiritually. Lucia changed the subject to the planning of the day's attack, postponing the debate over the merits of surrender.

Duilio suggested that Lucia should accompany him while Caio attacks the northern sentry outpost, so that both missions would have the greatest chance of success. Lucia insisted on staying with her brother. Caio trusted her plan, privately feeling more secure having Lucia alongside him. Duilio graciously agreed to his Dux Spiritus' wishes, and so they went.

The team made their way north along the eastern edge of the canyon and then west into the desert valley, staying as close as possible to sparse patches of vegetation to cover their approach.

Chapter 19:
The Earth Shaker and His Sea

ONCE WITHIN RANGE of the sentry outpost, they rushed into the cover of a thicket of bushes. The branches were razor-sharp, curling around in wild circles like an assassin spinning with curved swords.

Caio, Ilario, and Lucia huddled by the largest bush, panting. The warpriests hid behind other shrubs, watching Caio with deadly focus. The scarves protecting their bald heads from the climbing sun fluttered in the breeze.

Everyone else looks so ready for this, Caio thought.

He whispered, "I hadn't realized the mornings would be so cold." Caio didn't have whatever benefits of warmth came from the padding of armor, unlike Lucia. The goddess Mya and Lord Oderigo hadn't left behind sacred battle relics as Ysa had for her royal devotees. Caio's armor was spiritual. Oderigo entrusted the royal lineage with his sacred text, The Book of Time. The goddess Mya handed down to the royalty a wooden rod shaped from the first olive tree the gods gave the kingdom many centuries ago. Caio squeezed the solid, grainy wood of the healing scepter in one hand and felt its majestic aura.

This power was given to me so that I could heal. This is madness.

"I think this land hates us," Lucia whispered back, her sharp eyes remaining focused past the edges of the bush, up the hill. "Later, you'll be glad you dressed for the heat."

Caio squeezed one of his arms, feeling the loose sleeve of his unbleached cotton thawb, a long tunic running down to his sandaled feet. He thrust his head back and let the matching head scarf settle behind his shoulders.

"This is as close as we'll get," Lucia said.

"I pray none of them have to die," Caio said to himself as much as to the others.

Ilario had said little since they set out, keeping to himself most of the hike. Caio sensed his friend's fears about their mission and his conflicted feelings for

Lucia. Ilario's eyes focused on the Pawelon outpost and the steep climb leading up to it.

"You were right," Ilario said to Lucia. "There's no practical way to assault them. Their archers would have perfect positioning while we climb the hill, and they must have sages ready with a complete strategy for defense." He turned and patted Caio on the back, making brief eye contact. "Remember, you hold the goddess Mya's rod in your hand. Everything is possible for you, my Haizzem."

Lucia's gaze pried into Caio's soul, making sure her message was received. "Prevent them from seeing our forces behind us, and prevent them from alerting their army. You can do this."

Caio looked down on the intricate red and black lines the gods had painted on his palms while he was still in his mother's womb. As with all the other Haizzem before him, the patterns started at the center of his palms, wrapped around his hands, and wound along his forearms to his elbows. Gazing at the thorny lines centered his mind.

He gripped Mya's smooth rod with both hands and exhaled warmth onto his cold fingers. "Will our gods need to kill anyone to accomplish this goal? We only need to distract the Pawelons."

"I am sure The Ten will obey you," Lucia said, "though you know they aren't always compassionate."

"We will see a great miracle today," Ilario added. "Clear the way, my Haizzem, and let the gods decide the details."

Caio noticed that Ilario momentarily looked away from the hill, to Lucia's face. Earlier that morning, Caio had seen his sister relax and smile much more deeply than usual around Ilario. "I wonder what we'll be doing when we marry and grow old together," Caio said.

Lucia's and Ilario's eyes met for a moment before she said, "Caio, you should focus."

Caio stood up, still using the bush for some cover. "If anything should ever happen to me, know how much I love you both, and that nothing would make me happier than to see you together someday."

He knew they'd be uncomfortable hearing his words, so he gave them no time to respond. Caio ran into the open, up the long hill. If not for his trust in the gods, the empty distance would have been terrifying. He looked back, upset at seeing Lucia and Ilario chasing after him. The ten warpriests spread out to protect them, their flowing, white clothing snapping like flags in a strong wind.

The goddess Mya appeared three paces in front of Caio, wearing a lush green dress of leaves. Her enigmatic eyes quivered with a hint of moisture. She held up the palm of her delicate hand.

Caio remained upright but dropped to his knees. He heard the others stop and felt their eyes on him. He extended his open arms before his goddess, clenching her rod in one hand, with a plea upon his face. *If you will help us, Mya, what will you do to our enemies?*

He felt a sudden shiver of heat.

Must we kill them? Is that what I should ask for, and would you even grant such a thing?

No response came from The Goddess of the Great Waters. His heart was pulled deeper into her mesmerizing gaze.

How can I go against my own marrow?

Silence.

I am your chosen Haizzem, why can I not instead bring peace to this land?

Emptiness.

Do my wishes even matter? Can all this momentum toward bloodshed even be stopped?

Mya stepped toward him and caressed his face from cheek to chin. It felt refreshing all the way down to his toes, like cool water on scorched earth.

We only need the Pawelons incapacitated, so they cannot alert their army. I don't want you to kill them.

Mya faded from sight like mist warmed by fire.

The Pawelons stirred on the hill above. Caio knew he might have only seconds before their arrows or magic reached him and his friends.

Caio stood taller than he'd ever stood before, raised his arms, and closed his eyes. He squeezed the rod in his right hand and expelled his goddess's power toward the Pawelons. A booming, wet, sucking sound startled him, forcing him to open his eyes and witness Mya's miracle.

'*'

Lucia watched Caio raise the rod, then heard Ysa's sword and shield humming a barely perceptible tone.

Ysa, empower his prayers!

And then Caio was gone.

The Pawelon base became the epicenter of an impossible phenomenon. Countless water droplets appeared out of the dry air and flew toward the enemy forces as if in slow motion—yet the water covered the Pawelons in a matter of seconds.

Lucia felt her head spinning as she gazed at the divine handiwork. Something like a small sun covered the Pawelon fort, but instead of a fiery ball, the sphere was composed of deep blue water like the stormy Rezz Ocean. Its circumference chopped violently.

Muffled screams escaped the watery prison like a haunted chorus, emphatic but indistinct.

A sudden pain seized Lucia's heart. She raced toward the hill drawing her sword. "Caio!" *Damn you, father, you should have known he wasn't ready for this!* She held up her shield to block any incoming arrows or magic, leaving it up to her goddess whether she'd live or die.

The yelling behind her revealed that Ilario was close by and the warpriests trailed him. The sounds of her heavy exhalations and clanking armor almost drowned out the wails of the trapped Pawelons.

Strangely, her legs moved more easily as the climb grew steeper.

It's like I'm running downhill.

She felt a tangible force pulling her body upward toward the liquid sun, even with half the distance still to go.

From behind, Ilario screamed her name.

Chapter 20: Astrapios and Brontios

CAIO FOUND HIMSELF SUSPENDED ABOVE the Pawelon outpost, hovering in the air. Countless hostile faces screamed at him from below. He yelled back in their language, "I didn't come to hurt you!"

WHY, Mya?

The water droplets seemed to float toward him so slowly in that moment—so quickly in truth—accumulating rapidly, sticking to him, pooling around him, until he was submerged in the cool water, along with all the Pawelon soldiers. Water-soaked rays of sunlight cascaded around the edges, giving Caio hope that he might swim free. His legs kicked and his arms dug through the water—but his body stayed anchored in place.

I'm at its center.

I'm trapped.

Angry voices dribbled into his ears along with the rush of sloshing water. His already cool skin felt colder. Most of the Pawelons struggled to escape; some of them floundered, as if they didn't know how to swim. None of them got away. Caio realized that whatever force kept him in the center of the sea also trapped the Pawelons inside.

Two swam toward him with spears in hand and rage burning on their faces. Caio felt the spirit of the leading Pawelon, a veteran determined to see his iron cut through Caio's body. Caio's heart and chest heaved as the water swirled around him. The Pawelon drew close.

Caio jerked aside as the spear's tip thrust past his chest. A hard surge of water crashed the Pawelon into him and their bodies collided, grappling.

A fierce hand grabbed Caio's wrist. Fingers dug into his throat. He choked on cool water. Caio shoved the hand off his neck and tried to expel the liquid.

The second Pawelon swam close, ready to thrust his spear. The strong arms of the veteran wrapped around Caio's chest from behind, restraining him. Caio thrashed, overpowered.

I'm going to die.

The spear came at him. *I forgive you.* The blade pierced his chest, glancing off his ribs. Caio bellowed, bubbles erupting from his throat. Blood gushed from his chest, a murky red cloud in the blue.

Vine-covered Lord Oderigo flashed in his mind. Caio's eyes closed, his world fell away to nothingness, and death's long tunnel opened before him.

'*'

Lucia stared at the spot where Caio had been standing.

Whatever spell you've cast—her thoughts burned on the Pawelon sages—*I will break.*

She raced up the dry hill pointing Ysa's sword at the sky, her muscles alive with exertion. "Ysa, destroy them for whatever they've done to him!"

The sword discharged a shocking force into her body, stunning her senseless. The energy retreated back into the sword and shot from its tip toward the water.

Lucia collapsed in a quivering heap, battered lungs straining to breathe. Gasping for air, a vision of blond Ysa appeared.

'*'

Death's tunnel pulled Caio in, faster and faster ...

BOOM!

An explosion shattered the black tunnel. Caio became conscious of his body again. A shock wave sent blistering heat across his skin. His nose picked up the scent of sizzled hair and flesh.

Dozens of Pawelons floated around him, all but one unconscious. The first attacker floated away, twitching involuntarily. The young man who speared him struggled with weak limbs to grab his floating weapon.

Caio grabbed the spear with his right hand, Mya's rod still somehow in his left. As he pushed the weapon away, their eyes met. The boy wrapped his fingers across his own throat with terror contorting his face. Caio heard a garbled sound from him and knew the young man was nearly out of breath. By some grace, Caio no longer struggled to breathe.

His empathy reached out to the boy, and the Pawelon's story came to him in a flash of insight. His family lived in a poverty-stricken village in the

101

mountains near the city of Mathura. Caio saw his possible future. He saw the man someday with a large, loving family. His first son would become a respected spiritual leader among his people.

Caio watch the young man's agony as he drowned. He reached out just as the boy's body went soft, and put his arms around him.

Mya, protect his soul.

The rest were dead. Caio sensed, as he often intuited things, that the boy's spirit had been powerful enough to keep him conscious after the lightning spread through the water.

The water gave way and flooded down the hill's steep slopes. Caio crashed to the ground in the center of the outpost, clinging to the young soldier and bleeding on his enemy's soaked uniform. He rolled onto his knees and grabbed the boy's shirt with both hands.

Mya, I command you, raise this young man from death!

Chapter 21: A Rival to the Gods

Moments earlier.

ILARIO WATCHED SPARKS OF LIGHTNING flow from Lucia's sword, around her armored body, back into the blade, and then out toward the hovering mass of water.

"Lucia!"

He slid beside her, panting, his knees scraping against the desert floor. He dropped his sword and put his hands to her cheeks.

"Lucia, you're going to be all right!"

Her body writhed. She struggled to breathe. No air came in or out.

Ilario pressed against her breastplate, hoping to awaken her stunned lungs. A tortured sound escaped her throat, followed by wheezing, then choking breaths.

"I'm okay," her pained voice lied. "Stop their sages. Go find Caio." She squeezed her eyes shut and grimaced. "I'll follow. Go!"

Ilario grabbed his sword and stood, his heart slugging his ribcage. Lucia's suffering filled his mind with red rage. He wanted to stay with her, but he knew she was right. The warpriests would protect her while he searched for Caio.

With duty focusing his mind like the edge of his blade, he pushed his muscles to their limits and ignored the burning in his thighs. He sprinted to the wall of the Pawelon outpost, just beneath the chaotic waters. He dug his fingers into the stone walls, climbed, and jumped upward into the hovering sea.

The water sucked him in deeper before its force released him. His stomach hit the dry ground. A moment later, the sea crashed down over him, surging past his ears as it flooded the area. He jumped up reflexively, spinning with sword in hand. The water cascaded off the hill in all directions, revealing hundreds of dead Pawelons. Their outpost had become their graveyard.

Caio lay near the center of the structure, beside a Pawelon's body. Both of them were covered in blood. Ilario ran toward him as Caio came up onto his knees, grabbing the unconscious soldier by his shirt. Caio's face contorted in agony, revealing intense concern for the young Pawelon.

"Let me help you." Ilario approached him, tearing off his cloak to cover Caio's wounds. The warpriests were running in from behind.

"Stay back, Ilario. These men are dead because of me," Caio said.

"You did this so fewer will have to die."

"What about this one? Does he deserve to die?"

Caio put his palms on the dead Pawelon's chest. His hands and arms glowed red and black, projecting dark swirling colors into the daylight. The colors transformed slowly into pure white. The light spread over and around the soldier, sheathing him like a cocoon. The boy rose into the air.

A gust of breath punched its way into the Pawelon's chest, and his body rippled with an aftershock. The lights lifted higher, and he with them, turning him until his feet dangled just above the ground. The coat of light sank into his chest and disappeared. The young Pawelon landed upright.

We'll never see this miracle again. Ilario realized he'd been one of only a dozen to witness the single resurrection by the Haizzem of his era. The greatest miracle Caio could grant in this life was given and done.

"You resurrected a gods-damned Pawelon!" Lucia's voice bellowed from well behind Ilario. She flung down Ysa's helm and stormed forward.

Ilario envisioned two scenarios in which he might need to intervene, one involving an angry Lucia and the other involving a violent Pawelon. He took another step toward Caio and the pig. Caio bent over, hiding his face and breathing hard. The Pawelon's face revealed his enchanted state of mind.

Ilario said in stilted Pawelon, "Sit down. We'll not hurt you now."

Caio raised his head off the ground, and the boy sat as commanded.

Lucia raced forward, pointing Ysa's white blade at Caio. "You raised a gods-damned Pawelon from the dead?"

"He will have seven children," Caio said. "He will be a peaceful man, a good man. I couldn't—"

"Lucia, please put your sword away," Ilario said as he raised his free hand.

"You could have saved one of ours some day." She sheathed the blade with a resounding slam. "This is an outrage, an insult to our entire history."

Caio pressed his lips together, restraining his words. His eyes were locked with Lucia's, asking for understanding.

"Damn, Caio! How could you do this? How could you be so irresponsible?"

"I could not let this boy die! You don't understand how much he has to live for."

"Just one time, Caio. Just once. You've gone and used your power. How could you!"

Caio pushed himself up, revealing a long, bleeding gash on one side of his chest.

Ilario rushed to him and covered him with his cloak. "Lay down, Caio. You're losing a lot blood."

Lucia came forward and knelt beside her brother. Her red face turned pale. "I am sorry. I didn't know."

"We're going to take care of you." Ilario held the cloth to Caio's chest and watched the blood run down his hands. "Don't worry."

Lord Sansone, let him be all right.

Ilario glanced at the Pawelon. The boy stared at the ground with his mouth open, looking too stunned to move.

Caio's eyes opened wider in a defenseless, humble expression. "If anything happens to me, remember what I said to you. You should be happy together."

"Caio, don't talk like that." A sickening taste forced its way up Ilario's throat and into his mouth. "Stay with us, Caio. We need you."

What the hell have you gods done to him? All he's ever done is worship you.

Caio opened his eyes. "I feel Mya's healing presence."

Lucia's breathing was out of control. "Tell her you want to live."

"I couldn't let him die. I couldn't live with myself if I did."

Lucia's eyes softened.

"Stay with me, here and now," Ilario said. "Focus on your healing."

The warpriests had encircled them. They sat up from their prostrations and one of them began chanting a hypnotic prayer. The others joined in, uttering the specific, harsh sounds of the old tongue. Lucia placed her hands beside Ilario's on Caio's chest.

Ilario prayed in silent anguish to the backdrop of chanting, watching Caio smile despite his suffering. He looked down again and fought the churning nausea in his stomach as he watched the Haizzem's dark red blood stain his hands.

Chapter 22:
The Quieting of the Gods

HEARING THE WARPRIESTS' resonant intoning gave Caio tranquil distraction from the guilt and doubts thumping inside his breast. He felt Mya's invisible hands over his wound, soothing the bloody sting. Her spirit filled him like a cool spray of water tumbling off the canyon's edge.

Invigorated, Caio sat up on one knee. Ilario rested a heavy hand on his shoulder, his light brown eyes full of concern. Caio stood, ignoring the pain still burning in his chest.

Ilario rose with him. "Don't strain. Your duty is done."

"We'll call off the offensive." Lucia leaned against Caio and kissed his cheek, rekindling his will to press on.

"I can still pray. My body suffers, but my spirit soars." Each word Caio spoke intensified the pain in his chest. "These deaths should not be for nothing. We will push on."

The young Pawelon gazed at the spacious sky. Caio sensed everything the boy was feeling: stillness, gratitude, and wonder.

Caio addressed the boy in his own language. "Now you know the peace of death."

"What happened to me?"

"The gods of Lux Lucis brought you back to us. Your life means too much for it to end today."

The soldier came to his feet and staggered around, calmly viewing his fallen allies. "These men ... they are in a better place now." He turned his eyes to Caio and stared. "Are you ... ?"

"I am the Haizzem."

"You saved my life."

"I want you to return to your people. My army is coming. We intend to end the war today. You won't be safe unless you leave the area. Go north until you reach the lake. Wait there, and return to your people some other day." Caio coughed, causing hot daggers to stab his chest. "I've seen your future. You *must* live. You have so much to live for."

"I owe you my life ... so I will do as you say." The boy pursed his lips, deciding something. "My army will soon realize something is wrong. That we are not communicating with them. Only our sages can send signals back to them."

"Thank you," Caio bowed as he spoke. "My brother, not all of us believe in this war. I, for one, do not."

"Then go home. Go back to your lands and leave my people alone. If you are the Haizzem, why don't you make them all go?"

Ilario was still holding his cloak to Caio's wounds. He interrupted, speaking the Pawelon language with some difficulty. "Because this world is not yet right. Look how your people suffer. You believe in no greater power than yourselves, and look at the results. You live like pigs. You suffer—"

"And you mean to *help* my people? You wish to see us suffer *less*? We are happier than you think—"

Caio interrupted, "My father believes this war to be a religious act."

"Don't you command this army now? Take your people home. Let us all live."

Ilario spoke again, "Then you would come after us."

"We would not!"

Lucia commanded everyone's attention: "Our people believe it's the gods' will that we wage this war, because they want us to better our world. But if Rezzia is not guided by the gods of Lux Lucis, we will not conquer Pawelon. Soon, we will know what the gods wish for." She looked at Caio, and he understood her meaning: Lord Danato's vision, Caio's abilities, and the favor of the gods would be put to the test on this day.

"You, Haizzem," the boy said, "you have such power. You should follow your own truth."

Maybe you're right.

The boy had named the outcome Caio wanted most: a retreat with no further casualties. The young Pawelon could be the last to die in the war, even though he now lived. The miracle of life given back to him could be such a worthy, symbolic act if his resurrection were to be the final turning point in the war. How many lives could be saved?

But it's impossible.

The entire nation of Rezzia, as well as its army, expected the fighting to crescendo now that he was Dux Spiritus. History, tradition, and even scripture gave him a mission to fulfill, made necessary by his father's sacrifice. He was the son of King Vieri, the Dux Spiritus of Rezzia, the Haizzem of their faith, and no one in his proud nation would be willing to see him lose. He had only one option, an already decided fate—*and I despise that with my whole heart and soul.*

"Go!" Caio pointed north at the sun. The star blazed wine-red in the early morning haze. "Go north to the shore. Our armies are approaching. Run as fast as you can. Live for tomorrow. Live out your life!"

The boy walked away, then turned around again, out of words. His gape showed his sadness and rage. He glanced at the warpriests before racing toward the sun.

"If you insist on going forward," Lucia said, "we must pray for a great rain to conceal our advance. Now."

Mya ...

The Rezzian army could barely be heard marching in from the east. A gust of dry heat blew across the land as pregnant clouds formed and distant thunder rumbled.

Chapter 23: A Prayer for Accori

THE GENTLE CLACK AND CLANG of Duilio's waiting army centered his mind like a familiar song. The morning's cool breeze had turned warm and surprisingly humid, soothing his dry skin as he sat astride his horse and looked down on a young soldier.

The boy could barely grow a moustache, but reported as if he carried the burden of all the world's troubles. "Strategos, the sentries sent up their fire signals. Their citadel will know that we're here." The young man's intense vision focused in the direction of the Pawelon outpost.

Duilio's legions had been spurred on a hard march toward the southern sentry outpost. Now they waited, surrounding the enemy beyond the range of arrow fire, hoping to draw more of Pawelon's forces toward them.

The old Strategos leaned forward and pulled back his horse's tasseled red and yellow caparison. He dragged his fingertips along its warm chestnut neck.

We have some time then.

"We have seen significant movement in their southern contingent. We believe they are mobilizing to meet us," the messenger said.

"How rude. What is your name, son?"

"Accori, Strategos."

"And whom do you worship, Accori?"

"My family worships the goddess Vani, Strategos."

"Is that right? Do they approve of you fighting?"

"To be honest, not entirely, sir."

"Let's do something for your parents." *Since they've trusted your life to me.* Duilio pulled up his silver necklace from beneath his breastplate and dangled the ancient symbol. "Look here, son. Will you pray to Lord Cosimo with me?"

"Yes, of course, Strategos." Accori's wide, intense eyes focused on the holy ivory.

"Lord Cosimo, how did I forget to honor you earlier today? Where was my mind? You are a kind god to old, forgetful men. I beseech you, my supremely patient god—wait, would you say anything to him, Accori?"

"I ... I thank him for protecting us."

"A good thing to pray for. Because you will be fighting alongside me, rather than with your Haizzem or king, or even with our king's daughter. But we have a *great* purpose, you and I do, Accori, in support of our new Dux Spiritus. Are you prepared?"

The messenger's brow tightened as he nodded. "Yes. Lord Cosimo is a god of miracles, is he not?"

"Indeed he is." Duilio studied the earnest boy. *Cosimo might have no other choice but to protect you—you dedicate your whole being to your duty.*

"I put my trust in Lord Cosimo to look after you, Accori. At my age, the prospect of death is not feared. It is a constant companion. I believe it is not important how long you live, but that you give yourself to living. Live as only you can, with every part of you fully engaged. Tell me something, how does this air taste to you?"

"How does it taste, Strategos?" Accori sniffed, looking around dutifully, licking his lips. "Good, I suppose?"

"Try again, as if this breath might be your last."

The young man nodded quickly and his nostrils widened again. He looked up at the clouds forming in the north. "Like ... like the breath of unpredictable gods, warm at first and then cool. Sweet with the gifts of nature, and then ... foul."

"Outstanding. Though perhaps my horse has just relieved himself."

Accori's unforced laughter transformed his stern face for a moment.

Duilio tucked his necklace back under his breastplate. He dismounted and placed one hand on Accori's shoulder. The scent of the soldier's leather shirt wafted to his nose. "Live life as you just breathed in and you will not fear death, even though Lord Danato takes the young as easily as he takes the old. Think about the goddess Vani today. Do not be afraid to pray to her. It would please your parents."

"I will do it. Thank you, Strategos." The young man maintained his good posture as he stared back at Duilio with transfixed dark eyes.

Duilio patted his steed's shoulders. *Lord Cosimo, you've brought me through it all.* He rubbed along the underside of his horse's neck. *From a young soldier like Accori, fighting with my bare hands.* He stared at the colorful tassels decorating his steed. *Through the last nine years leading men either to their graves or back to their lonely beds in the desert each night. I pray that you bring this young man back to our camp this day, and back to his peace-loving family some other day. I know all the gods must be very busy, but please take care of this one.*

The young man glanced toward the Pawelon outpost, suddenly looking more uncomfortable than confident. "Can I do anything else for you, Strategos?"

"Go and spread my command. There's no use in attacking the outpost now. We'll spread out and do our part to look like a threat and see how many flies we can attract." Duilio tapped the holy symbol behind his breastplate. "We'll have The Lord of Miracles on our side."

Chapter 24: Lions Arising

RAO LICKED THE ROOF OF HIS DRY MOUTH. To take his mind off the blisters on his feet, he focused on the warm air passing through his nostrils and studied the greenery among the red rocks near the trail. The path itself had been trampled into a smooth, featureless road, but the tiny plants growing around the nearby rocks scented the air with a hint of life.

The northern path began its switchbacks even though surrounded by canyon walls, starting down toward the canyon floor. A few dozen soldiers scouted ahead while most marched from behind. Aayu walked next to Rao, bouncing forward with nervous energy.

Rao felt the tension in his clenched jaw, a product of his morning conversation with Indrajit. They had stood near a handful of other Pawelon officers at the forward-most edge of the cliffs due east of the citadel, looking down on the canyon. He recalled the conversation with detached emotions.

"I'll be taking my unit to reinforce our northern defenses."

Indrajit had been arguing with a couple other officers. "Excuse me, gentlemen, our prince has interrupted us." He did not turn to face Rao. Instead he looked down into the canyon itself. "Even though they are moving in a large force from the south?"

"I assume you will be rotating other troops from northern positions to southern ones." Rao worried that the northern defenses would be left too thin, but he didn't say it.

"Your father has given you the freedom to abandon your army and avoid confrontation at a critical time—if you must."

"He only asked me to follow my own instincts, General."

"Then get out of my sight."

Indrajit and Briraji led the bulk of Pawelon's army down the southern trail. Earlier, the southern sentry had signaled that a large Rezzian force surrounded them. Briraji said he would have another surprise in store for the invaders.

The further Rao walked the trail with his unit, the more his concern for the northern defenses felt justified. An unexpected rainstorm moved in from the northeast, blocking visibility. He suspected the worst.

A lanky messenger ran through the ranks to Rao and Aayu. Soldiers surrounded the winded runner as he spoke. "My Prince, there's something strange you may wish to consider. Prior to the arrival of the storm, we received no communications from the northern sentry for a considerable time."

"Thank you," Rao said. "Continue on and relay this to our commanders at the citadel."

The thick slab of rain crept toward them, churning darker and greyer, like the expressionless face of a sorrowful god. Steaming air pressed against Rao's cheeks, adding palpable sensation to the weight of leading men to face the storm.

Aayu's jaw hung slack as he searched the sky. "Was it like this when the royal daughter conjured the storm?"

"No. There was no rain at all. But I'm sure she's out there."

Rao commanded the men to increase their pace. When they reached the final slope, cliff walls blocked their sight lines to the valley. In another hundred paces they would see the canyon floor again.

As Rao rounded the final corner with his men, a warm gust carrying the odor of the rainstorm blew through his hair. Inauspicious dark weather stretched from the ground to the heavens, waiting near the base of the trail and blocking all visibility beyond it.

Without hesitating, Rao climbed the nearby cliff and balanced himself on a narrow ledge. He addressed his men. "There is something behind that storm, either an army or some spiritual weapon. I'm afraid we don't have enough forces here after some of our defenses were repositioned. If you go forward with me, accept that we are likely to be overrun." The words poured out only due to some kind of instinct. "If you join me down this hill, know the sacrifice you are making. If you cannot do this, go back now and fight another day. With luck we'll stop the dogs again, or at least slow their advance."

A thousand pairs of eyes looked up at him—probably an inconsequential number contrasted with whatever waited behind the storm. "Master Aayu and I will locate their leadership and attack those targets. We will indicate their position with a signal. Join us and kill their leaders and we might survive."

Rezzian roars and the clamor of pounding feet passed through the storm and rose to Rao's ears.

113

There are far too many of them.

"Run!" Rao yelled, and every one of his men sprinted toward the valley as Rao jumped to the ground.

Aayu stood before him, his eyes focused with a determined glare. "You are your father's son after all."

With no one else able to hear him, Rao said, "Is that what my fear sounds like? Courage?"

They joined the stampede and ran side by side. After dreaming of it for years, they were finally fighting together. In conjunction, their strength would be more than doubled. No one would hurt Aayu—Rao would see to that—and Aayu would defend Rao's life as if it were his own. The moment heightened Rao's bond with his brother and ally, his bhai.

Rezzian shock troops emerged through the watery partition and filled the air with their battle screams. Moments later, the storm literally vanished to a clear sky, revealing the armada of warriors and cavalry behind it. Ten lions led the Rezzians, bounding toward the Pawelon front line.

"Lord Galeazzo's lions," Rao said to his bhai. "Their king is here. Rezzia's Haizzem must be with him."

With his face red from running, Aayu panted and smiled. "Then we'll kill them."

Chapter 25: Struggle

ALBINA TROTTED HESITANTLY behind the dark sheet of rain. The mare yanked her head from side to side, reluctant to follow the weather. Whenever the wind stopped, Lucia heard the sounds of mass death at the Strategos's battle to the south. Duilio wasn't supposed to engage a large force. Something was wrong.

She rode between Caio and her father, with Ilario on Caio's other side. Her brother's grunts and grimaces were a constant reminder of his pain, but she felt powerless to help him. She could pray to Mya to comfort Caio, but Caio had already prayed to his goddess. The gods never answered Lucia's pleas for compassion anyway.

The army marched behind the wall of water and stayed dry, barely touched by its refreshing mist. No one could see through the rain. The army of Lux Lucis followed the goddesses' miracle until the storm halted, waiting ...

King Vieri bellowed the commands to begin the charge, swinging his falchion in circles through the air as if an ancient spirit possessed him. For the first time in her life, Lucia saw her father in his primal element, red-faced and roaring, commanding his legions like the storied kings of old. For once, she felt proud to be his daughter.

"Pray, children! Beg your gods for victory. Give strength to our men. Disrupt their sages. Destroy their arrows. When the enemy turns to retreat and reposition, finish them all."

The shock troops rumbled forward and disappeared through the watery plane first by the handfuls, then like a tidal wave crashing forward and swallowing the sands.

Vieri's eyes homed in on the battle. "Tell your goddesses to stop the rain. Now!" He kicked his chestnut steed into a gallop. "Follow me!"

For one moment, Lucia watched her father ride off into the crowded desert. His sword hung again at his side and he carried the glorious golden shield of Lord Galeazzo, a relic wielded by most of Rezzia's kings. He yelled a guttural yawp and raised the brilliant disc above his head. He stopped to pray, and Lucia pulled up beside him.

She asked Ysa to dissolve the storm.

'*'

Invisible to all mortals, Lord Galleazzo strode beside King Vieri, standing taller than five men. The body of the most commanding god was protected with a full suit of golden chainmail, though he wore no helm. Furry eyebrows and wild, white hair accentuated the aging god's possessed face. A thick vermilion cape billowed behind his shoulders, bearing an august image of the sun.

'*'

Ysa, carry me forward and watch over me.
Albina shot ahead at an extraordinary speed.
Not again.
Lucia leaned forward with one arm against her mare's right shoulder, keeping her shield close to her body. She sped past her father and rode under the waterfall. The refreshing sensation lasted only a moment. As she moved beyond the rain, the downpour vanished and a strong gust covered her face in dust.

Her vision shook as tremors rattled the canyon. From beneath the red dirt, the ten fabled lions of Lord Galeazzo emerged with full-throated roars, five males and five lionesses twice the size of their natural counterparts. They shook their bodies, sending clumps of red dirt flying in all directions. Lucia raised her shield to cover her face. She looked back to see her father holding his god's shield over his head, commanding the divine beasts: "Kill their foul sages!"

The lions bounded past Lucia and surged ahead of Rezzia's legions.

Pawelon's northern defenses were thin. Instead of clogging the area in front of the trail with long spear formations, the pigs crouched and waited behind the long mounds of dirt stretching across the wide trail's mouth. Following the lions, waves of Rezzian troops raced up the defensive hills and charged over the top, breaking formation and fighting man to man. Arrows flew from the rear of the Pawelon positions and from the cliffs, dropping a small number of Rezzian bodies to the ground.

Albina galloped with a ferocious spirit, putting the other horses far behind her. *What's gotten into you?* Lucia pulled on the reins with all her strength and screamed for the animal to stop. It was either too scared or too possessed to listen. Charging soldiers flew past and behind them.

Ysa, you are The Commander of Horses. Stop her!

Deep, conch-like horns blew from within the Pawelon ranks. An eerie tension crowded the atmosphere. Around the leading Rezzian soldiers, sandy air swirled up into small tornadoes, choking men and forcing them to cover their eyes.

Albina raced into the sages' dark magic.

A shower of tiny stones pummeled Lucia's armor. A dirty cloud infiltrated her helm, forcing her eyes closed and sending dust up her nose. Albina screamed, but the mare only raced harder.

Further ahead, the lions bawled carnal roars. Terrified Pawelons screamed. The tiny sandstorms dissipated. Lucia opened her eyes again. As the Rezzians advanced again, the army's rowdy cheer must have soared to the citadel itself.

Albina lunged forward like an elegant machine, climbing the first hill even though Lucia pulled on her reins to stop her. From the hill's vantage, she looked back and saw Ilario on his horse racing toward her, with Caio and her father following him.

Crack!

An arrow shaft smashed against her shield, knocking Lucia sideways. She squeezed the reins and held on, raising her goddess's shield. *Ysa, protect me and my soldiers!*

Her crazed horse surged down the first hill, into the little valley between the first two long mounds. Here, the Rezzian warriors enjoyed a great advantage against a dwindling number of Pawelons.

Albina began climbing the second hill. Having no control over the animal, Lucia pushed off and dove for the ground, clutching Ysa's shield. The ground knocked the wind from her lungs. Her fingers dug into the dirt, finding no purchase. She tumbled into the second trench, her armor bruising her skin. More dust and dirt coated her mouth and tongue. Unstoppable momentum spurred her down.

She looked up at the pigs.

In the second trench, enemy soldiers still outnumbered the Rezzians. Luckily most were far from her position. But not all. Ilario felt so far away.

Gods! Will they even be able to find me?

She unsheathed Ysa's white sword as two bearded Pawelon warriors approached and taunted her with feinting short spear thrusts. A Rezzian soldier ran down the hill behind her, yelling "Your Grace, come toward me!"

A spear cut across her cheek with stinging pain. As the Pawelon pulled his spear back, she stepped forward and bashed his weapon with Ysa's shield.

The attacker shifted back, keeping his grip on the spear. He threw his weapon into the charging Rezzian soldier's gut.

The second pig came at Lucia from her shield side.

She swung her arm to block his spear thrust and he lost his balance. With Ysa's sword leading, she lunged forward and slipped the blade past the edge of his shield, into his gut.

Deep pangs of betrayal came over his brown face as he dropped his shield and weapon. They fell together, her shield between them, his disgusting body beneath hers.

The other pig jumped on her with his knees digging into her back. He pounded her face with his rocky fists.

Her nose stung, her cheekbones felt crushed.

In a mindless rage, she swung an elbow at him, and he dodged toward her shield arm. With a yell, she brought the shield up with a crunch against his head. The pig's weight left her back.

Lucia rolled over. She tried to push herself up, but the Pawelon grabbed her arms and pinned her flat to the rocky ground. He came up on his knees, straddling her body and dominating her with his strength. His rotten breath engulfed her. His venomous face screamed. She twisted her body and struggled with all her rage.

You will not win!

She swung her sword away from her body, freeing her arm. One quick motion brought her sword around his back and through his body above his hip. He screamed, eyes stretched wide.

The pig released her other arm and swayed before her.

She removed the blade and scrambled to her feet.

She stabbed his chest.

Pulled out the sword.

Stabbed his heart.

Stabbed!

Stabbed!

Stabbed!

She backhanded Ysa's shield across his face and knocked him onto his back. Forever.

Lucia screamed involuntarily, releasing tension. Only madness helped her to ignore the pain. Her eyes watered. Her breath heaved.

More footsteps approached.

Three more brown men raced down the second hill.

I can't fight three. Ysa, why did you bring me here? Do something!

She looked to the other slope, hoping to see a miracle. Two Rezzian soldiers scrambled down. Behind them, Ilario on horseback.

She pulled Ysa's shield to her chest, barely in time to keep the first thrown spear from flying through her. The impact knocked her backward, stumbling. She met the ground again, and before she could stand, another heavy Pawelon body pressed down on her.

Metal clanked against metal. Men screamed, dying. Bodies crumpled with thuds.

The Pawelon fell off to her side.

Ilario pulled her up and into his arms.

He pressed his jaw up against the uninjured side of her face. "You're safe, Lucia. I'm here."

She panted and squeezed his sides. *Get me out of here. Carry me away from this nightmare and never let me go.*

A mysterious bright light flashed near them, rising up to the sky. Lucia's chest clenched with an oppressive sense of terror.

"Their prince is here with us. I feel his presence. It's evil. It's him."

'*'

Relief washed over Ilario as he embraced Lucia. The metal of Ysa's armor felt strangely supple against him. He smelled the sanctified oil used to polish her helm. His duty fought back against his reprieve, commanding him to look for Caio and rejoin the fight.

"Their prince is here with us. I feel his presence. It's evil. It's him." The gash across her cheek still bled.

"I'm here. I won't let him hurt you."

Lucia fell against his body, moaning.

"What's wrong?"

"Help ... help me," she said, her voice quiet and pained.

Approaching shouts came from both the Rezzian and the Pawelon sides. "Stand strong," he told her, not knowing what to say. "Focus." He held up her body with one arm and used his other hand to squeeze her fingers around the handle of Ysa's ancient sword.

Lucia's eyes closed. Her mouth hung open and she whimpered. Her unconscious body collapsed against him.

Ilario hoisted her up and over his shoulder, turning toward Rezzia's forces. King Vieri appeared at the top of the hill on his chestnut horse. Caio rode up beside him on his grey steed.

Ilario waved to them. "I've got her. She felt that same presence again before she collapsed." As he spoke, her body's weight lessened until she felt like nothing at all.

She was inexplicably gone.

Ilario searched for signs of her on the dusty ground, down the trench, and up the hills.

King Vieri and Caio rode toward him. "I saw you holding her. Where did she go?" the king demanded.

"I was—she said it was their prince. She begged for my help—she vanished. She was in my arms."

Caio's voice was weak, his conviction strong. "We must pray to our gods to help us find her. Now."

Lord Sansone, I'm no good at praying, but help me find Lucia. She was in my arms, in my care. Sacrifice me if you must, but take me to her ...

Chapter 26:
The Rape of Persephone

Moments earlier.

RAO AND AAYU DREW UP behind the first mound, beside a few sages already directing their powers at the dogs. The twangs of bowstrings and the swift flights of arrows peppered their ears. Their closest guards formed a square around them, shields and spears at the ready.

"Let's find the Haizzem." Rao stood on the balls of his feet, bent his knees, and rested his hands on his thighs. He exhaled a long breath, shaping the sound like a deep whistle to attune Aayu's mind with his own.

Aayu faced him and matched his posture. Each one gazed at the center of his partner's forehead, recognizing the self in the other, connecting his consciousness with the essence within his bhai.

Rao led, closing his eyes and relinquishing all sensory perception, embracing pure and untethered awareness. He returned to his body and his senses. The chaos of hustling bodies blurred around them. Dying screams arose from the trenches near the front. Above the heat and violence, the blue sky spanned calm and vast.

Rao lowered his eyelids with great mindfulness and focused on a bright point of light in the black void for seven breaths. The glow expanded over his inner vision and drew him fully into his subtle body.

The world transformed, as if painted over by one magical brushstroke, into a jumble of bright colors, audible thoughts, and tangible feelings. Rao's essence hovered, lighter than rarefied air.

Aayu's orange energy field expanded, nearing the same state. Rao reached out in his insubstantial form and touched Aayu between his eyebrows to quicken his transmutation. Once on the same plane of awareness as Rao, Aayu appeared much as he did in his physical body. Most of the thousands of other men appeared as red fields of energy, concentrated near the wide mouth of the trail.

Rao only needed to project his thoughts to communicate to Aayu: *Let's find him.*

His consciousness floated above the battle and scanned the areas thickest with fighting. He propelled himself forward until he found two unusual beings in the second trench leaning against each other. The first was an enormous black and red field, with intermittent yellow and white pulses. The second had a more regular aura, curved like an egg, a color between brown and gold. Rao visualized a flare of light around the two to signal their position to his men.

Go there. We'll capture the larger one.

The two bright Rezzians seemed to be embracing each other as Rao and Aayu surrounded them. Because of the colors, Rao realized he must have found the royal daughter again.

See her energy field shrinking and powerless. We'll bring her to us. The Haizzem will come looking for her if he's here.

Her colors dulled and her aura diminished briefly—before her spirit battled back, expanding and flashing its many colors again.

Focus! We'll pull her toward us ... Now!

The woman's being collapsed into a tiny point, as if it had been extinguished. An instant later she appeared, lying dazed at their feet in her subtle body.

It is her. I didn't see her face last time.

Should we send her spirit to another plane? Aayu thought to him.

Not yet. I hope to persuade her to retreat with her army.

She must be too disoriented to think clearly.

Two more unusual figures approached from the Rezzian side of the battle. One looked like the royal daughter, with a giant red and black field, though this one was surrounded with a smooth yellow-white aura. The other burned orange and red, with its edges flickering like flames.

The golden brown being began expanding its energy, attuning its consciousness to subtler realms.

It's coming toward us, Rao thought to Aayu.

How? They can't be trained for this.

I don't know, but look ...

Chapter 27:
The Fury of Agamemnon

"WE MUST PRAY TO OUR GODS to help us find her. Now." Caio dismounted. His chest clenched in agony as his feet hit the ground. He sunk onto one knee, then the other, and fell forward onto his forearms and crown. He clenched Mya's rod as he squeezed tears from his eyes.

Mya, I beg you, help me find Lucia.

"Ilario!" The king's boots rustled the earth as he spun, searching for the massive warrior. "Where ... ?" Ilario was gone.

Caio again buried his head in the inhospitable earth and prayed. *Lord Oderigo, we need your answers now.*

"Raise your head and read from The Book." Lord Oderigo's smooth, deep voice was like polished bronze.

Caio lifted his eyes to a vision of The God of Prophecy. Oderigo lowered the tome with his lustrous arms and slowly opened it. The words glimmered on the gold-trimmed pages, pulsing larger and smaller as if the book were breathing.

Even the most pure intentions cannot halt the fruition of forces began in generations past. Only in man's response to tragedy and destruction, this humbling crucible and cleansing of souls, can he find the power to renew his spirit and all the world.

On this day in Gallea's history, the gods' most beloved son would experience immovable denial, a submission to the demands of the past, to the totality of the divine instruments of Lux Lucis, who enforce the restoration of balance and the coming of the light. The Black One would have his due.

The towering god slammed shut The Book of Time. The vines trailing down Oderigo's arms slithered by their own power and wrapped around the great work before Caio's lord vanished.

His father stood over him, covering his son with Lord Galleazzo's golden shield.

Caio stood and pain sliced through his body again, a crippling he surrendered to and embraced. "Lord Oderigo refuses to tell me where they are."

'*'

Vieri glimpsed a fresh row of brown reinforcements coming over the adjacent western ridge with spears in hand. Dozens of Rezzian troops had already poured into the second trench, but the oncoming Pawelon infantry outnumbered his men.

"Run back, Caio. Go."

"I can't, I—"

Vieri unleashed an animalistic yell as three spears flew spinning toward them. He blocked two with his lord's shield, but the third grazed Caio's shoulder.

Pangs of horror filled Vieri as his son fell onto his back with a scream. Vieri stood in front of Caio with his shield before him and his falchion pointed to the sky. "I pray in Lord Galleazzo's name, every pig who comes near my son will die!"

The first Rezzian to make contact with Pawelon's front line deflected two long spear thrusts with his shield and knocked a third away with his sword. He advanced, ducked, spun, and cleaved his blade through the midsection of a Pawelon soldier as the same soldier stabbed down at him and ran his spear through the Rezzian's neck. As their blood spilled on the dry earth, the two armies collided and stabbed each other at close quarters.

Vieri roared with long syllables, "Gal-e-azz-o!" calling to his god's lions.

With coordinated efforts, the Pawelon spearmen battled their way through the Rezzian infantry and left dozens of corpses in their wake.

Berserk, Vieri swung Lord Galleazzo's golden shield, hacking down with his falchion on the long spears lunging toward him. His spirit boiled with feral wrath, lost in the brutal dance.

He sliced down clear through the neck of a stumbling enemy and burst forward, tackling two more to the ground. A Rezzian ally stabbed one of the Pawelons in the chest. Vieri squeezed and snapped the neck of the other with such force that the man died in his grip.

Vieri stood, searched for the lions, and found no sign of them. More Rezzians charged down from the hill as the dying screams and blood-spilling continued.

The Rezzian reinforcements beat back their foes. Retreating Pawelons found Rezzian spears in their backs.

Vieri called for medical help from the warpriests as his troops congratulated each other for surviving the skirmish. He tried to calm his panting and overcome the crazed lightness in his head. He removed his helm and crouched beside his son to collect his mind.

Caio reached up and put his hand on Vieri's forehead.

Vieri's world slowed. He noticed colors again: the bronze greaves on his soldiers, the red of their tunics and horsehair plumes, the ruddy browns of the dirt. He realized how tightly he was gripping his falchion. He sheathed his weapon and stretched the aching fingers of his red, cramped hand.

"I'll be fine," Caio said. "We need to find Lucia and Ilario."

King Vieri gathered his son's hands, with Mya's rod between them, and held them in his own. His son had come within an inch of dying and his daughter was gone. Rezzia's new Dux Spiritus lay wounded and defenseless on his back, with his protector nowhere to be found.

Vieri stared into his son's wide, undefended eyes and prayed, "Lords Galleazzo and Oderigo, goddesses Mya and Ysa, bring Lucia back to us now. Whatever the cost may be, please bring her and Ilario back. I pray in your name."

Caio's eyes were bottomless, tranquil pools. Vieri realized he had never before felt so close to his son. He continued, "Gods of Lux Lucis, I swear that Rezzia will retreat from this battlefield with haste if you bring her back to us. We will take my son to safety and make sure that he heals. I will personally guard my daughter from the evil that has raped her, if you bring Ilario and Lucia back to us now. Save her from Pawelon's dark magic."

'*'

His wild, white hair stirring in the breeze, Lord Galleazzo, in his golden chainmail, looked down on Rezzia's supplicant king.

Vieri's bearded face pointed to the sky. His deep brown eyes glared at the heavens, begging.

125

Chapter 28: Death and Life

LORD SANSONE, I'M NO GOOD AT PRAYING, but help me find Lucia. She was in my arms, in my care. Sacrifice me if you must, but take me to her ...

Ilario experienced the infinite black expanse of the universe, with only the presence of distant, burning stars to comfort him. A haze rose, a celestial grey fog, clouding his perception. Without warning, barrages of vibrant colors overwhelmed his vision, streaking around him, subduing his consciousness into dazed submission.

A muted thought floated through it all.

I am dead.

No body, no weight. Only consciousness floating, experiencing something grander and more confusing than he'd ever thought possible. The sensation might have been liberating if it wasn't so foreign.

Lucia, he remembered. *Where is Lucia?*

An all-powerful force sucked his being downward, into a body made of light. A strange landscape of glittering red dunes surrounded him. Ilario felt ill at ease, unable to feel solid ground. A sensation like burning went down into his throat and deep into his chest.

Three figures appeared in the distance. Dizzy, he propelled himself forward, though he wasn't sure how. It felt like flying, unsteady and easy at the same time. Somehow he understood what was before him: two sages trying to possess Lucia's spirit, and Lucia struggling against them.

Focused on the larger of the two, he propelled himself against the Pawelon sage. There was no sensation of colliding against him. Ilario entered the same mental space as his enemy. Its jumbled consciousness spliced with his own and he glimpsed an enemy much more confident in this realm—one annoyed at having his attention diverted. Their fragmented minds pushed against each other, wrestling for domination.

Helped by the distraction, Lucia's spirit broke free and arose.

Ilario! he sensed her thoughts as she recognized him.

Fight them, Lucia!

I love you.

I do, too. Now fight.

The big sage pushed Ilario away from him. Ilario tried to tackle the being again.

As he tried to grapple his opponent, Ilario's subtle body twisted around violently and slammed down, leaving him disoriented.

What just happened?

He looked for her. She was on her knees with the hands of the other Pawelon on her head, pushing her down and controlling her body.

Ilario found himself rooted and heavy, frozen in place. The larger sage stood over him and waved his flabby arms around like snakes toying with prey.

He felt as if he was being compressed into single point of light. Then came a nauseating shock, like having one's insides scattered by a swift wind.

Now I'm dying.

Somehow from this disjointed state, he sensed the conversation taking place between Lucia and the other sage, hearing it as if it happened all at once.

If you agree to retreat with all of your forces, we will release you.

Stop whatever you are doing to him!

Only if we can negotiate.

Fine. But send us back and fight us like men, in the flesh.

Take your forces in the valley and return to your camp, or we'll kill him here and now.

Your rajah will be given the chance to surrender. Under my brother's leadership, we won't humiliate you. Tell your people he will not slaughter them if they submit.

My father will not surrender. Agree to return and retreat.

Maybe—if you send both me and him back safely.

We have a deal then. Tomorrow, will you consider peace?

If Pawelon surrenders.

Tell your people to give up their war, before I am forced to hurt them, and you. The next time will be different ...

The nightmare faded away.

Ilario began to feel the limbs of his physical body, like heavy stones flat against the earth. He barely heard the shouting of excited men and moved his dry tongue against the parched ridges on the roof of his mouth. A smooth hand touched his face.

127

Bright sunlight blinded him as his eyelids opened. Caio looked down on him, smiling despite another wound, this one on his left shoulder.

"My father prayed to the gods to bring you back to us. Lucia is back, too. Come with me, brother. I've called for our retreat."

Chapter 29:
The Barren Fields of Ares

LUCIA'S SWEAT-SOAKED VERMILION HAIR covered her face and shielded her from the cruelty of the sun. She kept her eyes closed, let her body sway, and allowed her mare to follow the others. The discordant sounds of the wounded men wheezing in pain and the stomping of the crawling beast that was the Rezzian army merged into a single droning noise that sent her within.

Her body felt alien, jagged and stretched out in places where she had no flesh. She yearned to sleep in hopes of waking to a more coherent sense of self, even if it meant facing Lord Danato again. Maybe she would sleep in Ilario's arms.

The presence of Caio and Ilario, riding beside her, helped her feel sane. They either had no interest in talking, or they respected her need for quiet. Caio's difficult breathing stoked her anger over the day's events, but it had been a miracle of Lux Lucis they survived the day. Ilario's ability to rescue her from that dark dimension was an even greater wonder. These miracles made her think of Lord Cosimo.

I hope your god watched over you today, Duilio.

Drowsiness came over her, soft and gentle. A moment of rest, just for a moment ...

With a sudden jerk, she opened her eyes and found herself riding alone in the desert, hearing a familiar voice rumbling up from the dust below.

"My dearest Lucia."

What do you want?

"Tell me how you feel about what happened today."

You really want to hear what I have to say to you? She searched frantically for a sign of him, finding none. *Fine.*

"My spirit was abducted without warning." Her voice sounded coarse and dry to her ears. She hoped it sounded like anger rather than vulnerability. "I was completely unable to defend myself. My soul was nearly stolen away to another dimension, I can't think clearly, my brother nearly died, Ilario was lucky to survive along with me, and the entire mission was a failure. My goddess's own lightning nearly killed me. Caio's first attempt at military leadership went nowhere. Everything is horrid in my world and you are the most foul presence in it. Does this make you happy?"

"My daughter, I am sorry for your pain."

"All the other gods help us when we ask them. You are fixed on a vision of a war that never ends. Are you asking the rest of the gods to hold back their aid just so you can be right?"

Lord Danato's voice remained calm. "I only want you to see, Lucia—"

"I see evil everywhere, and it always starts with you." Tears poured out her eyes, over her cheeks.

"I am a patient god."

"Damn, you are! What do you want from me?"

"What do you feel about the war now?"

The horizon was hazy, as if windstorms were blowing in from all directions. "Caio and I want it to end. Again you didn't allow that." She raised her voice. "Why?"

"I want freedom for you, dear Lucia. I want you to see—"

"I have always seen what *you* wanted me to see. What kind of god terrorizes a girl and stays with her all her life? Will you never leave me alone?"

"Halt!"

"Halt!"

"Halt!"

Her body jerked—again she saw the waking world and heard the voices of soldiers. She rubbed hard across her brow with one hand, pushed her hair up, and smeared it back over the top of her head. She tugged back the reins.

From the south came a lone rider bearing the crimson Rezzian flag.

Her father trotted forward on horseback and motioned for his children to follow. They rode out and approached the thin soldier, a young man with only the beginnings of hair on his upper lip. His stretched-wide brown eyes, reddened by either his tears or the harsh winds, looked traumatized.

Ysa, please don't let it be.

"Report, soldier," her father drew up, but remained at a distance from the young man. No one else in the army was within earshot of the conversation.

130

The young man looked from face to face, his mouth twitching rather than speaking.

"Go on, report," King Vieri barked.

"Havah ilz avah Haizzem." He bent his head low in Caio's direction. "My King, my Haizzem and Dux Spiritus, Your Grace." His speech was uneven from tired lungs or a tired mind. "We ignored the sentry after they sent up their signals. A large Pawelon force came to meet us."

"Speak faster."

"And, it was all chaos, my King." The young soldier stared down at the legs of Vieri's horse. "We were overwhelmed by their sages. Our Strategos said he'd never seen such an effect."

"What was it?" Lucia asked.

"I can't explain. The skies went dark around us, Your Grace. We saw, we saw, almost as if the Pawelons were stars. We could not focus, couldn't see their forces approaching. Or their arrows. We couldn't see the terrain or the horizon. Bodies started falling. It was a total slaughter."

"Where is Duilio?" her father asked.

"Strategos Duilio asked me to remain close to him. Once their sages' magic ceased, we were surrounded. Eventually their general approached us."

"Indrajit," her father said with disgust.

"Yes. They were only interested in one prisoner, the Strategos. They slaughtered our remaining men. Their general introduced a sage named ... something, and gave him credit for their victory. They came for me with their spears and I lost consciousness. I was sure I was going to die." The soldier stopped again, with strain on his face as he fought through his emotions. "Later, I awoke on the battlefield. Everyone was dead—there were no wounds on my body. I don't understand what happened."

Lucia slowly turned her head from side to side as a painful realization began to sink in.

Danato's vision ...

"Everyone else was slaughtered?" Caio asked.

"Yes, Dux Spiritus. Yes, my Haizzem. I wish I had better news to bring to you. I am so sorry."

"I'm glad you're alive, my brother. What is your name?"

"Accori." He slowly approached the side of Caio's grey horse with watering eyes and humbly raised his hands.

Caio took Accori's hands in his own. "You and Strategos Duilio prayed to Lord Cosimo?"

The soldier looked surprised. "Yes, my Haizzem, at his request."

"I can tell you with certainty, Accori, this is why you are still with us."

"Praises to Lord Cosimo," the soldier said before he quickly lowered his head.

"Praises to him," Caio said as he rested his palm on Accori's crown.

Her father turned his face before Lucia could study his reaction to the news. He spurred his steed into a canter to rejoin the army.

'*'

From the moment Caio glimpsed Accori riding toward them, he felt leaden fingers squeezing his heart, much more painfully than the burning wound over his ribcage or the gnawing pain in his shoulder. He felt the horror of so much death in Accori's soul, but refused to accept the truth until he heard it from the young soldier's mouth. As he heard Accori speak, Caio saw a vision of Lord Cosimo standing beside Duilio and Accori as they prayed.

Caio rode once again between Ilario and Lucia, staring ahead at their camp.

Lucia spoke quietly, "It's on us to admit our plan failed, and miserably. The gods remain unswayed." Her voice trembled with frustrated emotion and tiredness. "We have no other choice now but to visit Lord Danato."

Caio hesitated to think it.

"You have to agree," she said.

"I do." He looked down at the trampled desert with a sense of dread choking him.

"I don't want to interrupt," Ilario said, "but are you talking about what I—"

"Yes," Lucia cut him off. "Danato's underworld realm."

Ilario's brow creased in confusion.

"My dear friend," Caio began, "I've recently learned that Danato holds a clear vision of this conflict. In his vision, the war rages for another ten years. Unless we appease him, our lot is to be doomed and ill-favored by our gods."

"But do you have to do something so extreme?" Ilario held back the strength of his conviction; Caio could feel it.

"Believe me," Lucia said to Ilario. "It is the very last thing I would ever want to do."

Hearing Lucia's words, Caio's heart felt strangled again.

132

Ilario scrunched his lips and clenched his jaw. "But there has to be some other way. Can't you appeal to him without visiting his realm? What is it the scriptures say about those who make that journey?"

"That he always *gifts* his supplicants with sorrow," Lucia said.

"We must give Lord Danato the greatest respect," Caio said and heard a huff of disgust from Lucia. "He is a god of Lux Lucis. His sole purpose is to protect us and guide us to the light."

Lucia shook her head and looked away.

None of them spoke again during the journey back.

The camp lay ahead, with the sun not long from setting in the north, to their left and behind them. Fires burned in the distance, first for cooking their meat and gruel, then to let the warriors stare into a flickering, ceremonial reminder of the day's dead. Under the tall white tents, thousands of well-worn beds would remain empty, haunted.

Chapter 30: Fading Sunlight

DEVAK'S BOOTS HAMMERED the stone floor as he marched in circles around his chamber, shaking his head, wondering if he should curse himself. Still no word from Rao.

Indrajit walked slowly, almost meditatively, near the center of the room. A layer of dust covered his uniform after his trek into the canyon and back. "It was a glorious rout. Briraji's help was invaluable. We massacred their legions."

"How many Pawelons were slaughtered to the north?" *I don't care what you detect in my voice.*

Indrajit's steely expression remained unchanged. "We had no chance to reach them. We only know the Rezzian army retreated."

"I want to know what happened."

"We should know soon." Indrajit stepped past the late-day shadows, to the highest eastern lookout inside the ancient tower. The opening had been worn down by wind and rain over the centuries. "No matter what happened there, we annihilated a considerably larger force in the south. This may be the greatest victory we've achieved in a single day."

Devak huffed out a breath and approached the side of his general. The sun sank too quickly toward the northern horizon. The northern troop still could not be seen—only pale green shrubs, red earth, and a darkening sky. "Once Rao is back, we'll call this day a victory."

"Oh, I expect he will be back." After a long silence, Indrajit turned his head to Devak. "I had excellent commanders there, too. Those men would be significant losses."

Devak squinted his eyes in response. "Rao was right."

"This time he was. But we cannot plan a war with caprice and whims." Indrajit looked to the sunset again. "Eventually your luck will run out."

Devak stepped in front of Indrajit and searched the world outside the citadel, finding too much calm. "We have been stuck here too long. I want to see Pawelon again."

"Hasn't my strategy allowed us to survive, Devak? Have I failed you?" Indrajit's breath reeked of his last meal, garlic and onions.

"No. But something needs to change."

"I've been employing new tactics, my Rajah. You even questioned me when I did ... I'm confused. Would you look to a boy for your answers?"

"For some answers maybe. He has his gifts."

Silence lingered after Indrajit walked away, his boots making slow progress.

A tall soldier in fine uniform interrupted the quiet from the stairwell. "Sirs, we have word some of our army is returning from the north. Prince Rao is with them. That is all I was told."

Devak's chin fell forward as his shoulders dropped. As he looked at the stone floor, his mental chatter went silent and gratitude arose instead. He looked out of the tower toward the northeast, searching, finding nothing. "Come with me to meet them."

Indrajit met Devak's request as they passed under the archway together. The odor of the guards' sweat lingered in the sweltering vestibule. Endless stairs descended before them.

Devak tried to stop worrying about his son's condition. "Congratulations on taking their Strategos."

"Duilio himself." Their voices reverberated inside the rocky stairwell, as did the powerful footsteps of soldiers ahead and behind.

"It's amazing they would sacrifice him," Devak said.

"They're overconfident. They must believe he is expendable now. Imbeciles."

"And Duilio said nothing at all?"

"He very cordially refused to speak of their plans," Indrajit said with a wry smile.

"I'll pay him a visit myself. We'll see how cordial he is after I beat him." Devak's heart wouldn't stop fluttering. "He'd better hope Rao hasn't been harmed." He felt his lungs shaking as his breath tumbled out. The monotony of the descent was so well established now, it had become like a meditation, though the silence failed to calm his lingering worry.

"My problem with Rao is that he is passive and an idealist." Indrajit broke the quiet with words that seemed carefully prepared. "He possesses the naivety of youth, but not the vigor. Were he to inform our tactics, we would not only remain trapped here, the dogs would take advantage of his inexperience. If you take his voice seriously, we will risk everything we have worked for."

"You've served me well, Indrajit, and I hope you will for a long time to come. But he is your future rajah—"

"Someday he will be ready to lead. For now, he is still a child in many ways."

"Remember who serves who here."

Indrajit's voice remained smooth. "Of course I do, my Rajah."

"Maybe it's not a coincidence—Rao coming of age at the same time as the dogs' Haizzem."

"I ... can't speak to that," Indrajit said.

"Maybe Rao was meant to counter him."

"Your son was a great help to us in that battle. Perhaps he helped our forces again today." Indrajit's breath still reeked.

"If so, I may double his command."

There was a pause before Indrajit nodded. The lack of discernable emotion on Indrajit's face told Devak nothing of his general's mood.

The two parted a sea of prized guards and stepped into the late afternoon. Shade filled the barren grounds. Far ahead, rows of men pulled the creaking eastern gates wide. Distant cheers arose from the soldiers stationed on the northern and eastern walls. Devak hustled toward the gate feeling lightheaded, his heart shaking like a rattle.

Chapter 31: Tempting the Light Against the Dark

AAYU CLIMBED THE LOW PEAK of the boulders and savored the wide grin stretching across his face. Maybe the hiking and fighting had made him delirious. He beamed his joy at the soldiers coming up the trail behind him.

Rao hiked at the line's front. The citadel's opening gates beckoned from only two hundred paces away. Jumping up and raising his fists, Aayu sang with a voice unfit for the task, making up the words as he went.

"The dogs fell down in the desert today.
They tucked their long tails and ran away.
O the dogs! O the dogs!
No more bones for the dogs today—"

Rao cut him off. "These men have already survived one deadly force, Aayu. Cease!"

"Don't cry for the dogs!
No don't cry, no, no, no.
Nooo, nooo, nooo ...
Nooooooooooooooo."

Rao and the leading troops caught up to him by the time their laughter quieted. "May I help our talented minstrel down from his pedestal?"

"No, I am full of energy." Aayu jumped and crashed down, taking the impact in his knees and across his palms as they scraped the ground. *That hurts.*

Rao lowered his hands to help him up with a smile that carried no hint of mockery.

"Thank you, my prince, sir, sage, master, sir, prince."

"Are you really all right in the head?"

"I may be a little strange."

"Worse than usual?"

"What is usual?"

"Right."

Aayu gave Rao a stinging slap on his back. "You ready for our heroes' welcome?"

Rao chuckled and touched his thumb to his lower lip.

Enjoy yourself, bhai. "I am looking forward to seeing the look on Briraji's face when he hears what we survived."

"We were really lucky," Rao said.

"I told you we were going to change this war. They've got no answer for us, bhai. Forget their Haizzem."

"*They* will not forget their Haizzem. They're going to keep coming at us, *because* he is here."

"Of course they won't stop. Once they see enough of your abilities, they'll start to believe he was born to defeat you."

A boyish grin stretched across Rao's face as creases formed around his eyes. "As if I were his opposite. He the light and I the darkness, the only thing standing between him and his destiny." Rao stared up at the cloudless sky.

"I can see you're contemplating something, you devious bastard. What is it?"

Rao covered his mouth and coughed instead of laughing. "Look, my father and your uncle are waiting to receive us. They'll want to hear my idea, too."

The surviving soldiers made their way into the citadel, greeted by ovations and heartfelt reunions with friends. A light wind blew more dry heat into the courtyard.

Aayu clapped his hands and then pumped his fists. "Live it up, bhai! We're the victors." He slapped the hands of three soldiers rushing to meet them.

"Victory!" the soldiers shouted.

Rao's guards quickly closed around their prince, as other men stepped forward to salute and congratulate him.

"Victory to Prince Rao!"

"Victory!"

The hawkish glares from the rajah and general pulled them forward. Both men loomed like ogres. Aayu found the rajah's gaze more comfortable as they approached. Relief even made a brief appearance on Devak's face moments before he bear-hugged his son.

Aayu held up his fist in salute before his uncle. Indrajit rudely paused before returning the gesture.

Indrajit's voice carried a hard edge. "We need to know what happened."

Rao, if you could finish up that father-son reunion ...

"Yes, General Indrajit. Of course," Rao straightened his saffron uniform and stood with a soldier's posture, at nearly the same height as the general. "It became clear the storm was not a natural event; in fact their army hid behind it. Probably the goddess Ysa was involved in the weather again and perhaps Mya as well. She is one of the Haizzem's patron gods. We saw Galleazzo's lions. The king and Haizzem must have been there, too. We might have seen them.

"My unit joined the fight after it had begun, but the Rezzians still outnumbered us by a drastic margin. It was not going well when we arrived. Aayu and I used my *sadhana* to seek out their Haizzem, but instead we found the royal daughter. We," he began moving his hands in circles, looking for the words, "pulled her into a parallel dimension. A Rezzian man followed her and found us—we are not sure how. But we had the upper hand and used our advantage to negotiate for their retreat. We don't know how they got away from us, but they slipped out of our control and immediately after they returned to their physical bodies, the entire Rezzian army headed back east. Once they were gone we tended to our wounded for some time."

"You made the right decision," his father rumbled slowly.

"I truly could not have done it without Aayu. Even with his help, we were lucky."

"We made a really big difference today," Aayu said. Devak looked stony and Indrajit unfazed. "That's why we came here. To help you win this war. We have great powers, Rao and I. The dogs expect they're going to conquer us now that their Haizzem has come. We have other plans." His uncle glanced at the rajah, but Devak's eyes remained trained on Aayu.

"Did our commanders survive?" Indrajit asked.

"Sir," Rao's face lost all traces of light, "Zakhil did not. The rest did."

A quiet followed. Indrajit spoke again, "In the south, we met a not insubstantial force. All of them were killed, to the last. We took one prisoner: their Strategos."

Rao regained some color. "That is incredible news, General."

"This was almost a disaster," his father said. "Isn't it a good thing, General, that Rao did what he did?"

"I suppose it was."

"It was," Aayu added.

Rao's eyes softened as he spoke to his father, "I believe we are in the right moral position. This gives us true strength. Look at what happened today. Instead of losing everything, we captured their Strategos instead. Our good karma favors us."

"We were lucky," Indrajit took a step toward Rao and Aayu and raised an outstretched finger. "They are more desperate than ever. Your moral high ground instills a false sense of security. We must keep a step ahead of them—not rest on false hopes. What do you think our ancestors thought before a Haizzem destroyed them? I'll tell you—it didn't matter."

"Rao, what would you suggest?" his father's question was like a command.

"I have two ideas. The first is that we continue to defend ourselves as before. We still have the same advantages as always, and I believe I can counterbalance their Haizzem."

"And his sister," Aayu added. "Rao and I fought both of the royal children today and we won."

"Yes," Rao said as his face became more animated, "and if we can continue to hold them off, they might agree to leave the valley. If even their Haizzem can't achieve victory, we might be able to convince them their war is unwinnable. We also have their Strategos as a bargaining chip."

"You expect sensibility from an insane people," Indrajit stepped even closer, and Rao lowered his arms to his sides. "You also assume you'll be able to neutralize this Haizzem. You intend to let them dictate the terms of engagement. You would give them the freedom to scheme against us as they did today. Don't let your early luck go to your head."

"What's your other idea, Rao?" his father held his fist against his lips, considering something.

"Father, General, maybe we could entirely avoid the fighting on a grand scale. We could make a proposition I don't think they would refuse. Tell them I will fight their Haizzem, alone. If I win, they must go back to Rezzia. If he wins ..." Rao looked each of them in the eyes before continuing, "They can take our citadel."

Chapter 32:
A Dream Between Dreams

LUCIA LIT EVERY CANDLE in the room, leaning close to each flame until the smell of wax and gardenia splashed some color onto her grey soul. The ritual provided distraction from the storm in her mind. With ten candles burning alone, she lay in her bed and imagined a simpler life with Ilario beside her.

Her eyelids closed drowsily. She bolted upright and opened her eyes wide. *Please, not yet.* She walked around the circular yurt with disgust simmering in her stomach, hoping she hadn't drifted off to another nightmare.

Servants had already cleaned and polished her sword and armor, but from out of the corner of her eye she saw blood dripping off the white blade.

No! She stared at the blade and it turned white again. *Is there nowhere you won't haunt?*

As the thought echoed in her head she heard a man's voice through the doors. "Your Grace, Ilario is here to see you."

She sat at the edge of her bed, facing the door, and dangled her legs. "Tell him to come in."

Ilario arrived with a warm, weary smile. "I hope I am not disturbing you."

"Of course not. It's good to see you."

He had changed into casual clothing. His rope belt framed his waist and helped to highlight his firm stomach and thighs. He lifted the chair by the desk with one arm and sat in front of her. Though his legs shook nervously, his sharp brown eyes looked relaxed as he gave her his attention.

She breathed a deep breath to calm her heart.

"I'm sorry I couldn't come sooner. The warpriests were healing Caio. He's in bed now. He actually ordered me to come see you."

"How is he?"

"He told me to tell you not to worry and said he's feeling much better."

"Thank the gods," she said. *Most of them.*

With his elbows on his bulging thighs, Ilario formed a fist and cupped it with his other hand. "I'll never doubt them again after what I saw today."

"I'm still seeing it, still feeling it." She ran one hand slowly over her hair, from her forehead down to her shoulders, feeling her body shake weakly as she remembered those awful sensations. "I can't thank you enough."

He spit out a grunt of disbelief. "You can thank Lord Sansone."

"You were brave. I was powerless." She heard the disgust in her voice.

"I've never experienced anything so evil." He stood up, shaking his head and body as if throwing off a spirit. "I don't understand why the gods allow Pawelon to remain standing against us. What kind of pact have they made, and with what sort of entities?"

"I can't pretend to understand our own gods, much less Pawelon's dark magic."

"I understand that this has all been very difficult for you," he said.

Don't cry. "Their prince has his mind set on me. He's found me twice." She fought off queasy sensations in her belly. "I'm sorry. You've caught me at a terrible time."

"Lucia, as we rode back, my heart pleaded for another chance to defeat their prince and his ally, but in this world—not theirs. I will defend your honor."

She felt expansion in her chest, a gentle sensation. "I may not want to see more dead, but their prince can be tortured for all I care." Lucia looked up at the round ceiling and let out an exasperated breath. "Do I even sound sane? I mean overall."

"Yes." A genuine smile stretched across his face, giving her all she needed— all her traumas and fears dissolved by his love, for one glorious moment.

"It's good to know I have some ability as an actress. Faking my moods seems to be the greatest part of my duty." A sudden wind blew against the walls of the yurt. "Come sit by me?"

Ilario stopped his nervous fidgeting and came across to sit at her left.

Lucia breathed deeply, savoring his clean-smelling aroma.

"I'm worried about you, Lucia. What's going to happen when you visit Lord Danato?"

Her mind froze. She looked at him, making sure he was real. "I'm not dreaming, am I?"

"What do you mean?"

She shook her head once. "Something evil. I'll tell you all that I know." She took a long pause, staring at a dark red spot on the rug. "After we enter his realm, we'll each face one of our deepest fears. It will be up to Lord Danato to decide what happens next."

"But there is no chance of anything good. Even I know that."

"Some good perhaps."

"Even if he helps you, his aid will be tainted with some kind of tragedy."

"So the warpriests would say."

"I don't want you to do this." Ilario took her hand in his. His large almond eyes softened even more.

"There are many things I haven't told you, Ilario. If you knew everything about me, you would understand just how much I *don't* want to do this."

"Tell me what's bothering you. I'll listen."

Lucia pressed her fingers into her forehead, looking down and wishing she could say more. She leaned her body closer to his, allowing him to press fully against her. With an arm like a tree, he wrapped her up and provided an oasis of affection.

Don't cry.

She laid her cheek upon his wide shoulders, staring at Ysa's armor.

He reached his arms around her and rocked her gently. Seconds later, her nose itched at the coming of tears. She let her weight fall against him. Her chest pressed into the furnace of his warrior frame. Lucia wanted to relinquish her tight hold on everything raging in her mind and heart. Instead she unleashed tears in controlled waves, one torrent after another.

He lay back and eased her body down, letting her rest on him. He kissed the top of her head, as her chest lurched with uneven breaths. Eventually her crying stopped, though she'd hardly dipped into the well.

"Can you stay?" she asked.

"Yes."

"Good. I will tell you what you can touch and see." She lifted herself and studied Ilario's patient face. He seemed peaceful, ready for anything. "Only half of my body, to symbolize that until our love is sanctified by my father and Tiberio, it is not full and complete."

Lucia came off the bed and stood before him, unfastening the buttons on her long skirt, beneath which she was naked. Her loose blouse remained over her chest, and her long black gloves ran under its sleeves. The dress fell to the floor.

143

Ilario came up sideways on one elbow. She turned just enough to give him another view of her figure. With one hand she pushed him onto his back again. She climbed onto the bed and knelt beside him. With her eyes trained on his, she untied the belt around his waist.

Chapter 33: The Hazards of Love

THE ELITE GUARDS stepped aside. Rao viewed his chamber and he remembered how lucky he was to have been born a prince, to be granted private quarters while most soldiers had so little comfort. He was also able to share it with his love. Narayani's presence meant so much to him now, more than he would have expected.

"Rao!" her voice exploded as she ran to embrace him. The chamber smelled of her healing herbs, which had been separated and spread out atop a yellow shawl on a low table.

"What do I get?" Aayu joked.

"Aayu, I'm so glad that you've returned." She opened her arms to him and squeezed him, too.

"I see you had some furnishings delivered," Rao eyed the new dark orange furniture. "Are you sure we can afford it?" He said with a wink.

"It was a gift from my father. He had it removed from his own quarters so that I would be more comfortable." She squeezed him again, then led him across the spacious room. "Try it. Sit down."

Rao leaned against the smooth fabric of the lounge and put an arm around Narayani, swooning at her exotic perfume. The closeness of her smooth neck aroused his senses in more ways than one. He knew it was all a temporary distraction from the nightmares trying to crowd his mind, but her warm heart and body, along with the presence of Aayu, created a momentary tranquility, a relaxed chest, and a sense of belonging.

Narayani covered her mouth with her hands and began sobbing. "I'd already convinced myself you were dead. A soldier slipped and told me you went off to an ambush."

He kissed her warm cheek. "My dear, Aayu and I saved ourselves with our abilities."

"And we beat their stinking asses back to their holes," Aayu said. "They outnumbered us twelve to one, but we made them run. Because we know things,

Narayani. We've been telling you not to worry about us—though you nearly had to worry about Rao after what he told your father."

"Aayu, don't—"

"What did he say?" She fidgeted as her face flushed with surprise. "What did you tell them?"

"Nothing to worry about, my love."

"He proposed a duel between himself and their Haizzem. They said no, very quickly."

Rao braced himself for her disapproval. Her lips twitched and showed feelings of betrayal. He knew she wanted him to feel guilty. He did. "They're coming back some time tonight. I asked them to consider the idea, and they agreed to do that, but I don't expect them to change their minds."

A disgusted sound shot from her mouth. "That is *completely mad.*"

"I thought it might be a way to end the war without more bloodshed."

"Except yours!"

Rao put his attention on his breath instead of the words he wanted to speak.

"Listen, Rao could handle him. But," Aayu paused, "if the Haizzem got lucky—"

"The Rajah and his general come!" Commanding voices spoke through the curved archway.

Rao stood, along with Aayu and Narayani.

His father wore a scowl, something that would have worried Rao just a few days ago, but with each interaction, his notion of his father was softening. Indrajit's presence, on the other hand, induced tension.

"Hello, Narayani," his father gave her a momentary glance. "Rao, you know our answer."

"I understand," Rao said with a bow of his head.

Devak looked over the three of them and said with finality, "We are glad you are safe."

"I only wanted the best for Pawelon,"—*this is my last chance*—"but you know what's best for us. Please understand, it was not a reckless thought. After what happened today, I feel convinced I could defeat him, and if I had the chance to fight him, this could all be over. They would be devastated, and I am sure they would interpret it as a bad omen, as the abandonment of the gods of Lux Lucis."

146

Rao maintained eye contact with both men, despite Indrajit's distracting stare. "And I thought the worst that could happen if I were to perish is that our men would really have something to fight for as the Rezzians made their final push for our citadel. Of course, if that were to happen, you wouldn't have stuck to any agreement anyway. It seemed like a scenario where our overall chance of success would improve either way. But I thank you for at least having considered my proposal."

Narayani's glare was burning into the side of Rao's head. He hoped that Indrajit heard something he would like, something that would persuade him. In those brief moments of silence, the general's eyes glanced sideways as the bottom of his jaw moved in contemplation.

As Rao's father started to speak, Indrajit interrupted him. "My Rajah, let me be more frank with you, as I should have been before. I am not entirely opposed to Rao's idea." Indrajit paused until Devak's head turned to face him. "I have seen Rao in the field, up close, and I have complete faith in his abilities as a sage. He is a true prodigy. I feel guilty saying this because he is your son."

"Say what you mean then." Devak's brow tightened and his eyes seemed to cut into Indrajit.

"I could never suggest for you to risk your only son's life. You would have so much to lose."

His father's breathing became uneven and his eyes betrayed uncertainty. Rao had never seen his father so flustered before.

Indrajit continued, "And you have already lost so much."

"I won't hear of my losses. How many children have lost their fathers? I'm not afraid to lose more. That's not what this is about." Devak walked to Rao and gripped his son's chin, holding it to secure his full attention. "I'll admit I thought you were a coward. I was wrong."

"I was wrong about you also, Prince Rao," Indrajit said.

At least you're trying to sound sincere. "You could tell the dogs that if they turn down the offer, their general will be executed. And that if their Haizzem defeats me, we'll surrender the general back to them." Rao knew that Narayani was in hell right now, that she dared not speak out with her father and the rajah dominating the room.

His father removed his hand from Rao's face. "The whole thing's a terrible idea."

"I understand," Rao said.

147

"Devak, while it poses a risk, it also provides a real chance for us to win this war and return home. You have a valiant son, willing to fight for his country's freedom. You are a blessed man. I envy you."

His father clenched his jaw as he relaxed his arms at his sides. "Rao, you no longer have to do anything to impress me."

"I know I can handle him. The Haizzem was there today, and he did nothing against us. Think of how it would shatter their spirits."

"They'd become even more determined," Devak said.

Rao suspected his father was right. "If their Haizzem dies, they would believe their gods have abandoned them. They couldn't defeat us all these years, and if even their Haizzem cannot defeat a savage boy like me, they will have to face the truth about the futility of their crusade."

"They'd come for us right away and fight to the death is what they would do," his father said.

"But they take their oaths very seriously. They would think, how can the gods favor us if our Haizzem dies *and* we go back on our word?"

Indrajit squinted so much that the white of his eyes were gone. He didn't seem to notice his daughter looking at him desperately. Aayu stood observing and let out a sudden breath that revealed his stress.

The rajah lowered his face again, directly in front of Rao's. "You're the Prince of Pawelon." He paused. "I will leave this to you." Silence again. "If you were to go through with this and succeed, you would never again have to worry about the support of your people. You would prove yourself to be a worthy rajah someday. And if you were to meet your end, you would die with honor and with everyone's respect, including mine."

A shiver traveled down Rao's spine. "Thank you."

"I want you to sleep on this. If your mind is still made up in the morning, we could dispatch a diplomat with a proposal."

"That is wise. I will think it over tonight."

"Pawelon is a better country because of you," Indrajit said to his rajah. "Your sacrifices are well known and admired."

"I have to say something," Aayu said. "Rao and I worked together today and that's why our men came home. It's why we won today. He and I are stronger together."

"I respect your loyalty to my son, but this is his decision."

Narayani fidgeted and flinched as she stood with no respectable exit.

Rao wondered how his father really felt. What did the old rajah truly value? How many emotions were beneath his proud veneer?

"Rao, come with Indrajit and me," his father said. "We have more to talk about."

"Could I join you in just a moment?"

A pause. "Fine. We'll be at the top of the tower. I expect you soon."

Rao kept his eyes on the soldiers outside the archway after the two men left the room, dreading Narayani's coming reaction. A solid blow struck him near his kidneys, and as he turned she turned too, rushing off toward the bed chamber.

Aayu's lips were pressed together in a flat line with his cheeks tight and bulging. "I'll go for a walk and be back later."

Rao exhaled forcefully and nodded. He followed Narayani.

"Why are you trying to kill yourself?"

His head shook almost reflexively.

"Why do you want to do this?"

"I want all of us to go home." He knew she felt abandoned. "I want all of this to end."

"You don't have to do this. It won't change anything, even if you kill him. This has all gone to your head."

"Narayani, I want to be with you. I want to live my life with you, and do all the things we've dreamed of together. I want to get you out of here."

She shook her head once. "You don't care about me. You care about your ambition. You're trying to make your father love you."

"That's not true! I can end this war."

"You'll be a footnote in history. The last Pawelon prince, whose death sealed the end of our culture. The Rezzians will mock your name forever."

"Then you don't believe in me?"

Conviction possessed her dark eyes. "If you do this, I think you're going to die. That's what I think."

Rao looked down and ignored the insult. "I'm doing this for all of us."

"You're going to do it?"

"Yes."

She pointed at him with one finger as she said, "I will hate you."

"I will never hate you, Narayani."

She slammed her palms to the sides of her head. Rao reached out a hand, only to be swatted away.

"I love you, and I would not do this if I wasn't convinced that I'd have the upper hand. Imagine the best scenario, please. It would mean so much to me."

"Even Aayu thinks it's a bad idea."

"Please. Calm. I have to go talk to my father."

"Fine, practice leaving me now so you'll be ready to do it again when you die."

"I have to go, he's expecting me."

Her eyes were bloodshot, her lips tight against her teeth. "Right. I know exactly what you care about."

Rao's stomach knotted with a sharp pain. *I will not desert you.* "I have to go now. I'll be back soon."

"I don't know if I'll be here."

"My father requested my presence."

"Goodbye."

Rao passed the guards outside. Some were Indrajit's prized men, and others belonged to his father. "There is no need to follow me," he told them. "I am going right up to my father's quarters."

After they reluctantly agreed, Rao climbed the curving stairs until he was well out of the guards' sight. He sat and leaned against the inner wall. Feeling a dull emotion he couldn't identify, he lowered his forehead into his hands. The pressure of his duty ached between his temples.

Chapter 34: The Blood That Binds

NARAYANI FUMBLED through her medicinal collection for her vial of bacopa powder and jar of honey. She combined the two with trembling hands and stirred them with a tiny wooden spoon before eating the mix of sweet and bitter flavors. Within seconds, she felt warm shivers, calming nerves, and a gentle buzz throughout her body.

She collapsed on the stained rug and lay on her side, surrendering to the tower floor. She eyed the crumbling grey ceiling and longed for the amenities of the palace in Kannauj.

When am I going to find one person who won't leave me?

If Rao were to die, she'd probably be forced to marry someone else for protection. Her mind kept wandering, remembering how utterly alone she felt when her mother left her.

I can't do this—I need help.

Narayani looked down at her comfortable dress, the plainest garment she'd brought with her, and decided to change into something more attractive. She dragged herself to the low table holding her personal items in the corner, and raised the mother-of-pearl hand mirror Rao had given her after they first met. Her eye makeup was smeared beneath her eyes and needed redoing. She struggled to keep her hands steady at first, but, with heart-pounding determination, finished drawing the dark blue paint on her eyelids and at the corners of her eyes. One thought intruded repeatedly.

Rao's the same as all the rest.

'*'

"Narayani, he—" Aayu said, then stopped himself as if it was hard to say it. "Of course he cares about you. He's doing what he believes is right for Pawelon."

"Who would be left to care about me? You probably do more than anyone else I know. That's depressing."

"Don't act like such a little girl."

151

"I'm leaving."

"Where?" Aayu pointed disbelievingly at the archway and the guards on the other side of it.

"Away from here. I'll walk all the way back to Kannauj." She began gathering up her medicines, pouring them back into their vials and pouches.

"You're not going anywhere. Not with your father's guards here."

"I am, and because you won't teach me your *sadhana*, I'll probably be taken by bandits and killed."

Dimples formed in Aayu's cheeks as he smiled and shook his head.

"Why won't you help me? No one else will. No one else even cares."

"That's absurd."

She let out a scream and stomped her way over to the mound of pillows. She threw herself down and fought back her emotions.

"Hey, you should be better than that."

"You don't know how much I love him. What am I going to do when he gets himself killed?"

"He is my bhai. You think I want him to do this? We can try to talk him out of it, but don't expect him to change his mind."

I can't believe I'm going to try to have a meaningful conversation with Aayu. Narayani sat and looked up at her cousin. "Why do people always leave me? Am I cursed? I'm not an ugly person."

"Of course you're not. Don't be so thick. Let's think about what happens if Rao wins. We should be optimistic."

"If he succeeds, he'll be taken with all of his fame and admiration and won't have any time for me at all."

Aayu shook his head with another smirk. "No, he would have *more* time. We might be able to get out of here. If he goes through with this, he's going to need our support."

Narayani huffed out an aggravated breath. *All I ever do is support him ... that gives me an idea.* "But, Aayu, I need your support."

"What do you want from me?" His eyes doubted her, even as he grinned.

"We both know this could be the end."

"But I don't think it will be."

"Well then, it won't matter." Narayani rubbed her fingers across her lips and chin, stalling. "Aayu, I need to learn your *sadhana*."

Aayu's eyes stretched wide, mocking her.

"When Rao fights him, I want to be close enough to see it with my own eyes."

Still looking at her, he shook his head and made no effort to conceal his amazement. "No, Narayani. No."

She pleaded with hurt eyes. "I love him. I love him more than I will ever be able to love anything or anyone else ever again."

"You want to get yourself killed. What an idea."

She clenched her fists and looked down at them, struggling not to collapse onto her back and give up on everything.

"I really do care about you, Cousin."

"I wouldn't get close to them! I want to see him defeat their Haizzem. Then when he talks about it, I will know exactly what he did. I will always be able to share that with him if I am there to see it."

"Be serious." Aayu's lips pressed together until they were thin.

"Let me love him. Let me be there for him. Please, that's all I want. I want to be there with him. Please. I will bring my best medicines. If he's harmed, I'll revive him. I can do that for him. I will be there to make sure he gets whatever he needs."

Aayu glared before looking away.

"Please try to understand how I feel. I am losing my sanity, Cousin. I don't know who else to turn to. You are all I have now."

Aayu tightened his already clenched jaw. She knew something was starting to get through to him, just a little.

"My father doesn't even want to look at me after how many years since I last saw him. I just want to be there for Rao. Whatever happens, I *need* to be there for him. He is all I have, Aayu. What have I ever asked you for? You have to understand how important this is. No one else can help me. Even Rao doesn't seem to care." *I'm sorry to do this to you, Aayu.* "It makes me want to kill myself."

"Don't say that!"

"But I do. I am in a really bad state. This is the hardest thing I've ever been through. I need something to keep me going." Narayani gritted her teeth. "Before I hurt myself. I'm really close to doing something."

Aayu walked away, put his hands atop his head, and began pacing the room. He grunted through clenched teeth. With their history, Narayani knew that he would have to take her threat seriously.

153

After countless trips around the room, Aayu faced the curved outer wall and slammed his forehead against it—not with full force, but enough to be audible. He kept his head against the wall and grunted some more. Narayani remained quiet and gave him time.

He turned to her and started speaking in a loud voice. "Listen to me. If I were to even consider helping you with this, I would have very serious conditions—"

"Of course I would agree, Aayu. If you'd help me? I'd do anything you asked."

Aayu took in a long breath through his nose and let out a longer one that sounded like the growl of a large animal. "You would stay far, far away from any large battle. And I never want to hear you talk about killing yourself again. Do you agree with me so far?"

"Aayu, I promise with all my heart and soul. I'm just asking you to help me do what I really need to do."

"Do you agree completely and totally to the terms I just stated?"

"Yes, of course I do."

"If you get hurt ..."

"I won't. I will stay far away from them. I promise. I just want to get a little bit closer so I can see whatever happens to him and be there in case he needs me."

"And that's the reason why I'm going to help you. If anything happens to Rao *and no Rezzians are near*, I want you to save him." Aayu closed his eyes, relaxed his shoulders, and sighed.

He knelt before her, lowering one heavy leg after the other. "Before I teach you this mantra, I am going to impart an energy to you. It will help you to focus more than you've ever been able to focus. You will see what it's like to have the mind of a sage."

He touched her forehead, between her eyes, and a cool, burning sensation spread from that point, throughout her head. Narayani's mind cleared of all thoughts and emotions. A pleasurable calm buzzed through her body. She simply sat. Nothing intruded: no analysis, no fears, nothing to protect, argue, or defend.

"Now repeat these words, out loud at first." Nothing else existed but the sound of Aayu's voice. "After you memorize them, see them in the center of your head, moving across your inner vision with a great light behind them ..."

154

Chapter 35:
The Ebon and the Moon

THE EMPTINESS OF MIDNIGHT in the desert seemed to tranquilize the Pawelon soldiers atop the high walls of the fortress. They gazed down into the widening canyon: a graveyard for men by day, where countless tiny creatures scurried at night, ignoring mankind. The walls lifted the men too high to smell the desert fragrances, but an occasional cool wind helped to keep them awake.

Indrajit felt no desire to interrupt their quiet as he walked past them. They deserved some moments of repose.

When he reached the center of the east-facing wall, he sent the four closest sentries away. While he waited for Briraji, the calm of night did nothing to penetrate the walls of his mind. Even after the day's great victory and the capture of Strategos Duilio, he dwelled only on the coming retaliation, his fear of the Haizzem's powers, and the guilt clawing around his insides.

"Their Strategos says little, General, and when he talks he lies." Indrajit hadn't heard Briraji coming. "He claims their southern force was only testing our defenses."

Indrajit leaned forward against the wall and stared down at the canyon. "I wonder. The prince's story indicates he may have caused them to retreat, but I find that hard to believe. The Rezzians still had the numbers. They could have killed every man and marched to the citadel."

"I don't believe the Strategos, but I think our prince believes what he says. Though I suspect he's deluding himself."

"I don't expect Rao to change his mind in the morning and I am quite sure the Rezzians will agree to his proposal. If Rao is killed, we will benefit from a perfect opportunity to inspire our troops before the onslaught."

"And if he somehow wins the contest, it could turn the war in our favor."

Indrajit agreed silently. "But I am afraid that could be the beginning of our next great problem."

"What would that be?"

"The rise of Prince Rao as a hero who will exert great influence over his father, and therefore our army."

Briraji made a sharp sucking sound. "I see your concern."

The moon was bright. It would be full tomorrow. From this height, the boulders and shrubs of the canyon were like objects in the field of a child's imagination. A sudden breeze swirled around them.

"Can you imagine him as our rajah? Taking meaningless orders from him, while he would fritter away our security?"

Briraji said nothing.

"In peacetime, he would be a fine ruler. But in all military matters, he would be a disaster. For how long have men ever known peace on Gallea?"

"I agree."

"Then can I trust you completely?"

"Always, General. You know that I understand my place."

Indrajit breathed a shallow breath. "We must be prepared for any potentiality, remembering that our duty is to our race and nation, not to any man. Whatever must be done to ensure our survival and independence, we must do. No one man, nor any boy, is more important than the whole of Pawelon. Forced to choose between one loyalty and the other, there can be no deliberation." Indrajit leaned against the short wall, looked downward, and spit. "Only decisive action."

"You command this army, General. I understand my place in it."

"Loyalty such as yours is too rare." Indrajit felt the weight of his contradiction after he'd said it. "I want you to be prepared for anything I might ask. You are a great sage and a great soldier. I will not forget your devotion."

For the first time, Indrajit looked at Briraji, who nodded.

The old general gripped the ebon handle of his grandfather's dagger sheathed inside his boot. He raised the tip of the polished steel to eye level and twisted it to catch the light of the moon, running one finger along its straight, blunt edge.

"Briraji, I may soon be in a position to reward you for your impeccable service."

Chapter 36
To Honor the Black God

CAIO'S THROBBING SHOULDER and searing chest wound tortured him throughout his fitful sleep. The warpriests said the pain would dissipate by morning, thanks to their prayers, though they warned him his suffering might peak overnight. It did.

He awoke to an overwhelming scent, mystical *myrrha*, sweet and smoky. He rolled off the bed and onto his feet with a groan. A spasm of pain seized his chest.

Lord Oderigo? he asked silently. *It's finally time for me to transmit your prophecy?*

No response.

He spoke softly, "Lord Oderigo, is this *myrrha* from you?"

No answer.

I believe I understand your message, my Lord.

The Book lay upon the dark wooden altar, wrapped with fresh vines. Caio willed his body toward it, breathing in deeply and embracing the pain. Before the altar, he bowed to the ten sacred objects symbolizing the gods. The two largest items honored his Lord and the goddess Mya; for the goddess, a conch shell, and for Oderigo, the very Book of Time.

Caio untied the vines sealing the god's book and felt a shiver upon contact with the cracked leather. He moved his thumb along its ridged spine. Reaching its base, his palm and fingers stretched out and grazed across its holy face before his fingertips ran along the edges of the hoary parchment.

His thumb ran up and down the pages until a sudden vision of light filled his mind. He pushed his thumb into the middle of the book, the pages parted, and the book flew open with a thud. A passage of text pulled his attention:

The evil deeds of men exist as unaware spirits long after the heinous acts are done, for such products of man's depravity can neither be dissolved nor diminished merely upon death. Such spirits must and will be transformed by future men, who rarely discover they are grappling with the ghosts. Lord Danato, Dweller in the Abyss, is the sole master of this serpentine process at each pivotal twist.

He folded the book shut and eased himself down to sitting on his prayer rug, in front of the altar. He kneeled on one leg and stared at The Book. *Lord Danato,* he prayed, *I have no doubt you have called us to journey to your realm. I accept this. Though you may be ready to see us suffer, I won't argue with gods and their gifts to men.*

He lowered his forehead to the floor in respect to The Black One. Caio's resistance to his physical pain had abated, if not the discomfort itself. After a long submission of his will to the gods, he stood and scanned the vines that adorned the walls. He snapped off a long section and used it to wrap up Oderigo's text once more. The vine went four times around the book.

Caio closed his eyes and images arose: drowned Pawelons lying on wet ground, the spear flung into his shoulder, his father nearly losing his own life to save him, Lucia's tormented face after she returned from her abduction.

Raw feelings coursed through his heart as he contemplated the crushing slaughter of Duilio's legions, the hopelessness of his soldiers masked by rage, his paralyzing fears about Lucia's and Ilario's safety, and, overall, his grieving over the total loss of his perfect world.

He fell to his prayer rug and prayed again. *Lord Danato, whatever suffering may be coming, I beg you to saddle it on me. Let Lucia suffer no more, let no one else suffer but me. I am your slave. Punish only me.*

Ilario's dauntless voice filled the room. "May we enter, my Haizzem?"

Caio filled his heart with love as he stood. "Yes, my brother."

Lucia followed Ilario, resplendent in her royal *cremos* robe. Caio sensed Ilario's guilt, so he embraced his stout friend. Caio warmed inside, knowing Ilario and Lucia had spent the night in each other's arms.

"I am so happy to see you together, and to see that you are feeling much better, Lucia."

She smiled enough for dimples to form in her cheeks, like drops of sunshine. Caio wanted to hug her, but didn't want to stain her pristine *cremos* robe.

"Now that I have begun to regain my strength," Caio said to Lucia, "I can pray to Mya to heal you."

"Save your energy. I'm feeling better. It's you I'm worried about."

"The warpriests prayed with me. My healing is progressing very swiftly. Please have faith in me."

Lucia squinted her eyes at him. "Are you sure you can you do this now? It can wait for another day."

"I'm ready. I've completed my morning prayers. But there is one thing. I need to change."

"We'll wait outside." Ilario laid a gentle hand on Caio's uninjured shoulder before he and Lucia left the yurt.

Caio undressed and washed his body with anointed clay soap and blessed oils before tying his *cremos* around him. He rolled up his prayer rug and placed it next to his bed, then laid in front of the altar a fresh white linen trimmed with embroidered gold. He spoke softly, "From here, Lord Danato, we will begin the journey. I hope this site is pleasing to you. It would be much more extravagant and better prepared if we were in Remaes."

He invited Lucia and Ilario to reenter, and her happiness noticeably dimmed when she spotted their ceremonial portal. Ilario sat cross-legged on the floor, facing the altar from the opposite wall. Lucia froze and eyed the floor.

"Maybe there is another way," Ilario said.

"No," Lucia answered.

"I would be crushed if anything happened to either of you," Ilario said.

No one spoke.

"It is time," Caio said. "Sister, when you are ready, please sit." He motioned toward the white linen. "Ilario, should anything happen to our bodies during this process—"

"I already told the healers to be at the ready," Ilario said. "I'll fetch them quickly if they're needed. Do you think that could happen?"

"We don't know what might happen," Caio said.

Lucia sat beside the ceremonial portal and Caio went to the altar. He held up a rough piece of obsidian, a sacred stone to worshipers of Danato.

"Lord Danato, we exalt you. We seek your audience. We bow before you." Caio placed the jagged stone in Lucia's hands, looking deeply into her guarded eyes. As she bowed, her hair fell and covered her cheeks.

Caio returned to the altar. He lifted a glass vial and removed its stopper. *We receive your blessings.* He splashed the sacred water around: on himself from head to toe, on Lucia's forehead and body, on the altar, in the air, and on the floor.

He used the burning oil lamp on the altar to light a pungent bundle of grey and green desert herbs. He left the sacred plants smoking in a wooden bowl.

"To bless our journey, I will now read a passage from The Book of Time in honor of Lord Danato." Caio unfastened the vine and turned to the eleventh chapter, the one dedicated solely to the tenth and final god of Lux Lucis. He began to read:

"In the earliest days of King Goro's reign, a great prosperity blessed the lands of Rezzia. The King was a most devout ruler, one who honored The Ten with extravagant ritual sacrifices, the building of great shrines, and support for their warpriests.

"In the fourteenth year of his reign, the gods came to King Goro on the eve of the Festival of the Golden Moon and invited him to a banquet prepared by their devotees. Just as the ambrosial delights arrived, Lord Galleazzo, The Commander of Lions, the Lord of Lords, asked the king which of the gods he believed was greatest.

"Being careful not to offend, King Goro told stories of the gods' grandeur, beginning with the power of Lord Galleazzo's golden discus and the devotion of his wife, the goddess Jacopa, queen of all the plants, animals, and birds. Next he spoke of the holy prophecies of Lord Oderigo and the healing waters created by his sister, the goddess Mya.

"King Goro told of the endless service to mankind done by Lord Sansone, and of his wife, the goddess Orazia, whose laughter filled the halls of the gods' pillared mountain shrine. He spoke of the amazing miracles delivered unto man by Lord Cosimo, and of the peace of the loving goddess Vani, who blessed all the world. Lastly, he spoke of the rages of the goddess Ysa, The Protector of Mankind and Commander of Horses.

"But he neglected to mention Ysa's brother.

"After the king's long and impassioned speeches, a brooding silence hung over the gathering. The sky darkened to black and one god stood: Lord Danato. 'You have spoken so well of the nine who dwell together, King, yet you have not once mentioned me, as if the Lord of all the dark processes does not belong at the same table as those who dwell on the holy mountain. Your ignorance and insult offend me. I hereby curse you for seven and a half years. You will learn for yourself the depravities which afflict the masses.'

"The King yelled out his disagreement with The Black One, insisting he made an understandable mistake and should not be punished. The debate

160

between Lord Danato and King Goro grew more heated and, as it did, the King called on the other gods to defend him. They said not a word. Not wanting to contradict Lord Danato, those four gods and five goddesses departed and left the king alone with The Black One. Still King Goro refused to submit and insisted he was right.

"Within a year, Goro lost his throne due to the treachery of his closest ally, Farinata. By the time seven wretched years had passed for the prior king, he was reduced to begging as a pauper, suffering from a crippling disease and unable to walk, bereft of all family and friends.

"Goro made use of his prior spiritual training to journey to Lord Danato's underworld, where he finally begged for The Black One's mercy. Lord Danato accepted the king's humble request and gave him some relief from his feverous aching, but told him he would have to suffer in isolation for another half of a year, just as he had initially decreed.

"Upon the completion of all the days of his curse, King Goro found himself miraculously healed and soon welcomed into the fold of the royal family once again. He lived the rest of his days as a guest in the holy palace, at the pleasure of his nephew, now King Lapo, who had reclaimed the seat of power from Farinata the Usurper.

"In a tale from the year 765, the Rezzian Queen Modesta also made the treacherous journey to Lord Danato's underworld. Her husband, King Remigio, lay dying of an incurable affliction with no male heir. Upon reaching Lord Danato's realm, she is said to have been subjected to tortures the equal of her greatest fears. Once her underworld trial was complete, Lord Danato appeared and gave Modesta his mixed blessing.

"The king's health gradually improved, but after he recovered, their daughter Pia died in a raging fire while visiting the province of Lympia.

"So it has always been. The black god always receives his due."

Caio closed the book and closed his eyes. *Lord Danato, we honor you and your power.*

As Caio prayed, he still sensed the fear coming from Ilario. "We must honor Lord Danato with all our being. He alone holds the vision of unending warfare. He holds the power of absolution over us all. Nothing further will be accomplished without his grace."

Ilario's face twitched as he nodded. "I will be here saying prayers for you and Lucia."

Caio lowered himself to his knees and sat beside Lucia on the floor. She still held the obsidian and glanced down.

"Let's begin the journey," Caio said.

Lucia blew out a hard breath. Her eyes burned red. "I love you, Caio."

"I love you, Lucia."

"I'm ready."

They lay on their backs, holding hands with their feet pointed away from the altar and The Book of Time upon it. Their spirits fell through the ground, through rocky earth and darkness, plummeting without a sense of physicality, wrenched down by The Black One's abyssal gravity.

THE SECOND STANZA

DEUS EX KARMA

Chapter 37: The River Styx

A MYSTERIOUS, SUBDUED LIGHT SOURCE lit the underworld sky. Most of the firmament alternated from impenetrable grey to flickers of soft light mostly eclipsed by the thick atmosphere. Above a crumbling building in the distance, turbulent clouds roiled like a boiling cauldron, spinning around the structure as if it were their axis. The effect dizzied Lucia and Caio. Chaotic shadows waltzed around them.

"There are clouds in the underworld?" Lucia asked herself quietly.

"No." Caio somehow heard her. "This is the plane between the surface and Lord Danato's underworld."

Their voices rang thin and hollow, as if there were no souls behind them. Their speech was nearly drowned out by eerily moaning whispers carried on the winds.

Tall, craggy mountains surrounded the royal daughter and son as they stood in the center of a great basin. Their bare feet chafed against the cracked floor and those winds—hot, biting, full of steam—forced them to keep their cream robes wrapped closely around their sensitive spiritual bodies.

"Danato's Lighthouse." Lucia pointed to the structure beneath the clouds.

Just ahead of them, the harsh ground became a polished natural floor. Close to the distant mountains ahead, Danato's fabled lighthouse literally glided around the smooth surface while the dark clouds followed it.

"It is winding across this plain like a snake," Lucia said.

"We must speak respectfully of him."

A surprising wave of static raised the hairs on their bodies. Lucia looked to her brother and he mirrored her look of indecision. Their eyes looked uncharacteristically tiny, as if squinting at some distant mirage.

Caio reached out to hold his sister's hand and they set off toward the mythologized portal. She slipped on the strange surface first; his balance supported her. He slipped next; her steadiness grounded him. They shuffled onward with their arms wrapped around each other's backs and approached the sliding structure. Its means of entrance: a swinging, dilapidated, black wooden door.

"We'll have to run to catch it," she said.

164

"I'm ready." Caio sounded certain. He pulled her forward.

Caio and Lucia stumbled ahead together, holding each other upright. He leapt over the few crumbling steps, through the door, and Lucia followed him as they squeezed into the dark vestibule.

Dim rays of light from outside revealed a much heavier door in front of them, one reinforced by tall bands of steel and decorated with round obsidian gems. It blocked the only way forward. Carved into it were the following words in the ancient script:

Truth is the only therapy.

"Shall we?" Caio asked.

Her eyes darted downward and sideways before she nodded.

Caio pressed the lever atop the rusty handle and pushed. The metallic hinges produced an echoing screech and another tiny room opened in front of them, this one crowded by musty texts lining shelves along the side walls. Lucia coughed painfully, a sound almost like vomiting.

"Don't touch," she paused to hack up rancid air, "even one book."

Caio nodded and pulled her behind him. "I remember." *His Truth can only be found through direct experience.*

Two paces ahead, an open archway framed their view of the main room in Danato's Lighthouse. They stepped forward into the tall space. Spiraling, moss-coated stone steps led up to the lookout. Pale green limestone tiles covered most of the curving walls. The eerie wind whispered from the windows of the level above. On the opposite side of the room, almost behind the stairs, lay a man-sized circular hatch in the floor.

"The myths tell us we should go directly downward," Caio said. Without hesitation, he stepped around the stairwell and pulled up the rotting wood by its metallic curved handle. The nether world exhaled from below, hot air like a pent-up cry.

"We must go, with open spirits, willing to meet whatever he presents to us," Caio said.

Lucia crouched at the edge of the hole and held her brother's gaze. "I'll go first. Please stay close to me."

With no wall or ladder to grasp under the hatch, Lucia lowered her legs into the circular maw and fell in. Her body disappeared in the darkness and Caio followed.

Down.

Chapter 38: The Curse of Memory

LUCIA PLUMMETED, swinging her arms around, hoping to grab onto something to break her fall. She found only darkness.

Panic.

"Caio!" she screamed. The sound became muffled in the suffocating black. It felt as if her stomach might fly through her throat.

"Someone help me!" she cried with long syllables as hot air rushed through her hair.

Ignored.

Lucia plunged and spun faster. The force overwhelmed her muscles. She couldn't control her arms.

Her shaking lips managed to mouth, "No," but only produced a squeak.

Breakdown.

Tears flew from her face.

With only a small part of her spirit intact, she waited for it to end.

Impact. Submersion.

Water!

A flesh-like weight pushed her down. She felt suffocated.

I will not surrender! You'll kill me first.

The water surged beneath her and pushed her straight up. She began hitting objects as she rose—*bodies?*—and threw her arms over her face in disgust. Her head emerged above the surface with a howling gasp, sucking in the putrid, sulfuric air. More impenetrable darkness met her eyes, though her wits began to return.

"Do you wish to see, Lucia?" Lord Danato's voice rumbled from above and to her left, calm and patient.

You want conversation?

"Let me know when you wish to begin."

Lucia swam instead, away from the sound of his voice. Almost immediately, she had to push a lifeless body away from her now naked flesh.

"Haven't you come to see me, my dear Lucia?"

Damn you! "Where is my brother?"

166

"What if dead? And floating near you?"

Her jaw clenched and she glared upward in his direction, her mind thinking of the goddess Ysa and the prayers she could make to her.

"Ysa will not help you here. My sister would not invade my realm, nor act against me. You do not yet understand that the gods are one."

"Where is he?"

"Caio's body is here." The Black One paused. "You will have to find him."

"I can't see anything!"

"Do you wish to see, Lucia? After all this time?"

A long silence followed, save for drops of water dripping upon the dark sea. Judging by the sounds, the body of water extended out a great distance, all around her.

"What I want is to find my brother. Then we will ask what can be done to save our people from this war and plague. I am talking about your people, we who honor you, the people of Rezzia."

"Do you honor me, Lucia? Then tell me how." Lord Danato's voice still bellowed from a towering height.

"When have *you* ever honored me?"

"I have always honored you."

You are vile.

"Do you wish to see, Lucia?"

"Fine! If that is the only way. Yes."

Hundreds of torches lit the air like fireflies and floated high and low, animated by an unseen force. A sea of corpses floated in the black ocean. Lucia spun about, her legs ready to give out and her skin still throbbing from the impact. She looked into so many pale, empty faces. Thousands of corpses, once Rezzian soldiers, surrounded her—women and children, too.

A sheer cliff loomed before her, stretching into the darkness. At the ledge of a cave high up the rocky surface, massive Lord Danato knelt on one knee and looked down upon her with eyes highlighted by the orange teardrop on his cheek.

"Where is Caio?" Her hysteria began to return.

"Why don't you find him?"

"There are too many bodies! Where is he?"

"If he is dead, does his body matter? What will you do next? What will you *feel?*"

I'd bloody kill you if I could.

"Can you raise him from the dead?"

Curse you! You know the answer to that.

"I gave you the markings. You bear the power."

"I want nothing to do with your gifts!"

"Could you be a Haizzema?"

"No!"

"Could you heal the children?"

Lucia almost punched herself as her hands flew to the sides of her head in frustration.

"Could you end the war?"

Shut your mouth!

"What lies beneath your rage, Lucia?"

"More!"

"And beneath that?"

"More!"

And beneath that?"

"Bloody more and more! Bloody gods damn more!"

"And *that* is why you suffer."

"Do you know how much I despise you?"

"Any emotion toward me is better than none, my dear. It brings us closer together. I have long watched over you for my sister. Before your mother died, Ysa asked me to take care of you."

Lucia wrapped her arms around her head and tried to exhale her insanity.

"You do not see. You do not know how I have loved you."

"You are a liar," she mumbled.

"And now Caio is gone. Haven't you always been afraid he would die, just as your mother left you?"

"Do not. Speak again. About my mother."

"She was your everything, Lucia."

"Shut your mouth!"

"What did you feel when you saw me standing over her? Do you remember?"

I loathe you.

"What did you feel? Was it like your feeling now that Caio is gone?"

"You'd better kill me before you take Caio." Her voice became weak and pleading. "He is not tired of this life. He has not yet begun to heal this world."

"Why don't *you* heal this world?"

Curse you, you vile bastard!

"You could do it."

"Bring Caio back."

"For once, you should consider my words, Lucia."

"What can I do to appease you?"

"Lucia, this is the way. The way is in your heart."

"Then tell me."

"Openness. Honoring me."

"Tell me what I need to do."

"You are doing it."

"What?"

"It is in your heart now."

"I only know that I need to find my brother and we need your help to end this war."

"Good."

"What else can I do?"

"Come to me, Lucia. Your subservience pleases me."

Chapter 39: Heat

CAIO PUSHED HIMSELF off the edge and dropped through the hole into the darkness. After falling a short distance he crashed onto a moist, clay floor, falling forward onto his hands and knees. The pitch black felt like some kind of oven. He felt a sizzling steam wash over his body, bringing with it the scent of mugwort. The environment was, at best, a sauna. At worst, inhospitable.

"Lucia?" Caio's lungs burned as the hot air entered them. He crawled, extending his hands looking for her body. "Lucia?" The silence lingered as it would in a vast cavern. "Are you all right?"

His intuition told him she was somewhere else, even though she had jumped into the same pit a moment before him.

I am praying for you, Lucia.

Caio dropped onto his stomach and stretched out his legs, pressing every available part of his body against the cooler floor to escape from the heat. Even this low to the ground, the air burned so much it hurt to breathe.

I could die here.

I could pass out and die.

The war would go on without me. The plague would continue to spread.

And I wouldn't have to kill another man or watch another diseased man die ...

No.

Please help me, Lord Danato.

A thin beam of light shone from far away and with it came strange sounds. Caio crawled toward the light with sweat streaming into his eyes. He tried wiping his forehead with his arms, but they too were drenched. The scalding heat and burning in his lungs lessened as he pushed on. A brief look backward still revealed no other light and no way back up to the lighthouse.

The sound eventually became clearer. Some kind of raucous gypsy tune played near the light, which looked increasingly like the outline of a door. Behind it, stringed instruments and drums were being played at a frantic pace, unlike any music Caio had ever heard.

Caio stopped crawling and turned an ear toward the tiny door. *Voices. Hollering. Eruptions of joy. Noises like animals would make–but these are men and women.*

Please be here, Lucia.

Caio hesitated in front of the door. The temperature was still uncomfortably hot, though more manageable now.

Behind the door, a fiddle screeched to a crowd of hands clapping in rhythm. Women shouted, but with ecstasy. A deep sound boomed over and over behind the frenzied music, the passionate thumping of a long, thick string.

Interrupted bright light streamed from the edges of the door. Dancing bodies moved behind it. Caio felt the door and discovered wet, coarse stone. He nudged it slightly open and the overpowering scent and taste of alcohol overwhelmed him, like a cloth soaked in red wine and dragged across his nose and lips.

His feet, he found, were tapping to the beat. The music—sultry, bouncing, pounding—grew louder. On the other side of the door, he anticipated finding an unchaste celebration. The door opened after a firm shove from his shoulder, revealing thousands dancing to the band of musicians playing on a tall wooden stage.

The instruments stopped all at once and a tan woman with long, curling blond-brown hair began humming a deep, seductive melody. Her red lace dress barely covered her supple breasts and no part of her shoulders. Tattoos of branches and leaves wrapped around her biceps in a narrow band.

The singer looked directly at Caio as she sang, though no one else seemed to notice him. The crowd kept dancing, acting crazed. The women wore scanty dresses and low-cut shirts. Their chests and thighs bounced and flexed. The men wore no shirts at all.

These denizens of the underworld won't know me, will they?

The warm air reeked of alcoholic spirits and human sweat. Caio drifted through the crowd looking for Lucia, but the farther he went in, the harder it became to get through. He wanted to go past the musicians, but as he approached the stage the bodies were more densely packed.

Without warning, a hairy man put his hands against Caio's face and shoved him sideways. Caio tripped and began to fall, but two full-bosomed women held him up by pressing their bodies against him. Before he could pull away, the darker of the two women put her mouth around his ear and pushed her tongue into it. As he turned to tell her to stop, the fair-skinned woman grabbed his cheeks and kissed his lips.

"You're such a beautiful boy!" the lighter woman said in a thick accent Caio didn't recognize. She pressed her heavy body against him and rested her hands on his hips.

"Get away!" he cried.

The olive woman's arm slipped around him from behind, and her firm hand rubbed his chest. Her breasts pressed against his back. She made as much contact as she could against his back and pressed against his buttocks.

The drums began popping and pounding, faster and faster.

Caio tried to remove himself from her strong grip, but other bodies pressed against them, leaving him no room to get away. Both women had him wrapped up and were holding him with surprising strength. The darker woman lowered her arms, dug her elbows into his stomach, and moved her hands up and down his inner thighs.

Caio found himself passive, unable to say no. The bass-stringed instrument slid up and down from higher to lower notes while two mandolin players picked their instruments with expert speed.

They'd managed to pull his *cremos* off his shoulders and the darker woman somehow yanked it off his arms, leaving him in his undergarments with his robe around his feet.

The women spun him around. He marveled at the glistening skin of the darker-skinned woman as she disrobed. Before Caio could move, she pressed her nude body against him. He pushed against her, trying to break free, but the other woman grabbed his waist from behind and the women pressed him and kept him upright between them.

He continued to struggle. The larger, darker woman tickled his neck with her snakelike tongue. Shivers ran across his skin. His muscles felt teased and weak. Her mouth jumped to his nipples and bit him. Caio looked away, to the stage, and saw the vocalist staring at him as she wailed.

This is offensive and wrong. It's madness!

The women squeezed his body between theirs, massaging him along his thighs, chest, and back with their four hands, sliding their bodies against him erotically.

The olive woman turned around again, bent at her waist and leaned forward, and thrust herself back against his pelvis as the first woman undressed

172

him completely. The light-skinned woman held the sides of his chest in her strong hands and restricted his movement from behind.

No one else around them seemed to notice what was happening to him. The bodies in the crowd pressed close to each other as they celebrated the music. Many of them danced passionately, rubbing against each other.

Caio put his hands on the buttocks of the woman in front of him and pulled her against him, rotating his hips.

My gods, forgive me.

Chapter 40: Trust in the Darkness

AN INVISIBLE POWER, one that felt like two large hands, groped at Lucia's body as it lifted her. Her limbs flailed as she floated. Helplessness and revulsion disturbed her body and mind. She flew past hovering torches that afforded her a view of the water below. The boundaries of the dark sea could not be seen, but an uncountable number of bodies floated beneath her. Despite an incredible urge to vomit, nothing came up her throat.

Lord Danato's shadowy form appeared larger and larger as she approached his lair. He stood and stared with unrepentant eyes, his face like coal. Danato's body was a tower of muscle and black leather. He appeared even larger than he had when she was a child.

Lucia was lowered softly onto the clammy cave floor, one pace away from the black god. She stood and trembled, coming up not even to his knees. His body dripped with either steam or sweat.

"I need Caio." Her body felt defiled. "How could you even think of harming—"

"Dear Lucia, how will you honor your Lord?" His voice was deeper and more miserable than she remembered.

"I—I've come all this way."

"Daughter, the greatest distance to travel is to your own heart."

"Please," and the next words felt like pressing hot cinders against her flesh, "Lord Danato, I need your help."

The orange teardrop stared down at her. "Over there. You will find Caio's body." Lord Danato stretched out his arm and pointed into the pitch-black bowels of the cave.

You won't even light the way?

Coals burned red in a nearby pit, but they gave off almost no light. A steamy blackness hung before her.

"Is it safe for me to go in there?"

"Of course, dear Lucia."

I will not trust you. But I'll go.

"Caio?" she called.

Step by timid step, she inched into the cave with fear suffocating her spirit. "Caio?"

The darkness surrounded her as she stepped forward and committed to discovering whatever lay there. She heard Ysa's voice inside her head: *Lower yourself. Crawl.*

Lucia dropped to the dank floor. The clammy dirt stuck to her fingers and knees as she clawed forward.

A hand grabbed her forearm.

She pulled back.

Lucia and Caio shouted each other's names.

"Thank the gods you're alive," she said.

He crawled closer and embraced her. His wet body felt warm.

She yelled back to Danato, "You said he was dead."

"I said, what if he was?"

"And why would you do that to me? Why?"

"Ah, dear Lucia. You ask your Lord exactly the right question. What did you feel when you thought Caio might be dead?"

"I hated you."

"That is why you must go deeper. When you do, you will know the answer to your question. Go back to the root."

Lucia locked one arm with Caio and stood, pulling him through the darkness. As they shuffled toward the red coals, Lucia pulled ahead of her brother and crossed her arms over her chest. She sat far away from the dim light. Glancing over her shoulder, she saw Caio sitting by the pit, wearing his cremos robe and sweating.

"Lord Danato," Caio began, "we seek your aid. We want to end the war. We want to heal our people of this plague."

A howling gust extinguished the torches. Lucia could only see by the bare light of the burning coals.

Danato remained standing at the edge of the cave, staring off into the darkness. "And you would accept my assistance?"

"Yes, my Lord," Caio said. "The truth is that we can find no other way."

"Truth," Danato held the sound at the end of the word, as if contemplating it.

"Lord Danato," Caio added, "If I may make another request. I beg you, please give my sister release from her suffering. She is innocent—"

"Innocence has no part in it," Danato interrupted. "Someone must pay the price."

Caio walked closer to Danato and prostrated before the black god. "Whatever it is, I will pay the price for her. Punish me, please, but give her absolution."

The god took two steps away from him to the edge of the cliff and looked away into the steamy blackness.

"Caio, stop it," Lucia said, not wanting to move any closer to Danato.

"You sense the truth, boy Haizzem. About absolution."

Lucia's voice erupted, "You're punishing me for something I had nothing to do with?"

"Misdeeds have consequences. Fairness is a lofty concept, Lucia. It will give you no benefit. But healing, that is something else."

"You speak of healing when you don't even let me fall asleep peacefully? I've been scared to get into my bed most of my life. Even now you come to me in nightmares and soak my sheets in blood."

"Lucia, I do speak of healing. There are many things that gods cannot speak of without invitation. We wait patiently for you to speak to us."

"You *play* with us," she said. "What can we say to you?"

"I do what I must. I swore to Ysa to help you."

"Nonsense!"

"Perhaps you will need time to consider your fears. Do you wish to find out the truth, Lucia? Caio?"

"Yes," Caio said right away.

Lucia hesitated deliberately. "Yes."

"Do you also wish to make matters right?"

Caio and Lucia agreed just as before.

"I'm proud of you, Lucia." Danato turned to face them. "So it will be done. I ask one thing of you, royal daughter and son. You will receive news soon from Pawelon. I am sure you will do the right thing. Tonight, I suggest you enjoy your time together. Ride all the way until you reach the lake. The moon will be bright and you will remember it forever."

'*'

176

Then came the silence, the black, and rest.

Ilario's handsome face greeted Lucia as she opened her eyes. He seemed unable to find words equal to the moment.

Lucia's hands went to her body, finding her *cremos* robe covering her and her arms still covered by her long gloves. She wondered how unappealing her face appeared after enduring Danato's trials. She only nodded, trying to say, "It's done."

Caio's glorious eyes made her smile a little and gave her some hope they had done the right thing.

"Whenever you are ready," Ilario said, "a message has arrived from Pawelon. Their sage-prince has challenged you to a duel, Caio. He has proposed total victory in the war to the winner of the single combat."

Caio examined his body with a look of shock, touching his chest and shoulders. "All my wounds have been healed." His brow quivered as he seemed to accept the reality. "Lord Danato healed me."

Chapter 41: Rites of Succession

VIERI WAITED FOR HIS SON at the highest lookout within the Rezzian camp, listening to the gentle wind. A white canopy provided shade for as many as a score, but Vieri paced the sunny western edge of the plateau alone, looking up from the ground now and then in anticipation of Caio's arrival—perhaps Lucia's as well—while weighing Prince Rao's proposition.

Vieri stared at the western horizon. He blew up his cheeks and released the air. Pawelon's citadel looked tiny and unimpressive, a false image created by the distance.

He looked at his aching feet. *Have they become harder than my shoes?* He removed his tough sandals and felt the crusted earth using his toes and feet. Even the most jagged rocks did little to penetrate the calluses. The hard dirt and stones rustled beneath him.

Contemplating the prince's proposal gave him new hope, despite Rezzia's bitter defeats the day before. After years of winless strategy, he wondered if his decision to surrender Dux Spiritus would finally tip the scales of history in his favor.

All your tests and tribulations, Lord Galeazzo, have they occurred to bring me to this moment? His heart ached to believe it was true. *I am still full of faith.* Yet uncertainty clawed at him from the recesses of his soul.

The soldiers far below came fully to attention, then knelt and prostrated. Caio passed between them and climbed the hill using the rocky makeshift stairs. He wore a long tunic down to his sandaled feet and a smile. Vieri waited, admiring his son's easy gait.

"Thank you for coming alone," Vieri said, posture erect.

Caio smelled of sweet orange and lemon. "It *was* difficult to persuade Lucia to stay away."

"I can imagine." Vieri led Caio to the smooth table beneath the canopy and they sat across from one another. Caio's attentive eyes gleamed. "Do you understand what they have proposed?" Vieri asked.

"Yes. Their citadel if I defeat him, plus Duilio." Caio untied the long scarf from his head and placed it on the table. "If I fail, Rezzia must flee the valley and accept an end to the conflict."

"And if we decline their offer, Duilio will be hung." The troubled creases on Caio's face indicated he had not been told this. "Word has already spread among our men about their proposal. I assume their messengers told more than just our diplomats. As more of our soldiers find out, it becomes harder for us to say no. The pigs know that."

"The decision is even easier then. The only difficulty is that Lucia won't accept it."

Vieri admired his son, wondering how much longer he'd be able to gaze upon his well-formed face. He saw a young man with a pure heart, someone with so much left to experience, someone with the charisma to achieve anything on Gallea. His son was ready to make a glorious impact on history.

Vieri scratched his scalp near his hairline. "I've spoken with our leaders and they were almost unanimous in their support should you decide to fight him. I find myself hopeful that you would bring resolution to us all, but what great deception might they have planned? Tell me, how can I sanction an event that offers your life to their trust?"

"Father, Pawelon is desperate and taking whatever chances they can. They may think a fair battle between their prince and me gives them their best chance of survival."

Vieri looked down to avoid his son's gentle gaze. "If they are so desperate, Caio, it must be becaue they believe they cannot hold out forever. One would think that capturing our Strategos would give them the confidence to fight on. Instead, they are afraid to wage war."

"Maybe they can hold out against us," Caio said. "Father, after yesterday's events, I have to question if our gods even want us to conquer Pawelon."

"Of course they do! The gods test our resolve with setbacks. By overcoming these obstacles, we prove our greatness to them. No victory can be magnificent in the eyes of Lux Lucis unless the hero is constantly tempted by thoughts of surrender—especially just before he reaches his goal. You will see, throughout your life, just before you reach any summit, the gods will make the final leg difficult. That is when you must grit your teeth, set your mind to your purpose, and forge ahead. You are not a weak-minded man, Caio. You are my son."

"I am not used to the gods testing me in this way. Perhaps you understand them more than I do."

"I am quite familiar with their trials, Son. I also know that you will win this war, whether after this duel or after a glorious siege."

"Then let it be with this duel."

Vieri saw his son again, a man too kind for his own good, a man afraid to fight, even in self-defense. The young man was incapable of guile and far too trusting. He could never have wielded his power and influence if the gods had not favored him as their Haizzem.

"Are you prepared to kill a dangerous man? You cannot feel any sympathy or doubt. You must focus yourself completely on the task, shut out all feelings of compassion, be as merciless as an animal. You must harden your heart to his pain, his screams, his begging for life. None of that can touch any part of you. He must be like an object, a pig to be slaughtered. Can you fight like a man?"

"I can defeat him. Whether I live or die will be up to Oderigo and Mya." Caio glanced to his right at the citadel in the distance, then turned back. "But I must ask you to hear me when I say this. After this combat, my wish is for no more blood to be shed. The fighting must end with me. Please hear my longing, Father. This is my prayer. I will need all of Rezzia to pray for me."

Vieri groaned inwardly as he took a difficult breath. "If you control your emotions, you will not lose. Don't consider any other outcome. The gods did not bring you to me so you could die a young man. You were sent to conquer Pawelon and to raise up all mankind. After you kill their prince, we will see if Pawelon's promises have honor. They may not, but if you humiliate them they will never recover. You must choke the life from the rajah's son and leave him with no heir."

Caio leaned back in his chair with a sad look. "Lucia believes he wields a dark magic we cannot defend against."

"That scum has assaulted your sister twice now. Don't give him another chance to hurt her. You understand?"

"Yes. But I'm concerned she might interfere. If she tries to help me, Pawelon would be justified with any response."

"You make a good point." Vieri searched his mind for a solution. "I will keep Lucia close to me. Any interference from her would render your victory foul and disgrace us. If the war is to end here, no one else can have a hand in this fight."

Caio's eyes seemed to grow even larger, more sensitive, more dazzling.

Vieri looked into them and felt a wave of divine energy, losing himself in sadness and love. *What are you doing to me?*

Vieri looked away and covered his eyes with one hand. *Guilt won't even allow me to look into my own son's eyes.* He suddenly longed to clutch his son to his chest as he used to do when Caio was a motherless baby.

Caio stretched his left hand across the table and turned up his palm to receive his father.

Vieri considered it, but stood instead with his hands face down at the table's edge.

"You will live, Caio. Later we will have time for celebration and emotions—after you fulfill your duty."

"I respect you, Father."

Vieri's throat knotted as he swallowed and tried to hold Caio's eyes before his own.

"And I you."

Vieri fled down the stairs, choking back his buried feelings, confused about the sadness within him.

Chapter 42: Into the Night

RAO, AAYU, NARAYANI, heard the news together. The Pawelon messenger spoke a flawless, high dialect of Pawelon as he read from the majestic scroll:

"I, the Dux Spiritus and Haizzem of Rezzia, address Rajah Devak, Prince Rao, General Indrajit, and the people of Pawelon. I accept your proposal for a duel with your prince. In three days as the sun reaches its zenith, I will meet Prince Rao in the center of the canyon, due east of your citadel. No man or woman from either nation may join us there, and only one of us will return from our single combat. Both nations' armies shall be permitted to march close enough to observe the bout, under the condition that no other warpriest, sage, or soldier will influence the combat. Anyone found impinging on the contest will be turned over to their enemy to be put to death. Any nation resorting to such interference would surely be disgraced by their actions.

"Should Pawelon's prince emerge as the victor, Rezzia will relocate its armies away from this canyon and away from Pawelon's territories and interests, furthermore agreeing to a truce of no less than ten years between our nations.

"Should I be the victor, Pawelon will have three days to vacate its citadel and will return Strategos Duilio unharmed to the Kingdom of Rezzia. I will then relate to you our terms for your surrender.

"I look forward to a fair combat, one which I hope will lead to the end of the bloody struggle between our nations."

The messenger tied up the scroll again and handed it to Rao. "The rajah and his general have already been apprised of Rezzia's agreement."

"Very well then." Rao raised his fist in salute and the soldier bowed before exiting the chamber.

This is really happening, he thought.

Without having another moment for the situation to sink in, Narayani raced past Rao, dropping a note at his feet. She picked up both of her bags. "I'm going to stay with my father."

Rao stared, speechless, but Aayu followed Narayani and grabbed one of her forearms, holding her under the archway. "What are you doing?"

"I can't be here with him!" she said as her voice nearly broke with despair.

182

"Narayani—" Rao began as Aayu cut him off.

"Where are you going, Cousin?"

"My father will take care of me."

"You'd better not—" Aayu began.

"Not what?" she said.

"If you go to your father, *stay with him.* Do we agree?" Aayu asked.

"Of course I will."

Rao approached them with his arms open. "Narayani, you don't have to go."

"I do," she said as Aayu released her. "Maybe I will see you tomorrow."

"I love you," Rao said.

Narayani turned away and raced down the stairs. Rao entered the stairwell and commanded his men, "Make sure she goes to her father. Follow her."

Aayu looked down the curving stairs and rotated his jaw in frustration.

"Let her go." Rao waved his friend in as he reentered his chamber.

"Leave me alone." Aayu clenched his jaw and two dour creases ran up his forehead as his eyebrows lowered over his eyes.

Rao thought better of trying him again. He picked up Narayani's note from the dusty floor.

My sweet Rao,

Know that if you go through with this fight, it will be too much for me to bear. I do not know what I will do. I feel capable of anything. If you are reading this, then I have already left you and gone to be with my father. He will take care of me if you will not. If you want to speak to me again, you must talk to him first.

I don't understand why no one ever seems to think about how their actions will affect me. You are yet another in a long line of such people that I have known. Is this my lot? It's becoming too much for me.

If this letter should be the last time I communicate with you, know that I would have gone to the ends of Gallea for you. All I want for my life is to be with you, loving you, supporting you, being the only woman for everything you need. Ask anything of me, and I will do it. I ask of you just one thing.

Do not fight their Haizzem. Please, Rao.

Your love,
Narayani

Rao exhaled a defeated breath and sent his thoughts to her, hoping they would register on some level: *Narayani, I'm sorry you don't understand, but I am doing this for us. Wait three more days and you'll see.*

"Let's get out of here." Aayu walked up to Rao, still looking unusually frustrated. "You've got to clear your mind and stay focused. If we stay around here, Narayani's going to keep you on this emotional ride." Aayu put a firm grip on Rao's shoulder. "Give her a day. Now, you can do anything you want. You've got three days of total freedom. What will it be?"

"Hm," Rao tried to distract himself and change his mood for the better. There was no use flogging himself about Narayani, even though he knew she was miserable. He didn't want to leave her alone, but at this point she wasn't going to understand. "Let's go to Lake Parishana. I'd like to see it."

Aayu whispered, "You and I will get out of here without anyone knowing about it. Leave that to me." He followed with a wink.

"Just for one night."

"Anything you want, bhai."

Chapter 43: Secrets

AAYU AND RAO WALKED along the western edge of the canyon, far below the citadel, against the stony, sun-drenched cliffs. It was still early enough in the day for the insects to fill the air with percussive clatter.

Rao's out of that neurotic hellbox, away from Narayani, away from his father, away from the generals, away from everyone who wants to touch him and ask him ridiculous questions—all thanks to me.

The air felt cool against Aayu's skin. "Just relax, bhai. If you observe anything in your mind, return your focus to your breath."

Having recited the same mantras for *shunyata* back in the tower, Aayu could see and hear Rao, and Rao could see and hear him.

"It's been a couple hours," Aayu said. "They can't see us even from the tower now."

"It's still safer to remain hidden."

"After this much time, my *sadhana* changes my sensory perceptions. Colors and edges aren't as sharp and everything sounds like it's coming through water. I want to experience the *full* scenery."

Rao sighed.

"This drains us of *ojas*, too," Aayu said.

"Slowly."

"And surely."

"All right," Rao said with reluctance.

Aayu focused inward and reversed the order of the letters in the mantra, from end to beginning. With a shiver and a sudden awareness of great weight, he found his body and senses returned to their natural condition. Rao joined him.

"Welcome back to normality." Aayu said.

"Thanks. You're not suggesting you're normal?"

"Are you kidding?" Aayu crossed his eyes. *At least you can still laugh, Rao.* "This," Aayu said while pointing his hand at the sky and the cliffs above, "is amazing."

With only a few thin clouds in the sky, soft blue covered the heavens. Aayu filled his lungs a few times, trying to stretch them past their capacity, distracting himself from the subject he'd been dreading.

"Do you think we'll make it there before dark?" Rao asked.

"Probably not, but at least the moon will be out."

"It should be full."

"Today, in fact."

"We need to keep a brisk pace. I'd rather not have to walk the desert at night."

Aayu thought again about their supplies. They'd packed enough hard fruit, flatbread, and water to sustain them for a few days—more than they should need. They brought two heavy blankets, and Aayu carried a tightly woven canopy that would keep them dry in the event of rain.

Aayu kept his awareness on his breath, stilling his emotions. "I know you have enough on your mind, but I've been thinking about something."

"What's that?" Rao asked.

"Some things I think you might want to know."

"I'm listening."

Aayu wondered, *How can two people be brothers if they keep secrets from each other?* Then he realized he shouldn't have thought that at all after what he shared with Narayani.

Rao continued, "I don't know if I'm going to be alive in a few days. You can tell me anything."

"It's about Narayani. I know she's pretty annoying sometimes—I think so, anyway—but there are some things you don't know about her." Aayu's pounding heart added to his anxiety. "She told you she never knew her mom, right?"

"Yes."

"Well that's not true." Aayu saw the hurt on Rao's face, but thought he deserved to know. "Her mom was around a lot until Narayani was six. The woman had a lot of problems. She was always mentally absent, to say the least." Aayu used his hand to pretend he was smoking. "She wasn't right in the head even when she wasn't intoxicated. And of course Indrajit never cared about her. My father told me that Narayani's mother was a whore Indrajit found in a brothel."

The two of them walked in and out of shadows cast by the trees. Long whip-like branches curved over them. Rao walked with his head down, apparently integrating the information.

"Narayani didn't have much growing up. My family looked after her a lot. Her dad's influence and money got her into one of the best programs at the academy, but other than that I don't think her parents ever did anything for her, and she tries to forget that she ever knew her mother."

"Where is her mother then?"

"She left one night. Narayani came running to our house. She ran all the way from the slum districts to the north end of town where we lived at the time and said her mom was gone when she woke up. We never heard from her mother again." Aayu looked his friend in the eyes and saw him dealing with another overwhelming reality. "Bhai, I know you love her. I'm glad you do."

"Thank you for telling me. She never likes to talk about how she grew up."

"I promised her I'd never tell you these things, but ..." Aayu stopped himself for a moment, then continued. "She's had some really hard times. When we were growing up, we had to hide all the knives. Otherwise she'd try to cut herself." Aayu's voice began to crack. "Damn." He wiped his eyes. "What am I, a girl?"

"The mark on her arm?"

Aayu nodded. "She did that before dinner one night—started pouring boiling water on herself. My father stopped her before she could pour it on her face." Aayu's lungs were working too hard and fast.

"And Indrajit never did anything."

"Every now and then he'd come by, but if their relationship wasn't public knowledge, I don't think he would've paid any attention at all. She lived with us for a few years before she went off to study. I think my parents made sure she stayed with us until she stabilized a little bit."

"Thank you for telling me this."

Aayu nodded and looked away with guilt nagging him. *I know you'll do the right thing, Rao.* "Don't hold any of it against her."

"Aayu, I would never do that."

"You won't say anything then?"

"Never. I promise you."

"Good, because you know I'd have to kill you." Aayu controlled his breathing again and savored the spicy scent of the desert. "She really blossomed after she met you. She's a lot calmer now, if you can believe that. You just have to be careful with her. Do you see what I am saying?"

"Aayu, I want to marry her someday."

"I know you love her." Aayu picked up a rock and felt its coarse, dirty surface in his hand. He threw it as far as he could up the path. "I had it so good growing up compared to what you and Narayani had."

"Our backgrounds are probably one of the reasons she and I can relate to each other."

Aayu laughed, trying to break the serious tone of the conversation. "You're going to need that ability to relate to her when you see her again." Both of them grinned.

"We both love her, Aayu. We'll always do the best we can for her. She's grateful to you. I hope you know that. She doesn't always know how to say it, though."

A warm round of contagious laughter bubbled up from Aayu's chest.

They pushed on at a strong pace the rest of the day. Well past daylight's end, they began walking downhill toward the enormous Lake Parishana that created the northern boundary of the canyon. The full moon lit their way north, approaching its zenith as they entered the sparse forest near the shore.

Chapter 44: To Ebon

WITH THE MOON RISING in the northern twilight, Lucia held the reins of the three steeds at the rear of the stables.

Hurry, Caio.

She heard quiet footsteps around the corner. Lucia silently drew Ysa's blade and peeked at two figures approaching; they wore black robes like hers. She whistled into the night, and another returned the call. Lucia pulled back her hood and Caio and Ilario did the same. Their packs, and Ilario's weapons, remained concealed.

"Religious duties done for the day?" she asked.

Caio nodded as Ilario occupied himself with scanning the darkness.

"These are the best and the blackest that we have," she said about the horses in a hushed tone. "Waste no time." Lucia removed the blanket and sacks from her heavy pack and stowed them in the horse's empty saddle bag. Ilario and Caio did the same. She fastened Ysa's shield to her ride and patted the animal, a mare named Ebon, at her neck. Lucia pulled herself up, slinging her right leg over Ebon's back, and centered her weight over the well-trained beast.

Ysa, grant us safe travel.

'*'

The goddess Ysa and Lord Danato towered mere feet away. Ysa wore her armor and observed Lucia's every movement from atop her massive steed. Danato, in his jet leather, looked into the darkness with an expression of melancholy. The black god stood close enough to lean against Ysa's great horse, though he remained upright.

'*'

"We will have to ride most of the night to reach the lake," Ilario said.

"It's an odd situation Lord Danato has led us to," Caio said.

"And not one I agree with," Ilario said.

Lucia had nothing to add, so she kicked Ebon's side and directed her onto a path that would lead north out of the Rezzian camp. Caio and Ilario followed behind her.

'*'

Lord Danato looked to his sister Ysa and she turned her head to him. Without another reaction she followed the three. Danato remained behind.

'*'

Once outside the random clack and clatter of the camp, all was silent save the croaking calls of the desert birds, the symphony of insects, and the clomping of hooves. The moon floated ahead of them, pointing the way, while the warmth of day faded to a chill.

"At this pace, we might not get there till morning," Ilario complained.

"I'll ask Ysa to speed our journey," Lucia said before the three went quiet. She prayed again to the goddess of horses and felt a strong response. "I think you should hold on tightly. Something is about to happen."

'*'

The goddess pulled up beside Lucia and touched the black horse's thigh. Ebon charged forward and the other horses raced after her. Ysa empowered the other horses, too, as they passed her. The goddess halted and watched the three speed along the desert trail.

The goddess blinked as her eyes clouded over with moisture.

Chapter 45: Memories of Home

BY THE TIME the horses made it through the sparse forest and stopped at a river close to the beaches, the moon glowed from heaven's vault. Ilario, Caio, and Lucia dismounted and the men dropped to the ground while Lucia leaned against her mare with her head down and her arms over the horse's back. All of them panted and shivered.

Ilario came up on his hands and knees and waited for his equilibrium to return, for the sensation in his head to stop spinning, for the ringing inside his cold ears to stop.

"Lucia, maybe," Ilario took a couple breaths, "for our return," again he stopped to breathe, "you could ask Ysa to slow them down."

"I tried, Ilario. It didn't work."

"That's been happening a lot lately," Ilario joked.

Caio's sweet laughter filled the air, even though Ilario assumed that Caio felt as tired, cold, and nauseated as he did.

The horses were inhaling water from the river. Ilario finally stood on what felt like solid ground and removed one of their rear saddle bags full of crushed oats and barley. "Let's feed them, but split them up so they don't fight over the food."

Caio and Lucia each led a horse further up or down the river and dumped feed on the ground. The horses seemed even more energized than before as they ate and shuffled, swinging their tails.

"How are they still alive?" Ilario asked.

"Only by a miracle," Caio said.

"I've seen quite a few of those in the last couple days." Ilario removed their blankets from each of the horses and handed them out. "Here. If I knew we were going to gallop like that, I would have packed a hat too." He put an arm around Caio's shoulders. "We've made it this far. Let's go down to the beach?" He stuffed his food sack into his backpack and untied his throwing spear. He walked with Lucia and Caio the short distance to the edge of the forest.

191

If not for the abundance of moonlight, it would have been hard to see where the water met the beach's dark red sands. The cove was shaped like a half circle that opened out to the lake. Moderately tall cliffs surrounded it on both sides, so the waves hitting the shore were calm compared to the deeper waters beyond the nook.

"It's beautiful." Ilario stopped to observe the image and sound of waves splashing up the sands.

"Have you seen a beach before?" Lucia asked.

"I have." Wonderful, stretched-thin memories stirred inside him. "When I was young, my family went to the shore north of Peraece every winter. Those were our best times. For some reason, my father loosened up whenever he saw the Rezz Ocean. The rest of the year was nothing but work until our muscles ached, and his lectures about purity and duty. But he genuinely loved the ocean. He should have lived there."

"I wish I could have met your parents," Caio said.

"You would have liked my mother. She wasn't the same after she got sick, though. My father wasn't easy for anyone to relate to. I don't think anybody did, not even my mom. He never passed up an opportunity to preach about Lord Sansone. You had to listen to him or face the whip, or else ..." He punched his left palm with a fist. "He respected religion, hard work, and obedience."

"Good thing you are a part of our family now," Caio said.

I still regret not seeing them at the end. Ilario's mind continued to wander, and his mouth with it. "I had to get out of there, and I did find a home in Remaes. I suppose all that hard work paid off in the end. The military was easy compared to my upbringing."

"My father bragged about you before he selected you," Lucia said. "He was very impressed with your, as he called it, 'perfect effort.' That's high praise, considering your Andaran blood."

Ilario stifled a laugh. "Too bad my father didn't live long enough to find out. I'm sorry for rambling. The water brings me back."

Lucia walked over and leaned against him, wrapping her blanket around both of them. Ilario realized that if he wanted to, and if he knew how, he probably could've cried.

"Let's go down," Caio said. "I want to feel the water on my feet. The lake's creatures won't swim into shallow waters."

192

Lucia and Ilario sat close to the water's edge, huddled under the blanket, and Caio went into the lake up to his calves.

"How are you doing, Caio?" Ilario asked over the gentle surf.

"Everything is more vivid, Ilario. Every tree, every sound. Every wave. Every word means more. I am nervous, but I am not afraid. I am not afraid to die. I don't believe death would be the end of me. I feel the gods have a plan, and I am hopeful. War has not resolved war. The more we fight, the more we have to fight. It can't be a coincidence that as soon as we came back from Danato's realm, you told us about Pawelon's proposal. Maybe The Black One is giving us a way out."

"What else did Lord Danato say about coming here tonight?"

Lucia answered. "Not much. He told us to enjoy our time together. He said ride until you reach the beaches, the moon will be bright, and you will remember it forever."

"It is beautiful here. It's a shame the lake isn't safe to sail on." He hoped that his brooding wasn't apparent. The influence of Danato was unsettling enough, but now the lake wouldn't let him take his mind off his past. He didn't think about his parents much anymore. He'd already done his grieving years ago, however unsuccessfully. Whenever he did think of them, he wondered if he had been a selfish son. He wondered if anyone had been there to comfort his father when the old man died.

Maybe he was thinking about them because of the duel. It would be a fair fight between the very best and most genuine man on Gallea versus one of the worst—all left to chance with nothing he could do to affect the outcome. His friend would either live or die, and he would have to watch it happen.

"How are you doing?" Lucia asked him.

"Oh, I'm fine."

"You sure?"

"Yes."

Caio walked to them and smiled with affection. "I'd like to go for a little walk, just up and down the cliffs. To see more of the lake."

"Why don't we stay together?" Ilario asked him.

"I won't go far. I need a little time to think."

How can I say no? "Stay close enough so I can see you, all right? If you need anything, call."

"Thank you, my friend. I will."

193

Lucia stood and embraced her brother. She didn't seem to want to let him go. She rested her head on his shoulder and sniffled, taking in quick breaths.

Ilario watched, thinking he should join her but not knowing how. Something felt wrong, absolutely wrong, but what use were irrational thoughts from an emotional man?

Caio has a lot more to think about right now than I do.

As Lucia pulled away from her brother, Caio said, "I love you both more than I can say. Now please, enjoy some time together."

"Very well," Ilario said. He watched Caio walk back up the beach to where the cliffs began.

'*'

Ilario and Lucia snuggled under the blanket. They faced northwest so that they could see Caio walking along the promontory, out above the ocean. She felt the warmth of his body and the strength of his chest against her breasts.

"You've gone quiet," she said.

"Just thinking about things."

She curled an arm around his biceps and cuddled closer. "You can tell me if you want to."

"I'm not going to be rational for the next few days. And if anything happens to him, I won't be rational for a long time."

"The whole idea is nonsense. It's a farce. I don't know how my father agreed to it."

"We agree—uh, not about your father, but I don't trust the pigs." Ilario blurted a grunt of disgust. "They must know about Caio's temperament and think he isn't up for it. They are too good at hiding things from us."

"No good will come from thinking about it now." Lucia raised her face and looked up at Ilario's wide jaw and distracted eyes. "Try thinking about something more pleasant."

He looked into her eyes and his expression softened as he leaned closer.

She wet her lips and closed her eyes, then received his kiss. She felt warm and relaxed in her body. Bliss arose in her heart. His knuckles moved sweetly down her cheek and his other arm pushed her closer. She paused to see his light brown eyes full of tenderness for her.

This is what I want, gods. This is what I want.

She heard a man's voice.

194

That's not Caio.

"Listen," she said. "I hear someone."

Ilario scrambled to his feet, picking up his throwing spear from the ground. Lucia stood, tying her belt back onto her waist along with Ysa's sword.

Two distant male voices came from the woods, laughing. "They don't know we're here," she whispered.

Caio wouldn't be able to hear the men from the cliffs. The sound of the waves crashing against the rocks might even drown out Lucia's and Ilario's voices if they yelled to him. Her brother sat quietly, staring out at the water.

Ysa, please alert him.

Wispy clouds swirled over the lake and a tiny fork of lightning flashed to the north. Caio looked back. Lucia waved her arms and Ilario waved his spear in the air.

The voices drew closer.

"They aren't speaking Rezzian," Lucia whispered. "They're speaking Pawelon."

Ilario headed back toward the forest and the horses, and Lucia followed him as he ran up the beach leaving heavy footprints in the sand.

Ilario readied his throwing spear. He entered the sparse forest and tried to conceal his body from the Pawelons behind a thick bamboo-like tree. Lucia positioned herself behind a tree just a few feet away from him and tried to slow her breathing. The sparse trees covered only part of the night sky, and the forest floor glittered under the moon.

The voices chattered, laughed, and drew nearer.

They approached from afar. Pawelon's prince and his companion, the ones that attacked her.

They tracked us here. Curse you, Danato!

Ilario seemed ready to attack. Her first instinct told her to follow Ilario's lead, but her mind wanted to direct him. She pointed the sword down, with her shield covering her chest.

Ysa, if there is to be fighting in this abandoned country, let us strike first.

Ilario elevated his spear and pointed it in the direction of the clearing the Pawelons were about to enter. Lucia watched in a paralyzed daze as Ilario flung the spear forward.

'*'

195

The god Sansone stood in front of them, invisible, ten paces away. The powerful, heavyset figure clenched his hard jaw and focused on Ilario. The god carried a compact metal hammer, the type that could bend hot metal just as well as a person's skull. In his left hand, he gripped a thick iron chain from which his holy symbol, a black anvil, dangled and nearly scraped the ground.

Ilario's spear passed through the center of Sansone's insubstantial form. The god, the tireless Servant of Man, frowned.

The spear hurtled toward the larger of the two targets, the man blocking their view of the prince, and sunk deep into the big Pawelon's chest.

Chapter 46: Throwing the Spear

"WE'RE ALMOST THERE!" Aayu yelled with joy, his hands pounding on Rao's shoulders as if beating on drums. "I'm going to lie on that beach and sleep *all day*. Good luck waking me."

Rao laughed while admiring the beauty of the moonlit forest. The gentle chaos of the rumbling waves told him they were close to the lake. His aching legs and feet told him he needed to sleep.

"Just lay in front of me in case the water level rises."

"Sure! I'll get wet and cold for you. We can't let the prince's beauty sleep be interrupted."

Their laughter rose and then quieted as they entered a glade bathed in silver-white light. Rao stared up at the moon and watched a thin cloud sprint across it like a silk scarf pulled across a dancer's face.

A piece of metal flashed at the edge of Rao's vision.

Toward Aayu.

Spear.

In Aayu's chest.

Rao raised his hand.

Aayu gasped, stumbled.

Rao's fingers formed a complex forked mudra specific to his secondary *sadhana*.

His mind pierced the weapon to its core, directing it to return to its sender:

Viparyas amrakh!

The spear flew out of Aayu, backwards, just as it went in. It flipped over in mid-flight and shot headlong in the opposite direction.

A man's pained cry curdled the night.

A woman screamed out in the Rezzian language, "Ilario!"

'*'

Blood spittle, bubbling over his red lips.
Warrior thighs rattling, shaking, failing.
Rasping, inhuman moans, heralds of death.
Extinguished like a wick's flame between two fingers.

'*'

Rao grabbed Aayu's arm and pulled him into the darkest patch of forest nearby. Aayu clutched his chest, but the blood and the wound were mostly gone. "It's the royal daughter," Rao said. "They followed us."

"Did we kill the Haizzem?" Aayu pressed one of his hands against the wound.

"I don't think so. Ilario is a Rezzian name." Rao sensed a hot flare of psychic content around them. "Do you feel that?"

Indomitable rage.

"I feel something."

A fog displaced the clear night air, whooshing in with an icy bite and electric tang. Moonlight sparkled through the sudden mist.

"This is a mistake!" Rao shouted. "We don't want to fight you."

"Pigs!" the woman screamed the common slur. Electricity crackled in all directions.

"The Storm Goddess," Rao said. "No time to shift. Stay in your center. You cannot be harmed."

Blinding light flashed as sizzling heat pulsed through Rao's body. He clung to an inner visualization of himself and Aayu standing upright and unharmed.

Breathe through the pain. Breathe through ... the pain.

As the blast stopped, Aayu swayed on his weak legs. Rao rushed behind him and held his friend upright, feeling Aayu's weight against his body. Rao grabbed Aayu around his chest and they stumbled together.

Flames licked the trees around them. Acrid smoke irritated Rao's nose. His eyes watered. Rezzia's royal daughter stepped into the now hazy clearing. The air buzzed quietly, chaotically.

A black cloak covered her body, except for her possessed face and vermilion-red hair. Yellow and red gems on her round shield reflected a distracting light. Her sword pointed away from her body, diagonally downward.

Rao clung to Aayu, who still recovering, and tried to stabilize both of them.

198

The Rezzian strode shield-first and elevated the blade, positioned to strike. Her murderous eyes fixed on Rao as she surged forward. She swung with a three-quarters motion across her body, screaming "Ysa!"

Rao stepped in front of Aayu in a martial stance. As the blade came down on his shoulder, he held a clear vision of his health. The blade sliced through to his opposite hip, as if his body had not been there.

Rao's hands shot to her sword arm and he focused his *ojas* on pushing her back.

She swung her shield all the way around.

It cracked against Rao's skull and down across his face. He fell to one knee, his nose and forehead stinging as if attacked by a swarm of hornets.

She swung the shield backhanded against his head.

He fell onto his back. She raised the blade, her lips tight against her bared teeth.

The sword came down through his right lung while he breathed through his visualization of perfect health. Her sword thrusts felt like icy shivers, passing through him like a violent ghost.

Aayu dove at her, and she screamed.

The Rezzian's white blade sliced across one of Aayu's arms—he screamed as he tackled her to the ground. Aayu grabbed a rock, pinned her sword arm down with his left hand, and swung at her face. She brought the shield up to block him. He sat on her pelvis and continued slamming the rock against her shield, trying to overwhelm her with his strength.

Aayu and the royal daughter traded grunts back and forth, punctuated by the collision of stone against metal.

Rao crawled to Aayu's right, gripped the leather sleeve of the woman's sword arm with both hands, and used all his weight to pin her to the ground.

Aayu used his free hand to pull the shield away from her face and pounded her skull with the rock.

Chapter 47: No Return

CAIO SAW THE FORK OF LIGHTNING in the starry sky and looked to the beach. Ilario and Lucia were running toward the woods with their weapons in hand, waving to him.

Gods!

He'd only wanted to give them some time alone. Caio hurried and tripped on the rocks, cutting his knees. He stood and pulled Mya's rod from the pocket inside his tunic.

After covering most of the distance to the forest, he heard Lucia scream Ilario's name.

"What's happening?" he screamed. "What?"

No answer. He ran faster, with the chilly wind raising goosebumps on his flesh.

They have to be all right. I am almost there!

The massive god Sansone awaited him at the forest's edge: black hair, eyes, and beard. Caio had only seen the form of Ilario's god through painting and sculpture. The deity raised his heavy iron chain and motioned for Caio to follow him into the trees.

Caio's heart raced as he chased the god. A strange fog hovered all around.

A violent explosion shocked Caio into cowering. Electric static warmed his body and raised the hairs on his arms and legs. A subtle buzzing hummed in his ears.

The metallic rustling of Sansone's dragging chain turned Caio's attention to Ilario, flat on his back—his own bloodied spear lying beside his body.

Sansone lowered his iron links and his holy symbol, the black anvil, onto the open wound on Ilario's chest. The god knelt by Ilario's head and with his thick fingers lowered Ilario's eyelids.

Caio fell onto Ilario's body and wrapped his arms around his massive chest. *No heartbeat?* Caio looked at his own tattooed arms, remembering the Pawelon boy he resurrected. *Oh no ...*

Soul and spirit had deserted Ilario's masculine face. His tight cheeks sagged. His firm jaw hung slack. Caio grabbed his face and shook it. He pressed Mya's rod against Ilario's chest and prayed.

Please heal him. You have to heal him for me.

Caio spun around to look for Ilario's god. He wasn't there.

Mya, do something, please! I am like a helpless child in your arms. Please save my brother!

He couldn't see Mya, couldn't sense or hear her.

For me, Mya? For your poor son? I am nothing without you.

"Ysa!" he heard Lucia's scream and pushed his body to its limits running toward the sound of her voice. Ahead, the fog sparkled in the moonlit clearing. Lucia yelled and grunted. As did an unseen man.

Lucia and the man screamed as a hard object hammered against metal.

The fog thinned as Caio approached. Two men held Lucia to the ground. The larger of the two struck her face with a rock.

Oderigo, Lord of the Book of Time, stop them now!

The ground began to quake. Caio lost his balance and stumbled to a nearby tree. He held its trunk as the earth rippled beneath his feet.

With a slithering noise like giant snakes pushing through the soil, two massive vines thrust themselves through the forest floor, throwing up dirt as they soared above the trees and reached toward the moon. The green stalks swayed like cobras.

The Pawelons had fallen to the ground. Lucia was crawling away from them. Oderigo's vines bent over and swung toward the Pawelons, wrapped around them three times, and lifted them high above the canopy of the trees. Their screams for mercy sounded far away.

Caio yelled back in their language, "You killed my brother? You attacked my sister? You expect quarter?" He ran to Lucia as she tried to stand and grabbed one of her leather-covered arms. Blood covered her forehead and nose.

Though the earth had stilled, Lucia's legs failed her as she tried to stand. Caio lost his grip and she tumbled to the ground, falling closer to Ysa's sword. She grabbed the sword's grip and lay on her side grimacing in pain. "They're the ones who abducted me, Caio."

"Lord Oderigo," Caio's lungs heaved like great flapping wings as he yelled into the cursed night, "finish them!"

201

Chapter 48: Whispers of Love

Earlier that day.

NARAYANI WATCHED Rao and Aayu pack. Her bags hung from her shoulders, but they felt much heavier before she'd used Aayu's mantras to activate his *sadhana*. She watched Rao leave notes for her and her father.

At least you're doing that much.

Soon after, they disappeared from her sight the same way she had from theirs. She followed the path she guessed they would have to take, down the tower's stairs and toward the gate that pointed toward distant Lake Parishana.

Narayani waited a long time for the gate to open to let some scouts in. She hoped she was leaving the citadel at the same time as Rao and Aayu, and headed for the wide trail leading below, along the way spotting vegetation she had never seen in the wild before.

Ghrita Kumari plants! I can't wait to return later and gather some.

Guggulu shrubs! Aayu could use these.

Narayani took short breaks to examine the plants, but pushed herself to keep walking. She guessed at the speed Rao and Aayu would be traveling, so she walked a little faster than her normal pace. If she couldn't locate them before they reached the lake, she would try to find them after she got there—though she had no idea how far she would have to walk.

Much later in the day, she heard their voices well ahead of her and hurried to catch up with them.

"It's about Narayani. I know she's pretty annoying sometimes—I think so, anyway—but there are some things you don't know about her. She told you she never knew her mom, right?"

Aayu, you stupid ...

"Yes," Rao answered.

"Well that's not true."

Narayani thought about emerging from hiding to stop him, but couldn't pass up the chance to eavesdrop on their brotherly conversation. Having her secrets revealed to Rao was infuriating—and oddly liberating.

"I hate crying," Aayu said. "What am I, a girl?"

Aw, you do love me.

"Don't hold any of it against her," Aayu said.

"Aayu, I would never do that."

"You won't say anything then?"

"Never. I promise you."

"Good, because you know I'd have to kill you. She really blossomed after she met you. She's a lot calmer now, if you can believe that. You just have to be careful with her. Do you see what I am saying?"

"Aayu, I want to marry her someday."

"I know you love her ..."

She felt it, from both of them, and wanted to cry.

The conversations between Rao and Aayu were surprisingly mirthful the rest of the day and night. After a while, Narayani felt glad she didn't normally hear their private humor. So glad, in fact, that by the end of the trek she fell back and let them walk ahead of her. She stayed close enough to hear their voices and see where they were, but felt guilty enough to allow them a little privacy. Their pace was too hard anyway. Even with Aayu's *sadhana* making her body feel lighter, her muscles ached and it was tough to keep up.

When they entered the wooded area in front of the lake, she increased her pace again, not wanting to lose sight of them.

"Ilario!" a woman screamed in a foreign language.

Is that Rezzian?

She rushed ahead, thankful that she'd maintained Aayu's *sadhana* even though her sensory perceptions were becoming stranger by the minute.

A beautiful white mist and an odd burning scent filled the forest. Cold shivers danced throughout her body.

A sizzling pop exploded. Narayani dove to the ground, lying flat on her stomach. To her right, a force like lightning fanned out in a wide swath and burned the trunks of a dozen trees.

Narayani froze with fear and watched the ensuing melee between Rao, Aayu, and the Rezzian woman. A Rezzian man came forward. The earth shook violently. Something she could not believe was real lifted Rao and Aayu into the air.

Narayani canceled the effects of the mantras and felt heavy in her body again.

She stood, her arms shivering, hearing a vivid, crackling hum.

"Stop it!" she yelled.

She waved her hands above her head and took steps toward the Rezzian man—a beautiful, but angry-looking man.

"Don't hurt them!" she yelled again.

The Rezzian stepped forward into the light and stared at her, appearing confused.

"Let them go!"

Chapter 49: Vengeance

CAIO WATCHED THE DARK-SKINNED GIRL come forward swinging her arms above her head. He heard her pleading voice, but couldn't focus on the words. He could only stare at her idyllic face as she looked back at him.

You appear just as I was going to kill them ... it's a sign of Lux Lucis ...

He realized if he killed their prince before the duel, there would be no surrender or truce.

Lord Oderigo, I retract my prayer. Show them mercy.

"Are there more of you in the woods?" Caio asked in Pawelon.

The Pawelon girl kept coming toward him. "No." She shook her head.

"Who are you?" Caio wasn't sure why he asked.

"I love them," she said. "Let me take them away from here."

Lucia's voice boomed from behind Caio, "You love them? Do you know what they've done to me?"

"They don't want to hurt you," the girl said.

"Then they've stolen your mind," Lucia strode forward with her sword pointing at the Pawelon. "Do you want to see the body of my lover? Right back there." She swung the sword back to point at Ilario.

The girl's face trembled as she backed away.

"Lucia, she had nothing to do with it."

"How do you know? Maybe I should balance the scales. A lover for a lover?" Lucia stepped forward in pace with the girl, pointing the white blade at the Pawelon's ample chest.

"Lucia, as your Dux Spiritus I command you to stop."

His sister looked back at him with narrowed eyes. "My Haizzem, why don't you raise Ilario from the dead?"

Caio dropped his head, balled his fists, and pulled his hands against his chest.

"Or did you use your ability on a worthless Pawelon boy, even though I still lived? Even though Ilario and Duilio and our father were still alive? Were you that stupid?" Lucia swung around again and raised Ysa's sword. She feinted a thrust at the girl, who cowered and begged.

"I will take them away," the girl whimpered in Pawelon. "They would not want to hurt you."

"They have hurt me. They have hurt me *very badly*, girl." Lucia surged forward and grabbed the Pawelon's hair, yanking her body to the ground. The girl screamed and begged. Lucia knelt on her left knee and brought up Ysa's sword in her right hand.

With a fierce yell, Lucia swung the sword down.

Just to the side of the girl's head.

The Pawelon girl's wailing haunted the forest.

Lucia kept her grip on the girl's hair and brought the blade against the back of the Pawelon's skull.

"Lucia, I command you, stop!"

Lucia pulled the blade up, stood, and turned back. Caio saw the full length of the girl's hair in Lucia's left hand. The Pawelon ran her hands along her scalp and continued sobbing. The Pawelon men continued their pained grunting as Lord Oderigo's giant vines swung through the air.

"Kill the men and let's leave this cursed place," Lucia said.

"We can't. Remember the duel."

"Kill the fat one then. He would have killed me if you hadn't stopped him."

"Let's just leave," Caio said. *There is too much risk now.*

"Ilario. Is. Dead." Lucia came so close she nearly bumped her chest against Caio's. "Dead. And you can't do a thing about it. Now someone has to pay for this."

"Lucia, I am angry, too. But when I defeat their prince that will be payment enough."

"Killing him might save Rezzian lives, Caio. He is dangerous."

"I am going to fight their prince. We've reached an agreement."

"One that will be worthless even if you win. And that fat Pawelon will still be there, looking for me and killing our men."

Is she right, Mya? Oderigo?

The tree-length vines collapsed onto the forest floor.

Lucia scrambled around searching for their foes. "Where did they go?"

Terror punched through Caio's heart. "I don't see them."

Lucia picked up her shield and stepped backward in the direction of the lake. "Caio, get behind me."

Caio's feet pressed against dried leaves as he walked backward and scanned for his enemies through the mist.

Lord Oderigo, protect us.

All at once, the girl's sobs stopped.

"I feel their presence," Lucia said. "They are still here. Stand back." She tested the sword through the fog, slicing through the air.

"Do not touch my sister ever again! If you intend to meet me for single combat, flee from us now."

As they stepped back through the forest toward the lake, the fog thinned. Smaller flames licked the trees. The icy air still smelled of smoke and hummed with a divine presence.

"I think they're gone. I don't sense anything," she said.

"I agree." As he began to feel safe again, Caio's heart filled with the black trauma. He stumbled on, each step toward his friend's body harder to believe than the last. Caio fell onto Ilario and pressed an ear against his still chest.

Lucia stood over him, gripping Ysa's sword.

Caio forced himself off Ilario's body and, still on his knees, put his head onto the cool ground instead. "I saw Lord Sansone. He laid down his heavy chain and shut Ilario's eyes. His god blessed him to live forever."

Lucia dropped the sword and shield and fell to her knees, pounding her fists on Ilario's bones. She kissed him on his lips and turned her head to Caio. "And you can't do a thing about it?"

"No!" Caio's insides felt pummeled and bruised. "No."

She ran toward their horses, saying only, "We need to bring his body back for proper burial."

The horses had been tied up, but by the time Lucia and Caio reached them, their midnight-colored forms were walking toward them.

"The goddess," Lucia said.

Caio understood that Ysa had possessed them again. They were still capable of doing the impossible. The steed Ilario had ridden sped up and approached his corpse. The horse lowered itself and touched its belly and then its nose to the ground.

Caio helped Lucia pull Ilario's body onto the horse until it balanced across the beast's back. Ilario's stomach rested where he had previously sat, his arms falling out to one side and his legs to another. Lucia and Caio carefully lashed him to the horse's saddle as they sniffled and wiped away tears. Lucia covered Ilario with her blanket and tucked the dark blue material under him.

She carefully removed Ilario's necklace. The holy black anvil of Sansone reflected a shard of moonlight. She tied it around her own neck.

They mounted their horses in silence and Lucia tied Ilario's horse to her own.

Caio's whole being was a jumble of worry, confusion, denial, and anger.

And guilt.

Chapter 50:
The Burden of Sacrifice

I COULD BE DREAMING AGAIN, Lucia thought. *I could wake up in Ilario's arms. It could be another test.*

The horses moved with such vigor. Lucia wanted to lie across Ebon, fall off, die. The lunging movements of the horse stirred her nauseated gut. Her ill stomach told her she would vomit again soon.

Her soul felt tender and gnawed through. *"Enjoy our time together under the full moon."* You're a bastard and thief—a force of evil. You deserve no worship, no love at all. Be alone in your hole with the dead. Leave the living alone.

"Lucia," Caio called. "Lucia." Silence. "Lucia, speak to me." She focused on the contours of Caio's voice, studying the sounds as if they were exotic, piped in from another world.

You have no idea what I can do, Caio. You have no idea the dilemma I face.

Lucia squeezed both her forearms, digging her nails into the leather.

"Why did Ysa speed our journey?" she finally asked Caio. "She must have known. She could have saved Ilario with her shield. Does my own goddess not care for me?" She slammed her eyes shut, ejecting tears. "Because Danato is her damn brother?" She yelled into the night: "I would kill the perverted god if I could!" The desert was quiet except for the horses' clomping and the insects. "Or he can kill me! It doesn't matter."

You won't kill me without a fight. I will draw blood from you before I die. I will see it on your sister's sword.

"It's my fault," Caio said. "I knew there would be a cost. Ilario told us not to go to Danato. Why didn't I listen?"

"Because you don't think things through. You trust and believe. You have too much faith. You knew Danato hates me. He'd kill you next just to drive me to the limits of sanity. We let him suck us into his corrupted world and now he's going to take you to punish me even more." Every word she spoke was a victory, keeping madness at bay. "In the underworld, Danato made me think you were dead. What if their prince kills you?"

"Lucia, he is a god of Lux Lucis. He is one with Ysa, with Galleazzo and Oderigo and Mya. He does not act against their interests or wishes. If the gods wish for me to do their bidding, they will not let another god kill me."

"You are insane. He is not one of us. The nine should banish him from their ranks. He punishes us. *He* killed Ilario."

Caio turned silent.

I could do something to make all of this go away. Fix everything.

She looked back at Caio's silhouette. She needed to keep him alive. She needed to be ready in case he died. She stared at Ilario's corpse, a mass of inanimate flesh.

Three days. Why did it have to be three days? Why not tomorrow? Why? Why? Damn it! Damn it forever. Why? Once I find out if Caio will need to be raised, Ilario's soul will have left this world forever. My chance to resurrect Ilario will be gone ... eternally gone.

Lucia pulled on Ebon's reins and stopped the black mare. She freed her feet from the stirrups and let herself fall to the ground. A rock jabbed into her back and her body writhed involuntarily at the pain.

Caio dismounted and rushed to her. She wanted to tell him to take Ysa's sword and run it through her. Lucia stood, gritted her teeth, and balled her fists.

She punched his chest over and over. He stood and took the blows.

Lucia let her body collapse onto the desert floor. Her face, already stinging from the Pawelon's blows, pressed flat and heavy so that her bruised cheekbones kissed the harsh earth. The sting was sharp and raw.

I could still save Ilario. But what if you must be saved after your duel, brother? I can only raise one person from death ...

Chapter 51: Dreams of Forever

RAO'S HANDS LOCKED TOGETHER under his skull as he stared up at the grey ceiling of his bed chamber, looking at nothing at all. The longer he lay there, the less dizzy he felt. Narayani covered his face with a warm, wet cloth. The otherworldly essences of some of Pawelon's most exotic flowers flooded his awareness. She removed the cork on a glass container with a pop and dabbed a cool cream on his temples and neck, over his heart, and at his solar plexus. He tried to breathe consciously while she rubbed the salve into his skin. It burned at first, but rejuvenating shivers soon followed the heat.

"You should feel proud that you saved Aayu's life," Narayani said.

The killing had happened so quickly it felt like a reflex—as if it wasn't even under his control. Did some invisible hand shape their destinies? Rao had even felt the Lux Lucis divinities there, but the only person who died was a Rezzian.

"I am not sure if *I* did anything," he said.

He thought he knew who died. There were only three Rezzians there, and the Haizzem's bodyguard went everywhere with him. It had to be him. It was still disturbing to remember the emotion in the air after the royal daughter screamed.

"Are you sure there isn't anything else you want to tell me about how you got there?" he asked.

"I *told* you. I came back and found your note and started walking to the lake. I didn't expect to find you until I got there, if I could find you at all."

"I can't fathom how you escaped the citadel. Aayu seemed awfully skeptical."

"I traveled all the way from Kannauj without anyone discovering me. All it took was the right disguise."

"Could you hear our conversations?"

"Once I heard your voices I stayed far behind you. I was afraid if I came closer that you'd send me back."

"Because if you want to talk about anything you heard, we can."

"I couldn't make out your words. I was too far away."

Maybe she was telling the truth. Though if she'd heard the conversation about her background, she probably wouldn't admit it.

"I want you to lay still and let the medicine work. If you keep following my advice, you can be healed before you have to fight."

"I feel much better already, physically, except for the sensation in my head."

"That's because you feel overwhelmed and your body is telling you to rest. You need to relax your mind and save your energy for tomorrow."

Rao exhaled loudly and felt a calm tingling in his chest. He recognized where she was right. His mind had been like a monkey stung by bees since the tragedy two nights ago. He'd never before known such guilt, and the feelings wouldn't leave him alone.

He inhaled the scents and let himself be transported by them. The recent days spanned across his inner vision like a panoramic timeline. He focused his attention on the last couple days, reliving the entire melee with the Rezzians. He breathed deeply as he recalled all that had occurred.

In the aftermath, he and Aayu managed to use Rao's primary *sadhana* to escape and take Narayani with them, but they didn't want to travel far in their wounded condition. They spent the night in the forest and the next day practiced intense healing breaths and ate medicinal herbs that Narayani found in the woods. By the end of that day, they were found by the soldiers his father sent. Even though Rao insisted on walking the next day, the men had orders to carry him on the throne they brought with them. At least the men had strong shoulders.

"I wish you weren't doing this. I wish you would change your mind and leave here with me." She took the cloth off his face and put it back in the wooden bowl. "Drink up." She handed him yet another cup of *ashwa* tea.

He puckered his lips before letting more of the soul-rattling bitterness trickle down his throat. "We'll be together when this is done, I promise you. We'll get away from here as soon as we can."

She fell to the bed and lay with her back turned to him. He heard a sob and then her voice carried the emotion. "I don't want to wake up tomorrow. Let's stay awake as long as we can. When they come for you, you can just tell them you're not going. Their Haizzem looked so angry when I saw him."

"After I defeat him and their army flees," Rao knew his voice sounded flat, so he tried harder to sound reassuring, "we can go anywhere together. Think about that."

212

"They'll find another reason. They won't stop." Narayani's brow relaxed and her eyes widened into pearls of compassion. She caressed Rao's cheek. "It wasn't your fault the man died. He attacked you first."

Rao didn't want to cry, but his chest clenched and he felt moisture escaping his eyes. "I was just protecting Aayu. We were walking and laughing and then I saw the spear go into Aayu's chest. Everything else was instinct. There was no deliberation behind what I did."

"You had to do it then. You didn't mean for him to die. It's not your karma."

"But I reversed the karma. I sent it back to him."

"Then it isn't your fault. He received the fruit of his own action. If he hadn't received it then, he would've received it later."

"But I became involved. Now I've entered that chain of reactions. It wasn't completely an accident. I knew what could happen to him, even if only for an instant."

"And what if you had let Aayu die? Wouldn't that be worse karma for you?"

"Yes, I think it would have been worse."

But I'm still involved now and I don't want to die.

"When you kill their Haizzem and end this, you will make everything right. That will be *good* karma if you are able to save so many lives."

"I hope so, for everyone's sake."

She snuggled closer and wrapped her warm legs around his, stirring his passion.

"Can you make me dream about you and make it last forever? I want to dream about going back with you, back through the mountains, past Kannauj and through the forests. I want to see the leaves flashing their colors. I want to go all the way out to the beaches in Ashown. I want to sit on the sand and watch you swim. We should make love in the middle of the day when no one else is around—hearing only the ocean. Slowly, so it lasts an eternity. I want to dream till the end of time, with just me and you together, only living on our love. Can you make me dream it?"

He wiped his face on her shoulder. "Narayani, we're going to have time to do all those things together. We'll do it when this is over, I promise. Someday when we have children, they won't have to grow up being afraid for their father's life as you and I had to. We are going to make life better for everyone."

213

"I don't want to live here anymore. I want to dream forever. With your powers, can't you control dreams? Can't you just make them last forever? We would be so much happier that way. You can let your father fight a duel. You're too young. We should just be happy together."

"Be with me now, my love. This is all we have. The future is always in doubt. Maybe I will die tomorrow. Maybe we'll die together a hundred years from now. The only thing we know is that this won't last forever. But I know how to fight him. His gods are a projection. They are just as false as this world. I know that. I will win."

Rao knew that reason wasn't going to get through to her now. She squeezed him so tightly that all he could feel was her soft flesh against his body.

"Just make me dream I'm with you tonight. Make it last forever. You can make it last forever."

Neither said another word as sleep overcame them. In the dream they shared together, they rode off in an old wagon toward the mountains, stopping whenever possible to buy fruit and trinkets from the farmers and merchants along the roads that led throughout the charming hills of Pawelon toward the western sea ...

Chapter 52: The Weight of Death

A COOL MIST filled the chamber along with hints of sunrise. Rao woke up long before the darkness turned deep shades of purple and the birds' songs welcomed the morning. He cherished the sound of Narayani's uneven breathing.

A very long time passed.

Heavy footsteps and deep voices echoed from the stairwell. His heart seized up, hard and cold. He'd savored the intimate warmth of Narayani's body against his own throughout the night, but those moments were gone forever. The day had begun. By nightfall, Rao would have either killed a beloved man or he himself would be dead.

"Narayani," he moved his hand gently across her warm back, "We need to get up. They are coming."

She sat up, startled, then her eyes settled into a caring mood. "You made me dream it, Rao."

"I didn't cause it, but I dreamed it, too."

The marching footsteps grew louder until a strong voice shattered the peace: "Rajah Devak has come to speak with you."

Narayani kissed him, leading to a long kiss that reminded him of all of their nights of passion.

"Prince Rao?"

He pressed Narayani's chest against his own.

"Master Rao, are you there?"

Eventually he broke away. "Yes. Tell my father I will meet him in his chamber soon."

"Very well, my Prince."

'*'

215

Rao's father was leaning against the front of his desk when Rao entered the chamber. The Rajah wasn't sitting calmly or reading reports. He wasn't staring out the window. His father was staring at the door.

Right away, his father made long strides toward him and wrapped his heavy arms around him. The rajah's chest felt like a rock wall against Rao's body and face. The old man had a human scent all his own, a smell Rao remembered from his youth, mingled with a musty odor from his battle uniform. It was strange, his father touching him. It could have been awkward—it was the only such intimacy Rao could remember—but it was more than a temporary refuge. The moment was a vehicle for a transcendent ecstasy, a bliss felt throughout Rao's being that assured him he could die knowing that he and his father had at least once expressed their love for each other.

"Come," his father said before breaking off contact and leading Rao across the room to the table against the opposite wall. "I'm sorry circumstances haven't allowed us to spend more time together."

"Me too." Rao felt like he was ten years old again, watching his father set off for the canyon with his monstrous army.

"Whatever happens, I'm proud of you. You are risking a charmed life with a beautiful woman. Because of this, our people already admire and respect you."

"You've been a good father."

His father expelled a puff of air in disbelief and his chest heaved with a brief laugh. "That's rubbish. You've turned into a good man despite me. By the way, you did a really stupid thing, leaving here."

Rao glanced down at the dark wood table. The surface looked as though it had been carved into at random places over the course of the war with a knife. "I feel good now. I've had just enough time to heal."

The rajah seemed to be struggling to find words. "Good." His father's face was so busy with pits and scars, but Rao focused on his emotionless eyes.

"You killed his protector," his father said. "We've confirmed it."

"Damn. That's what I thought."

"What do you think this will mean for you today?"

"It's possible it could help me. My opponent might be too upset or angry to focus."

"Anger is a good emotion, Rao, and it's essential when you're battling for your life. For a Rezzian praying to his gods, anger is the perfect emotion."

I'm afraid you're right.

216

"I'm going to tell you something now, something I had always intended to tell you. You deserve to know and now you need to know it. You need to match their Haizzem's passion."

Rao felt his chest tightening in anticipation. "Passion and anger may benefit a praying man, but it does not benefit a sage."

"Don't argue with me again." His father waited for agreement, continuing his empty stare.

"Yes, Father."

"King Vieri ordered the killing of your mother and your brothers. He ordered your killing, too."

Rao scrambled mentally, wondering how he should feel. Vengeful? Sad? Empty? Detached?

"We captured one of the assassins and found out as much as we could. Your mother hid you under her chair when it began. They were in the western section of the palace in a room that was built for you and your brothers. It was full of toys. The Rezzians hid in a closet. Your brothers were killed first and as far as I know your mother saw it done. They cut her straight across her throat." The painting of his mother still hung behind his father's desk. "There were two of them. Our guards quickly put them down, but too late."

Rao walked over to the window and placed his hands on its ancient stone. He looked down on the square formations of troops within the citadel, then to the east where Rezzia began. The scene played out vividly in Rao's mind. His father had given too many details.

"Where?" Rao asked. The location was an unimportant detail. Something for Rao to distract himself with while he tried to make sense of everything. Rao heard his father coming up behind him and then felt his hand on his shoulder.

"A room in the long hallway along the northwest of the palace. Rao, King Vieri won't rest until you and I are dead. This is something you need to fear until the day he dies."

"I am glad to know the truth. The timing is ... hard." *And either terrible or great.*

"You have the chance to fight the son of the man who killed three members of your family. Focus on your rage. You deserve to live a long and happy life, one much better than mine. I must ask you to do this for me, Son. Avenge their deaths. Kill the Haizzem."

Chapter 53:
Surrendering to Revelation

CAIO'S BED WAS A BITTER COMPANION. He slept only for brief stretches, rolling under the covers, unable to shield himself from the talons of memory. Images of the last three days kept smashing their way past the sentries of his consciousness. Ilario alive and warning him ... Sansone's hulking form closing Ilario's eyelids ... Lucia being attacked through moonlit mist ... black horses moving at divine command ... Ilario's body slumped over horseback ... his military burial.

Dim light began to invade the fabric around Caio's yurt. He dreaded the sun. He looked sideways at Ilario's empty bed. There was no breathing in the room but his own shallow breaths, not even shuffling or mumbling from the soldiers outside. Only suffocating silence.

He sat with his feet dangling off the edge of the bed, rubbing his cool face with both hands. He eyed his altar behind him and recoiled, looking down at the black and red Satrinian rug instead.

Why is it so hard to motivate myself? Is it a bad omen?

He slid around the bed until he faced the altar some ten feet away. As he glimpsed The Book of Time, he smelled sweet *myrrha*, the scent even stronger than a few days ago.

"You bring me to this state, and now you want me to transmit your prophecy?" He spoke quietly so that only the gods could hear him. "Now that you've broken me down?"

He felt too tired to stand, too tired to pray. A red and black image of Lucia flashed across his vision and burning knots tightened inside his chest. Of all the things that pained him, Lucia's suffering hurt the most. That he couldn't feel her pain with her only made it worse.

"I am sure you have your reasons and I strive to accept them, whatever they are. Reasons why you would take a great man and ruin two other lives at the same time. Why you would let the Pawelons follow us all that way, or find us in such a remote place. Why you would let them hunt my sister, bash her face, and again threaten her life. I am not strong enough to understand your reasons."

He ran his left hand forcefully down the side of his face, then pressed it into and around his neck. He surprised himself by standing suddenly and walking over to the altar. He lifted Oderigo's holy text and removed the vines. He prayed for a message from his god, opened The Book, and read:

Though man does not see it, and though he doubts, always the gods act in concert. The will of one is the will of the ten. If one has a purpose, the nine give support, often imperceptibly and surprisingly. The Ten are always mysterious, but always act with intent. With wisdom, man will come to appreciate and trust in the ways of Lux Lucis.

He held the ancient book with two hands and felt the edges of its crumbling pages with his fingertips. He closed his eyes and squeezed the book. Squeezed it harder. Harder.

He spun around and threw the book across the room with all his strength and watched its delicate binding crash against the wall.

His mind filled with the smell of hot *myrrha*.

Chapter 54:
The Power of Prophecy

HOT WINDS BLEW through Rezzia's camp like the breaths of a god, flinging Lucia's hair around her face. She hurried with her protectors toward the temple, a spacious white tent at the center of the encampment. Five stone pillars supported it, the tallest one at the structure's center with the other four pillars holding up its corners. Caio's duel loomed.

She was late to the special ceremony Caio had called for earlier that morning. The event was known as an *Ayot*, a gathering for revelation to be added to The Book of Time. Only royal patrons of Lord Oderigo could call for such a ceremony. Caio had never transmitted Lord Oderigo's prophecy before.

As Lucia approached the central entrance, ten bald warpriests prayed in the old tongue and sprinkled holy water over her. Cream tassels flapped against the tent. Her guards stepped aside and she entered the temple alone.

Upon her entrance, the highest-ranking warpriest stood and called for the men to kneel and bow in prayer. Sweet, smoky incense and *myrrha* filled the hall.

"Havah ilz avah Haizzem!"

Lucia shared the hall with more than a thousand of Rezzia's most powerful men. She stayed back and performed the prayers, waiting until the opening ritual finished before walking down the wide aisle to sit beside her father. Her father kept his gaze on her from the time she entered the aisle until she sat next to him. His austere eyes relayed his disappointment at her tardiness.

Look all you want. I'm not the one sacrificing my son to the pigs.

Her father's most powerful nobles and leaders sat all around her, but she chose not to look at them. She didn't want to remember how many he'd tried to marry her off to, nor did she wish to see the faces of any men she would be pressured to wed.

Caio wore his prized Haizzem *cremos* and sat tall in a white ceremonial throne. The divine words stitched into his robe shined with a golden brilliance. He glanced solemnly downward. A few moments after Lucia sat, he began:

"The gods, my brothers, act as one. Those who believe in them know they are gracious and merciful. We worship them alone. They give us their grace and keep us on the straight path."

Caio paused and let the words simmer. With only the sound of the wind beating against the canvas tent, the warm room overflowed with faith and melancholy. A long silence followed.

"The true religion belongs to the gods of Lux Lucis."

The silence itself became hot, a penetrating field of religious devotion. Lucia felt a holy presence around her, calming her mind, and her resistance to Caio's prophecy lessened.

"According to Lord Oderigo's will and direction, I transmit his living prophecy to you. This scripture shall be recorded and maintained within The Book of Time. Lord Oderigo called me to him three days ago with the scent of his *myrrha*."

He closed his eyes and sat calmly. The warpriest scribe readied his quill and prepared to transcribe Caio's words into The Book. The crowd bathed again in the holy atmosphere. Finally, the Haizzem began to speak in a powerful voice with an accent not entirely his own, channeling the god's prophecy.

"The enemies of Truth are persistent. They are many. They must be opposed with the greatest vigilance. Those who know wage a war against those who are blind. Those who believe and submit to the way of peace will be those who bring the will of The Ten to all men. This is your highest duty.

"The gods of Lux Lucis have powers great, but do not forgive those who forget them. The gods cannot. In their adamancy they are merciful. They call each believer to spiritual warfare, the highest calling. Men of faith must stand together in community, in strength. They pave the way for a perfect world."

Lucia felt hemmed in by the crowd and discomfited by the uncharacteristic words coming from her brother.

"Men of wisdom surrender to the gods of Lux Lucis, for without them men are literally nothing. All that has been corrupted and made vile can be healed only through the truth. So it is.

"Many thousands of years ago, when Gallea was barren, men were created by gods and scattered across the lands. Only one people, the people of Rezzia, were chosen by the divinities of Lux Lucis. The eternal Truth has been transmitted to you, the righteous given the task of preserving the prophecies through the centuries. You will always be protected by the gods and by the Haizzem the gods send to protect you and lead you to spiritual victory.

"The gods also call men to wisdom, for ignorance will not absolve men of dishonorable actions. What is given will be received. What is inflicted will be felt. What is ignored will be brought back. And bitter fruits, if resisted, will remain to rot and fester.

"You, men, are called to struggle and to strive to create a society where goodness prevails, to recognize the true limitations of other races of men, for only by addressing their weaknesses does real change becomes possible. Only then will Gallea become a perfect home where the gods can once again walk freely and openly among men.

"The gods are great. The gods are great. The gods are great.

"He who dies for them attains perfection."

Caio's head dropped as if he'd fallen asleep and the worshipers knelt and leaned forward. Lucia prayed with them, unsettled emotionally but unwilling to question the prophecy with her father beside her.

Caio's head rose with a deep breath into his nostrils. With one motion, he stood and stretched his arms out to his sides. The men surged forward for a chance to receive the Haizzem's grace before his combat.

Lucia stood and pulled her arms close to her body as the men crowded around her. Her father stood still beside her, gazing at Caio. She soon felt her father's eyes.

He who dies for them attains perfection. Is that what you would see, Father? Could you stand by and watch that?

"Lucia," her father spoke quietly in deep tones, as if his voice was raw, "Lord Oderigo has spoken through your brother. We must withhold our judgment until his combat is finished."

How convenient.

Still facing Caio and the crowd around him, she turned only her head to look at her father's face.

"Imagine the possibilities with his victory," he said, his face regaining its color and vitality. "Possibilities inspired by The God of Prophecy himself. I request your presence beside me during the battle. When your brother is victorious, I want to celebrate his triumph with you."

And I am sure you want to keep your eyes on me.

"I consent, father, for this reason. If anything terrible happens to Caio, I want to see the remorse on your face."

Without answering, he made his way forward through the crowd. As the others saw him, they stepped aside and allowed him to approach his son. Father and son embraced. Lucia stood on the bench behind her to have a clearer view of her father's sobbing.

Caio held his father with his hands behind the man's heart. They rested their heads on each other's shoulders and everyone in the temple seemed to be observing their tender connection.

As they began to separate, her father said to Caio, "Remember all whom you are saving. Remember your duty compels you to serve the people of Rezzia."

Caio did not answer, but pulled his father's face against his own and kissed one of his cheeks.

King Vieri made his exit down the central aisle and other men soon flocked around him. He looked back at Lucia and their eyes met for one expressionless exchange.

Lucia sat on one of the benches in the middle of the temple, watching Caio and waiting for all of the men to pay their homage to him and leave the hall. She wanted to be the last to approach him.

Once the hall emptied, she approached him alone.

"You've given up on everything you believed in, everything we once agreed on. Caio, where is my brother?"

Caio's countenance shifted from austerity to uncertainty. "Lord Oderigo's words are not my own! Who am I to question a god?"

Lucia stopped two feet in front of Caio. "Is it a coincidence that as you deal with Ilario's death, the god speaks through you those words of vengeance?"

"You've read The Book of Time. Oderigo has many moods, and righteousness is one of them. He came through me."

"How can you be sure? You're not yourself."

"I can't help that the gods have changed me. Clearly, I do not control my own destiny."

"But you can fight back. You have free will. You have your own mind. Lord Danato sent us to the lake to see Ilario die. *He* did this to us. Don't let him win."

"It's too late. We went to Danato because there was no other solution. Now we must follow his will. He has *already* punished us." Caio's eyes pleaded, shining like pearls. "Now he can help us."

"You think he won't punish us again? He has no sense of mercy. I would know! Look at yourself, Caio. He has already changed you. He hasn't killed you yet and already, Caio, you are dead. What is left of my beautiful brother?" Lucia ran her gloved hands down her face, trying to collect herself.

"I am accepting my responsibility. That is all. I am the Dux Spiritus. I accept that I have a role, a role you encouraged me to grow into. I'm embracing my duty."

"Which is what?"

"To struggle to create a society where goodness prevails. To see the realities of other races of men, so that we can address them and make this world a perfect one where the gods can once again walk freely among us. The gods keep us on the straight path and lead us to spiritual victory. Theirs is the way of peace."

"What happened to real peace? To healing? To love? I've known you all your life. Those are your true beliefs."

Caio shook his head in resignation. "I can't win. When I don't want to fight, I'm a child. When I meet my duty, I am not myself. You have to accept that I have changed. I am doing what our people need me to do and I am doing what our very gods have led me to do." Caio's voice softened as he said, "I am also doing what Ilario would have wanted."

"He would not have wanted you to kill yourself."

"Through his death, Ilario woke me and gave me life. He showed me reality. He had tried to tell me before, but I did not understand then."

"Nonsense!" Lucia turned around and kicked over the wooden bench behind her. It knocked hard against the bench behind it. "His death was nothing more than Danato's perversity. He only wanted to torture us! We practically asked him to do it."

Caio stepped forward to keep the same short distance between them. "Ilario told me the killing of fewer men is better than the killing of more men. Lives can be saved through warfare. It is a reality of this world I have to accept."

"Maybe, but Ilario wouldn't have wanted you to abandon your principles or to sacrifice yourself."

"Ilario understood the value of sacrifice. He would've gladly died for me. I'm doing my best and learning that I can't please everyone." Caio's eyes narrowed as his face grew serious. "Now please listen to me. Listen. If I die, I want you to fight on. I have already told Father this. You should continue fighting without me."

Lucia looked at him incredulously.

Then even your death wouldn't end this war.

"And if I am the victor, we will have an army to conquer. I doubt they will relinquish their citadel. But our victory would be made easier with the death of their prince. That is why I must go to fight him. He has assaulted you, and I will not allow it again."

"Neither outcome will end the fighting, then! And you think that is what Ilario would've wanted? Then he died for nothing."

Caio grabbed her arms and his eyes dove into her soul. "He wanted victory, Lucia. He wanted to see us help the people of Pawelon and he wanted our people to be proud."

"I've lost both of you now. Ten curses upon Lord Danato."

"Lord Danato is a god of Lux Lucis. As he acts, so do The Ten. They are one."

She pulled herself away from his hands. "I will protect you until the day I die—that includes today. I made that promise just before our mother died. You have no idea the sacrifices I have made for you, though I chose to make them."

"I thank you and I ask you to pray for me, Sister. But today you must leave me to fight the darkness alone. I am a man now. And I am called by prophecy and by tradition to win over this evil. If you were to interfere, our agreement with Pawelon says that you should be turned over to them and put to death."

"Of all the men in this world, I never thought I'd see you go insane. Here you are, just like all the rest."

"I hope to prove you wrong. Let me fulfill my own destiny."

"To die young?"

Caio gently raised his hands. "Why do you believe I will die? Don't you believe in the Rezzian tradition? Look at my hands!" Caio put forward his arms with his tattooed palms facing upward. "Do you think our gods will kill me?"

"Caio," Lucia dropped her head in defeat and resisted the urge to collapse to the floor. "Lord Danato came to me again last night. He promised me something." She breathed through a tight sensation in her chest and battled against her angst to speak the words.

"Whatever it is, I want to know," Caio said.

"He promised me that something will soon happen that will haunt me the rest of my life."

"We will heal it." Tears began welling in Caio's eyes. "Whatever it is, we will call on the goddess Mya. She will grant you her grace."

"The Black One promised me." She squeezed her fists tight as she raised them in frustration and felt the dark leather stretching around her fingers. "He promised me the war can end soon, but not without more senseless killing."

"And?"

She walked close to Caio again. "He said this war will not and cannot end before one of you dies—either you or Pawelon's prince."

Lucia placed her hand on Caio's cheek and put the sides of their faces together. She kissed him and pulled away.

Caio's eyes seemed wider and more sensitive than ever before. Lucia noticed every detail of his appearance. His wavy hair rolled beautifully around his ears and onto his shoulders. His smooth, full lips still formed an optimistic countenance. *You are innocent still.* She burned this image of him onto her memory as a tear crawled down her cheek.

Lucia wiped it away with one finger and pressed the tear onto Caio's lips. She held his hands in her own and searched his oceanic eyes for as long as she could bear.

She turned away, leaving him in the temple, alone.

Chapter 55: To Shape the World

BONE HORNS MOANED like the cries of woolly beasts, announcing the march to the duel. The armies of Pawelon had come down into the valley and assembled behind a disciplined front running from north to south. Rao took a step into the vast space between himself and the Rezzian army to the east. With no wind blowing, his face felt like meat roasting under the sun.

Anxious nerves electrified him as he prepared to speak to his men. He turned back to the west, looking left to right without seeing the end of the Pawelon front line.

He extended his right hand and Aayu clasped it with his own. Aayu pulled him forward and they reached their arms around each other's shoulders. Aayu wrapped a hand around the back of Rao's neck and pulled him closer until their foreheads touched and Rao could smell his bhai's breath.

"It's your time. Go and send the dogs away."

With intense, unformed emotions stirring inside him, Rao patted his friend's stocky chest twice by his heart. Rao breathed to clear his mind. He took seven deliberate steps backward into the dead valley and faced the wall of men. The soldiers' faces formed a stoical line above their armor and shields. Rao felt awkward and exposed with his arms dangling at his side, so he widened his stance and raised a clenched fist. A chorus of metal and motion ensued as Pawelon's army mirrored his posture.

Rao began, "The sage Naganjuma wrote these words more than eight hundred years ago: 'To the bold, to the shaper of worlds, goes the creation of the spoils. This is our greatest duty.'" He paused to let the words resonate, then spoke with as much conviction as he could command.

"The fruits of men's enterprises are not found so much as they are chosen. They do not exist outside of us like treasure, but are created out of our own beliefs and philosophies. This is why our desires must be questioned before we undertake any great endeavor. If our values are flawed, our actions can only produce imperfections.

"Pawelon is a land of mystical insight. We are shapers of reality, but only if we can accept this power and wield it with brave intent. Do we have the courage to examine the first cause?" He swallowed into his dry throat and attuned himself to the silence within.

"Have we fulfilled our highest duty if we accept the means of the past as evidence of future necessity? Introspection, clarity, and creative imagination must come before action."

He scanned the faces of the men before him and stopped at Aayu, noticing his friend's clenched jaw and piercing eyes.

"I have a better vision of life on Gallea, and that is why I go now to follow Naganjuma's call. To shape the world."

Rao turned toward the Rezzian horde massed on the other side of the valley, but he focused on the ground. He walked mindfully toward the conflict, feeling the contact between the heel and ball of each foot with the uneven ground, each step making his former life recede further from his being.

His days with Narayani existed only in the past, merely a memory, traces of smoke.

Far distant from his own men, Rao spied the form of his rival walking through the heat of the desert. Rao took seven final steps. Though his heart beat faster, his mind rested in a vast calmness within, an emptiness brewing with unsettled passion.

Chapter 56: Dying to Believe

THE RAISED PLATFORM at the front of the Rezzian line gave Lucia and her father, and their guards, an unobstructed but distant view of the conflict. Caio appeared smaller and smaller as he wandered out to meet Pawelon's prince. The waiting was too much to bear.

"There," her father pointed across the open space.

Lucia stood and squinted through the haze of desert heat. "I see their prince."

A sick feeling assaulted her stomach like a heavy club, and she fell awkwardly back into her chair to avoid collapsing and making a scene. Her fall did not go unnoticed. Two perfumed attendants brought her water and wet cloths and begged to help her. Lucia sat as tall as she could. Her left hand slowly massaged her belly. She drank the first glass of water quickly, then swatted the people away. "I am fine," she said. Her weak voice betrayed her assurance.

"Lucia." Her father looked at her with what she believed was a delusional gleam in his eyes. "We are to witness a Haizzem fulfilling his great destiny."

Then why aren't I with him?

Her father looked again at the distant figures. "Caio will be the one to find a way to win this war. If Pawelon does not surrender today, our men will win it gloriously under his command."

Lucia looked out to the west. "They are tricksters, all of them."

"Caio and I approved this, along with our commanders."

"This will not end well."

Her father almost pleaded, "It is with Lord Oderigo's guidance and the goddess Mya's protection. The Ten are with us. Pray to your goddess, my daughter. Do not fill your spirit with worry when Caio needs us most."

He extended his hand to her, resting it on the cushioned arm of her chair. She waited, knowing how he would interpret her hesitation, without caring about his feelings. She looked across at the blur of a massive Pawelon army to the west.

"I have faith in him," she said, finally placing her hand in her father's spacious palm.

It's the gods I don't trust.

Her vision lost focus as she remembered distant scenes ...

She sat, thirteen years old, at the feet of the guards, waiting for Caio to wake up. Finally, little Caio's feet pattered on the cool palace floor and she was given entrance to his chamber. It smelled of religious incense and the walls were painted with scenes of vine-covered Oderigo and Mya. She immediately handed him his favorite toy, a large wooden horse carved of oak, and his joyful exuberance warmed her young, troubled heart.

He hugged her legs as hard as his infant body could. "I want sweets now," he said.

"Not until you have soup and bread ..."

By the gods, she didn't want to cry, not in front of her father. But she couldn't stop the tears.

'*'

Caio heard the growling Pawelon horns, the distant, heavy bleating signaling that Prince Rao would be coming to meet him. Caio had been walking for some time, so he squatted to give his foe time to catch up. He wanted to meet him in the middle of the canyon, exactly as they had agreed.

Mya's rod buzzed with subtle spiritual energy in Caio's left hand. He stared at the smooth wooden shaft of Ilario's spear in his right hand. He placed the spear on the rocky ground in front of him and prayed to Ilario's spirit with both hands together:

Give me strength, Ilario, so there will be justice.

Caio rubbed his right palm flat on the crusty ground, feeling the gravelly stones press into him. A lone raven's heavy wings flapped above him.

After scraping his hand, his raised his dark palm close to his face. It looked even redder, stinging enough to remind him of the vulnerability of his physical form.

"I am ready to fight for you, Lord Oderigo. I am prepared for your spiritual war."

'*'

230

Vine-covered Lord Oderigo loomed over his unaware patron with frozen posture, watching with black eyes like tunnels stretching into a starry nothingness.

'*'

"I am not afraid to kill him. I am no longer afraid to kill any of them. I pray that this pleases you."

A mild breeze swept a dry leaf across the desert.

"Will you watch over me today, God of Prophecy? I seek to embody your word." Caio looked around at the giant red cliffs to the east and the west.

"Would you show yourself to me now? I go to fight, perhaps to die. Might I see your tall shoulders once more?"

No? I take no offense, my Lord.

'*'

The god walked the remaining distance with Caio, waiting until Caio glimpsed Pawelon's prince. The god halted and watched Caio walk to the west to meet his adversary. With no expression on his face, Lord Oderigo turned back toward the Rezzian army and walked away.

Chapter 57:
The Line Between Men and Gods

REZZIA'S HAIZZEM APPEARED as a distant figure holding a spear in his right hand, waiting for Rao in the desert. Rao recognized the flowing hair and assumed the robe was a *cremos*, but he couldn't make out his enemy's face.

The spear. A shiver of fear washed over him. *My karma returns to me?*

He shifted his attention to his body, feeling the pulse and hum of his blood and organs. As he went deeper beyond the physical body, he felt an energetic disturbance throughout his muscles. As he probed deeper he recognized the congestion as a dark inner vision, an imagining—or was it a remembrance?—of his mother's killing.

He returned his attention to the Rezzian's form and thought about driving the same spear though the Haizzem's heart.

Rao's being filled with purpose. He willed himself to change, then followed an instinct arising from deep within to expand his spirit far beyond his physical constraints and senses.

He felt himself merging with the sky throughout the valley. With a quiet intention, he transformed into a state of being lighter than air.

He was ecstasy. Ecstasy expanded outward. Space posed no obstacles. Time ceased, a state of consciousness he had never before achieved. He recognized the fuel burning in him, pushing him on:

Passion.

Rao's expanded being swept toward the Haizzem like an invincible gale force.

'*'

Caio watched the Pawelon's form disperse into the air as if consumed by a great wind.

A moment later, Caio's skull cracked against the earth.

He lay flat on his back, disoriented, pressed down by an irresistible weight. His fingers clenched; Mya's rod remained in his left hand, Ilario's spear in his right.

The invisible force dragged his body against the ground in a wide circle, scraping and punishing his skin. As his flesh grated against the hard earth, he watched Ilario's spear scraping over the uneven ground. Caio recalled his friend's death: Ilario lying on his back with his own spear lodged in his chest.

Caio clutched Mya's rod with all his strength, begging it to save him. The wooden rod felt like a raging waterfall in his hand. His body slowed. His own grunts became louder than the chaotic rustling of the desert floor. Caio stood with pain searing him and raised the spear above his shoulders, squeezing it. The muscles of his arms soon burned from exertion. Heaving breaths flew from his dry mouth.

The Pawelon's form coalesced before him like sands poured into a translucent hourglass. Caio brought Mya's rod before his heart and focused its power, pressing it against his chest. As the Pawelon materialized, a watery prison manifested around him. The Pawelon yelled muffled words as Caio's heart erupted with sorrow and rage. He focused his strength on the rod and spear to take his mind off his injuries and stormed forward.

"How many times have you attacked my sister?"

"How many Pawelon women would your people rape?"

"We'll crush your soldiers and show your suffering people the way of light!"

The Pawelon closed his eyes, apparently drawing on another power.

Goddess of the Great Waters, destroy him!

‘*’

Rao drew his attention inward again—

A chaotic racket roared into his ears. He found absolute blackness. Frigid cold submersion. Water pressed against his skull, threatening to crush him. The pressure escalated, casting pain all over. His skin and muscles caved inward, compressing. His lungs expelled every drop of air.

It barely registered that his body was at an inhospitable oceanic depth. His spirit detached, allowing him to witness his body's end.

The desert spun around him, soft blue skies stretching into forever, red canyon walls soaring like giants. Below his incorporeal awareness, his shriveled body lay. His spirit retained the barest connection to his pummeled flesh.

Though his mind and spirit remained agile, his body had been wrung to the brink of death.

Death.

It seemed so close.

Narayani, Aayu. My father, the rajah with no sons. How will they take the news?

Rezzia's bruised Haizzem walked to him, holding the spear low in his slack arm.

Rao focused his mind past the veil of the physical world. His spirit diffused into everything within thirty paces of his body. Feeling that space as a single whole, he whipped the ether into a frenzy, scattering the building blocks of matter until nothing would be comprehensible by the senses.

He knew the Haizzem would be caught up in the effect. He hoped the man would be trapped as Rao tried to locate his body and renew his life force again.

But Rao couldn't find his body. Instead, his subtle awareness was ejected from the space it had entered. The environment around him reverted to normalcy again. He could do nothing to stop it.

Rao remained a spirit without a body and could again see Rezzia's Haizzem walking toward his physical form. Time extended slowly, warping and stretching the appearance of everything around him. A preternatural figure appeared, standing beside his abused body. He looked Rezzian, but impossibly tall, with vines covering his shoulders.

Their god Oderigo, he realized. Rao sent his thoughts to the god, "Why do you come, phantom?"

"To witness history," the god thought back to him. Oderigo's words echoed with a deep and otherworldly timbre.

"Can a ghost do that? You are a children's story, a Rezzian dream."

"Your interpretation is equally subjective, though you do not comprehend the nature of belief."

"I see things as they are," Rao said.

"Pride fuels everything you do. To whom can you bow? What can you embrace that is greater than yourself?"

"I do not bow to myths. True seeing transcends such childish ideas."

"And yet your body lies dying."

"I admit myths have some power. But my people seek no crutches."

"You are a master in a tiny field. The ultimate truth still lies far beyond you. There is no end to evolution, to the unshackling of chains."

"Why do you favor them? Are you vain? Are you a creation enslaved to a self-absorbed master?"

"We arise together, the Rezzians and the gods of Lux Lucis. We do not always answer them, nor always give them what they seek. Though we always hear them. We assist them only as it suits their evolution. As they evolve, so do we. You would call this karma."

"So you are looking for a promotion. How godlike."

"We all play our parts in the divine play. Every being has its role."

"Gods who are slaves to duality. How inspiring."

"There is so much you do not understand, Prince."

"I know they created you in their minds."

"In fact, we arise together, interdependent. We were within them always."

"And they could have created any number of divinities, given them any variety of qualities or names."

"So it must seem to you. But man cannot create that which is not within him. You mistake them for being only that which they are aware of."

"No, I don't. We are much more than what we are conscious of. Sages know this."

"Yet you draw a line between the Rezzians and their gods. This line does not exist." A noise rung out like the slamming of a heavy tome. "Your vainglory is your end."

Time resumed and Oderigo faded from sight. Rezzia's Haizzem stood over Rao's body, holding a wooden rod in the air and the spear of his deceased friend.

Rao remained dazed from the encounter with the god of Lux Lucis. His awareness floated, watching the boyish-looking man grit his teeth, arch his brows, and raise his spear ...

Chapter 58:
Silent Misunderstandings

EARLIER IN THE DAY, Narayani had invoked the mantras and felt its strange sensations again.

Now, she could only watch as Rao's body convulsed and collapsed in the middle of the desert canyon, for no apparent reason.

My sweet Rao!

Everything supporting her was gone.

The Rezzian man—the same one she'd approached in the forest—walked painfully toward Rao's disposed body with spear in hand. Rao's body twitched.

An aftereffect of death, she told herself.

She ran as fast as her heart would allow toward her lover's body, but soon everything changed. Nothing made sense. The space between them became a clear vacuum—then a jumble of colors. She couldn't feel her own body. Couldn't see her body.

Disconnected patches of earth and sky reappeared seemingly at random and, within the span of three breaths, Narayani saw the material world again. She closed the distance and slammed down on her knees with Rao's disfigured head between her thighs. His face showed no movement. He'd stopped breathing.

The Rezzian murderer stood so close, even closer than he had at the lake. In his white robe, he looked possessed with the desire to kill, with dark eyes and jaw clenched. He readied the spear to strike Rao and sunlight glinted off the metal.

Abruptly, he looked directly to her. Narayani's breaths came heavier, then uncontrollably fast.

"Are you a ghost?" he asked in Pawelon.

"You see me?"

The Rezzian lowered his arm and the spear. The skin surrounding his eyes quivered as he stared.

'*'

Caio hadn't expected Mya to dispense of Pawelon's prince with such brutality. The prince struggled in the deep, black waters but his body soon succumbed to the force and the pain. Ironically for the Pawelon, the attack occurred only in his mind. Yet there lay his disposed body, ready to receive Ilario's spear. In the distance, Rezzian soldiers cheered.

Thank you, goddess Mya. Thank you, Lord Oderigo. I do this in your name.

The deep voice of Lord Danato emerged with an echo inside his skull. "You are doing that which you must do, Caio. This is your free will. You are beginning to understand that your wishes and choices cannot always align."

Is he dead or alive? Caio sensed the pain in the Pawelon's body, with every organ crushed and bleeding. *Alive. How is his soul still connected to his body?*

Caio's grip on the spear was so intense that he found his knuckles white. He looked to the vicious point of the metal and visualized the spear going through the Pawelon's bruised chest and into his heart.

Caio looked up one last time, spying the wall of far off Pawelon soldiers. In his heart, he felt the love and hope of the Pawelons for their dying prince. He couldn't help but feel sorry for them.

The Pawelon girl appeared out of nothing, sitting by the prince's head.

With his hand poised for killing, he lost focus in her face. She was like the goddess Vani with dark skin and clipped hair, a paragon of beauty. She looked and felt as shocked to see him as he must have to her. Oddly, neither army made a clamor after her appearance.

"Are you a ghost?"

"You see me?" she said.

"Yes, and if you are really here, you are violating the rules of the conflict. Others cannot see you?"

"No, I don't think so. I beg you, do not disfigure his body any further. And if you must kill him, then please kill both of us together."

The Pawelon girl was so innocent, so delicate. "Fair woman, I could never harm you." Caio's grip on the rod and spear softened. "Go and let me finish this battle, as we agreed."

Tears ran down her face. "And they say you are a spiritual man. You're a murderer."

"I am not! He dies so that thousands more will live." Thousands of Rezzians, he admitted to himself. He pointed at Rao's body. "He proposed this fight. Now the gods have punished his arrogance."

"I will not live without him."

"You must. Go now!"

"Why do your gods drive you to murder? Why would they want to kill an innocent people? What gods would do such a thing?"

"Gods who bring power. Gods who bring light and healing." Caio felt too keenly his own contradictions.

"Do not speak to me of healing! Do not tell me you think about families when fighting for glory, the widows and parents and children."

You have no idea. Then Caio realized he had not thought of any such repercussions since Ilario died. "Your prince *wanted* to fight me."

"And I didn't want him to! I will not leave his body." She stood and planted her feet, her eyes screaming defiance. "Tell me, if you are so spiritual, why can't you find another way to solve your differences? Rao didn't *want* to fight you. He only wanted the fighting to end."

Of all the things she could have said ... Caio wondered with a knot of guilt, is it possible this man wanted the same thing he did just days ago? "It's too late for understanding. You should look away."

Caio stood taller and gripped the spear again. Mya's rod suddenly felt sharp in his left hand as his palm cramped. The Pawelon threw herself completely over her lover's body, face down. For a moment, he considered giving her what she asked for. If they were both found there, it would be clear that she had interfered with the duel. He would win the contest for Rezzia, and Pawelon would be exposed for breaking the rules of the single combat. He yanked the spear back over his shoulder.

"I will give you until the count of three to get up. At three, my spear will strike. Do not be in its way."

Caio felt the sun burning his hair and back.

"One."

"Two."

His clenched arm shook.

"Three."

Chapter 59: Kill the Haizzem

RAO'S BODILESS AWARENESS continued to observe Rezzia's Haizzem standing over his disfigured body. After his last power left him scattered, Rao found himself unable to focus on any abilities that might rescue him. He felt ready for death, and only sad for those who would mourn him.

The Rezzian jumped away from his body and began speaking in Pawelon.

"Are you a ghost?"

Had the Haizzem gone mad? Rao's body was all but empty.

"Yes, and if you are really here, you are violating the rules of the conflict. Others cannot see you?"

What? Aayu?

"Fair woman, I could never harm you." The Haizzem loosened his grips. "Go and let me finish this battle, as we agreed."

Narayani! How?

"I am not! He dies so that thousands more will live." The Rezzian pointed at Rao's body. "He proposed this fight. Now the gods have punished his arrogance."

Aayu taught you his sadhana.

"You must. Go now!"

Then I have to do something. Anything.

"Gods who bring power. Gods who bring light and healing."

Your gods may be powerful, but they are not all-powerful.

"Your prince *wanted* to fight me."

I did. Now I will find another way.

"It's too late for understanding. You should look away."

The Haizzem stood tall and gripped his spear again. Rao tried to gather and focus his spirit, but failed.

"I will give you until the count of three to get up. At three, my spear will strike. Do not be in its way."

I have to risk coming back into my body, Rao decided.

"One."

239

The pain inside his body would be beyond overwhelming. That pain might destroy his mind, too, if he couldn't recover ...

"Two."

I have to save her. I'll hit him immediately, before the pain overcomes me.

Just before the Rezzian said "Three," Rao sunk his consciousness back into his body. The physical torture consumed him. He gathered the last ounce of his soul to form the mudra for his secondary *sadhana* with one hand:

Viparyas amrakh!

Even after sending back his pain to its sender, his mind clung desperately to one small tree in the middle of the raging hurricane: the intention that he underwent this suffering for all sensitive beings. He wished that his torment would lessen the pain of all the worlds, seeding his suffering with purpose.

As he succumbed to the pain, it grew larger. It became in his mind the pain of every being. Death was coming, but the Rezzian would be distracted and Narayani would get away.

Rao forgave Rezzia's Haizzem without any further blame. He simply forgave him for doing what he had to do.

Immediately, Rao's pain subsided. It became duller and duller, further and further removed from his direct experience. It was becoming something other than himself, as it should have been all along. Rao barely opened his eyes and saw the Haizzem flat on the ground. His foe appeared unconscious, but between the two of them stood a stunning woman with fair skin and exposed shoulders above a tight-fitting dress made of green vines.

Her voice was high and kind, with an otherworldly resonance. "Because of your prayer, I must heal you now, Prince of Pawelon." Rao felt a wholesome and cool sensation in his mind, like minty, sweet milk. He closed his eyes and his whole being was embraced, feeling a total lack of censure. The pain receded. Sanity reemerged. This love made his spirit soar, so much that he struggled to remain conscious of his physical body. He forced himself to stand and open his eyes.

He saw no goddess. But he looked behind him and found Narayani, looking amazed.

"Narayani, remain in *shunyata!*"

"I am! You see me?"

"Yes. And even if you are still hidden, I want you to go away to safety."

"You will need my help."

"Go!" Rao stepped forward and picked up the man's spear. He glanced momentarily at the metal and recognized it. It was terrible thing to think of doing to another man, but it had to be done.

May his death bring peace to him and to all of us.

"Rao, no!" Narayani pleaded.

He thrust the spear's point through the body beneath him and felt it go deep within the flesh. He saw Narayani flash before his eyes as she unexpectedly dove toward the Rezzian's speared body.

After that moment, everything changed.

THE BLACK GOD'S WAR

Chapter 60: Changes

MIGHT THE NINE TRUE GODS act rightfully after all? Lucia wondered.

Though the figures appeared the size of children's toys at such a distance, she clearly saw Caio standing over the fallen body of Pawelon's dark prince with Ilario's spear in hand.

'*'

Beside Lucia's throne, the petite goddess Ysa stood with arms crossed over her silver breastplate. Her eyes looked to the west, more above the action than focused on it. Unfelt by her devotee, Ysa laid a palm atop Lucia's head. The goddess pressed her index and middle fingers into Lucia's eyes.

'*'

The melee zoomed into Lucia's vision, leaving her feeling bodiless and dizzy as she watched. The body of Pawelon's prince lay bruised and discolored. Caio's eyes glowered with vengeance.

My goddess Ysa, I pray for the greatest good.

Another Pawelon appeared out of nothing, the girl from the forest. She'd trimmed her hair, but looked just as beautiful.

Caio jumped back and began conversing with the girl.

Lucia could barely feel her lips, and mumbled as she spoke, "There is another Pawelon there."

"Where? I don't see it," her father answered.

"On the ground by their prince. It's his lover, the one we told you about. They've broken the agreement."

"I don't see her."

"I am telling you, she is there. Caio is talking to her right now. He is telling her to go."

"You don't sound well, Lucia. You are imagining things."

Caio raised his spear again above the body, and the girl threw herself over the prince.

"One," Caio said.

"Two."

Ysa, may this act bring peace.

"Three."

Pawelon's prince underwent a miraculous and instantaneous healing, no doubt to Lucia a product of the dark magic wielded by him and perhaps the girl as well. Caio dropped the spear as he slumped to the ground and convulsed. His chest and arms heaved as if in dying spasms. Caio's moans curdled Lucia's blood.

The Rezzian crowd gasped and screamed in disbelief. The prince and his lover spoke to each other in their language.

Lucia called out to her father, "She has used some dark magic to conceal herself. She is there!"

Pawelon's prince picked up Ilario's spear—*don't you dare touch that, you bastard*—and stared for a moment at the metal.

The prince strode to Caio's body and raised the spear.

"Rao, no!" the Pawelon girl screamed.

The prince swung back the spear with deadly force as the sun glistened off his bare chest and, with two hands, he drove the blade into the center of Caio's chest.

In the briefest of moments as the spear came down, Lucia's heart called out, *Ysa, take me instead!*

Lucia's head and vision rattled like a pounded drum. The arid desert pressed flat against her back, and then Ilario's spear entered her chest, under her right breast.

The prince's exposed teeth and gums showed his horror. Caio and the Pawelon girl were gone. Her enemy pulled the spear from her chest and Lucia fell into darkness.

THE THIRD STANZA

TO HEAL THE SCORE

Chapter 61:
In the Hands of the Enemy

INDRAJIT STOOD BESIDE HIS RAJAH, searching for the combatants with his bleary vision. Between them and the single combat stood the bulk of Pawelon's great army: pockets of sages, archers in square formations, spearmen in rectangular groupings along their front and at their flanks.

Indrajit elevated his plane of vision to the Rezzian army beyond. His heart fluttered with twinges of excitement.

Briraji had used a power to gain extraordinary sight. "Something has happened." The sage's hands formed a vault to keep the sun from his eyes. "The Haizzem falls and ... Rao rises again."

Indrajit noticed the gasp of hope on Devak's face.

"Rao picks up the spear. He pauses, raises it. He stabs the Haizzem—wait—the Haizzem is gone. Rao speared a woman instead, one with dark red hair—"

"The royal daughter." Devak simply spoke the fact.

"Dogs!" The word exploded from Indrajit. *No honor. They sacrifice a woman instead.*

"Rao has disappeared. He must be using Aayu's *sadhana*. And now the royal daughter is gone."

"None of them are there? No one is there?" Indrajit asked.

"No one."

"My Rajah," Indrajit said, "there *must* be a price to pay for their treachery."

"Rao won the combat." Devak crossed his arms over his massive chest. "We'll wait for their next move."

'*'

Narayani's world spun around her dizzy head, blinded by the red ball of the sun. Fighting the throbbing in her temples, she placed her hands on a smooth, hard surface and raised herself to look at her surroundings.

Below the raised platform, the Rezzian army spread out farther than her eyes could see: long-haired, dirty men bearing shields, many of them dressed in crimson shirts and capes around their armor; bald men in loose, white tunics; decorated officers upon horses.

Two men sat in chalky white thrones before her, the Haizzem and a man that could only be Rezzia's king. The king's golden armor reflected the sun as he stood. He glared down on her with unkind eyes framed by his thick hair. Narayani fell flat and clung to the wooden floor, fearing the crowd of soldiers would spot her and tear her to pieces.

The king's gaze shot to the Haizzem. The young man writhed in agony.

"Healers!" screamed the trembling, red-faced king. He placed a powerful hand on his son's shoulder. "What happened?"

The Haizzem spoke with his eyes closed, clenching his teeth in pain. "He defeated me. He stabbed me. I should be dead. I don't know how I came to be here."

The king put his other hand on Caio's forehead. "Lucia was in your chair. She said a Pawelon woman interfered with your combat. Was it this pig?"

Caio opened his eyes and fixed them on Narayani. "This girl, she told me to kill her if I was going to kill the prince." Caio spoke slowly, breathing painfully. "I couldn't do it. Father, where is Lucia?"

"She took your place. I saw her hair. She took Ilario's spear in her chest." The King nearly choked as he uttered the words, "She is dead." He pointed at Narayani, flinging his arm toward her like a whip. All of his exposed skin seemed flexed and hard, from his fingers to his neck and forehead. "She'll be the first one to pay the price."

"How could it be?" Caio cried out as bald men in flowing cream robes rushed onto the platform to minister to him. Narayani tried to focus on the mantras Aayu taught her, but terror and nausea paralyzed her.

Focus!

"She sacrificed herself for me," Caio said softly. His eyes seemed to be searching for an answer, then focused on his father again. "Lucia interfered, too."

The king roared, "By dying for you?"

"My King," a high-ranking soldier in a crisp red uniform interrupted the conversation from the opposite end of the platform, "soon after the Pawelon stabbed down, he removed his spear. Then we all saw him disappear. Her Grace disappeared soon after that."

"Then where is she?" the king asked.

"We have not seen her since, nor the prince."

"Gods damn all of this." The king lunged forward and grabbed the back of Narayani's dress.

Narayani fought him, trying to stay down. The king yanked her up onto her knees, then onto her feet. Her wobbly legs would have collapsed again without the king forcing her upright. Thousands of eyes feasted upon her like starving wolves to prey.

"Warriors! The royal daughter of Rezzia has been taken from us. Just now, in the center of the valley, she was stabbed in the chest by the Prince of Pawelon." His voice then wavered as he said, "My daughter may be dying this very moment, or she may already be dead."

The king raised his open left hand and turned as he spoke, facing different sections of his army. "Your Haizzem is weak and wounded." The king's rough hands pressed against Narayani's back as he turned her to face each section of the crowd. "This Pawelon pig went into the valley, violating the rules of the engagement, and distracted your Haizzem just as he was going to kill the prince. *She* caused him to lose his combat!"

Wails of hatred and woe arose from the army. Narayani's heart burned like a funeral pyre.

"Let every one of us get in her!" a soldier yelled from the crowd, quickly joined by a chorus of cheers.

Focus, damn it! Focus!

"Make the pretty pig squeal!" another voice shouted from the throng. Narayani heard ugly voices throughout the mob imitating crying pigs. Terror gripped her so much she couldn't feel her body.

She twisted her head to focus on the Haizzem as he tried to stand. He collapsed into his seat, but the bald men around him helped him to his feet and held him upright. The army quieted and waited for his words.

"Father, what if Lucia still lives? Perhaps we could still exchange her for this girl."

The king held Narayani up as she tried to fall again, pulling on her dress with one hand. "You are right, my son, but she will pay for her crime. Now sit and rest." The king called to some men beside the platform, "Guards, we have a prisoner. Take her away from here and guard her life with your own. One way or another, she has value to me."

Narayani fell onto her hands and knees as the king released her. Her leather medicine bag lay nearby. Her brain stammered one desperate thought after another, trying to concoct a scheme for survival.

"Now we will have *our* battle!" The king said in Caio's direction. Caio sat with the aid of the bald men; he closed his eyes again and lowered his head into his hands. "Yes," the king nodded as he hissed the sound.

He looked to the west and walked to the edge of the scaffold, shaking the floor. "Now we will have *our* battle!" he announced with a muscular arm and clenched fist shaking above his head. "Now we will have *our* battle!"

The crowd raised countless swords and yelled with fury.

Helmeted soldiers with dark beards and hairy arms grabbed Narayani, lifting her off the floor. She squirmed in their grasp. She looked to Caio, but his face remained buried in his hands.

"My bag!" she managed to say in Rezzian. She understood their spoken language better than she could speak it. "I am healer. I can help Haizzem. I need my bag."

The king turned around. "You lying bitch!"

"Father!" Caio came to life and stood. "She speaks the truth. She is desperate and scared, but she believes she can heal me."

Narayani nodded repeatedly.

The king seemed to bite his tongue and shook his head. "She will not lay a finger on you with any of her dark magic."

"You will need me," Narayani stumbled over the words. "Caio injury from Rezzian magic. Not Pawelon. Your medicine not heal him. Mine will."

The king clenched his jaw and flared his nostrils.

"She tells the truth as she sees it," Caio said. The bald men supported Caio in case he might fall. "And she is definitely a healer."

"What on Gallea is she talking about?"

"Their prince turned Mya's divine power against me."

The king walked back to his seat and picked up a golden helm on the floor beside it. He held it under his right armpit, squeezed between his body and arm. He said to his guards, "Take her bag. Under no conditions will you allow her to get anything out of it. Is this understood?"

The men nodded. A heavy soldier picked up Narayani's leather bag.

"Make sure she does not come near Caio." The king looked to the Haizzem. "Go and rest and let our warpriests heal you. Do not fall under her enchantments. She brings only death."

The king stepped closer to his son. "While you heal, I will command the army. We will fight them and if Lucia is alive, we will find her. Do I have your permission to do so, my Dux Spiritus?" The king leaned his head forward in a bow.

"Yes." Caio looked down, then winced in pain and rubbed his face again.

"I pray for your swift recovery, Caio. So that you will be able to join the fighting again."

Narayani tried again to visualize the mantras. Her terror made the effort useless. For now.

Caio collapsed into the arms of the warpriests.

"Lay him down!" one of the warpriests commanded.

The Rezzian healers laid their hands on the Haizzem and uttered strange words Narayani did not understand. Caio's body only twitched. He began to moan. The king looked again to Narayani and sharpened his glare.

"Your magic not heal him," Narayani said.

The king knelt beside his son. "We do not practice magic! Say that again and I will cut out your tongue."

Without this Caio, I am surely dead. "I can heal him. I can heal Rezzian"—*not magic, what else*—"divine power."

The king gave her no answer. He told the warpriests, "As soon as you can move him, carry my son to safety."

The bald men bowed in agreement as the king prayed over his son.

Rezzia's king placed his golden helm over his head and stood again. He began issuing commands to older, higher-ranking men on horseback, below the platform.

The king turned once more to the warpriests and pointed at one of them. "You! Pray to Lord Danato for this: I want the pig unconscious but alive, so she cannot use her foul magic."

Narayani saw one of the warpriests step forward and bow to the king. The warpriest faced her and she noticed an orange tear tattooed on one of his cheeks. He began muttering in a strange tongue ...

Chapter 62:
For the One or the Many

AAYU COULDN'T BELIEVE what he was seeing, but he saw the saffron sage's uniform. Rao stood up from the canyon floor, lifted the spear, and thrust it down. After that, something about the Haizzem's body changed. Then Rao disappeared along with the body beneath him.

Aayu closed his eyes and visualized the letters of his primary *sadhana* on the black canvas of his mind, against his forehead. He heard the sacred syllables. His body transmuted and felt light. When he opened his eyes, the world appeared as it did before, but in less focus and with duller colors.

Aayu ran into the wide-open valley after Rao. He soon slowed to recover and pace himself. As he came closer, he was surprised that he was able to see Rao, who was also using his *sadhana* to conceal himself, kneeling beside the body.

"Rao!" he yelled, still a great distance away.

Rao turned his head. "Aayu! Come here!" Rao's barking showed his anger, an emotion Aayu wasn't used to from his bhai.

Aayu felt too out of breath to continue running, but he walked at a quick pace the rest of the way. He soon saw the deep red hair of the heavily armored royal daughter. She lay flat against the ground, unconscious.

"You taught Narayani your *sadhana*?" Rao's eyes were furious.

Oh no.

"Why, Aayu? Why?" Rao's angry voice turned to sadness.

"Where is she?"

"She's gone. She was here. She tried to help me."

"What do you mean she's gone?"

"Just before I stabbed the Haizzem, Narayani was here. They both disappeared."

"Damn! *Damn!*"

"The spear went into her instead." Rao pointed at Rezzia's royal daughter.

"Damn!" Aayu stomped around the desert. "Rao, I'm so sorry. She made me—ah! I let her convince me. She promised me she wouldn't come this close to you. I never should've trusted her. Damn it, Rao, I made a huge mistake."

"I don't think she's nearby anymore." Rao stood. "I can't feel her presence in any way. The only thing I can think of is that the royal daughter changed places with her brother and somehow Narayani went wherever the Haizzem went."

Aayu's blood burned as he thought about what they might do to her. He looked at the fallen Rezzian. "Is this one alive?"

"She is. I used your *sadhana* on her to slow her injuries. I don't know how long it will last. I don't have much *ojas*."

Aayu closed his eyes and beheld the *shunyata* mantra in his mind. He directed its power into the Rezzian, her sword, and her shield. She would remain concealed. "I've taken care of it."

"Good."

"Rao, if Narayani is with them, they won't do anything to her if they want to see the king's daughter again."

"Right. I agree. That means we need to get her out of here. We'll carry her."

Aayu rushed to grab the woman's feet and lifted her while Rao grabbed her under her shoulders. She bore bruises on one side of her face and on her nose, where Aayu struck her three nights ago.

You forced me to do it, woman.

"I am sorry," Aayu said.

Rao lowered his eyes.

Aayu continued, "She told me she was going to kill herself if I didn't help her. I thought it could help. Maybe she could use my *sadhana* if she needs to hide or get away from anyone."

"I really hope you're right."

The woman's body felt considerably lighter than it would have if they were in their physical bodies.

"Except for one thing," Rao said. "The Haizzem could see her."

"He could?" Aayu spoke the words so quickly all his breath went with them.

"He talked to her just before he was going to kill me. She argued with him. That gave me enough time to stop him."

"Then she saved your life?"

"I would've rather died than see her taken."

251

"Maybe she'll return. She can use my *sadhana* and come right back to us."

Rao nodded. "Aayu, it's hard to explain what happened, but I talked to his god. Then just before I was going to be killed, I saw his goddess and she healed me."

"That's—"

"I know. Maybe I imagined it. But why would I imagine that? And something definitely healed me. He destroyed me, bhai. It was horrible. My entire body was crushed."

"Let's sort all of that out later."

"I'm telling you, the only reason I won is because his goddess saved me. She saved me so I could stab him?"

"Yet another reason to stay far away from their foul religion. It curses them."

By the time they reached the army, the soldiers were stirring. Soon they stood at attention, ready to march. Aayu looked to the east and three breaths later, the Rezzian army began to charge across the valley.

"What do we do?" he asked.

Rao looked around, clearly thinking through his options.

"We need to help our army," Aayu said.

"And we need to get this woman to our citadel. One of us can take her. Please take her."

"What if she wakes up? She's deadly."

Rao gritted his teeth and shook his head. "She'd be a lot heavier for one person, too. You're right. We need to stay together. We may need her to get Narayani back, or we may need her so we can negotiate with Rezzia from a position of power."

In front of the Rezzian army, the desert floor rumbled as if the ground were on the verge of a collapse.

This isn't good, bhai.

An enormous golden creature shot up from the earth, scattering dirt and rocks all around. The male lion stood up on all fours, appearing taller than twenty men. It raised its black mouth to the sky and unleashed a deep, guttural roar.

"Rao?" Aayu said.

A similar beast arose beside it, this one a lioness, followed by eight more of the divine monsters.

"We have to trust our army," Rao said. "Trust Indrajit and Briraji. They have faced this enemy before."

"Not like this, bhai."

"What will happen to this woman if we leave her here? What if we die and she escapes? What if she returns to her physical form and dies? We've got to take her to the citadel. She's too valuable. The Haizzem will be too weak to fight and we have the royal daughter. We'll leave this to Briraji."

The Pawelon army held its formation. The archers readied their arrows. Aayu and Rao carried the royal daughter toward their citadel as the lions of Lord Galleazzo took careful steps toward Pawelon's army.

Chapter 63: The Loyalty of Lions

DEVAK JUMPED OUT OF HIS CHAIR when the lions emerged. Undisciplined voices from around the Pawelon army murmured. In the middle of it all, the sun burned down its cruelty on their heads.

Here comes hell, Devak decided.

"Briraji!" Indrajit commanded.

"I will deal with the beasts, General," the sage answered.

"Briraji," Devak interrupted, "Can you send the king a message?"

Briraji's dark face frowned and nodded. "I can find a way."

"Tell him we have his daughter. Tell him I will beat her until she is at the brink of death, and punish her every sick way that I can. Tell him I'll do her ten times, unless he calls off his army and his lions. Then tell him his entire army must retreat from the valley. I'll keep his daughter safe if he does. Otherwise, I make her my battered concubine."

"The king's lions, Indrajit," Devak changed the subject. "Have they ever appeared at this size?"

"Not since the beginning of the war, My Rajah. The king may have regained some of his power."

"No honor. None," Devak said with disgust. "Though I didn't expect any. Do we go forward or back?"

Indrajit walked to the forward edge of the hill and peered eastward. He spoke in his calm, assured voice. "We dig in, drink water, and wait. The dogs will exhaust themselves if they want this battle."

Indrajit looked back to Devak. "If they come, we'll finish them right here."

'*'

King Vieri leaned forward on his horse, his rear slamming against the saddle with each galloping lunge. The hot gusts blew dust into his eyes. He swung his father's falchion above his head and issued commands from deep within his chest. "Fall in behind the lions!" he commanded his leading cavalry. Two

254

warpriests flanked him on horseback. "Their bodies will protect you!" As his horse-riding officers reorganized and fell in behind each of Lord Galleazzo's towering beasts, the early waves of troops followed too, trailing the ten divine creatures.

The air filled with the ominous whispers of arrows, filling the sky like a swarm of black birds gliding off a peak. The arrows fell like rain, but were mostly absorbed by the pelts of Galleazzo's great lions.

Vieri heard a deep howl deep inside his skull and noticed his steed slowing. A gust of wind swirled around him, circling him with dancing leaves. Other cavalry outpaced his own horse. He shook his head, feeling mentally slowed. Soon, charging soldiers passed his horse as well.

What is happening, Lord?

The resounding moan increased its noise between his ears, like a ghostly owl screaming over his shoulder. A powerful gust descended on him, forcing him to halt his steed and close his eyes, forcing him to listen to the persistent and ethereal tone deep inside him.

Protect me from this foul spirit, Lord!

Vieri opened his eyes to a windy, darkening haze. Smoky strands of grey, black, and purple swirled around him. A smell like rotten eggs crawled up his nostrils. The outline of a face appeared before him, twisting and shifting in the thick smoke.

"Aren't you the king of Rezzia?" The creaking voice rose and fell, the syllables flowing like an uneven stream of gravel.

"What is this?"

"I bring a message from Rajah Devak."

Lord Galleazzo, free me!

"He has your daughter. She lives, for now."

"Where? Where is she?"

"She is with our prince. He contains and limits her powers."

"Gods! We have the Pawelon girl. The one who went into the valley and interfered with the duel. I offer her back to you in exchange for my daughter."

The voice hesitated for the first time. "What girl do you speak of?"

"She is ... beautiful, young. She is a healer. She carried a leather bag."

"I cannot address this matter now. I have the rajah's message. He demands you call off this battle and this war. Call off these lions, all these men. Then leave

255

the valley. He told me all that he would do to your daughter if you do not comply. Do you wish to know?"

Gods! Vieri was thrown into confusion. He couldn't find an answer.

"He will personally beat your daughter, break her bones. Then ride her ten times, causing as much pain as he can—*if* you do not agree. Leave here now and your daughter will be safe."

How do I even know he has her?

He visualized the battle: the lions tearing through Pawelon's forces; the great clash of armies; the holy power of the gods against the dark magic of their sages. Then he thought of Pawelon's giant rajah with Lucia beneath him ...

Caio and I will find a way to save her.

"What say you, King Vieri? I have seen your daughter's long, red hair. I know our rajah would find her young flesh appealing."

"Whoever you are, my army's charge ends now. Tonight, we will talk about an exchange of prisoners."

"Then call your men off."

The cruel face vanished into undifferentiated smoke, then into thin tendrils.

The fog within Vieri's head cleared, too, replaced by the cacophony of colliding armies and oppressive heat beneath his armor. He looked to his sides; the warpriests still flanked him. Behind him, a cadre of officers and messengers waited for his orders.

"Total retreat! I'm calling for a full retreat! Go!"

Soon dozens of messengers rode off on horseback, yelling and giving signals with their hands. The drummers pounded out the call to fall back.

Vieri kicked his steed into a gallop and called to the troops in front of him.

"Get back, all of you! Pull back! I promise you, we will fight another day!"

Lord Galleazzo's lions stopped in the desert and stood tall. Five males and five lionesses shielded the Rezzian troops as they turned back to the east, as the warriors of Pawelon cheered and celebrated Rezzia's withdrawal.

Chapter 64: The Drawing of Lines

RAO DREAMT OF VAST OCEANS rising up and covering the lands of Gallea. The global tsunami surrounded Pawelon on all sides and spilled inland until it swallowed the palace in Kannauj, leaving every parcel of dry land submerged. Every living creature drowned in the flood, ending the world of men. Directly above it all, the sun flashed, consuming everything in its light.

The soreness throughout his body woke him, overwhelming him. Before he could open his eyes, unique and overpowering herbal scents told him he was in the medical ward. Confused, he looked around the room. Long feathers from various birds believed to be auspicious for healing covered parts of the grainy wooden walls.

"Over here, bhai." Aayu sat in a chair in a far corner, concealed by shadows. "You collapsed."

"I did?" Rao sat up in bed and noticed the comfortable robe someone had dressed him in. The simple act of pushing himself up caused his back and arms to ache. "Some of the healing from the Rezzian goddess has worn off." He relaxed his muscles and fell back onto the bed. "It hurts to move."

"We carried the woman into a cell, then you passed out."

Ah! That is the last thing I remember.

"Good. She's here," Rao said.

"Indrajit has some of his prized soldiers and sages guarding her. The healers are working on her wound."

"Is Narayani back?"

Aayu shook his head and spoke softly, "Not yet."

Rao's heart became leaden again, and his battered body flooded with disgust. His limbs felt too heavy to move.

"Maybe she'll escape," Aayu said. "But I'm ready to do something."

"Me too, but," Rao realized his body wouldn't allow him to do much, "it hurts to sit up."

"You'll heal fast, bhai. We'll do the breaths together."

"Thanks. I'm sure that will help."

A young soldier walked in front of the open doorway. "My Prince, you are awake?"

"Yes."

"The rajah and his general wish to speak with you."

Devak and Indrajit had been waiting at ground level within the nearby tower. It didn't take long for them to walk across the courtyard to visit with Rao and Aayu. They immediately questioned Rao about the events of the day and explained how Briraji was able to convince the king to call off the battle, leading to minimal casualties for both sides.

Rao's father and Indrajit stood near the end of his bed. "There's another matter," Devak continued. "They say they have a beautiful young woman who claims to be a healer. They say she interfered with your combat and saved your life."

"It's true," Rao said.

Indrajit's face began to ripple with hot venom. "Explain this."

"It's my fault, Uncle." Aayu was already standing out of respect. He took a step forward and looked directly at Indrajit. He spoke with confidence in his voice, "I taught her my *sadhana*. She told me she wouldn't put her life in danger—"

"But she saved my life," Rao interrupted. "It's true. She distracted their Haizzem."

Rao couldn't keep their gaze for long. He looked down and felt his shame like a rancid stew in his stomach. Indrajit was steaming. His father's face looked empty and stunned. Rao remembered the terms of the conflict.

"Then she interfered," Devak stated the fact with reluctance. "They would be acting within the terms if they killed her. But," he looked sideways, staring at the wall, "they have offered her back to us in exchange for the king's daughter."

"Excellent!" Rao felt lightness in his body, down to his toes. Aayu's face turned sunny with his smile.

"No," Indrajit spoke with finality. "We can't allow the king's daughter to rejoin their army. She is far too powerful. You know that."

You despicable bastard ...

"Father, can't we use the royal daughter to negotiate? What if we tell them they need to flee the canyon?"

"I already did," his father's dry, throaty voice said softly. "We can't swap the prisoners. We have the upper hand now. They have to leave."

258

Rao couldn't find words. Neither could Aayu.

Rao's lips and arms trembled. "If they're willing to give us Narayani, let the king have his daughter back. We can defend ourselves."

"Absolutely not," Indrajit said. "If he wants his daughter back unharmed, he will treat Narayani well."

"How can you be so cold? We're talking about your daughter." Aayu's voice shook with rage. "Don't tell me—"

"Don't you ever question me again, Master Aayu. You have already been warned."

Rao spoke up to divert Indrajit's attention from Aayu, "General, with respect, I think it's only fair to exchange the women. We *were* in the wrong. Narayani interfered."

"Thanks to her idiot cousin, and thanks to you almost getting killed. The royal daughter interfered, too." Indrajit turned from Rao and glared at Aayu, who stood close to him. "You had your chance, Rao. Now they are going to have to end this war or fight without the king's daughter on their side. We have their leading Strategos. They will not harm my daughter if the king wants to see his own alive again."

Aayu stopped just short of bumping into Indrajit. He yelled into Indrajit's face. "What do you think they could be doing to your daughter right now?"

Indrajit swung his open fist.

Aayu tried to dodge the blow, but only turned enough to take the hard slap against the back of his jaw and ear.

Rao's father moved in to separate them. "Soldiers!" his angry voice boomed.

Aayu stepped back, holding a hand to the side of his head. His breaths huffed out loud and hard.

Devak stood between Aayu and Indrajit. He pointed at Aayu as he spoke, "You were warned." The room filled rapidly with armed soldiers. Devak told the men, "Take Aayu to confinement. Aayu, accept your punishment. You will have another chance."

Rao watched, helpless. "Please, Father. I need Aayu's help to heal."

"No you don't," his father said, keeping his eyes on Aayu. "Aayu needs time to think about respecting his superiors."

Aayu looked at Rao with a tight jaw and confused eyes as the soldiers approached him and grabbed his arms. He moved as they directed him, willingly.

Rao nodded at his friend. "Then please don't keep him long. I need to work with him."

Indrajit stood behind Rao's father, watching Aayu leave the room. Rao had never seen Indrajit so flustered and red-faced.

"We'll get her back, Aayu. Don't worry," Rao said. Indrajit turned his aquiline glare to Rao. Everything was changing too fast, spinning out of control. "You know," Rao said to his father and Indrajit, "the royal daughter is probably more powerful than any of our sages. You need to be careful with her."

"Briraji is among those watching her," Indrajit said. "And she is very weak."

"I need to watch her to make sure she stays under our control." Rao looked Indrajit in the eye with a challenge. "She is the key to getting Narayani back—or to outright peace."

"And you will let me and your father handle these matters."

"You'll also need my help to keep that woman in confinement. I'm still healing, and I can heal better with Aayu's help. My whole body is sore."

"We'll need you if there's going to be more fighting," the rajah said. "Find another way to heal. I'm sure you can."

Indrajit began walking out of the room. "They may attack again when they discover we have refused the exchange of prisoners. Come, my Rajah. Important matters call."

They do for me, too.

Chapter 65: Prisoners to Men

LUCIA AWOKE, ALMOST DELIRIOUS FROM FEVER, lying on a wooden slab in a drafty cell that smelled of feces and urine. At least a handful of small torches scattered around the room cast flickering light on the grey stone floor and walls. She lifted her head enough to see perhaps a dozen Pawelon men, soldiers and sages, standing or sitting against the walls of the room. She found herself wearing nothing more than an unclean robe.

Ilario's necklace was gone.

Much worse, her gloves were gone.

Danato, am I dreaming?

On her forearms, she saw the black, thorny vines, the markings of a Haizzem, markings she had borne since Danato first visited her in her dreams sixteen years ago. Her red and black palms were exposed. She dragged an arm across her body to touch her other forearm, staring at both limbs with panic.

Lord Danato, tell me I am dreaming!

Lucia remembered the other two times people had seen the markings. The first time it was a servant who found her sleeping after she'd dozed off without wearing the correct robe. The second time, a decade later, her lover in Peraece had pulled her sleeve down without any warning. Both times, they'd believed her when she denied its spiritual origin and told them they were tattoos in honor of her brother.

An ugly-sounding man's voice rattled on about something.

Wait, he is speaking Pawelon.

She focused on his voice: "Yes, awake. She is touching her arms."

She lowered her chin and lifted her robe to try to see the wound under her breast. A heavy cloth had been wrapped around her chest, reeking of exotic herbs. She kept her nose inside her garment, preferring the smell there to the one in the cell.

My goddess! How did I live?

She wondered about Caio. Was he safe and alive? She lowered her head against the hard thing they'd given her as a pillow, some kind of dense object wrapped in a coarse brown cloth.

Does my father even know I'm here?

The hinges of the heavy door whined. Lucia stayed flat on the wooden 'bed,' but turned her head sideways. Three men entered the room. In front walked a sage in a saffron officer's uniform; his features were hard to make out in the dim light, but what she could see of his face was an unattractive nose and a scowl. Close behind him came a tall general with a stern face and powerful, beak-like nose. The third man stood taller and heavier than any man she'd ever seen who wasn't obese; he loomed like two men combined in one body. His pockmarked face was motionless, like the calm preceding a storm.

"See for yourself, my Rajah, General," the sage said in a low, monotone voice.

The men only made it halfway into the room before stopping.

"Raise your arms," the general commanded in the Pawelon language. "I will not say it again. Raise your arms."

Lucia did it, though her whole body ached with fever. The sleeves of her robes fell down against her elbows. She watched the men staring at her.

They remained silent for some time. "What is the meaning of this?" the giant man's deep voice filled the room. "Answer me, woman."

"They are tattoos," she lied. "In honor of my brother."

"She's not telling the truth," the sage said.

"I am!"

"You cannot fool me, you dog. I sense too much."

Gods!

"They *are*," Lucia paused, "tattoos."

"She lies," the sage told the others.

Lucia shook her head.

"If they are not tattoos," the giant said, "what does this mean?"

The general answered, "That she is another Haizzem. She has already done incredible damage to our army. It seems reasonable." He raised his voice. "Tell us, wasn't it you who commanded the storm?"

"I don't command gods," she said.

"Give me a straight answer or you will suffer another wound," the general said.

"I worship the goddess Ysa. I asked her for help. She controlled the storms."

"Why wouldn't we know of these markings?" the giant asked. "How could they keep this secret from us?"

The sage answered, "She wore black gloves covering the length of her arms. She wasn't showing them to her men either. Perhaps it was a secret to most Rezzians."

All of them, in fact.

The giant addressed her again. "I told your father that if your people continue his war, you'll become my slave. You wouldn't enjoy that. Not most of the time anyway. Your father will choose your fate."

And that was unthinkable.

"He retreated with his army after he heard my message today, after the duel," he added. "There may be hope for you."

If Caio is still alive.

'*'

Narayani awoke confused, surrounded by darkness. She heard muffled male voices.

Light shone through the outline of a door before daylight flooded in and revealed an empty room with wooden walls, a moderately large box with no furnishings other than the dingy blankets beneath her. The air was stagnant and hot.

Heavy boots clomped and shook the wooden floor. Too many.

See the mantras, she told herself. *Now.*

The first three sacred syllables appeared in her inner vision, but large hands and long fingers squeezed her arms and forced her to stand.

"Where you take me?" she asked in Rezzian.

"To die, pig," said an armored soldier with a large, bald head.

As the men dragged her out of the box, a structure she took for a detention cell, the landscape of the Rezzian army's camp unfurled. Hundreds of tents sprawled in every direction, made of white cloth stretched taut and convex. Unarmed men in common Rezzian tunics wandered about, some keeping to themselves, others engaged in conversation. Most of them turned and stared, inspecting her with rough eyes set between crooked noses and bushy brows.

Hundreds more stared as she was dragged through the camp. They passed a tent with a handful of half-naked whores sitting outside of it. The women narrowed their hardened eyes and studied her.

Narayani's heart pumped hard and fluttered. Her panting breaths made her feel lightheaded. *What are they going to do to me?*

The smell of roasting meat found its way to her nose. Concentrating on Aayu's *sadhana* was impossible while walking.

They led her farther from the common tents, past five massive ones, to a more decorated, heavy, and round tent. Dark green vines had been painted around the cream fabric that encircled the structure. They stopped in front of double wooden doors and knocked.

"My Haizzem, we have her."

"Bring her in," Caio said from inside the structure.

Still outside, Narayani examined how the walls met the ground. She found no loose sections. Too many stakes tied the structure down tightly.

The door opened to foreign smells carried on smoky incense, both spicy and sweet. The Haizzem sat at the edge of his bed, facing her, with an empty bed beside him. At least a score of warpriests and soldiers either sat or stood around the room. Narayani found herself shoved into the tent from behind, and all eyes swung to her.

"Please, sit down," the Haizzem said in a smooth, easy voice. He motioned to the empty bed and coughed.

Narayani hurried over and sat facing the Haizzem. It allowed her to turn at least one side of her body away from the men.

Caio turned his body to face her. "Please tell me, what is your name?"

Should I?

"It's all right," he said. "I'm not going to hurt you."

I should. My father needs to know I'm here.

"Narayani."

"Narayani, you must be scared. My father was very angry yesterday. He may still be angry. I will not let him hurt you."

A tenderness in Caio's voice somehow convinced her of his sincerity. She kept all her attention on his handsome face to shut out the others' stares. His soft skin was tan for a Rezzian, but light compared to her own people's coloring. His nose was strong, but drawn with smooth, curved edges. Hollow dimples showed in his cheeks whenever he smiled. And despite his pain, he seemed to smile most of the time.

"Narayani, I know you can help me to heal."

"Yes. How do you know?"

"I can feel people's hearts. It is a gift the gods have given me."

Does he know I'm attracted to him?

Caio smiled in a way that made Narayani feel comfortable and accepted. "You told the truth when you said you are a healer. I know this. Many of our warpriests are great healers, but they have not been able to help me yet."

"Because Rao hit you with your power." She moved her finger in a circle to illustrate, "He made it go back to you. I trained to heal Rezzian magic—sorry, divine power."

Caio's cheeks shone as he smiled and nodded. "Will you please help me to heal?"

Why would I do that?

"If I am strong, I can protect you. You can stay with me instead of wherever you were last night," Caio said.

Narayani felt her shoulders relax. "If you don't help me, my father will try to take you. I don't know what he would do."

"Yes. I can help. Then you let me go home?"

"I hope so, yes."

Though it made no sense, she trusted him instinctively, throughout her body and down to her toes. She'd never met a kinder man. How could this be? The leader of Rezzia's army was either a gentle soul or he had her under a powerful spell.

No, he is a good soul. I know it.

Narayani looked at some of the other men. All of them seemed content to remain silent. They stayed back, giving Caio freedom to do whatever he wished. Many of them kept their glances downward in submissive postures.

They respect him, too. They will do whatever he says.

"In fact," Caio said, "my father has already offered to exchange you for my sister. We await your people's response."

Hope bloomed in Narayani's mind. Might this all be over soon?

"I need my bag." She did her best to project sweetness and defenselessness.

Caio turned his head just a touch and nodded. "I must ask for the bag. I will tell my father I commanded you to give it to me."

The soldier holding her medicines looked to all the eyes waiting to see his next move.

"Yes, my Haizzem." He turned around and picked it up. The leather purse sat on the floor, next to the tent's wall behind some kind of religious altar.

"Give it to her," Caio said without any apparent pride.

The soldier followed the order and handed Narayani her medicines. He quickly walked away, as if frightened by what might be inside it.

She untied the three strips keeping the bag closed and felt the contents.

It feels full. Good. Now should I really heal him, or just relieve his pain for a time? Or wait until I find out if I am going back? The longer I am with him, the better my chances of survival.

"It's important that I recover fully and quickly," he said with more seriousness in his eyes. "The stronger I am, the more I can help you."

She was beginning to feel persuaded when a voice interrupted, shouting from outside the door. "King Vieri seeks your audience, my Haizzem."

Panic began rattling around her chest and limbs. She looked to Caio.

"Try to relax. Remember, I will protect you," he said with his enormous brown eyes assuring her. He carefully shifted his position on the bed to face the door, as if it hurt him to move. "Please let him in."

Narayani swallowed.

The king entered with his thick hair messy, his countenance flustered. He spoke right away, "They said no. They," he paused, "said no."

Caio's head dropped in shock.

The king looked at her with contempt. "They don't want you. Your people don't care what we do to you. Your pretty face isn't worth anything to them. Not even to your prince."

It felt as if a sword cut through her heart and out her back. A deep wound opened, an old, crushing abandonment that she remembered too well.

"What in Danato's underworld is she doing with her bag?"

Caio answered right away, "Their prince turned Mya's power against me. None of our prayers or treatments helped. But I know she is a healer, and she knows how to remedy the damage done by Lux Lucis. She's promised to help me."

The king opened his mouth for a moment, staring at Caio, then slammed his mouth shut and turned his glare around the room. "None of you can help my son to heal? Your one and only Haizzem. All of you, get out of here. Now!"

The soldiers and warpriests scurried out of the tent. The solid wooden doors collided, shut from the outside.

Rao? Aayu? Not even my father? None of you believe I am worth saving?

Narayani closed her eyes to try to hide from the pain, but found no sanctuary.

She opened her eyes to find the king's gaze focused on his son. Caio stared back, earnestly, but with no apparent positive or negative emotion.

"I have already sent a message back to the pigs," the king said, dominating the room with his unyielding posture. "I told them that if they lay one finger on Lucia, not only will we punish this girl, you and I will defeat their army and pour over the lands of Pawelon, burning every forest, claiming every woman and child as our slaves, destroying every temple, and killing every man. If they will not surrender her, we will erase every bit of evidence that Pawelon culture ever existed."

Caio dragged a hand through his hair and over his scalp, looking just to his father's side.

You said you would help me, Caio.

"You won't touch her," he told his father. "She's innocent. I also need her help."

"What are you going to do to my son?" His father's eyes quivered with accusation.

"I help him heal."

"That's ridiculous. Why would you do that?"

"Caio help me."

The king shook his head and let out a long, aggravated breath.

"She is not lying, Father. She just wants to help me so she can go home."

"Is there anything in your bag that could harm him?" the king asked. "Caio, tell me if she lies."

"Only if he takes too much. But all these herbs are for healing."

"She speaks the truth," Caio said.

The bearded king walked closer to Caio, then knelt on one knee before him.

"Caio, how would you know what too much is? You must watch her every move. She caused you," his voice became rough, "to lose. You *cannot* trust her. Do you know this?"

"I understand."

"Do not let her evil seduce and deceive you. Have your way with her, if you want to. But do not think for a moment that she is not plotting to either kill you or escape. And never leave her in a place where she can use her magic to hide and sneak away."

"I will watch over her and keep her here. Everything will be fine. I believe she will help me."

"You know I am ready to assign another protector to you."

"Please, not yet. I'm not ready. Soon, though."

The king twisted his head, almost looking at Caio sideways. "If she heals you, you must join me. We will pray to the goddess Mya, to Lord Oderigo, to Lord Galleazzo, and we will find a way to overwhelm their forces and gain entry to their citadel. We will win this war and we will find Lucia. If we do not—"

"We will find a way, Father. We will save Lucia. I prayed throughout the night to Lord Oderigo and he showed me that she is alive, in a cell inside the citadel. They are nursing her wound and they have not harmed her."

"Maybe not yet, Son." The king's face became long, as if contemplating a great horror. He glanced at Narayani again, then back to Caio. "Rest and heal and continue to pray for Lucia's safety."

The king stood again, wincing as if his knees hurt him. He walked close to Narayani, his boots thudding against the carpet. He squeezed her jaw with his powerful hand and made sure she looked into his heavy eyes. "If you hurt my son in any way, I will do to you what your rajah has threatened to do to my daughter. Believe me, you will have never known such pain. No man could do to you what I can."

Narayani shot a glance toward Caio. She felt the tears building, ready to erupt.

"Father, let her go." Caio voice remained soft. "She understands you."

The king squeezed her jaw tighter, then pushed her head back. Narayani lay down on her side and curled her knees to her chest as her tears began to flow. She heard the king exit the room and the doors close behind him.

Caio touched her shoulder. "I am sorry, Narayani. Everything is going to be okay. I promise you, everything will be fine." He fetched a fine, white cloth from atop his light wardrobe and placed it on the bed before her. "In case you want to wipe your face."

How is it that you can calm my mind so quickly?

Narayani sat up, dried her wet face, and cleaned up around her nose.

Caio put the palm of one hand forward and gently took one of her hands in his. He covered it with his other hand. He turned his head away and coughed again, a wet, painful cough. He looked at her again, smiling as if he were not in pain.

"I worship a goddess called Mya. She is the divinity presiding over water and healing. She heals both bodies and hearts. If you would like me to, I will pray to her for you. She might help soothe your feelings."

"You do this for me?"

"Close your eyes. Invite Mya into your heart and feel her presence. Wait and she will come."

They sat together in silence. The atmosphere felt strange to Narayani, but sweet and wonderful.

She didn't know where the words were coming from, but she thought them: *Come into my heart. I am broken. Help me.*

It began with silence, a penetrating, easy silence throughout her mind, heart, and soul. Her body filled with a warm presence, as if a kind spirit had entered and filled her body with a profound love. The clouds cleared away, clouds of terror, of heartache, of rage. Feelings of dignity, wholeness, and peace took their place.

She opened her eyes and lost herself in Caio's radiant eyes.

"Feeling better?" Caio smiled, still holding her hand.

"Thank you." She quickly reached out to hug him. She felt his heart beating and knew that neither of them wanted the embrace to end.

She brought her face around to his and kissed him.

I am sorry, Rao. He is the only one who can save me.

His sculpted lips were perfect against hers. She kissed him harder. He kissed her back, opening his mouth and caressing her tongue with his own. She moaned softly, dropping sweet hints of ecstasy. She pulled her body closer to his, feeling totally surrendered to him.

She leaned harder against his body, pulling away her robe to let her firm breasts press against him. They lay down together, wrapping their legs around each other. As their tongues danced, she grabbed up his robe and pulled it over his head. She threw her own robe off and pushed her whole body against his.

As he kissed her neck, more moans of perfect pleasure escaped her lips.

"I'm very new to this," he said.

She rolled onto her back and held Caio so he stayed above her. She grabbed between his legs, squeezed him, and guided him to her ...

Chapter 66: The Veil of the Enemy

LUCIA WOKE AGAIN TO VOICES. She guessed the men were coming to see her and sat up, leaning forward over the edge of the raised wooden board that was her bed.

Sunlight streamed through a window, illuminating the dust floating in the air of her cell. The reeking air assaulted her stomach. She pulled up her robe to inhale the herbs the Pawelons had pressed against her with their cloth bandage. She shivered, her body still suffering from fever.

She knew the sages had used some of their healing magic on her during the night. She had been vaguely aware of it while she slept, a presence like a warm cocoon, circulating energy throughout her body.

The same number of soldiers and sages stood around the room. After some commotion beyond the door, the warriors stood at attention. The hinges screeched again and a man entered by himself.

Their prince!

"Your Grace," the prince said in Rezzian, "I am Prince Rao. Let me say first that if you cause me any harm, you will be killed."

That's how I'm going to die then. "What do you want?"

"Please start by telling me what happened yesterday. I stabbed *him.* I didn't stab *you,* but you were there. I had no time to react. Did you willingly trade places with your brother?"

You want me to admit it so you can have me put to death.

"Well?" he asked.

"I don't know what happened. I only know I'm here."

"Your brother is alive."

Thank you, Ysa!

"You're saying you didn't cause your brother to disappear?"

"No," she lied.

"Then was it the gods themselves?"

You think I know what the gods are thinking? "I suppose it was."

"I had no time to react," he said.

"What are you saying, you wouldn't have killed me anyway?"

"I could have easily killed you after I stabbed you. I worked very hard yesterday to keep you alive."

He had a point. "Why?"

"Because I need your help to end this war."

Liar. "And that's why you tracked and hunted us at the lake?"

"Of course we didn't." The prince's face flushed with some frustration. "We had no idea you were there. Your friend threw a spear at my friend—remember? Why would we try to hunt you down after you agreed to the duel?"

"So that you wouldn't have to fight my brother fairly?"

"No." The bastard was either a very good actor, or telling the truth. "I wanted this war to be over *after* our duel. The single combat was my idea. Remember?"

Then it was all due to Lord Danato. Lucia slouched back against the wall as the realization sunk in.

The prince rubbed his forehead as if accepting difficult facts. "You're telling me you weren't hunting us?"

"No!"

"Then it was a perfect coincidence?"

Lucia remembered Danato's directions that sent her and Caio to the lake that night. *No, not such coincidence at all.*

Lucia was surprised to find the prince, at least to this point, different than she expected him to be. His act made him seem reasonable. He also seemed to be wounded, dragging his legs as if it hurt to walk.

"Your people are the ones who keep this going," he said, pointing.

"I'll have you know my brother and I were trying to stop this war. That's the only reason he agreed to your duel."

"Funny, the day before I proposed the duel, you and your brother ambushed our men after you hid behind the rainstorm. I wouldn't call that an act of peace."

Lucia put herself in Prince Rao's place and understood his thinking. "A lot changed after that battle. After what you and your friend did to me and Ilario."

"Ilario. The one who died. Was he the Haizzem's protector?"

"Yes and much more. Because he died, my brother's no longer in the same mind. He wants to conquer Pawelon now."

271

Prince Rao paced the room with difficulty, drawing and exhaling long breaths.

"You're saying your brother wanted to attack us on the day you came for us hidden behind the rainstorm. Then soon after that he changed his mind, so that by the time I proposed the duel, or soon after that, he wanted peace. Then after Ilario died, Caio wanted to conquer Pawelon again?"

"That's mostly true, except he never wanted there to be a war in the first place. When we hid our army behind the storm, we were hoping to deal such a powerful blow that it would shock your nation into surrendering. And it was my idea. He went along with it." Lucia rubbed her aching temples, aware she needed more rest.

The Pawelon prince continued his slow pacing, apparently sorting out the details in his mind. "I want to make sure I understand. You're saying that Ilario's death changed everything for Caio. And you're saying it was a coincidence that we found you at the lake. I find that impossible to believe."

This bastard's mind is sharp. Lucia hesitated. "The truth is ..." She looked to her right at one of the many soldiers staring at her. "One of our gods told us to go to the lake that night."

"Mya? Oderigo? Or Ysa?"

And he knows a lot about us. "No. Lord Danato."

"Interesting," he said.

"You know our gods?"

"Oh yes, I've studied them." He stopped his pacing. "Then your black god was trying to hunt us."

He was hunting his own people. "I don't think so."

"Why else would he send you there?"

"Lord Danato is a perverse figure. I've given up trying to understand him."

The prince tilted his head to one side. "And you had a relationship with Ilario?"

"That's not your concern."

"You said so to my lady."

Lucia scrolled through her memory of that night. *I did say something to the girl about him.* "I'm not going to discuss my private life with you."

The prince's eyes widened, looking compassionate for a moment. "I am sorry for your loss. I didn't want to hurt Ilario. In that instant, I had no choice. It was either my friend or yours. I am very sorry."

Lucia stared down at the dirty stone floor and fought back her emotions.

The prince looked over Lucia's body. "How are you? Are our healers helping you?"

Lucia's entire body ached with fever, but she had to admit that her health had improved. "Considering I should be dead now, I won't complain about anything yet except for this gods-forsaken cell."

Rao nodded. "And you should, but we don't have a better place to hold someone like you."

"Is Duilio here, too? Our Strategos?"

"I shouldn't talk about that." Rao stepped closer to the bars of the cell. "What about your arms? Can I see them?"

Realizing it made no difference anymore, Lucia pulled back her sleeves. A moment later, she pulled the sleeves down again.

"Amazing," he said.

"They are tattoos."

"Briraji has canny senses. He said you would say that, and that you are lying."

The sage is called Briraji. Remember, the sage is Briraji. "Well then I can't convince you, can I?"

"Would you try?" he asked.

Lucia became aware of herself shaking her head in frustration, then stopped, not wanting to give the prince any more clues. "They are tattoos."

"There has never been a time with two Haizzem, has there?"

"Exactly. It's impossible."

"Unless this is the first time in history." Rao's hand shot to his chin. He scratched it as if experiencing a revelation. He took slow steps, a few in one direction, a few in another, keeping his head turned toward his prisoner.

"Let's talk about something else then," he said. "Think back to the day you and your goddess created the great lightning storm. Do you know I'm the one that stopped you?"

"I felt an evil presence around me before I fell down unconscious." The prince smiled, but Lucia continued, "We found out later you had taken credit for stopping me. So it *was* you."

"Your Grace, I did stop the storm, but as I did I sent you a message of peace. I could have really hurt you or killed you. And then at the ambush, after the rainstorm, I could have killed you and the man who came after you. You said that was also Ilario?"

"Yes." And Lucia realized he was right, that he could have hurt her and Ilario much worse that day. *But he wanted our army to retreat. That's why he didn't kill us.*

"I am a man of peace. I wanted to negotiate a conclusion to this war, but you were gone before we were able to discuss it."

His words were very, very hard to accept. She knew he was a skilled liar. "What do you want from me?" she asked.

"I want your people to go back to their homes and leave Pawelon alone."

Gods! Could it be? Could she have misjudged him this much?

"Your father offered to give back to us my lady Narayani in exchange for you. Our general and my father said no."

"How did my father capture her? I have to tell you, I saw her there, interfering with your combat."

For the first time, the prince looked afraid. "What do you mean you saw her?"

"I saw her arguing with my brother. She saved your life."

The prince's face stretched long in shock. "I have to go now. I want you to consider something. Remember I did not hurt you or kill you the first two times I had the chance—"

"Except when your friend tried to smash my face."

"We were defending ourselves. You came for us. Your Grace, I want to work with you." The prince looked around the room and continued speaking in Rezzian, as before, "My general has his own ideas. Your father does, too. But think about what we can do together to end this war. Consider this."

Lucia watched Prince Rao exit the room without another glance or word for her. She needed more time to think over their conversation.

Chapter 67:
The Measure of Old Dreams

DUILIO FELT GRATEFUL staring at the jagged stone walls of his ancient prison cell. The old Strategos had been granted another miracle, another day of life. He had a bench to sit on, a little bit of water to drink, and a little bowl of lentil soup, even if it hadn't been seasoned with any of those wonderful Pawelon spices.

He had been stripped of everything. His horse and armor and weapons, even his necklace bearing the ivory symbol of Lord Cosimo. His dear father had given it to him during his youth, in an era that felt as if it occurred many lifetimes ago.

In his solitude, away from soldiers and weapons and unbearable sun and a king and his two royal children, Duilio found his entire life to be a wispy memory, something once so important: every love, every pain, every near-sighted hope and dream. Had those old dreams mattered? Attaining his station? Raising three beloved children? Winning a war? He couldn't decide. Either those old dreams had mattered not one bit, or their measure was and always would be boundless.

Now, on what could be the last day of his life—he still didn't know what the Pawelons would do with him—he felt grateful for another breath of air, however soiled by stale urine and new feces, because each breath gave him another chance to remember his god, The Lord of Miracles, and to hope he was a worthy recipient of Cosimo's divine grace.

Footsteps and low voices sounded from outside his cell. The act of sitting up reminded Duilio how emaciated he felt by his impoverished conditions. It was a hoary creak, the moan of the door's hinges. He wondered how many centuries the metal had labored.

General Indrajit entered. Duilio stood and bowed his head just enough to salute him. The enormous rajah entered the room after the general.

The two Pawelon men stood side by side, a little closer to the cell than to the center of the room, close enough to be intimate, but not uncomfortably so.

"I have a question," the rajah said in his rumbling voice. "We have taken the king's daughter—"

"Lucia?"

Rajah Devak nodded. "I threatened King Vieri, told him that if he does not retreat I will do unthinkable things to her."

The rajah's threat reminded Duilio how many horrors were committed in the dark corners of their world.

"Your king replied," the rajah continued, "saying if we lay a finger on his daughter, he will not stop until every Pawelon woman and child is a Rezzian slave, until every man and every bit of Pawelon culture is gone."

Rajah Devak took two more steps toward Duilio. "Tell me, knowing how we have threatened him, would King Vieri attack us again?"

Duilio licked his lips and realized he was probably smiling. "Vieri loves his son and his daughter. He also loves his war. I am sorry. I really can't tell you which he loves more."

Chapter 68: Choosing War or Peace

CAIO WANDERED THROUGH THE DESERT VALLEY under the dome of night, toward Pawelon's citadel. The moon filled the canyon with sparkling white light, illuminating each tiny leaf and red stone. He hiked up the northern route to the fortress and closed the distance with ease.

The goddess Mya beckoned him toward the massive citadel with a wave of her hand, her pale back facing Caio as she walked in front of him.

"Mya, wait for me."

The goddess maintained her steady pace. Caio ran. Her soft shoulders reflected the milky light of the moon. Once Caio reached her, she stopped and looked up at the great stone walls.

Keeping her gaze upon the Pawelon fortress, she asked, "What is your wish, my son?"

"I want Lucia back safely. And I want to make my decision, to choose either war or peace."

"I can help you have whichever you wish." Mya paused. "My son, if you would destroy your enemy's citadel, witness how I would have it done."

Mya moved no limb, nor diverted her gaze, but her hair and the leaves of her vine dress flew and fluttered in the sudden storm. The enchanting light of the moon was eclipsed behind expanding brown clouds condensing out of a clear, black sky. The scent of heavy rain blew on the gusting wind.

Caio pulled his *cremos* robe more tightly around himself just as the storm's rains began to pound the hard desert. A wicked squall knocked him down, flat against the earth. The storm wailed and howled like the fury of the god Lord Danato himself. Caio found himself unable to stand upright in the wind. He crawled through the downpour to a rock formation and wedged himself between two boulders leaning into each other.

Unrelenting waves of rain crashed against the citadel's walls like a swell devouring a child's sand castle. Mya's form had already vanished.

A square section of the leading wall broke down and collapsed, spilling rock onto the ground. The hole grew larger with each gust from the storm, until the east-facing wall disintegrated into a mass of rubble.

'*'

Caio awoke lying on his side, with warm, smooth legs rubbing against his own. A moment later, he felt Narayani pressing her chest against his back, draping an arm over his body. He turned over and smiled.

She smiled back. "Did you have any dreams?"

He remembered the storm against the citadel. "Yes," he said.

Caio held Narayani close and felt her heart, both physically and spiritually. He sensed all of her emotional swings, more acutely than he had with anyone he'd ever known.

He knew she felt safe with him in that moment, but she remained confused underneath her attempts to persuade herself she could commit herself to living with him. She would need to confront those emotions later. Not now. Her instinct for survival motivated her to make love with him and to heal him, but he knew she felt love for him and might consider remaining with him.

"I can't remember if I had dreams," she said.

You did. You dreamed of Rao. You were at a beach with him. You were happy together.

She lowered her lips to Caio's neck and left a soft kiss. Then another. Another ...

"My Haizzem!" a man's voice from outside the yurt interrupted them. "Forgive me. Your father wishes to see you immediately. He is at the pavilion."

"Very well. I'll be there soon."

Caio tried to pull away from Narayani, but she held onto his painted arms.

"Don't go," she said.

"You are safe here. I'll return as soon as I can."

The light pouring in through the ceiling indicated the morning was young. Narayani threw off the sheet and lay on her side in the nude, facing him. Caio dressed himself in a long, light blue tunic and walked to his altar.

"How do you feel?" she asked.

"Even better today. Thank you for what you've done."

278

He splashed scented oils on his skin and tunic and stared at The Book of Time. Though he had thrown the book against a wall three days ago, its spine showed no sign of tearing.

He knelt and prayed to Mya and Oderigo, prostrating and kneeling, prostrating and kneeling, prostrating and kneeling.

When he stood up, Narayani was clutching a pillow against her chest with a trickle of tears wetting her face. He sensed what was in her heart: she worried he would not come back.

He sat on the bed beside her and caressed her hair and cheeks. "I command these men. This is my army, and I will not let anything happen to you."

She sniffled and gazed at him with those dark, sensual eyes. He pulled some of her wet hair away from her cheek.

"There's plenty of fruit and bread on the table. Eat as much as you like. You *can* trust me, Narayani. I care about you."

Caio kissed her forehead and exited his yurt. The soldiers knelt all around him. He blessed them, touching the crowns of their heads while thinking of the gods.

"I am your Dux Spiritus and you will obey me. Let no one enter my yurt until I return. This is an irrevocable order. Is this understood?"

"Yes, my Haizzem," they said together.

"It is also very important that you not let her out for any reason, no matter what she says. She has everything she needs inside that room. She has food. She has water. She has everything she needs for hygiene. She has the power to conceal herself so that you cannot see her. Do not open the door, no matter what she says."

The guards agreed.

Caio began the walk with a contingent of ten soldiers around him. His muscles felt almost normal again, just a bit sore, after just two full days with Narayani.

He asked the soldiers accompanying him how they fared, and comforted two of them who had not seen their families in years. He asked the men to join him in praying that they would meet their loved ones again soon. Caio prayed he would be alive when it happened.

He enjoyed the walk; it gave him time to contemplate everything happening with Narayani. Lucia's last words still echoed in his mind: "*He (Lord Danato) said this war will not and cannot end before one of you dies—either you or Pawelon's prince.*" If

279

true, if Rao were the one to die, Narayani would need someone else to love and protect her. If she wished to remain with Caio in Rezzia, he might someday take her as his queen. Caio had never known such sweet intimacy.

His thoughts turned to Mya's words. *"I want to make a decision,"* he told her in his dream. *"To choose either war or peace."*

"I can help you have whatever you wish," Mya told him.

He marveled at his words in the dream realm. In waking life, he had already made his decision. He found his father at the lookout and waved up at him. More soldiers lowered themselves to the ground in waves as Caio approached the stairs. He touched their heads and imparted the spirit of Lux Lucis to them.

"How do you feel, Son?" his father's rich voice carried on the gentle wind.

"Healed, father," he yelled as he began to climb. "She has healed me."

His father said no other words until Caio met him. They exchanged a Rezzian handshake, grabbing each other's right forearms. His father squeezed Caio's uninjured shoulder and led him to the west-facing edge of the pavilion.

The sky opened out. An unusual panorama of white clouds spread out like wings embracing the heavens. The morning air remained crisp and cool against Caio's skin. They stood side by side, staring at the Pawelon citadel in the distance.

Caio sensed his father wanted to convince him of something. If Caio's guess was right, convincing him would not be difficult.

"Then you are ready for the next phase?" his father asked.

"I am ready for whatever comes next."

"Have you had enough time to think over our last conversation?"

"I have. You are right, Father. We may never see Lucia again if we leave this valley. Who knows what cruel things they would do to her? If they are going to harm her, we must stop them. If she is suffering, we owe her that."

His father smiled and glanced at him. "If our gods will not obey us now, with Lucia and Duilio in a Pawelon dungeon, then when? We can appeal to Ysa, too. The Protector of Man must be enraged."

"Mya came to me in a dream last night. She showed me that she could destroy the walls of the citadel with a divine rain. Perhaps Ysa would contribute as well."

"I won't wait while Lucia suffers."

Caio sensed his father feeling a great fear. "What are you afraid of, Father?"

His father straightened up his posture and his face grew intractable and proud. "We cannot trust their rajah. He is a vindictive man."

Caio rubbed his father's back with his right hand to comfort him. He prayed to Mya to soothe his father's pain. "Give your worries to Lord Galleazzo. Ask him for his grace."

His father awkwardly raised his left hand and rested it on Caio's back. The sides of their bodies touched one another.

"The army is prepared to leave at any time," his father said. "We should fight today."

Be with us, Lux Lucis. "Very well."

His father placed his hands on Caio's cheeks and turned him until they faced each other. "It is good for the Pawelon girl that she has done a noble deed for the gods of light. She has healed you. She has healed our very Haizzem. This will be good for her soul."

"Father, I do not want her to be harmed."

His father stepped back and searched his son's eyes. "She is a political prisoner. I will do with her as I wish."

"Isn't she a military prisoner? She was captured on the field of battle. I believe she falls under my domain."

"She is a girl, not a warrior. She is the lady of Prince Rao."

"Yet you are saying she can be put to death for interfering with a military matter."

"Exactly what would you do with her then?" His father raised his voice and spoke more harshly, "She nearly got you killed. And she prevented you from killing their prince and winning your duel. Our people demand full justice."

"I don't want her to be harmed. No. Under no circumstances." Caio weighed out whether to say it or not, then spoke his mind. "I could love her."

His father threw up his hands and showed his teeth as he opened his mouth in shock. "Gods be damned! She's a witch, taking control of your mind. Her foul herbs are further means of her dark magic."

"No they are not. She healed me. I can feel her heart. She only wanted to heal me." *And to save herself.*

"She may be killing you, Caio. Not all poison acts quickly."

"No. She is scared. Like many, her life has been ruined by this war. She deserves a good life, like anyone else."

"Damn, Caio, you have gone mad." His father stared at him with pained eyes, trying to make Caio feel ashamed. "Do not. I repeat, do *not* get attached to this pig."

The king walked away with an air of finality. Caio accepted that he would not hear another word. He sensed that his father intended to make Narayani pay for what happened to Lucia and for the outcome of the duel.

I will change your mind.

Chapter 69:
Killing in the Face of Death

SANYAT, A YOUNG PAWELON SOLDIER, pressed himself against the mass of bodies trying to squeeze through the narrowest section of the southern trail. The stench of thousands of unwashed soldiers lingered throughout the tightly packed unit. His spear tip pointed upward, as did all the others.

Random voices yelled:

"Keep moving!"

"Move!"

"They're nearly here!"

The Rezzians had marched straight into the valley with their forces, not giving away their destination, then turned suddenly en masse toward the southern trail leading up to the citadel. The soldier's commander decided, perhaps too late, to retreat with all of the southern spearmen to defend the trail at its narrowest point, supported by the archers hiding throughout the cliffs.

The soldier finally passed between the two cliff walls and continued pushing forward. "There are many behind us! Move faster!"

The ground almost seemed to shake as the pounding feet and roars of the Rezzian army arose from below. Sanyat felt the rumbling noise in his chest.

The Pawelon soldiers hiked up the trail, filling the area to create a dense wall of bodies. As the Rezzians approached, the Pawelons raised their shields into a tight tapestry to block the Rezzian throwing spears.

The attack began with the sounds of arrows and the screams of injured men.

A spear banged against Sanyat's shield, just above his head, and knocked him onto his knees. The man to Sanyat's left grabbed his armpit and lifted him up again. Sanyat found his shield more difficult to keep steady with the spear embedded in it.

"Hold strong! Hold position!" a Pawelon commander yelled.

A resounding cheer arose down the slope from the Rezzians.

"What's happening?" the soldier asked.

"I can't see," the dark-skinned soldier beside him answered.

Screams arose from the Pawelon forces, in one section after another, followed by the disturbing howls of injured and dying men. Sanyat felt his heart beating faster, his mouth dry from his quick breaths.

He pulled back his shield just enough to see what was happening. He watched a massive golden beast leap over his head. A lioness, larger than five normal lions, landed on nearby Pawelon shields and knocked over dozens of men.

"Their king is here," the soldier beside him said, "and his lions are huge again."

Sanyat fell as the men behind him pushed forward. He cried out as heavy Pawelon boots stomped on his legs and over his back. The harrowing sounds of dying men surrounded him.

He was just beginning to stand again when one of the golden beasts leapt toward him.

Its paw knocked the wind from his chest and pressed him to the ground. Sanyat squirmed beneath its incredible weight, unable to breathe.

He screamed as the beast's fanged mouth tore into his skull.

‘*’

The Rezzians marched on to higher ground, to the citadel itself, as Pawelon stocked its high walls with archers and sages. The Rezzians stopped within view of the fortress, outside the range of bows and arrows.

The great storm began with gale winds howling around the great fortification. Every now and then the wind carried an audible hint of a woman's screams. Moisture rapidly condensed throughout the area. The wetness stuck to the walls of the citadel, collected along weaponry, and slid down soldiers' bodies under their armor. Expanding brown clouds tumbled in from the east like fat ghouls seeking souls, darkening the earth and sky.

The wind and rain slammed against the fortress, wave after wave. Pawelon's archers struggled atop the walls to keep from being thrown to their deaths. Many failed. Pawelon's sages focused their powers to weaken the elements, but the storm of the Rezzian divinities raged on.

‘*’

Indrajit climbed the stairs of the tower at the northeast corner of the fortress with two impressive guards behind him and two more ahead. The scent of rain brought an ironic freshness to the musty chamber. The viciousness of the storm echoed throughout the stairwell from far above, interspersed with the shouting of commands. Rezzia hadn't threatened the citadel so convincingly since the early years of the war.

They walked in silence. Indrajit preferred to think. He recognized the turning tide. He'd hoped that with the royal daughter in a Pawelon prison, the Haizzem would not have the power to overwhelm Pawelon's defenses by himself. Making matters worse, the king's lions had grown in power and Rao was still too injured to concentrate on his abilities. Perhaps if Rezzia could be kept at bay a few more days, Rao would be able to keep the Haizzem's power in check.

Indrajit carried another burden. He worried about Rao's wishes and plans for the king's daughter and Strategos Duilio, but especially matters regarding the royal daughter. His soldiers had relayed to him the topics of Rao's daily conversations with the Rezzian woman, and each day the trust between Rao and Lucia seemed to grow.

The severity of the storm surprised Indrajit as he neared the tower's top. Its force seemed greater than he had expected in every way: the remarkable strength of the wind, the explosiveness of rain smashing against stone, the haunting woman's screams.

Briraji stood where he had been assigned, in the protected chamber at the top of the tower. He stood with eyes closed in a meditative posture surrounded by three other sages and far too many archers trying to hide from the storm.

"Briraji, come with me."

The other sages and the soldiers stood at attention and saluted Indrajit with their fists raised high. Indrajit turned away.

Briraji followed as they headed back down the stairs to the first alcove that would afford them some privacy. They sat on uncomfortable stone benches against the walls, facing one another. A small candle flickered, battling the cool draft, in the deepest corner of the tiny room. Indrajit's guards were sent to wait for them at the top and bottom of the tower.

"How does it look?" Indrajit asked.

Briraji scowled, looking down and then up again. "I can do nothing against the storm. None of our sages can."

"Why not?"

"There are two Rezzian goddesses working together to create the storm. Their powers are combined, much greater than the sum of the two."

"Then the king's daughter is invoking her goddess's powers."

"Almost certainly, General."

"As I feared. We can't risk her presence any longer, not with those markings on her arms. Kill her."

Briraji bowed. "Right away, General?"

"Yes. We've waited too long." Indrajit stepped outside the alcove to make sure no one else was nearby, then returned to his seat. "I'll tell you what I have heard about Rao. He has been speaking with the king's daughter every day. She still doesn't fully trust him, but she has softened her doubts. He continues to hint to her they should find a way to negotiate a peace—"

"And by that," Briraji interrupted, "he likely intends to return this female Haizzem to the Rezzian army in exchange for Narayani."

"Of course Rao would be fooled."

Briraji shook his head in disgust and swung an arm through the air in frustration.

"Kill her now. The storm should weaken once she's dead. Knowing that Rao is around her makes me uncomfortable."

"I will, General." Briraji stood and saluted.

Indrajit remained seated. "And relay this order to my trusted officers around the prison before you kill her. If our prince gets in your way or theirs, if he does or says anything that indicates he wishes to free any Rezzian prisoner, kill him too. Without another warning, those soldiers and sages must kill Prince Rao. He will not use our prisoners to negotiate with."

"What if our rajah finds out?"

"These men are loyal to me. If it comes to that, tell them to blame his death on the king's daughter. If that fails and I need to deal with Devak myself, I will."

Briraji looked down at Indrajit, drawing and releasing one long breath. "I will certainly follow and relay your orders."

'*'

Briraji gave Indrajit's orders to the two trusted officers stationed at the prison. The long-serving officers had been reassigned from their combat duties after the king's daughter was captured. Briraji watched them relay the orders to the men under their command.

The sage walked up and down the wide hall of the prison, staring at the metal doors to the cells and the stone walls. Water still dripped from his uniform. The handfuls of soldiers patrolling the hall wore the finest Pawelon armor, combinations of leather and plates covered in dark blue and purple cloaks, and carried only well-maintained shields and spears. Indrajit had taken the prison's defense with the utmost seriousness.

Briraji reflected on his orders. The woman was still recovering from what should have been her fatal wound, but he was convinced her markings showed her to have the powers of a Haizzem. She had not used any of her magic since being captured, not overtly, but she had most likely contributed to the storm outside with her prayers.

He decided how he would kill her. He would suffocate her in a black psychic field, searing her consciousness with burning embers.

Once he decided how it would be done, he couldn't keep his thoughts away from Prince Rao. The prince was old enough to take his father's position, should anything happen to Devak.

Briraji stopped in front of the door to the royal daughter's cell.

"Do you wish to enter, sir?" The soldier standing beside the door asked.

Briraji centered his mind and visualized her death. He saw it clearly, giving him confidence he would be able to do it whenever he wished to.

"Not yet," he said.

He began walking the hallway again, one persistent thought tempting him.

I will find out where the prince's loyalties lie.

Decided, he stopped at Duilio's cell instead.

"Let me in," he told the nearest soldier.

The old Strategos was sitting up when Briraji entered.

"Good day," the old man said in Pawelon. "What is going on with the weather?"

Briraji smiled a little. "Your goddesses."

The Strategos showed no reaction on his face.

Oh, I know you're happy to hear that. "And that is why Lucia is going to die."

Ha. You can't hide your emotions this time.

The Strategos ran forward to the metal bars of his cell and pleaded, "You don't need to do that. She's much more valuable to you alive. If you hurt her, you *will* suffer the wrath of my king."

"He's not your king anymore. You're our prisoner and slave."

"Please think this through. Think of how Pawelon will suffer from Rezzia's vengeance."

"We don't intend to suffer."

"Our king has fought a noble war, focusing his efforts only on your army. Kill his daughter and he will do everything he can to make your people suffer. Think about what you're doing."

"We are not intimidated by your impotent king."

"Think of the Haizzem then."

"I will match your Haizzem. Our young prince almost finished him."

"This will be a grave mistake, sage. I swear to you."

"Good day, Strategos."

The doors closed behind Briraji as the old man continued to beg.

Briraji exited through the front of the prison and began walking through the raging storm. He pushed through stiff wind and stinging rain to find Prince Rao and tell him he intended to kill Rezzia's royal daughter.

Chapter 70:
Honor Among Enemies

A DRENCHED PAWELON SOLDIER entered Rao's room. The balding man stopped just past the doorway and sneezed as he saluted.

Rao interrupted the old healer who was massaging a warm oil along the length of his body. He stood, wearing his simple loincloth, and returned the soldier's salute. "Thank you for surveying the battle."

"Of course, Prince Rao."

"How does it look?"

"I've never seen such an effect. Both armies have become spectators. The storm is doing actual damage to our eastern wall."

"How much damage?"

"I would guess it's possible that sections of the wall could be destroyed within days."

Unbelievable. "Have our sages been able to do anything about it?"

The soldier frowned and shook his head. "If they have, not much, my Prince."

A terrible fear had been gnawing at Rao throughout the day, ever since the storm began: was Lucia's goddess involved?

"Have you seen any lightning today?"

"Yes, my Prince."

"How much?"

"Some. Not a lot."

"Thank you. That will be all."

If Lucia's goddess was responsible he needed to speak with Lucia right away. He told the healer, "Please leave. I need to rest and regain my strength. I want no interruptions. No one can enter my room. Go tell everyone else I am not to be bothered."

The healer bowed and exited as asked.

289

Rao dressed himself again in his sage's uniform. He stretched his arms over his head and twisted his torso. His muscles still ached severely from head to toe, but at least the pain seemed to be lessening a little each day.

Unsure about what would happen when he spoke with Lucia, he couldn't risk being seen by anyone until he reached the prison. Rao closed his eyes and visualized the sacred syllables of Aayu's *sadhana* across his inner vision. He felt his body becoming lighter—then his body shivered, his musculature clenched in pain, and the benefit of Aayu's *sadhana* failed. His stomach felt ill. He sat on his bed to recover his strength. The failure reminded him that his body was still drained of *ojas*.

Try again.

He concentrated perfectly for seven long breaths and activated Aayu's *sadhana* successfully the second time. He slipped out through the barely open door, and shut it behind him. With luck, no one in the building would know he'd even left.

Once outside, Aayu's *sadhana* allowed him to walk through the courtyard without the vicious downpour touching him. The soldiers who were trying to walk between buildings dealt with the stiff gusts. Many advanced slowly as they struggled against the wind; those moving with the storm stumbled forward like drunkards.

A figure coming from the prison walked toward him. Rao looked down at his body reflexively to see if he remained hidden. *Of course I am hidden. The storm has no effect on me.* Briraji came into view. The sage looked even more intense than usual as he fought the storm, heading toward the same building Rao had just left.

Should I find out if he is coming to speak with me?

Rao watched the great sage dig into the dirt with his heels, pushing himself through the terrible storm with gritted teeth.

No. He wouldn't approve of what I am about to do.

Rao felt another shiver just as he neared the entrance to the prison. His stomached rippled with sickness again. The effect of Aayu's *sadhana* dissipated. The storm winds blew against his body, drenching his uniform.

He approached the building and walked under the cover of the parti-colored canopy, which normally created shade from the sun. Three soldiers and one officer blocked the entrance. As he approached, one of the soldiers, a heavy man, put his hand on the pommel of his short sword. The rest of them stared.

Something feels wrong.

"May I enter?"

The men stepped back enough to allow entry, each with a solemn look on his face.

"What brings you here, Prince Rao?" The strong-jawed old officer raised a sharp eyebrow. His hands rested on his belt.

"You won't need your blade, will you?" Rao asked the soldier whose hand remained on his weapon.

"Of course not, my Prince."

The officer nodded as the soldier lowered his arms to his sides.

Rao searched the men's eyes, but found no camaraderie. "I would like to see the prisoner again. I want her to answer for this storm."

"Aye," the officer said, "she cannot be trusted."

Rao exhaled, releasing some tension, and nodded in agreement. "She is a Rezzian dog, after all. What do you think about this storm, men?"

One of the soldiers spoke slowly while looking at the others as if to gauge their reactions. "It's not right, is it?"

"No, it's not right," a different soldier said. "It's not right at all—"

The third soldier interrupted, sounding more certain. "We have our duties, no matter what may come."

"Right," Rao said. "I heard our losses were severe among the southern defenses today."

"They were," the officer said. "I spoke with Briraji not long ago."

"He was here?" Rao asked.

The officer pursed his lips and his jaw muscles twitched as he clenched them. He nodded just enough to indicate yes.

"Do you know where Master Briraji went? I need to speak with him."

"I don't know, my Prince," the officer said. "I am certain he will be back soon."

"So many men dying." Rao looked around, shaking his head. "It doesn't have to be."

"It is a war," the officer said. "And anyone foolish enough to stand against Pawelon must die."

"Yes, of course. All of you are fully committed to your duty, then?"

The third soldier said, "Yes, we are."

"You are good men." Rao raised his fist in salute. "You make my father proud."

The four returned his salute.

Rao walked further into the building, still feeling the tension from the previous encounter. He wondered what Briraji told the guards. They seemed to eye him like a threat.

He stopped to focus on his breath and recall the place's layout. The ancient structure had been adapted to hold prisoners, so there would be no places to hide. He took a sudden turn into the wide hallway to his right, toward the guards' chambers. Streaks of grey light streamed through a few small windows at the end of the corridor. At the end of the hallway, three armed guards paced the shadows.

Two of them stepped forward and halted, blocking entrance. "Honorable Prince Rao! Please stop! We have orders to allow no one into this area."

"My brothers, have you heard what is going on out there? It's a nightmare. We can do nothing against this storm. I have been sent by order of my father, your rajah, to claim the arms of the Rezzian prisoner. She once used her goddess's sword and shield to create a deadly lightning storm. We believe I may be able to use these objects to *end* this storm."

They glanced at one another, avoiding responsibility.

"You'll let me in then?"

A second soldier spoke up, "These were strict orders from general Indrajit. No one, he told us, no one can come in here."

"Of course he did, and you are in the right. But now things have changed. The rajah himself commanded me. Please. Open this door for me." Rao walked toward them, doing his best to seem relaxed and confident. "Or give me the key."

Two of them looked at each other for an answer while the third looked aside and scratched his head.

"Please hurry," Rao said. "Our citadel is being battered by the Rezzian gods. Men are dying."

The third soldier walked up to Rao. "I will not disobey my rajah," he said as he procured a key latched behind his breastplate. He opened the lock to the room where Lucia's arms were being held.

"It's dark in there," Rao said. "Where are her things?"

The soldier stepped into the room with Rao. He pointed to the opposite wall. "All the way over there, sir."

Rao waded into the mess, stepping around small piles of clothes, boots and shoes, and personal items from bags to trinkets. His eyes continued to adjust to the darkness.

Rao heard the soldier step outside the room and hoped he hadn't misjudged the man's intentions.

Ysa's sword and shield leaned against the far wall, above a pile of her armor. He hoped for the best as he picked up the sword and then the shield. He was relieved to find that neither object blasted him with any divine protections.

Thank you ... Ysa?

His fingers curled around the soft yellow and white handle of the sword—a surprisingly sensual experience—and he had to restrain himself from his sudden desire to swing the white blade in circles through the air. He also admired the shield's face, its concentric red and yellow circles. He could feel the pith of the object's history and wondered how many tales it would tell if it could. He gripped the shield's leather-wrapped metal handle in one hand and carried the sword, pointed down, in the other.

Just as he turned to leave, he noticed a brown necklace and two black gloves beneath the armor. He rested the white sword against the wall and picked up the masculine twine, from which hung a black anvil. *Sansone's holy symbol,* he remembered. His intuition told him he would need it, though he couldn't imagine why. He tucked the necklace into a pocket along with the gloves and left the room with Lucia's sword in hand.

"Leave this door open," he told the men as he exited. "I'll be back soon."

He felt the eyes of the soldiers he'd initially encountered as he walked past the central axis of the building toward Lucia's cell. Outside her detention room, another handful of prized soldiers stood still and watched him.

The tallest soldier, a powerfully built young man, drew a long knife from his belt and held up his other hand. "What are you doing with her weapons, Prince Rao?"

"You would question your prince?"

"Yes, I have to. Those arms are not to come anywhere near the prisoner."

The other four soldiers quietly spread out and raised their own weapons, circling Rao.

"What is going on here?" Rao asked.

"We were told you might try to save the prisoner before she's killed."

"She is to be killed?" Rao worried that he sounded too surprised.

"General Indrajit's orders." The soldier did not flinch as he stared and searched Rao for a reaction.

"Good. Then you won't stop me from doing it myself." Rao transformed his face with a relaxed grin. "I figure what better way to kill the bitch than with her own sword. She's killed enough of ours with it."

The soldier let go his own tense expression and smiled. "Briraji was going to do it himself."

"Yes, he was. Then he came and talked to me. I told him I would do it for him, and let him return to serving our general, fighting the storm. He agreed, saying he was needed elsewhere. Look at this blade." Rao stepped back and twisted the immaculate white metal, raising and lowering it. "Imagine her blood upon it."

The soldiers looked to one another. One of them nodded.

"Very well, sir," the tall soldier said. "We will come in and watch you do it."

"Excellent," Rao said.

Not excellent.

‘*’

Lucia heard the voices outside the room and thought she heard Rao's voice among them. She stood and wrapped her fingers around the discolored metal bars. Soon the door opened, but slowly. Whoever was coming in paused for some time. An ominous sensation sunk into her belly.

My goddess, I trust in you. May your will be done.

Lucia glimpsed an impossible image.

Gods!

The silver-armored goddess entered the room, Ysa herself. The goddess's helm covered most of her blond hair, but her face appeared as it did in books and paintings, pale with pointed, petite features.

Lucia dropped to her knees and expelled her breath in shock. Shivers ran down her arms.

You've come to me, after all this time?

The image of her goddess disappeared, and in her place walked Prince Rao, carrying Ysa's white sword and her shield.

294

Five soldiers followed behind Rao. The dozen men already in the room stood. One drew his short blade, and the others drew their weapons too. The room filled with silent tension, no one wanting to initiate whatever was to come.

"Your Grace," Rao said in Pawelon. "I am here at the order of my general. Because of this storm, and because we believe your goddess is behind it, he has ordered you to be slain. I am here to do it myself, using your own sword."

Why did I ever consider a word you said?

"Relax, men," the prince told the fourteen soldiers and three sages. They didn't. "Now, you murderous dog, continue to stand where you are. Don't make me come into your cell. Stand still and die with dignity."

The prince took one step forward with Ysa's shield on one arm and her sword pointed down at his side.

Where are you, Danato? You hideous black bastard. Am I dreaming, or are you going to kill me now?

The prince took another careful step toward her.

Wherever you are, you must be enjoying yourself. Laughing at me. Not caring one bit for 'your daughter.'

Another step.

Fine then. Go ahead and take me. I'll find out soon enough if I'm dreaming or not.

Another.

And if I die, then take my blood for Caio's. Let my brother live.

The Prince leaned forward and whispered in Rezzian, "We're getting out of here. Take the sword. If I'm attacked, protect me." He turned the pommel of the sword toward Lucia and handed it to her through the prison bars. "To prove myself, I turn my back to you."

Rao spun around and leaned his back against the cell. He held the shield to protect his chest. Most of the soldiers came forward a few steps and pointed their weapons at their prince.

"Wait!" Rao said. "General Indrajit gave you your orders. I know this. But hear me. No one has to get hurt. Pawelons killing Pawelons is insanity."

The leading sage answered in his smoky voice, "Surrender, my Prince, and your life may yet be saved. You know that we could blame your death on the prisoner."

"You are going to let us out of here," Lucia told the mob. Standing behind Rao, she raised Ysa's sword and felt a shock through her arm, invigorating her entire body. "You don't want to see what I can do with this."

A handful of soldiers stepped backward toward the entrance to the room. Two soldiers brandishing long daggers stepped toward Rao from his left and his right. Rao turned around and whispered to her, "Help." Lucia remembered the prince had suffered his own injuries at the duel.

Either Lucia saw an image of her goddess flash before her, or her eyes were lying to her again.

Protect both of us.

The two soldiers' boots thudded as they advanced along the stone floor. One yelled, "Go!" and ran forward.

Rao swung the shield in front of him, swatting at both daggers as they came for him. The steel blades clanged against ancient metal. Both attackers took a step back, one of them grimacing and shaking his hand and wrist. The sages closed their eyes and the semi-circle of men closed in.

"I will give you all one more warning," Lucia said in Pawelon. "After that, I will kill you all. That is the ancient shield of the goddess Ysa. It *will* protect your prince."

A sage standing against the opposite wall asked, "Why have you allied with our enemy?"

"That's not it at all," Rao said while turning his head to watch the men surrounding him. "She can help us end the entire war."

"You can't trust her," the sage said.

"My brothers, we don't have a better option."

Lucia stepped to her right to be in position to stab anyone charging Rao from that direction, knowing she could be attacked at any moment by the sages or a thrown weapon.

"One of you step forward and let me out now. This is the last time I will ask." Lucia held her sword in two hands and raised it, hoping she looked menacing in her filthy robe.

"These are good men, Lucia. They are following orders. They are only doing what they've been told." Rao nonetheless kept Ysa's shield close against his body. "We don't want to hurt you, just as we don't want to get hurt. If you let us out of here, you'll have my word that I will go to Rezzia and negotiate peace with them. Then all of us can return to our homeland. You can tell General Indrajit we escaped. You can blame it on me."

Silence, save the stirring of nervous feet.

The sage at the opposite wall spoke again. "Let's put down our weapons for now. Our rajah's only heir deserves a better death than this. Maybe he *can* stop this war."

No one spoke. A few soldiers lowered their long daggers.

"All we know is that Prince Rao came here, took her weapons, forced us to free her, and then left with her. Their magic kept us locked in here, so we could not chase them nor see where they went. If anyone disagrees with this, or isn't willing to tell this same story, say so now."

A soldier, a young man with a thick beard and black eyebrows, shot a look at the sage. "You're going to let her out of here?" He raised his blade in the air as he spoke.

"No, our prince is going to let this woman out of here. It's his choice. We should let him make it."

Another soldier, a thin man with long hair, said, "Prince Rao saved our entire unit from the lightning storm—"

"And we have our orders from the general himself," the bearded soldier fired back.

"My prince's orders are enough for me," the sage said. "I won't stand against him and I won't kill him while he is trying to save our people."

A middle-aged soldier, a man with a large, ruddy face, spoke from across the room, "If we do this, everyone must agree to tell the same story. If any one of you breaks this trust, you had better flee this place before we find you."

A sage came forward slowly, watching everyone around him, and unlocked the cell. The others stepped back and cleared a path to the door, though their faces looked much less generous. A soldier pushed the door slightly open.

Lucia walked with some difficulty, keeping her eyes moving around the room as she stayed two steps behind Rao. She turned to look behind her, to her right. She heard a clash of metal in front of her, then grunting.

She instantly brought her sword across her chest to defend herself. Rao held up Ysa's shield in front of her. The bearded Pawelon soldier lay on the ground in front of him, his dagger knocked out of his hand.

"Scum!" The insult flew from her tongue.

The soldiers tensed again and readied themselves for a confrontation.

"Stand back!" Rao spun, turning Ysa's shield in all directions. "Everyone calm down and no one will be hurt. Please."

Voices yelled from outside of the room, a great commotion. Among the words spoken, Lucia heard the word, "Briraji!"

The sage who unlocked the door raised his voice, "I am sorry, my Prince. Briraji is back."

"Wait," Rao said. "Give me three breaths."

Rao stood still with his eyes closed.

Ysa, save us!

Lucia felt her body disappear. She glimpsed everything around her for one instant as if she had eyes on the sides and back of her head. Then she felt her body again, but much lighter, as if it were air. The persistent pain in her chest was gone.

Rao's body wavered before her and then his form returned vividly. She realized then that she was seeing everyone else through a slight haze, but Rao looked solid and colorful.

"They can't see you anymore. You are invisible to them. We need to go now."

"Can we get my armor?"

He said with a quick turn of his head, "No time." Rao led her out of the room. The sage Briraji stood across the hall, close to a door. Soldiers ran around, positioning themselves outside the entrance to her former cell.

"How about my Strategos? Can we save him?"

"I'm sorry. I don't know how long this effect will last. We have to keep moving." Rao walked past Briraji and out the door. Briraji looked around quizzically as they passed by him, as if smelling something he couldn't locate.

She saw the great storm and heard the wind, but felt no rain against her 'body.' The weather was more dramatic than she'd expected.

"Your brother is fighting again," he said as he led her across the expansive courtyard.

"I see that. You can expect him to do everything in his power to rescue me. My father, too."

"That's why we have to talk to them."

"Where are we going?"

"We need to talk to my friend Aayu first. This might not be easy. He got himself locked up, too."

Chapter 71: Brotherhood

RAO'S STOMACH CLENCHED. He clutched his belly and fell to his knees. The downpour drenched his uniform a second time. His tight muscles throbbed again, all over his body.

Lucia returned to her physical form, too. "Ugh." She sounded like she might empty the contents of her stomach.

"It will get better." Rao looked around the courtyard and yelled to a group of four hooded soldiers running through the storm. "Come here!" He turned to Lucia. "Get down. Cover your head with the shield. I'll return soon."

She gave him a piercing look before she followed his directions. Rao left Lucia alone and ran out to meet the soldiers, the strain aching in his legs.

"I need two cloaks now." *You look like you're about my height. And you look like hers.* "All right, you two. Give them to me now."

"Yes, Prince Rao," they said together as they handed over their best protection from the rain.

A godlike gust of wind exploded against Rao's ears and knocked him sideways. It nearly blew the sopping grey clothes from the soldiers' hands.

As the blast settled down, Rao saluted the men. "Thank you. It's very important that you do not go near the prison right now. Briraji has asked everyone to stay clear of it. Instead, return to your barracks and stay warm."

The members of the crew saluted before running off again.

Rao returned to Lucia and handed her the smaller of the two cloaks. "Put that on and hide the sword in it." Rao covered himself and the shield as best he could. "We're going to that building there. It's a much nicer prison than the one you were in."

"Now you tell me."

Amazing. The Rezzian almost has a sense of humor.

"My friend can help us remain hidden just as we were before. Then we can easily get out of the citadel."

"This is the heavy man from the lake?"

"Yes."

299

"The one who almost killed me?"

"You attacked us first. Remember the lightning that nearly burned the forest down."

"Don't talk about that night."

You brought it up. "Now I just have to figure out how to get to him."

"Do you know what you're doing?"

"I only know I'm improvising."

Covered in grey from head to foot, Rao and Lucia entered the building from a side door just large enough for them to fit through. Rao shut the door and shivered as rain rolled off his limbs.

He knew the guards would be much more lax in this building. The structure was only used to detain Pawelon's own soldiers for punishment. The locked door around the corner, at the end of the short hallway, would pose the first obstacle.

"Give me the sword," he told her. "I might need it."

"I have to trust you with the sword *and* shield?"

"We'll trade," Rao said with the hint of a smile.

They moved close together and opened their coats. She wore a ratty earthen robe beneath the heavy cloak; Rao tried not to notice her athletic figure. She passed him the sword; he gave her the shield.

"You're my prisoner, all right?"

She grumbled, but followed him. They rounded the corner and walked down a few paces to a finely carved wooden door. Rao pulled Lucia's hood down over her face before he knocked.

An old man with a trimmed grey beard opened a hole carved into the door for two-way communication. "What do you need?"

"I have a new prisoner."

"Prince Rao, is that you?"

"Yes, my good man. I also have to see my partner, Aayu. My father ordered this soldier to be held with him."

"Come in." The old soldier removed the heavy length of wood barring the door. It fell with a loud knock against the floor.

"Do you want me to hold this man while you speak with Aayu?"

"No, thank you. We'll go in together."

"What offense has the new prisoner committed?"

"Just a little treason."

"Oh." The old man didn't seem to know what to say. "Very well."

"After you let us in, give us privacy. We'll let ourselves out."

"I can't—certainly, Prince Rao."

They advanced halfway down the hall, passing six other cells. The old guard searched inside a pocket at his hip. Metal clinked against metal before he produced a rustic key and opened the door.

"Thank you," Rao said and took the key before the soldier could change his mind. "My good man, if you see anyone coming, please let me know right away. It's possible I may be needed in the fighting."

"Certainly." The jailor nodded with uncertain eyes as he backed away.

Rao held his coat open while he entered the room, showing Aayu the Rezzian sword.

Aayu sat in a dark corner on a bench that looked too small for his frame. His mouth dropped as he stared. "You stole her shiny toy. Thank you, Rao, I didn't expect such an expensive gift."

Lucia entered the room, pulled back her hood, and removed the shield from her cloak. "Don't lay a finger on these objects."

Aayu jumped up and raised his hands in front of him as a reflexive defense.

"Everything is good. She and I are working together," Rao said.

Aayu rotated his head to one side and then the other. "You're wha-what?"

"We might not have much time. The storm outside is from the gods. It's eventually going to break down our walls, perhaps within days. So she and I are going to go to her people first thing in the morning to negotiate a truce with an exchange of Lucia and Narayani."

"Rao, I'm just going to say that I'm glad you're holding the big sword right now."

"I'll take that back," Lucia stepped forward and took the sword as she handed Rao the shield.

"I meant I'm really glad you're holding the big shield, Rao."

"I might actually need this one," Rao said. "I haven't healed as much as I'd like to."

Lucia opened her coat and robe enough to show her heavily bandaged side. "I know the feeling. Though I have to admit, your healers have helped me."

"Aayu, I need your help to conceal us. I haven't been able to maintain your *sadhana* for very long. She and I need to remain hidden, but only throughout the night. Tomorrow, we need to be visible."

"You want me to make the most valuable prisoner we have ever had, the royal daughter of Rezzia, invisible to all senses? Did I hear you?"

"Yes."

"We could also hit her over the head with that shield and stuff her in a sack."

Lucia interrupted. "Listen to your prince. We are going to find a way to speak to my brother and father and convince them to end the war."

Aayu threw up his hands and slapped his thighs. "Oh, well that sounds simple. Good plan."

"I am sure they want her back. If they do, they'll talk to me," Rao said.

"Then I suppose even if I did have a vote I would lose," Aayu said.

"Please, bhai. I can't explain everything that's happened over the last few days. She and I have been speaking. Her brother never wanted the war. We completely misunderstood his intentions, as they did ours."

"Are you kidding?" Aayu asked.

"No, and we don't have time to talk this over right now."

"Listen," Aayu said. "If I do it, this was your idea."

"I accept that. We're going to leave. They will probably be looking for us throughout the night. Our best chance is to go into the canyon and head east."

"I'm more than ready to get out of this dungeon."

"Bhai, I'm sorry. I need to ask you to stay in the citadel."

Aayu looked like someone punched him in the stomach.

"Indrajit ordered me to be killed at the prison. Briraji delivered the orders. I need you to tell my father what happened, and then I need you to watch over him. I was attacked by some of our own soldiers when I freed her. They were going to blame my death on her."

"What?" Aayu stared with his mouth open, blinking hard. "My uncle did that?"

"We convinced the men to let us go. They're going to say that I broke her out, that I used my powers to restrain them and escape. It's going to look bad for me. It's going to look like I've sided with the enemy, that I let her go."

Aayu sat on the bench again and leaned over, staring at the floor.

"It's very important that my father understands the truth. If Indrajit wants me killed, my father might not be safe either. I can't risk talking to him now. I need to get out of here with Lucia right away. So I need you to talk to him—"

"I'll do it, and then I'll meet up with you."

"Bhai, I need you to stay with him. Guard his life. Use your *sadhana* if you have to conceal him. Please. He'll understand once you explain everything. If you don't do this, I'm afraid he's going to be killed."

"You want me to let you go off into the desert with Rezzia's royal daughter, and you're planning on talking to the king and Haizzem of Rezzia, while you're weak like this? They will kill you."

"I would say I'm offended," Lucia said, "but I don't know how they'll react. This will be very dangerous for you, Rao."

"I understand that. But, Aayu, I need you to watch over my father. Even if I fail, their armies could be inside our citadel soon. They would come looking for him. But Indrajit is already here, and we can't trust him. Please protect my father."

Aayu shook his head, looking to his right, and exhaled a defeated breath. He grabbed his nose, squeezed his eyes shut, and scrunched up his face. "How are you going to protect yourself from them? You know this is ridiculous."

"I will protect him," Lucia said. She walked toward Aayu and knelt two paces away from him. "I give you my solemn word, on the honor of our entire kingdom."

Aayu raised his head and looked her over. "Curse the honor of your foul kingdom. It's worth nothing to me."

"I give you my solemn word. I will not allow any harm to come to your prince."

Aayu sucked in his cheeks and looked skeptically at her.

"Bhai, we need to get out here before we're found. Please do this for me. You and I came here to end this war. Let me try."

"I'm all right with it, Rao, but you need me at your side."

"I do. I won't lie to you. But I trust her. I have talked to her every day. She wants peace, just as we do. She is powerful, too, Aayu. We have her sword and her shield. Her goddess's powers are with us. And I can still use your *sadhana* for short periods of time. I've been feeling better every today. Tomorrow, I'll be even stronger."

"Rao ..." Aayu dropped his head again.

Rao walked back across the room and cracked open the door. He looked down the hall. The old guard was seated, looking in his direction.

"Is everything all right, my Prince?"

"Perfect, actually. I'm nearly done in here."

Rao closed the door again and walked over to Aayu. He sat next to him on the bench.

"I will owe you one." Rao put his hand on Aayu's shoulder. "I am going to get Narayani back."

Aayu sat up and stared solemnly at Rao, remaining quiet for many breaths. "Promise me you will get her back and return here alive."

Rao embraced his friend, feeling comforted by the warmth of Aayu's thick frame. "Thank you, bhai. You are my true brother."

Aayu pressed his lips shut and nodded many times.

"Thank you for helping us," Lucia said.

Rao squeezed his friend's heavy torso. "This is why we came here."

"You're right." Aayu sounded like he was trying to convince himself. "Go do what you have to do." He raised his voice as he said to Lucia, "And if anything happens to him, I will find you and kill you. I may not look like much, but I promise you I'll do it."

Rao pulled back and watched Lucia stare at Aayu. "She's given her word. That's enough for me. If not for me, she would've been killed. She knows I saved her life."

"I do," she said. "Now use your magic, Aayu."

Aayu stood and took in a deep breath through his nose. "It's not magic." He closed his eyes and released the breath through his mouth. "Briraji won't find you after I do this."

Chapter 72: Faith

INDRAJIT SURVEYED THE EMPTY CELL where the royal daughter had been confined, grinding his teeth together. His vision darted around, unfocused from his rage.

The reckoning will come.

This was no time to think about cosmic forces. He took three steps back and drew the dagger from the inside of his left boot. He flung the weapon cleanly through the bars of the cell and heard the explosive thwack as it sunk into the light wood of the bed.

"Get it," he ordered the closest soldier and headed for Strategos Duilio's cell, hearing and feeling his own boots clomping against the stone floor. He took the dagger back and tucked it into his belt.

There will be consequences, my Prince.

The old Rezzian lay on his bed, staring at the ceiling. He pushed himself up to a seated position with a hint of a smile.

"My former adversary." Indrajit stood in the center of the room with a perfect view of Duilio's cell. "Your war's conclusion is near."

Duilio also spoke in Pawelon, "Who do you think is going to win?"

"You and I have been scheming against each other too long. *Your* war is about to end. I will remain."

Duilio cocked his head to the side, staring and listening.

"Why are Rezzians so stubborn? You continue to charge into the teeth of our defenses, battle after battle, year after year. Explain this stupidity and pride to me."

"Ah." Duilio raised his bushy white eyebrows and rocked forward and back. "We think and worship differently than you do. We have faith. We don't want victory through cunning, or hiding behind walls, or guile. We believe in the courage to fight on no matter the odds. In doing so, we prove ourselves worthy."

"To your gods?" Indrajit began pacing in front of Duilio's cell, keeping his eyes upon his enemy. His footsteps beat out a hypnotizing rhythm.

"Yes, and also to ourselves. You see, we know we can always push ourselves to do more, to be stronger than you or any other enemy."

"Are you really that simple?"

"We are singularly focused on the very greatest things, on faith and courage."

"Strategos, you will be glad to know the royal daughter escaped from our prison. Though it embarrasses me to say this, she was aided by our prince."

"Well, isn't that a surprise?"

"Unfortunately it was a surprise to me, too. Just today, because of the storm, I had ordered her to be killed."

Duilio frowned and his eyes nearly shut. "Where is Lucia now?"

"We don't know. I have sent men to find and kill her and our prince. Because of her interference in her brother's duel, her death is owed to Pawelon."

"I couldn't possibly talk you out of that, could I?"

"No. I'm here because, in the meantime, Rezzia must pay interest on its debt. Beginning with you."

"I see." The old man rotated his jaw as if he were chewing something, but he seemed to accept Indrajit's statement.

"I won't risk losing two prisoners. Before I end this war for you, is there anything more you would like to say?"

"Would you allow me such an indulgence? My final words?"

"After this long," Indrajit said as he began walking toward a flimsy wooden chair against the left wall. "You deserve to speak your piece. What will it be?" He pulled the chair back to the center of the room and sat, waiting.

"This is it, then?" Duilio's eyes looked up to the right, up to the left, and then back to center.

Indrajit nodded once.

"Understood." Duilio came to his feet and dusted himself off. "All these years, I found you a suitable foe. Congratulations on your victory. It has been good to spend these final days in solitude. You have my eternal gratitude for that."

Duilio became more animated as he spoke, walking in front of his bars like a veteran orator, moving around his left hand, often holding up a single finger. "Now for that indulgence, General. I worship The Lord of Miracles. Of course, I have prayed to him while here, and naturally I have asked him for help. His grace

306

must not be coming to me, then, but I know that men do not control the gods. Perhaps the miracle has gone to Lucia instead."

"We'll see."

Duilio nodded and continued, "You asked me about our *stubbornness*. Let me tell you about our faith. My god, Lord Cosimo, has taught me what faith really means—yes, he has. We have a word for faith in our ancient tongue. Originally, faith did not have much to do with belief. The ancient meaning of the word has to do with loyalty and commitment to something." He paused for dramatic effect. "To an ideal. It meant to deeply value something noble, to do your best to uphold those values. It is when we have such faith that we attract miracles."

"Then perhaps I, too, could be blessed by a miracle," Indrajit said, enjoying the sarcasm in his voice.

Indrajit pulled out his long dagger from his belt, focusing on the center of Duilio's chest. He brought his arm down, his hand forward, and released the handle. The knife flew to its target and passed between the iron bars, landing deep within the old Strategos's gut.

Duilio released an involuntary, wet scream and fell to his knees. Blood ran down his legs and pooled around him on the stone floor. The old man crumpled.

Indrajit watched until his adversary closed his eyes and stopped twitching.

"Get my dagger," he yelled to the soldiers outside the room. He started for the prison's exit and the tower. He was late for his meeting. Devak would be, too.

Chapter 73: The Old Dagger

INDRAJIT CLIMBED THE TOWER STAIRS to the second floor. There he expected to find his highest-ranking officers waiting to discuss the day's events. Quiet conversations echoed above and below him in the stairwell. Despite having worn a heavy cloak in the rain, his uniform dripped streams of water onto the stone steps. His body still shivered.

His strongest guards surrounded him. For this, more than ever, he was glad. He stepped into the conference area and saw each person he'd hoped to see. Around a wide, crumbling stone table lit by tall candles sat his six brigadiers, but no Devak. The officers stood and raised their fists. Indrajit saluted them as he walked to his high-backed wooden chair. The seats to his left and right—Devak's and Briraji's—were empty.

"I had some business to deal with," Indrajit said as he sat. "Any news?"

Stern-faced Brigadier Karikala put his calloused hands on the table. "There's been no change in the storm since the Rezzians retreated to their camp. In some areas, the stone is actually crumbling and falling."

Curse you, Rao.

Indrajit nearly screamed involuntarily as he said, "If it goes through the night, and if the storm's power should increase tomorrow, we may have to worry about tens of thousands of Rezzian dogs climbing over that wall."

"Then we'll be ready for them," said his youngest brigadier, Sudas, a man who still believed sheer force could accomplish anything.

"Perhaps, but we cannot let this happen. Today, I gave Briraji the order to kill the king's daughter. Unfortunately that did not happen. Before he could do it, Prince Rao freed her and used his powers to assault our men and escape the prison with her. He left one Pawelon soldier dead inside the prison. Based on my conversations with Rao and the things he has told the Rezzian woman, I am certain he intends to go to Rezzia's king and exchange the king's daughter for mine. I don't know where he is."

No one wants to follow my words. Good.

"I gave Briraji a new mission, to hunt them down, most likely outside the citadel, and kill the royal daughter."

"What do you intend to do about Prince Rao?" asked Samudragupta, his darkest-skinned general.

"Prince Rao has committed treason. He probably believes he is doing the right thing. This is exactly my problem with our young prince. He possesses the ignorance of youth, which leads him to believe that Rezzia might actually give up the war after they give us a simple girl in exchange for a woman who commands their gods, a woman who appears to be another Haizzem. Rao should have never joined the fighting here."

All eyes remained on Indrajit. Two of his men nodded.

"Our rajah is not here yet because I wanted to speak to you all first. I am concerned that Devak will not take this news well. He listens too much to Rao, and I fear this has made him soft." Indrajit laughed. "He believes Rao was sent to save us."

Chanakya, his most veteran brigadier, spoke in his venerated tones, trying to be a voice for reason. "Let's hope Briraji can find them. Once she is dead, the storm may weaken."

"Agreed," Indrajit said. "Strange times are upon us. Unfortunately, at this time our rajah cannot be relied upon. Until this storm is defeated, I must ask you all to follow my command, regardless of what your rajah tells you. Do we agree that he cannot be objective about his son at this time?"

The men nodded in affirmation. A few of them said "Yes."

"Good. We are going to need a strong leader to get us through this, for the good of Pawelon. I will not allow a rogue boy to undo all that we've fought for."

"General, I mean no disrespect by this question, but Rao has helped us in our fight, hasn't he?" young Sudas asked him.

Of course you mean to disrespect me.

"At times, but he's never intended to see us actually win. In his first battle, he wouldn't attack our enemy until we were nearly routed. Even before then, he was pushing for some kind of passive settlement. He still believes the Rezzians can be reasoned with, and he is about to take this notion and destroy us with it unless he is stopped. He's going to give Rezzia their royal daughter, who bears the markings of a Haizzem, at a time when we cannot afford to give any ground."

The six officers either looked at the table or looked Indrajit in the eye, but none disagreed.

"Does anyone have a problem with following my orders?"

"Of course not, General Indrajit," Sudas said.

"Then be prepared for anything. You all know our assignments should Rezzia breach our walls, but let's go over them again tonight. I will meet with you all here when the moon rises. In the meantime, let's hope our sages find a way to stop the storm."

Indrajit stood and gave his salute. The brigadiers did the same.

"You are all dismissed."

The six vacated the room and took their guards with them. Indrajit took slow steps around the circular table, reflecting on what was to happen once Devak found him.

He brought his left boot up to rest on one of the other officers' chairs. With two fingers, he felt the cold, black metal handle of his grandfather's dagger tucked into the fabric.

Indrajit continued stepping mindfully around the table with one hand clasping the wrist of his other arm behind his back. Occasionally, he heard a unit of soldiers run up or down the stairs outside the sealed room. Mostly, he heard his own deliberate footsteps.

The sages can't counteract the storm, and there's nothing we can do about it ... This war is likely coming to its end. A great fortress that has stood for centuries, crumbling under the powers of two Haizzem. Two.

He fell into his own chair and leaned his head back, looking up at the ancient stone ceiling.

Nearly ten long years pushing myself to command these men, to defend Pawelon. Each painstaking step, for thousands of days, and now this.

He remembered the ceremony when Devak promoted him to his position, two years before the war began. Indrajit had been living in this tower ever since. Devak joined him after the war began, and it had taken some time to get used to answering to another man again. But Devak was fair-minded. He allowed his general to set his own strategy and rarely interfered.

All this time. Everything changed when Rao appeared.

The soldiers removed the slab of wood blocking the door. Devak entered with his thundering voice. "What in death's name is going on? You said you would meet me in my chamber."

310

Indrajit rose to his feet and saluted him. "I apologize, my Rajah. Too much has been happening. I briefed our generals and then I remained here when I should have gone to meet you."

"You didn't even send word."

"I humbly apologize. It has been a very difficult day."

Devak took his customary chair, to Indrajit's left. "Tell me what's happening."

"The storm continues and our eastern wall is slowly crumbling. Have you heard about Rao?"

"No."

"He freed the king's daughter and escaped with her. He killed a Pawelon soldier in the prison. Rao is now hiding. I assume he and Aayu have already left the citadel. Aayu is no longer in his cell."

Devak grabbed the arms of his chair and swung his head around, clenching his jaw. "Impossible."

"I wish it were a joke. One of my men explained that Rao intends to negotiate with King Vieri. He wants peace, and I am sure that he and Aayu want Narayani back."

Devak stood and threw his chair far across the room. It smashed against the grey rock. One of its legs broke off.

Soldiers poured into the room.

"Get out of here," Indrajit said. "Leave us alone and *don't* interrupt us again."

"Do you think he would go to them right away?" Devak asked.

"If he does, we may not be able to stop him. I have already sent Briraji and a team to look for him. He has orders to kill the king's daughter."

"We didn't discuss that."

"No, my Rajah, we didn't. Our sages found two Rezzian goddesses were responsible for the storm. I had to act quickly and I gave the order to have her killed right away. But Rao," Indrajit restrained himself, "interfered."

Devak lunged around the room, grunting and building up more anger. Light from the candles and shadows danced across his body.

"Rao may also be waiting for the morrow." Indrajit remained seated and watched his rajah steam. "In fact, that seems more likely. If he goes to them tonight, he's more likely to be captured. If he can signal to their army from the empty field, he might be able to arrange a neutral meeting to negotiate. He

311

would also have a much better chance to escape during the day in case they do not grant him an audience."

"Maybe you're right. Rezzia's less likely to try their tricks during daylight. Rao and Aayu are likely concealed right now. They won't be easy to find."

"If anyone can do it, Briraji can."

"You think we need to kill the royal daughter to weaken the storm?"

"I do."

"Fine then," Devak said.

"We can't risk her being used as a negotiating piece. That's also why I killed the Strategos today."

"You did what?"

"I couldn't risk him being freed. Perhaps Rao and Aayu are still inside the citadel with the king's daughter."

Devak let out a grumbling roar. "Eh, you're right."

Indrajit massaged his calf muscles, through his boots. He loosened the strap around his dagger and visualized how he would stab his rajah.

Devak sat down at Indrajit's right, in Briraji's chair. "If we don't find him tonight, I'll find him myself tomorrow.

... Now that might change everything. "What if the only way to do it is for you to chase him into the valley in front of their army?"

"If I'm killed, Rao will take my place as rajah. If neither of us makes it back, the position will fall to you."

Indrajit took his hands off his boots and sat upright.

"Why would you do this?"

"What would you do?" Devak asked. "He's my last son. It's my duty to protect him."

"You're more sentimental than I thought, Devak."

"More than that. He'll do great things for Pawelon when he's rajah. If they are going to take one of us, it will be me. I won't let that dog Vieri take him."

Indrajit smiled inwardly. Maybe he wouldn't have to deal with the mess of a dead rajah? Maybe Devak could even be made into a martyr, killed by the Rezzians themselves—whether in truth or at the hands of his own men tomorrow.

"You've surprised me, but I respect you for this." Indrajit stood and adjusted his belt. He adjusted his uniform back over his shoulders. "I will keep you informed if we discover anything else about Rao. Be ready to leave early in the morning, before sunrise."

Devak stood and stared down at a candle on the table, expressionless, lost in his thoughts.

Indrajit moved a step closer and waited until Devak looked him in the eyes. "My Rajah, if you should make the ultimate sacrifice, I will always remember it, and I will make sure your memory is honored as it should be."

"Thank you, Indrajit, for all you've done for me and for Pawelon."

Indrajit bowed to him. "My duty is also my desire."

Chapter 74: Sadhana

AAYU STOOD NEXT TO HIS UNCLE, INVISIBLE, ready to act if Indrajit meant Rao's father any harm. He watched his uncle massaging his calf muscles, through his boots. Then Indrajit seemed to be doing something else with his hands. Aayu crouched and tried to see what the general was doing.

His uncle loosened the straps around a concealed dagger.

Unbelievable.

Aayu focused on a thought-form that would knock Indrajit into oblivion.

Rao's father sat down at Indrajit's right. "If we don't find him tonight, I'll find him myself tomorrow ..."

Wait, big man! You and I need to talk first.

"... If I'm killed, Rao will take my place as rajah. If neither of us makes it back, the position will fall to you."

Indrajit took his hands off his boots and sat up straight.

Heard something you like, did you?

"Why would you do this?"

"What would you do?" Devak asked.

"I don't know."

"He's my last son. It's my duty to protect him."

The big guy is growing on me.

"You are more sentimental than I thought, Devak ..."

Aayu followed Rao's father when he left the room. They, and the rajah's guards, climbed the stairs to his quarters at the top of the tower.

Aayu slipped into the room at the same time Devak entered it, and felt relieved to be the only other person with him this time. Earlier, before Devak went to find Indrajit, the rajah met with some of his advisors, discussing the citadel's stock of food and water, among other mundane subjects.

While Devak stood near the large window watching the rain splash onto the floor, Aayu took a seat by the finely crafted table against the wall. He took in a deep breath and canceled his power. He immediately felt his body pressing into his chair.

"My Rajah, I bring news from Rao. He sent me to speak to you."

Devak turned with fierce, focused eyes. "How did you get in—" and then he seemed to realize the answer.

"It's a long story, my Rajah. Rao asked me to protect you."

"Why? Where is he?"

"By now, I hope he's far away from here. He left with the Rezzian woman."

"Why aren't you with him?" Devak began walking toward Aayu.

"He practically commanded me to stay here to protect you. Indrajit ordered him killed, along with the woman."

"How do you know this?" Devak towered over Aayu.

Aayu stayed in his chair. "Sir, I am going to tell you exactly what Rao told me. He wanted me to tell you this—"

"Get to it."

"Briraji took my uncle's orders to the prison, where he ordered Rao and the woman to be killed. He said they were going to blame his death on the king's daughter. Rao convinced the soldiers to let him escape, but he knew they would say he used his powers against them."

"Where was Briraji when this happened?"

"I'm not sure. Rao didn't say. But he said it was going to look bad for him. He wanted you to know the truth."

Devak took one huge step forward and kicked an empty chair five paces.

I'm just the messenger, big man. I'm just the messenger.

"*Why* did Rao do this?"

"He's going to try to try to talk to the king and Haizzem, and see if they can—"

"Enough." Devak turned and walked over to his desk. With his back turned to Aayu, he put his hands on it and leaned forward with his head bent low.

"My Rajah, if I may, I wanted to go with Rao to help him, but he insisted I talk to you and protect you."

Devak swung around. "Protect me?"

"He's worried because of what they intend to do to him."

"I see." Devak crossed his arms over his chest and looked away.

"I have to tell you something else." Aayu's mind froze with fear as Devak stared at him again. "I've been with you for some time now. I was there when you met with Indrajit."

"You'd better explain."

"This is the first time you've been alone. I couldn't reveal myself and, trust me on this, I believe Indrajit was going to kill you while you met with him."

Devak's eyes narrowed. "What in death's name?"

"He was playing with a dagger he had tucked into his boot. It's well-concealed. He loosened the straps. He gripped the handle. And then you said you were going to go find Rao. I think that's when he changed his mind."

Devak turned his back to Aayu and crossed his arms again. "It makes sense. If he was going to do it, he might've decided to have me killed tomorrow instead."

"Or he thinks maybe you'll get yourself killed."

Devak let his arms hang and walked back to the table. For the first time, he took a seat. "If anything happens to me tomorrow, Pawelon is going to need a leader. It might as well be Indrajit."

Even though he wants you dead?

"I'll deal with him later," Devak said. "First, we need to get Rao."

And Narayani. "I agree." Aayu nodded so hard his chair rocked. "When I saw him late in the day, he still wasn't doing well. He couldn't focus his powers for long. She had her sword and shield, though, and she swore to protect him."

Devak slammed his fist on the table and shook his head. "You shouldn't have let him go."

"He insisted."

"Indrajit ordered Rao to be murdered by my own men?"

"That is what Rao told me, my Rajah."

Devak's pockmarked face looked drained of hope. "It's too late to reach the patrols searching for him. They must have orders to kill him."

"The good news is that I used my *sadhana* to conceal Rao and the woman. That effect should last until the morning. That's when he's going to try to meet with the Rezzians."

Devak made eye contact with Aayu. His eyes turned from hopeless to merely emotionless. "Good."

"You'll let me come with you in the morning, then?"

"We need to reach Rao before he talks to the king. Did Rao," Devak paused and let out a shallow breath, "tell you what I told him, about what happened to his family?"

"No, my Rajah."

"Their king sent the assassins who killed my wife and his brothers. I didn't tell Rao that King Vieri has tried to kill him many more times since. Their king is determined to eliminate my lineage. If he sees Rao, he'll kill him on sight."

Aayu's throat seized up. Moments later, he breathed again. "The woman said she knew Rao saved her life. She said she'd protect him, on the honor of her kingdom."

Devak looked up, with very little color in his cheeks, and breathed through his mouth. "Rao would believe her. I intend to bring Rao back to us one way or another. If Rezzia's king gets to him before I do, I intend to at least give him the burial he deserves."

"He *is* coming back. Please focus your thoughts on that outcome. He wanted me to protect you. Maybe he knows more than we do about the Rezzian woman. Maybe she will protect him." Aayu smiled a bitter smile. "Now, about what Rao asked me to do. I have an idea."

Chapter 75: The Rage of Achilles

RETURNING FROM THE DAY'S EXCURSION, Caio's eyes rested on Rezzia's military city after dark. Torches burned atop tall poles throughout the site, throwing shadows on the complex of white tents. Smoke rose from the kitchens, carrying the succulent scents of roasting goats and pigs.

Caio felt once more the emotions of the army behind him. Morale remained strong, despite the long march with the extra climb to and descent from Pawelon's citadel. Faith carried them on. Many perished in the fighting earlier in the day, but thanks to Lord Galleazzo's lions, far more Pawelons fell in the rout. After Caio summoned the storm promised by the goddess Mya in his dream, only small skirmishes around the citadel claimed any lives, and then only in small numbers.

"Can you tell if the storm still rages?" His father's voice surprised him. They'd barely spoken during the journey back.

Caio nodded and visualized Pawelon's incredible citadel. He saw the storm pounding the structure, but weakening throughout the night. "I believe it does for now, but perhaps not for long. It's amazing that it seems to have continued even though I am not there."

"Ah, but Lucia is there. The gods can do their work through her presence."

"That must be why. I'm certain Ysa is also involved."

His father sat tall in his saddle, scanning the sights in front of him. "Do you see anything about Lucia?"

Caio remembered Lucia's face the last time he saw her, after the *Ayot*.

Lord Oderigo, how does Lucia fare?

Caio saw a vivid image of Lord Danato dwarfing Lucia, one arm crossed over his chest with his other hand on his jutting chin. The black god leaned forward, looking down on Lucia with eyes that revealed the god to be in pain.

"Nothing much, Father."

Caio and King Vieri rode on to the entourage waiting to welcome them. Out in front of the camp, the gathering of elite soldiers and warpriests chanted a monotonous prayer.

"Havah ilz avah Haizzem!" the leading warpriest exclaimed. The crowd paid their obeisance, either kneeling and bowing or prostrating the full length of their bodies.

"We achieved a great victory today!" Caio called out just as his horse slowed to a stop.

"Yes we did, my Haizzem!" His father stepped comfortably into his role. "We marched to the pigs' fortress and our gods assaulted the very walls. The stone itself began to crumble, and continues to do so! We may have reached the final days of this great war."

The men in the crowd stood again and cheered, most of them clapping their hands above their heads. Caio scanned their hearts. He felt their burning hope that his father's words were true, whether because of their faith or because of their longing for the fighting to be over.

Caio and his father dismounted at the same time. His father walked toward him awkwardly on sore legs and took Caio's left hand in his right. Vieri raised their hands together. "Together, we are unstoppable, king and Haizzem! My daughter still suffers for us all, but I swear upon the gods of Lux Lucis, we will rescue her soon."

After his father released his hand, Caio walked through the crowd, giving his blessings to each person there. He noticed his father waiting beyond the gathering, squinting at him with his face clenched. Caio sensed the emotion beneath his father's glance: guilt.

Caio pulled away and met his father with a quick embrace.

"Let's walk, Son. We should eat."

"I'll walk with you, but then I must go to my yurt and check on Narayani. It's been a long day."

With a wave of his hand, King Vieri signaled for their entourages to follow behind them.

"Do you ever get accustomed to it?" Caio asked. "Knowing how many men died or were maimed?"

"No, but you harden yourself to it. Even so, I still see them in my dreams. It helps to have some release. That's why the Pawelon whore was good for you."

"She's not a whore."

"Did you have to force her?"

"Father!"

"Then I'm right. She is a valuable whore now. Her body belonged to the Prince of Pawelon. She has great value to us."

"Don't speak about her like this. I wouldn't have been able to come with you today if she hadn't healed me."

"We've talked about this before. Let our spirits dwell on something else. You made our ancestors proud today. I will make sure the people of Rezzia know what you have done. Soon, you will destroy a Pawelon fortress that has stood throughout history." His father turned his grave eyes to stare at his son.

"It is Mya and Ysa who should be thanked."

His father shifted his glance forward and downward. His nose twitched. "Someday you will have your own children, and you will understand that fathers must do what they believe to be best for their sons and daughters—that they cannot always do what makes their children happy."

"I know you seek the best for Lucia and me."

"Yes. As the political leader of our people, I must sometimes do things for the welfare of our kingdom, even when it interferes with my children's wishes." His father looked at him intently again with quivering eyes.

An ill feeling washed over Caio.

"If you want to speak any more tonight, I will be here, dining with our soldiers. After that, I will retire."

"Very well. I'll come and eat soon. Tonight we can discuss Narayani."

His father's left hand rushed to scratch his beard, on both sides of his face. "Remember that above all, you are my son and I love you. Remember that I have a duty to uphold our proud lineage. You remember that."

"Of course, Father." Caio felt the tension in his father's body. He decided to give him space. "I'm going straight to my yurt then."

"Go and change. Make yourself presentable, then meet me for your meal," he finished with a hard slap to Caio's back.

Caio completed the walk to his yurt, near the center of the complex, still feeling unsettled by his father's emotions. The ten guards protecting his yurt knelt, but silently and without joy. Caio felt a great melancholy within them.

"Find joy in your service, my brothers, for Lux Lucis."

One man raised his head just enough to look at Caio. "We have done as we've been told, my Haizzem."

"Of course you have. Is everything all right?"

No one answered.

"I asked if everything is all right? Speak!"

The same soldier looked up frowning, with his neck and cheeks quivering. "We've only done as our king commanded us, my Haizzem."

Caio opened the doors and heard the old hinge creak. He stepped into his dark, candlelit yurt. Only silence and emptiness met him.

"Narayani?" Caio forced a difficult swallow. "Narayani?" He felt the beds for her, finding nothing, then hurried back outside. The men were standing again. Caio addressed the same man, "Where is she?"

"My Haizzem, she was taken at the direct orders of the king."

"Where? By the gods, where?"

Another soldier spoke up. "She was awarded to Pexaro."

Caio's gut split apart, as if a crevasse opened through his insides. He bent over and vomited on the ground. Two soldiers scrambled to check on him while another rushed to get a cloth and water to clean him.

"When did this happen?"

The soldiers hesitated.

"I asked you a question!"

"This morning," one of them offered.

His father ignored Pexaro's lecherous sins because his province recruited so many young men for Rezzia's armies.

Caio took the clean cloth from the soldier and wiped his mouth. He drank from the offered waterskin and spit on the ground, his mind filling with rage. He began to run back to the tent where his father was dining, beset with nauseating pangs of betrayal. He heard the footsteps of the soldiers following him, but couldn't bear to look at anyone.

Someday you will understand that fathers must do what they believe to be best for their children, his father had told him.

Men fell to their knees and onto the ground as Caio ran through the camp, but he didn't stop for any of them.

Remember that I have a duty to uphold our proud lineage, his father's words careened around his skull. *You remember that.*

Indignity flew through Caio's veins.

He entered the dining tent and saw his father across the space, sitting between Manto and Alimene. Men began falling to the ground in respect. Quiet followed the chatter.

"You betrayed your own son?" Caio yelled across the assemblage.

His father stood, putting his hands on the table and shaking his head.

"You can forget your cursed war! My soldiers are leaving this valley."

Before, the quiet still included rustling feet and bodies. Now, the silence hung over them like a smothering fog.

"Don't make this about yourself, Caio. Think about the good of Rezzia."

Caio ran toward his father's table. "You betrayed me!"

"I do what I believe is best for my kingdom, whatever is for the glory of Lux Lucis." His father threw down his spoon. It bounced off his wooden plate and landed on the ground.

"Handing over innocent young women to corrupt slobs? Whose divine glory is served by that?" Caio noticed his balled fists as he leaned forward.

"You will speak to me with respect!"

"I will not! You are fortunate we are related."

His father's face burned red, heaving with vigorous breaths.

"Then you are going to let your sister rot in a Pawelon prison?"

Mya, cool my fever. "My sister is there because of you. What if they have done to her what you did to the Pawelon girl?"

"Do not speak of such a thing!"

"You will free the Pawelon and bring her to me. You will never harm her again. Her welfare is my province—never yours. Agree!"

"Son, I am freeing you from her grasp, before she kills you, just as she got your sister stabbed on your own spear."

That was Ilario's spear! "Go do what is right and do it now. If you don't, not one of our men will march back into that valley to fight your war. Not a single one but you."

Caio turned and walked away.

"I will give the whore back to you." His father's dejected words soured the uneasy silence. "She will be your prize then."

Caio's stopped. He turned and locked eyes with his father once more. "*Never* call her that again."

His father stepped around the table. He lowered himself, first to his knees, then placed his head and hands on the ground. He stood slowly. "Will you forgive me, my Haizzem?"

Caio moved his gaze across the shocked faces of the hungry men surrounding him.

"No."

'*'

Narayani lay nude, curled on her side, on a dirty rug inside the accursed Rezzian tent, staring at the sagging, white ceiling. The men behind her continued laughing and bragging about the number of times and ways they'd violated her. She tried again to focus on Aayu's mantras, nearly visualizing the first syllable, but again her anguish ruined her concentration.

Commotion, outside. Yelling. Door flaps opened. Many more men entered. Many more.

No more!

"Stand!" a gruff Rezzian voice commanded her.

Her arms and legs shook from the trauma, but she leaned her weight onto her forearm and tried to sit up with her legs folded beneath her.

Two soldiers grabbed her arms.

"No more!" she cried. *Please kill me.*

The fat Rezzian, the leader inside the tent, argued with the soldiers. She overheard the soldiers respond, "We come at the king's direct orders." The argument continued as they dressed her in her robe and carried her out of the tent.

She screamed in tortured bursts as they carried her, wailing out her suffering like vomit from her deadened heart. Her eyelids squeezed shut and she hoped they'd stay closed forever.

"Narayani?"

Caio?

Facing her, he placed his hands on her shoulders. "I am going to help you." He yelled at the men carrying her, "Bring her in here. Put her on my bed."

The door slammed after the gruff men put her down and she sobbed. Caio knelt beside the bed, his face next to hers.

"I am going to take care of you now. I promise, no one will ever harm you again."

"Kill me." She could barely speak through her crying. "Please. I don't want to live anymore." Her lips parted and quivered as she began to cry. Her eyes shut, ejecting a flood of tears.

"I am so sorry." Caio placed one hand over her heart and the other over the crown of her head. She felt an almost searing heat from his palms, but it comforted her. She heaved a tortured sigh and sank down, onto the bed.

The tiny hairs all over her body stood up as a vibrant sensation washed over her flesh. She felt an invisible presence surrounding her, penetrating her heart, holding her. Images of lush vines flashed behind her closed eyes. The image shifted to a waterfall, pouring down on her, cleansing her body and soul.

Chapter 76:
Hades's Dark Processes

Earlier.

LUCIA AND RAO HURRIED to the western gate of the citadel, away from the brunt of the storm, and waited there for the gate to be opened. Lucia waited nervously; what happened to Rao's lady during the duel told her that this power of concealment did not work on everyone. As Rao predicted, once the Rezzian army began its march down into the valley, the western gate opened to allow some Pawelon scouts to exit.

Lucia and Rao took the northern trail down to the valley, expecting fewer scouts along the route the Rezzian army didn't take. Once they began their descent, they noticed the storm weakening. Lucia accepted that the goddesses' power would be limited by her leaving the area; the gods could only perform their miracles in the presence of their devotees.

As they walked in silence, unaffected by the weather thanks to Aayu's help, her mind worked to catch up. So much had changed in such a short stretch of time. Their prince seemed unlike everything she believed him to be, unless even her escape had been a complicated ruse. But she found it impossible to imagine Aayu wasn't legitimately shocked by what had occurred. If they wanted her dead, the Pawelons could've already done it. Maybe Rao had an unspoken plan to use her to win major concessions, but she didn't doubt Rao really was hiding from his general's men.

Rao was persuasive enough to be able to trick her, but she still found herself believing in the sincerity of his ideals. The weight of that irony gripped her heart. When Caio wanted peace, Rao had wanted it, too. Lucia had rushed Caio into his first engagement as soon as he arrived, at a time when she still believed in an outright Rezzian victory. Maybe everything was her fault. Because of her, everything happened so quickly and both men assumed the other intended to fight. Neither side understood the other, and the cost ...

She wondered if Ilario's soul had found peace with his father and mother.

At least grant him that, Danato, you heartless monster.

The supernatural clouds dissipated more rapidly than real clouds would have, allowing some starlight to shine down. The moon would rise later. For now she had to trust Rao to guide her down the path that he himself didn't seem to know all that well.

He was the first to break the silence. "I'm sure some of the things that happened when we initially fought frightened you. I want you to know my first intention was not to harm you. The first time, I wanted to defend my men. The second time, I wanted to speak to you."

Lucia shivered with an ill sensation. His reminder made her question herself again for trying to work with him. "I wish we had been able to finish that conversation. My father told me he prayed for me to come back. He told the gods he would retreat if they returned me."

"So that's why your forces left?"

"Yes."

"And that would explain why our conversation was cut short." Rao chuckled. "Your gods didn't give me the chance to say more."

Lucia stared off at the dark cliffs, forgoing any effort to understand the gods' motivations.

"Lucia, on the subject of your gods, I haven't told you what happened at the duel. At least not everything." Rao waited for her to look back to him. "I had interactions with two of your gods that day. First, Lord Oderigo and then the goddess Mya."

"What do you mean?" she blurted out.

"Oderigo seemed to chastise me. We discussed metaphysics, of all things, including the origins of the gods."

Spare me.

"But the most surprising thing," he continued, "an ironic thing, is that your goddess Mya saved me."

"What?" again her mouth moved before she could think.

"Your brother nearly destroyed my body. The pressure was unthinkable. My spirit left my body and I hovered, watching. Your brother held his spear over me—this was when he started arguing with Narayani—and I forgave him. I dedicated my suffering to a higher purpose and forgave him. That's when your goddess appeared. She healed me. I've been trying to make sense of this. Can you tell me why she would do that?"

Caio's own goddess? "I told you before, I don't understand the gods at all."

"Mya is a goddess of healing, isn't she? You call her The Compassionate One?"

"Yes."

"Maybe that's why she responded to my, well, my prayer. Your beliefs have always seemed odd to me. I always thought they were just figments of your collective imagination. I've always thought it was spiritually immature, like a childish dream or a story someone wrote down and then took literally. But that childish story seemed to save my life."

"If you are telling the truth, all of it surprises me." Not entirely, but she wasn't about to tell him that. "About your lady, Narayani? I'm sorry you've lost her. You must feel horrible."

Rao mumbled an affirmation. He looked away and Lucia looked off in the opposite direction to give him space. "I try not to think about her, and try to focus on what needs to be done. Do you think she's all right?"

"I am sure she is." Lucia had no idea. She remembered Danato's message. If true, then either Rao and his lady or she and her brother would not be reunited for long, if at all.

A stray thought slithered through her mind. If she killed Rao, would it not satisfy Danato's latest prophecy? She put her hands on the hilt of Ysa's sheathed sword. With the prince dead, Rezzia might crush Pawelon and take their fortress. But this was a problem, too. Her father would keep pushing for more conquest and when she last spoke with Caio, he was of the same mind as her father.

I can't believe I have more in common with the prince of bloody Pawelon than I do with my own brother.

"If I can help it," she said, "you will see Narayani again soon."

"Thank you."

"You've done some things for me."

He seemed nothing like she believed him to be. Rao was principled, and either brave or foolish. And he still seemed sincere. Pawelon was lucky to have him.

"I would have hated you forever for what you did to Ilario, and a part of me always will. But it changes things, knowing that you didn't come to hurt us, that you weren't hunting us. Is that really the truth?"

"Completely."

She could distract her mind for short stretches, but she always came back to Ilario. She could still sense his lips, see his face. But the image was a mirage, only a flash. It never lasted.

"I am sorry for your loss," he said. "It's something I still can't comprehend."

"Neither can I." She heard her voice bend with emotion and regretted revealing her sorrow.

"I've never wanted to hurt anyone. I have no idea about the depths of what you must be feeling, but I can tell you that what happened to him haunts me, too."

That only made it more depressing. "I am glad you still have someone, if we can get her back for you."

"How does it make sense that one innocent person dies and leaves others behind, while another continues? How can we live with that? You lose a love forever and life just goes on? I don't know how to make sense of it. What would your religion say about this?"

"You're not asking the right person."

"Why not? You are the royal daughter of Rezzia. You have a divine patron."

"I don't really care. I tried to protect him. I was right there next to him, holding Ysa's shield. It did no good at all." She was saying too much. Death was Danato's province. She'd never understand anything under his domain.

Rao waited some time. "I understand how hard that must be to accept. Oh, Lucia, I forgot something. Here, is this yours?"

Unsure of what he had for her in the dark, she slowly reached out toward his hand.

"It's a necklace I found near your armor."

The holy black anvil of Lord Sansone fell into Lucia's dark palm. She clutched it and looked away, fighting off her emotions.

"These gloves are yours, too."

They didn't speak again until the moon rose and they found a place to camp for the night. A dry ravine that must have once been a riverbed gave them an opportunity to conceal themselves. They walked along the rocky ditch until they found an area with dry tree branches arching over it.

Rao said they would have to get up very early, before the sunrise, to watch out for Pawelon patrols. They remained invisible due to Aayu's power, but by morning the effect would expire. Making a fire would have posed a huge risk, so

Lucia prepared herself for a cold night with little comfort in the desert. She insisted on keeping the sword and shield next to her and lay against the wall to hide from any scouts.

Rao sat two paces away, facing the opposite side of the ravine. "Lucia, I've been wondering about something you said about that night."

"Go ahead." Lucia opened her eyes. "You don't have to look away."

Rao nodded and turned around to face her. It was too hard to make out his features in the dark, but she could see his mop of brown hair. "You said that your Lord Danato sent you to the lake that night. Of course, your religion says he presides over death. That part makes sense, but why would he take away someone that you and your brother both love? Don't you believe that his duty is to watch over you, especially you and Caio?"

"I said it before. I *don't* understand them. I pray to my goddess, and sometimes she answers those prayers. Sometimes she doesn't. Lord Danato," Lucia hurried through a deep breath and fought the ridiculous urge to tell him more, "I don't understand."

"Has he done things like this before? Has he done anything else that has hurt you?"

Ha! "Yes."

"Interesting. Things that didn't involve death?"

"Sometimes."

"I was thinking about this. He is your god of death, but he is a complicated figure in your myth—" he corrected himself, "in your religion. I remember reading about him and wondering," Rao paused as if gathering his thoughts, "his domain also includes the dark processes of life, including the balancing of what you might call sin. Our concept is karma. It suggests that whatever we do returns to us because in truth there is no separation between us all. So when we act upon another, we truly act upon ourselves. Evil acts come back to us, while good deeds bring good karma. As I understand your Lord Danato, it's as if he is a god of karma."

"This is the kind of thing I have no interest in. You might as well be talking to yourself right now."

"I'm sorry. I ..." Rao sat back and looked up at the stars. Moonlight revealed his handsome face and clear, dark skin. "I was just trying to make sense of something senseless. I shouldn't have brought it up again."

Lucia turned onto her back. A bright star drew her attention and she stared at it for some time. She turned onto her side again and tried to ignore the rough ground against her hip and shoulder. "Listen, if you have any answers for me, I'll entertain them. I shouldn't have bristled at you."

Rao looked back to her and his facial features became blackened again. "It just occurred to me that if Lord Danato effectively took Ilario's life that perhaps it has to do with some kind of karma, or balancing."

"What are you suggesting?"

"I don't know if I should talk about it. It's just speculation. I don't know if you know—"

"About what?"

"Do you know about what happened to my mother and my brothers?"

"No."

"Your father never said anything to you?"

"No." *Why?*

"According to my own father," Rao paused as he looked up at the moon, "your father sent assassins to kill them. They nearly killed me as well. I was the youngest of the three boys. I was a baby."

Lucia's mind twisted and turned. Was he lying? Would her father do such a thing? She thought he could have, but didn't want to believe it.

"So," Rao continued, "wouldn't your Lord Danato be the one to enforce the balancing of this sin? He would be the one to bring that karma back to your father."

"Then why would he do anything to me?" Lucia blurted out, then regretted revealing too much.

'*'

Lord Danato crouched in the ravine, beside the tree branches, hidden from all forms of life. His midsection came up to the level of the ground above Lucia and Rao and the rest of his body stretched above it. He stared at Lucia.

'*'

"Maybe the burden was passed around—to you, and to Caio also. But, most likely, someone would need to die."

My mother.

330

Rao continued, "Ilario was almost like a son to your father, wasn't he? He was chosen by your father to watch over Caio."

"How do you know that?"

"I know a lot about your royal family. We have good sources in Remaes."

"Then you know my mother died."

"Yes. I'm sorry. You were young. It happened when you were ten, soon after your brother was born."

Gods! What else does he know about me?

Lucia sat up and leaned against the rocks. "Well if what you are saying is true, then that could be—"

"Karma, maybe. My mother died. And Ilario would be like a son."

"And his death hurt me, and Caio, and my father. So, would it be possible that this debt would've been settled with his death?" *If this whole thing isn't completely ridiculous.*

"Perhaps. That might be true. For your sake, I hope so."

Lucia rolled onto her back again and found the same star. Its twinkling looked yellow sometimes, then blue, then yellow again. *I'm sure he could've done it.* An image of Rezzian blades cutting through the chests of Pawelon boys forced itself upon her.

"I am going to meditate for some time. I'll sleep later, but we need to wake up before the sun rises."

That shouldn't be hard. I don't expect to be able to sleep for long.

Lucia looked at Rao once more as he sat tall in his sagely posture. She saw his profile, as he faced the moon. She thought about mentioning Danato's message to her ... *either you or Caio* ... but decided against it.

'*'

Lord Danato sat beside Lucia's head and Ysa's shield, leaning against the side of the ravine, the miniature canyon. The black god closed his eyes and waited for morning.

Chapter 77:
The Passion of The Black One

RAO'S EYES OPENED to the penetrating calm of the pre-dawn sky. The moon shimmered in the south, preceding the sunrise.

Lucia was gone. The goddess's shield and sword were gone, too.

He leapt to his feet and looked north and south along the ravine for her.

You deserted me. You did exactly what I should've expected all along.

His heart and mind stilled. His body froze.

I'm alone.

His fingers danced nervously on his chest, trying to keep himself present and in his body.

I've freed the royal daughter of Rezzia. She'll help Rezzia destroy the citadel's walls. If I return, I'll be killed for treason—if Indrajit's patrols don't kill me first.

Rao drew a crisp breath into his cold body, and followed the breath up his nostrils, down into his expanding lungs. He heard a voice. A woman's voice. He crept along the dry creek bed to a sloped edge and climbed out.

He found a dim figure in the distance that appeared to be Lucia ... *with a horse?* The white beast stared in his direction. Putting disbelief aside, he jogged toward her. The horse stirred, and Lucia turned to look at him, too.

She walked toward him, pulling the animal with her. Under the otherworldly light of the dark purple sky, the scene appeared strangely like a dream. As they met, the horse lowered its head obediently.

"This is Albina, my possessed horse. The goddess Ysa must have sent her. Or Albina escaped."

"And somehow found you?"

"Could be. I prayed to Ysa before I fell asleep."

Rao admired the enormous creature. With some exceptions, his people had chosen not to make much use of horses. Most Pawelons had a superstitious fear of the animals. "We can't very well hide with it, so we need to move on."

"Maybe we'll need her." Lucia held the horse's reins with one hand, and stroked its cheek and neck with the other. "Albina's a strong mare. If she'd allow it, she might be able to carry both of us for short distances. But I doubt she could move quickly with both us unless Ysa intervenes again. But she's done it before."

"For now, let's walk. We don't need to make it any easier to find us. Keep looking and listening for anyone that might be following."

Rao thought the sunrise seemed slower than expected, much slower than sunset the night before. Exotic birds emerged from the night and sang slowly to the rising sun, a patient symphony greeting the changing colors of dawn.

"Let's talk about what's going to happen," Rao said. "I've thought it through."

"I'm listening." Her voice sounded as cold as the morning, but at least she'd stayed with him.

"We'll continue east, outside the direct line between your army's camp and the citadel. That route should give us more cover. We'll have to time this perfectly. We'll turn to the south and come straight down the center of the valley, in front of the Rezzian army. This will keep us far away from Pawelon's defensive positions."

"That sounds reasonable."

"The horse should help us attract your army's attention. When they send a delegation to meet us, we'll demand an audience with your father and your brother. We won't discuss matters until we speak to them, and we will only speak to them if they come alone. Of course, I will rely on your protection if anyone attacks me."

"You have my word I will protect you, as long as I am able to."

"When we speak to them, you must convince them that your life is in danger unless Rezzia agrees to end the war. Tell them your honor obliges you to return to Pawelon with me if they do not agree. Say that you have only been given your freedom for this one purpose, to negotiate with them. If they do not work with us, the 'magic' I placed in your body will destroy you unless I personally cancel it. That means if I am killed, you will die."

"Fine, I will lie to them. You should know that my brother is uncannily perceptive. He will probably be able to tell if you're lying, however he can't read my emotions." Lucia began pulling her horse to the east. "My brother would have agreed to your proposal before Ilario was killed, but now ... I don't think so. My father will not agree to your offer, and he may even attack you. When we meet them, you should carry the shield for protection, even though my father will be infuriated to see you holding Ysa's relic."

"If we *can* get them to agree, we will ask for Narayani also. In exchange for her, I will agree to turn your Strategos over to Rezzia. I will remain visible, at least at first, to conserve my energy."

"I honor your bravery, Rao. Whether you live or die."

Rao understood the risks, but he couldn't think of a better plan. Surviving the duel was a miracle, bestowed by a goddess of Lux Lucis. Whether it was his destiny to fulfill this mission or whether he was now a pawn of the Rezzian gods, he hoped his actions would at least contribute to some greater purpose. And if he were to lose his life now, he could accept being just one among many more to fall in the coming days.

So be it.

The air wouldn't remain cool for long. The sun's rise in the north created long shadows behind the little hills and shrubs as they hiked eastward, facing the distant lands of Rezzia.

'*'

Lucia had already gone back and forth another handful of times, thinking over Rao's accusation. She wanted to ask her father before she believed the prince, but her feelings told her Rao's story was probably true. Her father sent the assassins.

Something even more disturbing rattled her soul, the question of Lord Danato's purpose in her life.

The clamor of a distant army reached her ears. "The Rezzian army is mobilizing. If you listen, you can just barely hear the marching feet."

"I heard them some time ago," Rao said, walking on the other side of the horse. "Your army is definitely coming for you."

Not for me. For themselves.

Rao's plan seemed sound, or at least the beginning of it did. They had a good chance of an audience with her father and Caio, but she had no guesses as to what might happen after that.

"This might be far enough," Rao said. "Let's turn south."

Lucia followed Rao as he started on the course to intercept the Rezzian army. The sun shone behind her, warming the back of her head and casting her shadow in front of her.

Rao crossed from Albina's right side to the horse's left. "We'll keep the beast between us and Pawelon now. I'm not worried about your army seeing us anymore."

Lucia felt uncomfortable with Rao behind her, with Ysa's sword still tied to Albina. "You lead then." She stopped and held the reins out for Rao.

"You still don't trust me?" he asked.

"I don't trust anyone."

Rao's expression conveyed his acceptance. He took Albina's reins and exchanged positions with Lucia. Rao tried to pull her forward, but the mare stopped and swung her head away from him in defiance.

Lucia slapped Albina on her thigh. "Go! Go!" The horse moved reluctantly at first, then settled into a walk. Albina bumped into Lucia, and the jewels of Ysa's shield scratched her arm.

Damn horse.

Lucia untied the sword and shield of Ysa as they went. She felt the weight of the shield on her arm and gripped the smooth handle of Ysa's perfect blade.

I'll let him hold the shield later.

Albina became like a statue, again refusing to move. The white horse whinnied and raised its head looking west, toward Pawelon.

Lucia spoke in a hushed voice: "She notices something."

Albina's legs shuffled nervously. She waved her head to the west and snorted.

Rao pointed up ahead to their left, at a hill. He held the reins out for Lucia. "We'll hide back there," he said.

A wet thwunk startled them just before Albina reared up and screamed. Lucia took two steps backward. An arrow stuck out above one of Albina's front legs.

"Archers!" she yelled as the mare ran away.

Rao sidestepped with impeccable reflexes as an arrow flew just to his right. Lucia held the shield over her chest and stepped in front of Rao to protect him.

At least two dozen Pawelon soldiers emerged from behind the desert shrubs and advanced on them with readied arrows and outstretched spears. In their midst stood the high-ranking sage she remembered from the prison.

335

Briraji barked at them, "Come forward, Rao. Men, hold back."

Rao pulled on Lucia's robe and they inched backward as the soldiers advanced. "Briraji, Indrajit doesn't understand what we're doing. We are going right now to negotiate a peace. I am doing this to save Pawelon."

"I know what you are doing," the ugly sage answered. "It's idiocy. It's treason. I command you to step forward."

"How can you doubt your own prince?" Rao asked. "If you question my loyalty, watch me now."

Lucia surveyed the men creeping forward. The spearmen were at least five paces away, but the archers behind them had their arrows trained on her.

She lost control of her body and slammed to the ground without warning. Ysa's shield fell beside her. Lucia struggled against the power, but the force acting on her froze every major muscle in her body.

"She is our prisoner," Rao yelled. He stood over her with his hands focused in sage mudras. "I didn't want to do this to her yet, but you've forced me. I can still negotiate with Rezzia. If they have any hope of getting her back alive, they will have to obey my demands."

She tried to fight Rao's power, but the noise came out like a muffled whimper.

Rao continued, "I can't negotiate with them if she's dead—only if she looks close to death."

The Pawelon troops continued surrounding them. Briraji stepped forward, more slowly than the rest. "I've heard enough from your lying tongue. If you are on our side, follow Indrajit's command and kill her now. Do it, or I will. Be quick."

"Master Briraji, she is useless to us dead. She means much more to Pawelon alive."

"If you truly belong to this army, you will follow these orders from General Indrajit immediately."

Lucia struggled to move, but her effort was useless. She heard a familiar voice inside her head:

"Betrayal, dear Lucia. Can you feel it?"

Bastard! Am I dreaming?

"No, you are not. Tell me, can you embrace this feeling of hopelessness and helplessness? This pain? It has become a part of you."

"Tell me," Rao's voice became that of an orator, "is there anyone here willing to kill your own prince before he would risk his own life to save Pawelon? Would anyone here be willing to bear the burden of this karma? To live with the knowledge that you have slain Pawelon's only prince, a young sage who journeyed to this canyon against his father's wishes to defend his people? If there is such a person among you, step forward."

Rao's fingers tightened more deeply into his mudra. He glared down into Lucia's eyes. She grimaced as more force pushed her against the ground.

"Betrayed again, Lucia. Don't you want to know how to be free?"

Yes!

"Find your therapy in the truth of your own battered heart."

Lucia felt tears leaving the corners of her eyes.

"Betrayed again, my daughter, but you are stronger than what you fear inside of you."

Briraji's voice rumbled with annoyance, "You each have your orders, direct from General Indrajit and also from me. Refuse them and I will punish you myself."

"The eastern wall of the citadel could crumble before the day is over. Haven't you heard the Rezzian army coming? They will not stop for anything except to negotiate for this royal bitch. Briraji will not be able to punish you if you are dead. My brothers, if you kill her—or me—you will seal Pawelon's fate. Our lands will be overtaken. Your sisters and mothers will become their whores. Do not be the one—"

Briraji interrupted, "Don't listen to this traitor—"

"Do not be the one responsible for the subjugation of our proud people. The karma would plague your descendents for a hundred generations—"

"You have direct orders!"

"Is anyone here willing to—"

Briraji screamed over Rao's voice, "It is your duty to perform as commanded, not to think. If your prince does not kill her now, kill him."

Rao's feet shuffled in the uncomfortable quiet.

"Soon, my daughter, you may be freed from all that has plagued you."

Freed from you!

"I have not plagued you, Lucia. I am only an instrument."

Briraji spoke again. "It's not my duty to weigh out consequences."

"That is always your duty. That's true of all of us! Please give your young prince this one chance to save Pawelon."

"Defend yourself," Briraji growled.

Lucia regained control of her body. She scrambled to stand for one moment, then thought better of it and stayed down, as if still under Rao's power. Her fingertips searched the ground for the handle of Ysa's blade.

An undulating field of darkness surrounded her, blacking out the light of day and then the ground beneath her.

What's happening?

"Darkness," Danato answered, *"the only thing that can free you."*

Lucia felt evil all around her, seeping into her mind. She continued fumbling in search of Ysa's sword, but the pliable blackness beneath her rippled to the touch.

"Rao?"

"He cannot help you. He is too weak." Briraji's silhouette appeared some distance away, a purple outline with flames flickering at its edges. "You are inside my universe now." With those words, searing red lights dotted the darkness like stars. "This is all you'll see before death."

Help me, Lord Danato.

"Good, Lucia. That is step one."

The form of Danato appeared behind Briraji, towering over him at twice his height.

"Close your eyes and embrace me."

I need you to save me!

"Then do as I ask!"

Briraji took one step closer. "This is what your Strategos saw before he died."

An image of the curly haired old man arose in her mind, sitting on horseback and holding his holy symbol.

Gods, bless Duilio on his final journey.

Briraji stepped forward again, but this time Lord Danato followed him. "You should not have escaped," the sage said. "Your corpse will be abandoned in the desert, a carrion feast for insects and birds."

Help me!

"Close your eyes and embrace me."

Lucia trembled as she swallowed and exhaled. She closed her eyes and felt the terror, a boiling, acidic squall raging within.

"But I'm not going to kill you. My men are." The sage's voice entered her ears like sand shoved into a wound. "They can see you. You cannot see them."

Lucia stood on the shifting blackness, still holding Ysa's shield. She swung the metal around in a great circle to scare off any attackers, then covered her chest with it again.

"That won't do you any good when you cannot see your assailants, my daughter. Close your eyes and embrace me."

And let you kill me?

"If you want my help, do as I say. You see, you do have free will."

Lucia crouched, facing Briraji's form, and positioned the shield to cover her front. She closed her eyes again and saw Lord Danato standing over her mother in the bloodied birthing pool. Her mother's face was the very picture of torment: bloodshot eyes, lips stretched above gnashing teeth, clenched muscles and skin.

Mother!

Lucia ejected tears from her eyes.

The black god stood over her in the red-dotted blackness with deadly countenance and clenched fists.

You would kill me, too? Why do you hate me?

Lord Danato raised one glistening, muscled arm and bellowed like a tempest from the underworld. With all his power, he dropped his fist straight down.

A man screamed.

Danato swung his fist with a backhanded swing, circling in a perfect arc.

Another scream.

"What is happening?" Briraji's voice quivered.

Lord Danato raised his elbow above his head, grabbed his fist in his other hand, and heaved the elbow down.

Another scream.

He bared his gritted white teeth, turned and punched forward with all his fury.

A fourth scream.

He yelled as he used his other fist in a sudden backhanded blow.

Five.

He gathered both hands and slung them downward like a hammer.

339

Six.

The god stood and relaxed his back. His chest heaved with his vigorous breaths. Both arms stretched straight out, striking out to his sides.

Seven. Eight.

He slung back his head and slammed it forward, as if cracking someone's skull with his own.

Nine.

The god fell down.

Chapter 78: The White God

"... PLEASE GIVE YOUR YOUNG PRINCE this one chance to save Pawelon."

Briraji snarled. "Defend yourself."

Rao closed his eyes, held his breath, and projected the sacred syllables of his primary *sadhana* into the depths of his consciousness.

His field of vision altered. He saw the soldiers as fields of red energy, but could not find Lucia or Briraji. The soldiers advanced toward the spot where Lucia had been.

A new form appeared, a massive, solid white field of energy, taller than two men. Its only distinguishing feature: a yellow tear on its left cheek.

The black god's soul is white?

The god followed behind the leading soldiers. As the spearmen rushed forward, the suddenly white god swung his heavy arms about, killing the them one by one.

Stop! Rao sent the god his thought.

If Lord Danato heard him, he did not answer.

Rao focused all of his limited *ojas* on the Rezzian god. The god cocked back his head and slammed it forward into a Pawelon soldier's skull. Rao projected as much force as he could to disrupt the god's presence in the physical world.

The god fell down. His white face lifted to look at Rao. "I will come for you today, Prince, but not now. You have a purpose to fulfill first."

"You're going to kill me?" Rao asked.

"No. Another god will. Then I will come for your soul."

The god's promise awed Rao's consciousness like a blazing pyre. "Lord Danato, stop killing my men. They're only following orders. Briraji is the one you need to stop."

The Pawelon soldiers stayed back, clearly afraid of attacking Lucia and meeting the fate of their dead brethren.

"I cannot stop him," Lord Danato said. "The gods of Lux Lucis respect his accomplishments too much to see him die at our own hands."

"Then I will do it."

341

"Your power is depleted, Prince."

Rao lowered his subtle body to ground level and knelt. "Then please give me strength."

The god stood and smiled with his lips closed over his teeth. "A request I cannot refuse." Danato leaned down and picked up Ysa's white blade. He held the sharp blade itself, and as he did the god's blood trickled down the white metal. Danato's long strides carried him to Rao, to offer the sword's handle. "This blade is a part of my sister. It is a part of me and of all the gods of Lux Lucis, for we are one. Take it and it will give you sight. You will see Lucia and the sage."

"Wait—why did you send them to the lake?"

"You know the answer, Prince."

"You are the god of karma."

"That is not incorrect."

"Then did Ilario's death settle the king's debt?"

"No, Prince, but the debt will be finished this day."

Lord Danato held the sword's handle just above Rao's outstretched hand. Rao stood and took the blade. Darkness overcame his vision and the god's form disappeared. Within the blackness Rao found Lucia and Briraji.

"Rao," Briraji said, "Welcome. Your *ojas* is drained already? Can't hide any longer?"

"I am still weak from my combat with the Haizzem."

"I know."

"Briraji, you win. I will do it." Rao stood with Ysa's sword in hand and approached Lucia.

She still crouched with Ysa's shield in front of her. "You're a bastard, Rao. We had an agreement."

"I talked to Lord Danato. He told me he could not stop Briraji." Rao turned to look at the sage. "The gods of Lux Lucis respect Briraji's power too much to interfere."

Briraji smiled, a sight Rao had not seen before.

"And if a god cannot kill him, you might as well surrender, Lucia. I have a future, to protect my people."

Briraji walked forward again. Rao stood within sword's reach of Lucia.

"You might want to pray to your goddess now," Rao said.

Rao prayed: *Ysa, Danato, lend me your divine power.*

342

Rao spun backward and pointed the blade at Briraji as he visualized the relic's power shooting toward the sage. Although he hadn't intended to let it go, the sword escaped his grip and flew into Briraji's chest.

The darkness lifted and the sun burned down on Rao again. The remaining soldiers looked upon Briraji's fallen body, impaled by Ysa's white blade. Lucia still crouched behind the shield.

"My brothers, the men who died ..." Rao pointed at the nine dead Pawelon soldiers as he stood. "Were killed by the black god of Rezzia. I stopped the god myself, saving the rest of your lives. The god told me he would kill you all unless I killed Briraji, our greatest sage. I was forced to choose the lives of many over the life of one."

The soldiers looked at him and at each other, some of them backing away from him.

"Let me go do my duty. I need to take this prisoner to Rezzia's king and Haizzem. They will talk to me, and with some luck Rezzia's war will end on this day."

Lucia's horse walked toward her. *Think fast.* "I am controlling this beast." *Not at all.* The mare moved awkwardly with the arrow above her front leg, and stopped near Lucia. Rao gathered his spiritual strength and found that, after holding Ysa's sword, he had more *ojas* than he thought. He focused his hands in mudras to control Lucia's body again and send a psychic wind to cause her to fall as before.

"Brothers, help me put her over the horse. I have weakened her greatly. She can't resist you." Rao approached Lucia, and as he did prayed to Lucia's goddess for her cooperation with the animal. With his back turned to his men, he looked down on Lucia's face and winked. He squatted beside her and whispered, "Play along."

He released her from his power. "But before you raise the dog onto the horse, you should spit on her."

Rao spit in Lucia's direction, being careful to miss her face. He mouthed to her, "Sorry."

She narrowed her eyes in anger. She grunted, pretending to resist Rao's power.

Three soldiers came forward, with their spears lowered. "If you insist on going, we will come with you, Prince Rao. We will protect you."

"You can't come with me. If I have soldiers behind me, their king and their Haizzem will not meet with me. I must go alone to negotiate for our freedom. Do not follow me. Do you understand?"

The men nodded and a line soon formed at Lucia's feet. Rao picked up the shield from the ground and stood beside her. Each soldier, more than a dozen, came forward and spit on her.

"Lift her onto the horse's back. Position her so she lies across and tie her to the saddle."

Lucia played the part, acting as if she had no control of her body while they lifted her onto the horse.

Rao walked to Briraji, gripped the white and yellow handle of Ysa's sword, and pulled the blade from the sage's chest. The dripping blood made his muscles weak and his stomach queasy.

Peace to you, Briraji.

"Go back and carry a message to General Indrajit. Tell him Briraji and the other men fought bravely against Rezzia's black god, and tell them I have gone to talk to Rezzia's king and Haizzem to bring an end to Rezzia's invasion. If I succeed today, you will see your families again soon. If I fail, you must defend Pawelon in my stead."

"Then we will be with you in spirit, my Prince," a soldier said.

Another raised his fist in salute. "Victory!"

"Victory!" the crowd said together.

Rao motioned the first solider over to him. *You've got a trustworthy face.* He whispered to the young man in private. "Also, find my partner, the sage Aayu. I want you to tell him the truth about what happened to Briraji."

The soldier nodded and saluted him again.

Rao continued with a smile, "And tell him I said his *sadhana* doesn't work."

With Lucia tied above her horse, Rao began to pull the white mare forward. The beast followed. *Thank you.*

Rao looked back. The soldiers watched him, a few of them with their palms pressed together in a spiritual gesture of blessings and respect.

'*'

Lucia found Albina's motion beneath her oddly comforting. As Rao led her further into the desert, she continued chastising herself for believing Rao had turned against her.

"We've gone far enough, haven't we?" she asked.

"I'm sorry about the spitting."

Bastard. She mostly believed him, though. "If you hadn't saved my life—"

"Lord Danato was doing a fine job of it."

"You saw that?"

"I did. I was in my subtle body. Most human auras appear red. Yours is different, by the way. It must be because you are a Haizzem. But Danato's entire being was solid white."

I've had enough irony for one lifetime.

Rao continued, "I actually did talk to him."

Lucia shook her head. "Let me down." She wanted to watch his face while he explained.

"I think it would be better for you to stay where you are. If your army sees us, I want them to see exactly this: you draped across your horse, tied down."

He's probably right. "Then what happened when you talked to Lord Danato?"

"He really did tell me your gods weren't willing to kill Briraji. He said they respect his power too much to do that. So I offered to do it and asked for his help. He gave me Ysa's sword. When I took it, I was able to see you and Briraji for the first time. I also felt stronger."

Lucia's mind stopped, arrested by confusion. *He helped both of us then.* She gazed at the shadowed ground passing beneath Albina's hooves, enjoying the scent of the desert.

"I asked him why he sent you to the lake—"

"And?"

"He confirmed my suspicion. Then he told me your father's debt would be settled today."

More cryptic information I do not need.

"He also told me he would be coming for me today, after my death."

Cryptic information you did not need.

"Lucia, if he speaks the truth, I *will* need you to protect me."

"Don't worry. Are you holding Ysa's shield?"

"I am."

Then with your shield protect him, Ysa. "Keep her sword, too."

345

"I will."

"At least untie me, so I can get up when I need to."

Albina halted. Rao loosened the rope binding Lucia's midsection to the saddle.

They stayed quiet for some time after they resumed. Lucia worked again to reconcile what she knew about The Black One, her torturer since she was a girl, with what the god had done today and Rao's theory of the black god.

"Help me understand something. Lord Danato has never been a friend to me—in fact he's been a harsh companion. If he is who you think he is, why would he torture me?"

Rao said after a pause, "Perhaps you were suffering someone else's karma. Every stray bit of karma in this universe must be resolved by someone, sooner or later. Karma can never be destroyed, only transformed."

"And Danato promised my father's debt would be resolved today? Does that mean someone else is going to die?"

"That's hard to say."

"Could it mean my father is going to die?" *Or Caio? Or me?*

"I don't know, Lucia. My advice is to keep your thoughts on a positive outcome. We create this world out of the power of our own consciousness. Now we must use this power to create a solution."

I wish it were that easy, Prince.

'*'

Rao raised the skin and sipped the last of his water. An expanse of barren desert stretched eastward toward the Rezzian army. The temperature had begun to warm, though the sun would not reach its zenith for some time. The Rezzian army looked like a mirage through the warming air, a shifting mass of human darkness.

"Lucia, we've been sighted."

"What's happening?"

"Four men on horseback are approaching."

"I wish you luck."

He'd managed to control his mind most of the day and keep his thoughts centered on his breath and body, but now the Rezzian threat was real and buried

346

fears pricked his spine like icy needles. He continued to pull Lucia's horse with her draped across it.

"Thank you for this chance," he said. "If your black god comes to me in death, I hope it will be so that our people can live in peace again. For this, I would gladly sacrifice my life."

I should have died when I fought Caio. Every breath since then has been a gift from Rezzia's gods.

Rao wondered if his vision for this world would not take root, if the soil of Gallea was not receptive to his imagination.

I have to try.

Rao pulled the horse to another stop. He held the bejeweled shield and white sword of Ysa for protection and also to show the Rezzians he was in control.

Goddess Ysa, if you can hear me, I only wish what is best for your people—and mine. Please give me the strength I will need.

'*'

The goddess Ysa, her slight frame covered in silver armor, sat calmly upon her giant steed. Her lance's tip pierced the harsh earth. She faced the east and stared with stoic restraint into the heart of the Rezzian army.

'*'

Rao felt stronger with the blade in his hand, as the black god suggested he would, but he knew the weakness in his body would still limit the power of his spirit.

The four riders approached warily. Rao planted Ysa's sword in the dirt, within arm's reach, and waved with his palm open. One Rezzian wore the fine red and yellow uniform of a diplomat. The others were hardened soldiers, each with a sword hanging at his side and a throwing spear in hand.

"I am the Prince of Pawelon. I seek an immediate audience with the king and Haizzem of Rezzia. Across this horse I have the royal daughter Lucia, devotee of the goddess Ysa. She is under my control, and should any harm come to me she will immediately suffer for it. I have afflicted her body with a deadly magic that will kill her if any harm comes to me. I will not speak to anyone but the king and the Haizzem themselves. Go send for them and tell them to come soon and alone or not at all. Tell them to bring the Pawelon girl they took after the duel. If they refuse, I will disappear with Lucia and they will never see her again."

The delegation looked disgusted. They looked at Lucia, who played her part by hanging lifelessly over her mare.

"We will tell them," the diplomat said before he yanked his horse's neck around and galloped back to the east.

Chapter 79: After the Deluge

Earlier that morning.

NARAYANI AWOKE IN CAIO'S BED, cuddled in his arms. She remembered Mya's rod had been in her hands when she fell asleep. She found it near her pillow and held it again. Her body shivered from a sudden rush of energy before her mind and body sunk into a profound calm. She remained aware of the trauma within her, but felt numb to its sting. Caio's healing powers had deadened her raw emotions and restored sanity.

She rolled over and rested her forehead against Caio's. His eyes opened, revealing his unguarded soul.

"How are you feeling?" he asked.

"You can't leave me alone again."

"Never again."

She pulled his body against hers and savored the warmth of his skin.

Caio used two hands to massage around her heart, with one hand on her chest and the other on her back. "Can you use your ability to make yourself invisible again? I need you to come with me today. I don't know what is going to happen, but if anything happens to me, I want you to go back to Rao."

She sensed sadness in his voice. "Why do you say that?"

"Last night I dreamt this would be the final day of the war. Of course, I want you to come back to Remaes with me. I want you to see our palace. There's so much space there: tall ceilings, atriums revealing the stars, white clay walls. And love. Everything there is full of devotion. It is paradise."

She tried to visualize it, but couldn't stop worrying about the fear beneath his words.

"If anything happens to me, I want you to be happy, and that means staying away from my father and going back to Rao," Caio said.

The commotion of soldiers readying themselves for another march surrounded their tent.

"Let's go to Remaes today, then. I want to see your holy city. I want to see the temples and minarets."

"I would give you anything you ask of me. But now I have a duty to perform." He kissed her lips softly three times.

Stay with me. Hold me. For once, let other men fight.

Caio sat up near the edge of the bed, keeping one hand over her heart. "I must fulfill the duty before me. Lord Oderigo assured me in my dream that on this day, the will of Lux Lucis will be done."

After Caio dressed himself and completed his morning prayers, Narayani activated Aayu's mantras and followed Caio through the Rezzian camp. The sight of each officer's tent generated feelings of unease, but no one seemed to be able to see her, other than Caio.

She stayed with him after he mounted his grey horse and set off with his father riding beside him. The entire army terrified her, but her invisibility made the experience thrilling at the same time.

She noticed the king's guilt, something he could not conceal behind his golden armor: the tightness of his jaw, his shifty eyes, his awkward attempts at conversation with his son. She noticed the sword Caio's father wore across his back and wondered how she might be able to slit his throat with it.

Caio looked down often, to make sure she was keeping up with him. Narayani carried all she had brought with her, one leather bag hanging near her belly, with its strap wrapped around her left shoulder.

The army marched at a brisk pace throughout the morning. The sun had traveled high when the Rezzian drummers began pounding their instruments and the army halted its progress. Messengers arrived to explain to the king and Haizzem that a white horse had been spotted with one Pawelon pulling it. The army took a needed rest while a diplomatic party investigated. Eventually a man in a fine red and yellow uniform rode through the Rezzian ranks to address the two Rezzian leaders.

"Havah ilz avah Haizzem. It appears Pawelon's very prince walks alone through the desert with Lucia on horseback—on her own horse, in fact." The diplomat continued and explained Rao's demands.

Narayani felt ripped in two when she discovered Rao was risking his life to rescue her. She knew then that Rao must have argued for the exchange of Caio's sister and herself. His pleading must have been denied by his father or, much worse, *her* father. Or both of them.

350

"Where is the girl?" the king asked.

"She's gone. I let her go." Caio looked down at Narayani and nodded as if talking to himself.

His father stared at him, his mouth open in the sea of his beard. "You're going to need to find her."

"That's impossible." Caio sat tall in his saddle. "I have no idea where she's gone."

"You lost a valuable prisoner, and you're telling me there is nothing we can do to find her, to bring back your own sister?"

"I am sure we can find another way."

"We are talking about your sister's life, Caio. Surely you can think of some way to find the Pawelon."

"Impossible." Caio looked back toward the Rezzian camp, away from the king.

Narayani felt heartened by Caio's refusal, but her mind spun with confusion over what outcome she should hope for.

"We will just have to take Lucia from him," Caio said.

"It is obviously a trap, my Haizzem." The king turned from Caio to address the diplomat again, "How sure are you that he has Lucia? Did you see her up close?"

"Yes, my King. She seemed to be under some kind of spell, unable to free herself. And," the man put his lips together and waited a moment, "I neglected to mention, their prince holds the relics of Ysa, her sword and shield."

The king slapped his saddle in frustration, leaned back, and bared his yellow teeth as he shook his head. "Caio, do you believe we can take him together? Tell me."

"Yes, but we would have to act quickly and finish him before he can react."

Narayani walked a handful of steps away from Caio, to the west. He didn't seem to notice. "Caio, why don't you talk to him first?" she asked. He gave no indication he heard her.

"Thank you, you are dismissed," Vieri said to the diplomat. He looked directly at Caio for one of the first times that day. "They must have men hidden out there, some sort of ambush prepared for us."

Caio's wide eyes narrowed into a determined look. "Then pray we'll be ready for them."

"If we get far enough, we'll talk to him, ask him about this magic he claims to have implanted in Lucia. You'll use your senses to find out if he is lying. If he is, we'll slay him then and there. If he tells the truth, we'll find out his demands. And if he insists on the Pawelon girl, you had better be able to find her. Do not admit that she is gone, even if she is. Not that I believe you."

Caio ignored his father's jab. "Before we do this, I have something to speak with you about. Ride with me." Caio gave his steed a gentle kick. He and the king rode together past the soldiers and into the open desert, far enough from the front line to gain some privacy. Though Narayani walked with him, Caio looked about nervously, as if he could no longer see her.

She waved her hands at him. She called his name.

No reaction.

She remembered something Rao told her back in Kannauj, that the ability to see through Aayu's *sadhana* had something to do with the depth of a person's meditation and their state of mind. She wondered if something in Caio's mind had changed.

"I would like to forgive you for what you did to Narayani, but I don't know that I can. I see you more clearly now. I know you have always loved me and Lucia, but now I see the full truth, that you have never been ashamed to cause suffering to other people to further your own agendas."

"In time, Son, you may understand me and my actions."

"Not all of them."

"It has not been easy, Caio, being your father, and failing to achieve even one great victory. Meanwhile, my people suffer yet another plague." His father lowered his defeated eyes. "I struggle to understand many things."

Caio looked at Vieri, whose gaze continued to focus on the ground. "There is nothing I have that I wouldn't share with you. There's nothing I am that I wouldn't be without you. We are different, but we are the same. You truly love your people. You want the best for them. I do, too. We only go about it differently." Caio looked around as if searching for Narayani, but clearly he could no longer see or hear her.

Hearing Caio capitulate to his father's feelings, Narayani's jilted gut churned with abandonment.

"Caio, I would like to say that I have done everything for you and Lucia, or for the people of Rezzia. In some respects that is true. But I wanted to be the one to save our people and elevate them. I have wanted to know that my legacy is greater than any king before me. For being a selfish man, I am sorry. I'm not a spiritual man."

Caio's eyes softened and his face turned kind. "Since my earliest memories, you have always been my hero. You always will be. I no longer agree with everything you do. I can't. But you have always loved me. And I will always love you, no matter the things you've done. In time, I may forgive you."

Narayani's discomfort turned to an expanding rage.

You could still love this man? You would pad his ego and soothe his pride?

The king's eyes looked wet. From his horse, Caio grabbed one of his father's hands even as he continued searching for Narayani.

"Lucia told me something after the *Ayot*. Lord Danato gave her a message. The Black One said that only one, out of Pawelon's prince and me, would survive this war. He said the war will not end until one of us is dead."

Now I understand what you said about going back with Rao ...

The king looked terrified as he stared into his son's eyes.

"Then it is time we rescue your sister. Pray with me, Son. Pray with all the feeling and devotion your heart possesses."

Narayani's mind dropped into certainty.

She ran toward Rao.

She saw him up ahead, standing beside the white horse, holding a decorated round shield. "Rao!" She held her bag with her left hand and forced her legs as fast as they could go. "Rao!"

"Narayani!" he yelled back.

"Rao, they are coming to kill you! If the Haizzem senses you are lying, they will try to kill you."

Rao pulled the horse forward as Narayani ran. She stopped before him and they stared at one another as if looking at mirages. Narayani closed her eyes and reversed Aayu's mantra. She felt heavy and solid in her body once again. She fell forward into Rao's arms.

Chapter 80: The Trojan Horse

CAIO WALKED BESIDE HIS FATHER, holding the sacred rod of Mya in one hand. His father carried Lord Galleazzo's golden shield and his own thick, curved falchion. Caio felt his heart beating nervously and noticed his shallow breathing. It seemed surreal to see his mortal enemy again so soon, once again approaching from the desert, this time pulling Lucia's limp body across her own horse. He recalled Ilario being in the same position not long ago.

The prince yelled, "Narayani!" as if calling to her.

Caio searched all around, but he still could not find her. He'd assumed she ran away, back toward Pawelon, while he was speaking with his father.

"Shall we?" Caio's father said.

"Wait."

The prince stopped. Narayani appeared out of nothing and fell into Rao's embrace.

"And there's the pretty pig," his father said. "Outstanding!"

"Don't go yet," Caio said, putting his arm in front of his father. "Give them some time."

His father grunted, but Caio refused to move. He remembered holding Narayani as she slept. He could still see her soft face and dazzling eyes.

How could I expect anything at all after what my father did to you? You've finally come to your senses about me and what I represent.

Rao's and Narayani's voices became louder. They seemed to be arguing. Rao shoved Narayani away, behind him.

"Now," Caio said.

Caio walked westward with his father beside him, praying to Mya and Oderigo to protect them from hidden dangers. His scans of the area found nothing unusual, just Prince Rao holding Albina's reins.

"Wait. Lucia's moving," Caio said.

She climbed into her horse's saddle and waved. She wore a dirtied Pawelon robe and her customary long black gloves. Rao watched her and did nothing. Caio and his father exchanged confused glances.

The white mare approached at a walk.

"Lucia, thank the gods you have returned to us!" Vieri said.

Thank you, Ten of Lux Lucis.

"Pawelon's prince freed me from their disgusting prison. He wants to speak with you. I've agreed to accompany him and protect him—"

"But—"

She spoke over her father, "He has saved my life three times already. Do not harm him."

Farther ahead, Rao pleaded with Narayani to stay back. She remained where he asked her to, but with her face molded into an indignant expression. "I come to speak about these prisoners," Rao said in Rezzian as he strode forward holding the sword and shield of Ysa.

Lucia directed Albina to step backward until Rao caught up with her. Caio and his father stood side by side.

Caio gripped Mya's rod and felt its power coursing through his veins.

The king raised his sword slightly as he took a sudden step forward. "We will take my daughter back and you can have your lady."

"It's not that simple. I've saved your daughter's life more than once already. I know what she means to you, to your kingdom, and to your army. My lady is but a civilian."

She's not good enough for you? Caio thought.

"You can't bargain for more now, Prince," his father said. "We have already exchanged our prisoners. I believe you're holding two relics that belong to my family."

"Father," Lucia said, "there's more to this. He cast some form of dark magic into my body. I experienced it going into me and I still feel it inside me."

Caio looked to his father. *You know I can't read Lucia's emotions.* Rezzia's king pursed his lips before exhaling forcefully.

"What do you want then?" Caio asked, surprised at the venom in his own voice.

"An end to this war. Your entire army must leave this canyon as we agree to end our conflict in a stalemate," Rao said.

Just as we are about to defeat you. Just as Lucia returns to us.

"What will you do if we refuse?" Vieri asked.

"He's promised me he'll kill me," Lucia said. "He promises he can do it even from a distance."

"Would you do that?" Caio asked.

The prince looked at Lucia. He did not answer.

"He has told me over and over that he would," Lucia said.

Why won't you answer me?

"Let the man speak for himself," his father said, then gave Caio another glance.

"Speak," Caio commanded him. "Would you do this to my sister?"

"Your sister has already explained my position. I will not repeat myself. Your only option is to agree to lead your people far away from the canyon for good."

"Maybe I will," Caio said though he did not mean it, "but I promise you I won't do so until I hear you say it yourself. Tell me you would kill my sister, that you have implanted some foul magic into her so that you can end her life at your whim."

Rao widened his stance, as if preparing to defend himself.

Caio sensed the prince's fear and embarrassment. *You're lying. You lied to Lucia about your power, too.*

"Caio, you know this conflict is unnecessary and cursed," Lucia said. "There was never any reason for it. We can finally have the peace you've wanted."

"That's not why we're here, Lucia," her father answered. "We came here for you. Rezzia's soldiers still have their honor to uphold. Don't you know their citadel is beginning to crumble, thanks to your brother?"

"Caio is the commander of what *was* your army," she said. "He can make his own decisions now."

"Are you really telling us the truth?" Caio asked Pawelon's prince. "Tell me about this foul magic you have used against my sister."

"Caio, he's saved my life three times already. Once after the duel. Once when he freed me from their prison. Once this morning, as he fought his own men to save me."

"And yet I don't know if I believe him now," Caio said. Caio continued probing Prince Rao's emotions, but discovered only anxiety and fear beneath his calm exterior.

"You would actually risk your sister's life?" Rao asked.

"Says the man who ran a spear through her chest," Caio said.

After a brief pause, Narayani yelled, "Rao, use Aayu's *sadhana*! You can't trust them. Come back with me."

"Caio, I swore to protect him," Lucia said. She threw one leg over Albina and dismounted.

"Let me show you again that I am a reasonable man," Rao said. He handed Ysa's sword over to Lucia.

Lucia took the white blade and pointed it downward. She took a position between Caio and Rao and held up her other hand to call Caio and her father off. "Can't we agree with his proposal, Caio? We are on the verge of winning, aren't we? We can leave with our pride intact, knowing we showed our enemies mercy."

"I think he lied to you, Lucia. He hasn't put any magic in your body that can kill you. Aren't I right, Prince?"

"Can you take that risk?" Prince Rao asked.

"Father, he's lying."

'*'

Four gods surrounded them. Behind Caio stood Lord Oderigo and his sister Mya, the vine-covered pair. Lord Galleazzo stood to King Vieri's left; the god's crimson cape hung flat against his back. The silver-armored goddess, Ysa, watched from atop her own white steed, beside Lucia and Rao, facing the other gods.

Caio's father surged forward with his falchion raised, around Lucia's right, to strike the Prince of Pawelon.

Lord Galleazzo took one long stride in sync with the king.

'*'

Lord Danato's message to Lucia flashed in Caio's mind: *"He said this war will not and cannot end before one of you dies—either you or Pawelon's prince."*

Time slowed for Caio just as he desired, after he called on The Lord of The Book of Time. Caio observed the panic on Lucia's and Rao's faces. He gripped Mya's holy rod and prayed: *My goddess Mya, if I have ever been a good servant to you, finish him now without warning.*

Mya appeared, stepping forward beside him, wearing her dress of vines. The goddess's eyes were wet with tears. She tilted her head to the right as she stretched out her right arm and pointed her fingers at Prince Rao.

357

Caio saw an image of the prince submerged in the deepest ocean water, quickly surrounded by the freezing darkness. The prince expelled an involuntary scream as he fell to the desert floor, crushed by the depths of the ocean in his mind.

King Vieri caught up to Prince Rao as the Pawelon fell, swinging his falchion down at the sage's chest.

'*'

Lord Galleazzo crossed his powerful arms as Lucia swung Ysa's blade upward to crash its white metal against her father's steel. The goddess Ysa's cold face merely observed without flinching.

As her father stepped backward, Lucia looked over her shoulder at Rao's corpse.

'*'

Narayani watched the king run forward swinging his sword. She watched Rao crumple to the earth.

She ran for him.

"Caio, you did this?" Caio's sister said.

"I knew he was lying. He didn't use any of his magic on you."

Lucia turned around to look at Rao's body and looked up at Narayani running toward her. She raised her white sword and pointed her open palm at Narayani to tell her to stop.

"Let me help him," Narayani said. She dropped onto her knees beside Rao and felt a burning sensation traveling from her stomach to her mouth. Rao's face had been instantly bruised into hideous shades of purple and blue. She turned away from him and somehow managed not to vomit, then rubbed her eyes and forehead, hiding from the sight of Rao's corpse.

"We did this together, Son."

Narayani felt Rao's body. His body was already clammy and cold from Caio's magic.

Caio stepped forward with his arms and chest open. "Narayani, it had to be one of us, either him or me. Now you can come back with me."

"Do what I asked you to do last night. Kill me! Right now. Let me fall against him and die."

MOSES SIREGAR III

Still two paces away, Caio raised his palms as if he intended to heal her.

"No more," she said. "Don't touch me with your gods."

"I'll do it." The king raised his blade above his head and stepped forward.

"Don't you touch her." Lucia bent her knees and brought Ysa's sword in front of her forehead, horizontal and ready to block the king's weapon.

"Have you gone mad?" her father said. "She nearly got you and Caio killed. She is evil, nothing but bad luck."

"Don't touch her, Father," Caio said. "She is distraught. She doesn't mean what she's saying."

"I do. I could never go back with you." Narayani didn't want the king to be the one to finish her, though. She ran her hands along Rao's body to look for a weapon, but found none.

Caio extended his hands outward and stepped close to Narayani. "Please. I want to take you far away from here, so you'll never have to experience any place like this ever again. I want you to live with me in peace and luxury in Remaes. Please let me make it up to you for all you've endured."

Caio put his hands on her cheeks. For one brief moment, she considered his offer.

"Viparyas amrakh!" yelled a Pawelon voice.

Caio's skin shook and rippled and, like Rao's, turned dark, sickly shades of purple and blue. Caio collapsed in a lifeless heap before her, beside Rao's body.

Narayani swung her head around. Rajah Devak stood ten paces away, in a sage's stance, holding his fingers in a forked mudra. Aayu stood near to him, holding a great spear.

What?

Rezzia's King took two great steps forward and hurled his sword at the rajah. The blade found its mark.

The rajah screamed in pain, but—he didn't sound like the rajah. The rajah fell backward and slammed down flat.

Narayani looked back toward Aayu, but Devak stood where Aayu had been standing. She stood and looked again at the rajah's fallen body. Aayu lay there instead, with the king's sword in his chest.

She felt Caio's neck. *Exactly like Rao's.*

Just as the rajah stepped forward holding his great spear, Narayani ran to Aayu. Her cousin writhed on the ground, grunting and screaming in pain.

"What just happened?" Narayani asked as she yanked the king's sword from Aayu's shoulder. Her cousin squeezed his eyes shut and unleashed a horrible cry.

Narayani fell to her knees and opened her bag. "This will hurt." She found her tincture for treating deep wounds and poured the oil into the bleeding wound. Aayu opened his mouth like a dying lion, suffering a silent scream. She grabbed a handful of cloth bandages and held them against the deep cut.

"I used my secondary *sadhana*," Aayu mumbled with incredible speed. "I appeared as the rajah, he appeared as me."

"Rao is dead, Aayu," Narayani said as her chest heaved from her misery. "And you just killed the Haizzem."

"He was about to touch you. I killed him with Rao's own *sadhana*." Still on the ground, Aayu turned his head and spit out blood. "What is Devak doing?"

The rajah of Pawelon thrust his great spear forward, backing Lucia and the king away.

Chapter 81: Choosing Death

LUCIA WATCHED AS Aayu's body became the rajah's, and as the rajah's body became Aayu's. She had no time to consider the sage's power that made it possible. The rajah pointed his long spear and raced for her.

Her father came forward. The rajah's spear clacked as her father's holy shield deflected it.

Lucia fell back. She lifted Ysa's shield from Rao's limp arm.

"Who killed my son?" the rajah asked in his own language, stepping around her father with his spear poised to strike.

Lucia remembered her power as a Haizzem. The one she'd chosen not to use on Ilario, the ability she would have to use now.

"My son killed him, as it should have been when they fought." Vieri raised his voice as he said, "Now look at my boy." He threw one arm backward, pointing at Caio. The sons of the two men lay beside one another, badly disfigured and bruised. Vieri pulled a wide dagger from his belt.

"Then you will finally bury a son, too." The rajah stepped back and lowered his spear. "I'll make you an offer. You bury yours and I bury mine?"

Lucia knew her father would feel naked without his falchion. She crept forward with knees bent, prepared to dodge or deflect the rajah's thrusts. "Listen! Rao rescued me so we could negotiate. You can choose to let their deaths be the end to all this fighting."

The rajah's black eyes searched her and her father. "That *is* what my son would've wanted."

"Not mine," her father said, "My son was sent by our gods to conquer your people and we will do it in his name, even if in death."

"What nonsense," Lucia blurted out. "Caio never wanted to kill anyone."

"It didn't take him long to realize his duty," Vieri said.

A frightening idea hatched in Lucia's mind, to use her power against her father.

"Father, Caio is dead. Duilio is dead. Will you keep fighting until I'm dead, too? Our gods do not support your cursed war."

Her father stepped backward, away from the rajah, motioning for Lucia to follow him. The rajah held his position. Narayani tended Aayu's wound. Lucia and her father stood close to Caio's body.

"Whether you want the fighting to continue or not, we must bury our sons," the rajah said. "You've taken all three of mine. At least give me this honor."

Vieri's nose twitched as he sniffled. He rubbed his nose with the back of one hand.

"Then what the prince told me is true," she said. "You had his brothers killed when they were little boys."

"I did what any worthy King of Rezzia would have done."

Lucia stabbed Ysa's sword into the ground. She grabbed one of her gloves, near her shoulder, and pulled it down and off. The black fabric fell beside the white sword.

Her father's lips twitched as he stared at the markings on her arm. "What in Danato's underworld?"

The rajah still held his spear in two hands. "So you didn't know."

"I am a Haizzem, or I suppose I would be a *Haizzema*." Lucia picked up Ysa's sword again. "These markings appeared long ago, a few years after Mother died."

"What are you saying?" her father asked.

"I have borne the signs of the Haizzem all of my adult life. And I believe this means I can raise one man from death."

A quick smile flashed on her father's face.

The rajah raised his spear and leaned forward, as if ready to charge.

"Wait," Lucia commanded. "I want the two of you to work out a settlement here and now."

"Lucia, we are winning now. Bring Caio back to us so the three of us can finish their citadel together."

"I won't raise him unless you agree to end your war."

The rajah lowered his spear again.

Her father let out a huff of irritation and pointed his dagger at her as he spoke. "Do not blaspheme, and do *not* threaten me."

"If I do not raise Caio, I will be the living Haizzema. If I tell our army to return to Rezzia, they will."

"Madness! You are not Dux Spiritus."

"Neither are you," she said. "You've relinquished your position."

"And I would have it again if Caio were to fall, but the thought that you would let your brother die is *unholy!*"

"Agree to end your war. You can still end it proudly because you now have Pawelon on their heels."

"That is why giving up is unthinkable!"

"The only reason I am still alive is because their prince saved me, and he saved me so that we could have peace. That is what I believe in, too, Father. I warn you, if you do not agree to peace," Lucia said, then swallowed. "I will save the rajah's son instead."

Her father ignored the rajah for the first time as he stepped in front of Lucia and faced her. "I resent your attempt to coerce me. This is a *sacrilege.*"

"I don't care one whit about what you think or what you want. Think whatever you want about me, but I mean what I say. I have never meant anything more. Agree to a final peace with Pawelon, now, or I will raise their prince instead."

Her father's brow furrowed with wrath. "Don't you gods damn lie to me, and don't you dare play with your brother's life."

"Get out of my face." Lucia pointed east, at the Rezzian army. "You've played games with his life already, and countless more lives on top of his. I give you one last chance."

"Lucia, you have always been stubborn and now you are angry. Think about what you are saying. Think of the consequences."

"I will not tell you again. You are the one who had better think. If you want to see your son alive again, make a lasting peace with their rajah. Right now."

Vieri threw up his hands and turned his back. He began walking toward the Rezzian army, then spun around again and pointed his dagger at her. "You will not kill your brother. And if you do, I will make sure all of Rezzia knows about your decision."

The rajah rested the base of his spear against the ground; its tip pointed toward the high sun. Her father, some distance from both her and the rajah, lowered both his shield and dagger and watched her with great focus. Rao's lady still tended Aayu's wounds, though she also watched and listened.

Lucia knelt by Caio and Rao. She closed her eyes and drew a deep breath.

She opened her eyes. Lord Danato's massive form stood by the feet of her brother and Rao. He smelled of Rezzian incense. The sky shimmered with a deep shade of purple, not unlike it had been before dawn. She and Danato were alone with the bodies.

"They can't see me, Lucia. They can't hear us either."

"You've come for their souls?"

"Only one. As to which one, I leave that to you." Danato took one step and put his foot down near Rao's head. "You know the truth now, something you were never truly willing to ask me for."

"Why would I ask you for anything after all that you've done to me?"

"It only seemed I was doing it to you, my daughter. I am an instrument in the hands of inexorable forces."

"You've tortured me more times than I can remember."

"Your father killed two boys and one mother. Someone had to pay for his sins."

"Why me? Why not him?"

"He has suffered, Lucia, but the answer to your question is that you were the only one capable of suffering for him with the power to heal the stain. And you still have this power."

"What are you saying?"

"Your father knows what he has done. For you to process his karma, as the Pawelons say, means much more in the eyes of the gods—especially to my eyes. Because to you the pain makes no sense at all. You did nothing to deserve it. It feels totally unfair, just as it did to that man." The black god pointed at Pawelon's rajah.

"Is that why you killed Ilario?"

"I didn't kill him. I suggested that you go to the lake. The rest worked out naturally, because it was time. Time for this debt to be resolved, for both your father and for you."

"This is entirely unfair. I had nothing to do with any of this."

"To understand what is truly *fair* requires a god's perspective."

"Yes, my perspective is that of a little girl whose bed you entered, whom you tortured physically, mentally, emotionally, spiritually. If the way things are is that little girls suffer for grown men's sins, then your world is wrong."

"I understand that it feels that way, Lucia. If you could only see things in the proper perspective, the truth of existence as it really is. It seems you are distinct from others—"

"Of course it does. *I* am the one who has suffered! Don't tell me I haven't. Don't belittle me."

"Of course you have, Daughter. The gods are not indifferent to your suffering. There's far more love for you in the kingdom of Lux Lucis than you know. But we do not wish to deny you the chance to heal your kingdom from the affliction it has attracted to itself. Now that you understand, you must either heal this black mark or remain sick."

"Then tell me, Black One, how do I heal?"

"Fully meet the truth *and* meet the pain. I can help you if you open yourself to me." Danato looked down at the bodies and waved one dark hand over them. "What will you do? You can only save one." Danato put a heavy fist on the desert floor and squatted. The god examined the two bodies.

Danato being so close made Lucia's skin feel cold and sensitive, but for the first time in her life, she felt safe in the god's presence. "You've tried to help me all along?"

Danato did not look up, but said, "I have always been here for you. You were not ready to receive me, so I had to take extreme measures."

Which only turned me away from you. "I can't let my brother die, but I swore to protect Rao. He saved my life, multiple times. And he actually wants peace. My brother doesn't."

"Sometimes, dear Lucia, choosing and wishing are very different things." Danato turned his deep, dark eyes to her. She knew he saw through her soul. She wanted to look away, but then recognized, for the first time in her life, compassion in the god's eyes.

"I never wanted to hurt you, Lucia. The more you resisted me, the harder it had to become."

"Why? Where is the compassion in that? You're a god."

"Compassion has many faces. Some things you must learn on your own, for your own benefit." Danato looked down again.

Lucia removed Ysa's shield and placed her hands on Rao's sunken chest. "Rao would agree to have peace. I would only need to fight my father for control of the army."

Lord Danato looked at Rao's bruised face. "Have you decided then?"

Lucia recalled Caio as a baby in her arms. She pulled back her hands. "No. Even if Caio is enamored with war, he is my brother, our true Haizzem.

She put her hands on Caio's corpse.

THE BLACK GOD'S WAR

Danato's eyes rolled to gaze on Caio instead. "Very well, Lucia."

Lucia closed her eyes and felt her own buried suffering, first as if it were an echo, then as a hardening of every bit of her chest, from her neck to her ribs, to her belly. "What is this?" she asked the black god.

"Pain you have carried for a long, long time. Since I first came to you."

"My mother's death?"

"Her passing was the seed, Lucia, the core of your suffering."

The sound of his words caused subtle ripples throughout her body, like shivers, but much deeper. She felt something stirring, wanting to arise.

"What? What do I do?"

"Do not look away. Lower yourself into it. For once, soften. Then you can give it to me. You can give me all of your pain."

I am so tired of fighting you.

She only saw darkness. Her body slowly sank into something like thick, stinging mud. She struggled to stay out of it. As she fell in deeper, she struggled to swim. Nothing she did stopped her from descending into the mire.

Lower yourself into it. For once, soften.

The oozing blackness covered her eyes, ears, nose, and mouth. It enveloped her flesh, burning her skin.

She let go of struggling, and fell in deeper.

She saw the bloody birthing pool again. Sunlight streamed into the sacred chamber of the ancient minaret. She smelled the holy herbs and scents of Caio's birth. She heard her own ten-year-old screams as her mother died in her father's arms. Her sorrow expanded ... until nothing else existed.

I give this misery to you, Lord Danato.

A great shiver rocked her body and her awareness returned to the physical world.

She looked at her colored hands on Caio's chest. Lucia looked around at everyone watching her. Even Aayu watched her, lying on his side. Narayani stood and stumbled toward her, as if she could faint at any moment.

"You are going to kill Rao?" the girl asked. "Even though you swore to protect him?"

"Caio is my brother. I have loved and protected him all my life. I let my lover die so I could save Caio some day."

"And I have no one," Narayani said. "I've never had anyone that loved me, not until Rao."

366

Lucia remembered Ilario sleeping in her bed, his face, his lips. She remembered his death. "You are young and beautiful. You will find another love."

Narayani fell forward and down, collapsing her body into a heap of sorrow.

"Have you decided, my daughter?" Danato asked.

"Yes." Lucia picked up her hands again and placed them on Rao's chest. She looked up at the cloudless sky and tears poured from her eyes like a gentle rain.

I am sorry, Caio. What you really wanted, before your heart was twisted and broken, was peace. I only sacrifice you so that so many more will live.

Chapter 82:
Return to the Underworld

A MYSTERIOUS, SUBDUED LIGHT SOURCE lit the underworld sky. Most of the firmament alternated from impenetrable grey to flickers of soft light, mostly eclipsed by the thick atmosphere. Above a crumbling building in the distance, turbulent clouds roiled like a boiling cauldron, spinning around the structure as if it were their axis.

Rao stood in this great basin surrounded by tall, craggy mountains. His bare feet chafed against the cracked floor and hot, biting winds—full of steam—assaulted his subtle body.

Lord Danato loomed over him, all black skin and leather.

"You've come for me," Rao said.

"This remains to be seen."

"Is this your underworld?"

"No. This plane exists between the surface and the netherworld. Your life remains in Lucia's hands."

"She is considering saving me?"

The black god nodded once.

Just ahead, the harsh ground became a polished natural floor. Close to the distant mountains ahead, Danato's fabled lighthouse literally glided around the smooth surface while the dark clouds followed it.

"Follow," Danato said, leading Rao toward the structure. The black god's strides lengthened and Rao's raw feet ran to keep up. He stumbled and fell once, twice, three times before he reached the swinging, dilapidated black wooden door.

The black god stood near the entrance, facing Rao. "You have only one chance at life. To exercise it, you must enter."

Without another thought, Rao leapt over the few crumbling steps, through the door, and squeezed into a dark vestibule. Dim rays of light from outside revealed a much heavier door in front of him, one reinforced by tall bands of steel and decorated with round obsidian gems. It blocked the only way forward. Carved into it were the following words in a calligraphic Pawelon script:

"May the spectre of death be your ever-present liberation."

Rao pressed the lever atop the rusty handle and pushed. The metallic hinges produced an echoing screech ...

'*'

The light of the sun blinded Rao's eyes, but a transcendent calm precluded him from feeling any pain.

Clang. The sound of metal against metal. Clang.

The washed out, white sky slowly differentiated into a field of blue and a burning sun.

Clang. A man screamed, dimly.

"Rao ... Rao ..." The voice echoed like drops of water dripping into a tub.

Two hands lifted him from under his shoulders. Narayani's face blocked out the blue heaven.

"Your father needs you! Get up." She lowered her face to his and kissed his lips.

The world spun around him in a great panoramic vision. There: Lucia holding Ysa's relics, Narayani lifting him, Caio dead, Aayu prone, and his father fighting the king of Rezzia.

With Narayani pushing him from behind, he rose to a sitting position.

Rao's father looked at him for a moment before the king charged the rajah and brought down his curved falchion. Devak had just enough time to block Vieri's swing; holding his spear in two hands, he received the king's sword against the shaft of his weapon, and then pushed the king back.

Why? Rao wondered.

The king and rajah danced around each other. Devak bled from one forearm.

Rao worked his way to his feet and put aside his shock over the presence of Aayu and his father. He looked down at Caio's body and saw his horribly bruised flesh. He looked down at his own skin and saw he was unharmed.

"Stop," he said.

"Don't interfere, Rao," Lucia answered. She pointed her sword, almost directly at him, as she spoke from five paces away.

"We came here to work this out," he said.

"And that's what they are doing," she said.

Devak thrust his spear forward and Vieri dodged sideways. The rajah stabbed forward again and the king blocked with his golden shield, then hammered his weapon down on the rajah's spear. Devak maintained his grip and pulled back again.

"Why?" Rao yelled.

"Until this man is dead," his father said, "your life will never be safe."

Rao checked Lucia. She stood away from the combat, seeming content to let it play out.

"This won't solve anything," Rao said.

Vieri roared as he came toward Devak, hacking down and then pulling back quickly and swinging from over his other shoulder. The rajah held his spear with two hands and blocked the rain of blows, screaming.

Devak swung the butt of his spear forward and jabbed, catching Vieri in the face and opening a wound on his cheek. The king rushed forward and sliced his blade low at the rajah's leg and opened a gash.

Devak stumbled sideways and held his spear in front of his body at an angle to defend himself. The king of Rezzia hacked as he came forward, once, twice, three, four, and five times, finally knocking the giant rajah of Pawelon down onto his backside.

Vieri fell forward, leading with his blade straight down into Devak's gut. Devak expelled a dying bawl and swung his spear once more weakly, cutting across Vieri's shoulder. The rajah's eyes seized up with crippling pain.

Devak dropped his spear and slumped flat against the earth. Blood poured from his midsection, onto the dry desert.

Rao closed his eyes, unable to watch.

He couldn't erase the scene from his mind: the slaying of his invincible father ... his father's gagging, guttural scream.

"Rao!" Lucia yelled.

He opened his eyes. Narayani raced toward the King of Rezzia.

With the king's back turned to her, Narayani picked up Devak's spear and thrust it fully into his back.

The king spun and fell backward, removing his falchion from Devak's body and slicing it across the front of Narayani's neck.

Aayu screamed, "No!"

The king fell to his knees and looked at Lucia before he closed his eyes and slumped forward.

Narayani clutched her neck and crumbled to the ground, convulsing, beside the king.

Their blood spilled onto the ground and ran together.

Rao ran to Narayani. Lucia ran to her father.

Narayani tried to speak. At first, only gurgling came from her throat. Then she said, "Now you'll be safe."

"My love," Rao said as he held her head with both hands.

Narayani clumsily grabbed at Rao's face and mouthed, "I love you."

He kissed her for the last time.

Chapter 83:
The Temple of the Gods

THE SUN'S RAYS shone a deep golden color through the aspens. The Temple of the Gods appeared as Caio remembered from his visions, except for one great difference. The holy structure had been utterly pale and white before. Now each column of the gods' temple shined with vibrant images of The Ten.

He turned his head slowly, taking in the tiny leaves fluttering in the mountain breeze. The air smelled fresh and moist despite the arid climate. Songbirds flew between the trees, filling the air with a ballad of eternal morning.

Caio walked to the high stairs of the temple and studied the colorful marble steps, vibrant shades of yellow. He heard a pleasant hum within the temple and climbed toward its towering, open entrance.

In his visions, the great hall had always been empty, save for the presence of Lord Oderigo. This time it was full of men, women, and children standing in rows, thousands smiling, warm and receptive. Those seated near the aisle held out their hands to him.

He walked the central aisle and gently held one hand after another. Each face brought back vivid memories of lives he had touched with one kindness or another. Some he had healed, some he had comforted as a counselor, some he had prayed with, and others he had made laugh.

He came upon a Pawelon man and held his hands. Caio recognized him as the young man he resurrected. Behind the Pawelon sat a short woman and a dozen Pawelon children.

The entire congregation began to cheer.

"What is this?" Caio leaned in to hear the man speak over the sound of the applause.

"I am still alive on Gallea. You are experiencing my spirit, the spirit of my eventual wife, and the spirits of my future children. We want to thank you."

Caio looked to the third child and somehow recognized him as the boy he saw in his visions, the one who would be a great soul among his people. "You're most welcome."

Ilario, he remembered.

"Your friend who died because I lived," the young Pawelon said, pointing further down the aisle.

Caio turned, greeted by dazzling faces as he walked toward the front row. His old friend's eyes drew all of Caio's attention. They were spinning portals of light.

Caio hurried forward and knelt. He put his hands on Ilario's knees. "Will you ever forgive me for not being able to save you?"

His broad-chested friend didn't move, but looked down with warmth that filled Caio's soul. "From where I am now, forgiveness is not a question. And very soon it will not be an issue for you either."

"How did I get here? Are Lucia and my father all right?"

"Lucia is leading her army back to Rezzia. Your father has taken his final rest."

"Where is he? Can I see him?"

"Not for some time. He must journey through Danato's underworld first."

"What about Narayani, the Pawelon girl?"

Ilario looked over Caio's shoulder.

Caio turned and saw Narayani standing close behind him, more beautiful than any flower, more divine than any mountain range, more magnificent than any sunset.

"What happened?" he asked. "Are you still alive?"

"I died soon after you, Caio."

"How?"

"That doesn't matter." She reached for his hand and lifted Caio to his feet. "We're going to be together now, together forever."

Caio's field of vision became restricted to Ilario's eyes. Their glow deepened, becoming a cone and then a corridor of soft light. He felt himself traveling the dazzling tunnel, holding Narayani's hand. He flew in further, faster, then felt a rush like the cooling sprays of a thousand bright blue oceans.

All that remained was acceptance and love.

Chapter 84: Mother of the Night

Kannauj, Pawelon.

RAO KNOCKED on the rickety, thin wooden door. It seemed to be 'locked' in place by a ratty piece of rope on the inside of the brothel. He looked Aayu in the face. Neither said a word.

"Who goes?" a hoarse woman's voice asked.

"I have money."

"How much?"

"Enough for all of you." Rao smiled at Aayu.

The lady of the house swung the door open, letting out a musty smell tinged with stale liquor. Three dilapidated pink couches covered in white shawls comprised the furniture of the waiting area. A dusty wooden stairwell led up to the second floor, where a hand-carved red railing ran in front of a handful of rooms.

"But I have a request for one in particular," Rao said. "Halima is her name."

"Boy, we've got younger, prettier women. Do you want to see them?"

"No thank you, she is the one we want."

The woman nodded, mainly to herself, and called up the stairs. "Halima! You have two customers." She narrowed her eyes upon Rao. "You don't get a deal for two. It's full price for each of you."

"That's no problem."

The lady held out her hand and took Rao's heavy copper coins. She flashed him a questioning eye before waving them up the stairs.

Rao wore common worker's clothing, oversized grey trousers and a long, scratchy wool shirt that ended above his knees. Aayu wore a matching 'uniform,' with a bulge at his right shoulder from all of his bandages. No one here would recognize them for who they were, not from their dress anyway.

A greying woman stepped out from the door at the end of the walkway. "Come on in."

374

Rao heard what sounded like a heavy man screaming in pleasure as he passed the first door. He increased his pace. "Come on," he said to Aayu, then turned and saw his friend about to break into laughter.

Rao and Aayu entered the room and the lady stood before them in the center of the room on an old rug, peeling off her long gloves.

"Please—" Rao said, holding up both of his hands.

"What sort of pleasures are you looking for?"

"Aunt Halima, it's Aayu. I'm your nephew."

The woman stiffened up like a board and her voice deepened, "Aayu? What are you doing? I am not about to—"

"We're not here for that." Aayu shook his head side to side. "Believe me."

Rao fought back a smile. "We're here to give you something." He produced a copper medallion from his shirt pocket. It had been carved into the form of a sun with seven curving rays streaming out from its center. "This is the highest medal our army can offer."

"Who are you?"

"I'm the Rajah of Pawelon, formerly your prince."

The woman's mouth flew open. Rao took her hand in his and placed the medal in it.

"Why are you giving me this?"

"Because your daughter can't receive it herself. She's dead. But in dying, she saved Pawelon from Rezzia's crusade. She saved my life and slew Rezzia's king."

Narayani's mother scrunched her lips into sour confusion.

"I wanted to make sure you know your daughter was a great soul. She didn't know how to find you while she was alive, but we managed to track you down."

The woman's voice turned weak. "How did she die?"

"The king killed her," Aayu said, "as she killed him."

Halima walked, with legs that seemed ready to crumble, over to her bed. She collapsed onto the heap of colorful, stained pillows.

"There's one other thing," Rao said. "I don't want to impose anything on you. But if you would like to leave behind this lifestyle, I've set up a private residence for you, a few streets away from our palace. If you'd like to, you can live there, and I've also arranged for a stipend so that you will never have to worry about working again. If Narayani had lived, I'm sure she would've wanted something like this for you."

"Was she your lady?"

"Yes. I loved her very much."

"Where is her father?"

"He served the lands of Pawelon with distinction, throughout the course of the war against Rezzia. He has since been released from his duty. I don't know where he is anymore."

Rao produced a small parchment from his pocket and placed it at the edge of her bed. On top of it, he laid down enough coin to pay for ten visits to the brothel and a small metal key. "The address is written there. And that note will get you access to the palace, if you wish to draw your stipend."

He nodded to Aayu and began to leave the room.

"Thank you," she said. "I was in the middle of a terrible time, Aayu, when I left."

"It's all right," Aayu told her.

Rao led the way back down the stairs. The old lady of the house smirked and winked as they approached the front door. "That was fast, gentlemen. That's easy money for my girls. Next time, one of you comes for half the price."

"Hey, it was our first time," Aayu said.

"Sure it was, son. I've heard that one before." She lowered her voice to a whisper. "Don't worry about it. Believe me, it's no problem."

Aayu couldn't seem to stop himself, "To tell the truth, my friend couldn't, you know, get excited. I'm the one who went too fast."

"Don't feel bad about it, son, it's your money," she said as she winked and opened the door.

Rao erupted into laughter as the door closed behind them. The two walked through the dirt alley together, laughing despite their watering eyes.

Chapter 85: In Requie

Remaes, Rezzia.

ONE HUNDRED CONCENTRIC WHITE CIRCLES rose and widened out above her, hardened clay rows of seating filled with countless thousands of grieving pilgrims. Far above, at ground level, ten shaggy palms formed a great circle; their leaves shook in the gentle wind. The bones of kings and Haizzem had been buried here for centuries, but never before had the remains of a Haizzem so young been brought to The Reveria.

Lucia stood in its center, at its lowest level. A hole had been dug in the cracked clay floor. She held two jars of human remains, one painted maroon and yellow, the other green and blue.

The Reveria hummed with quiet prayers the faithful muttered to themselves. The smoke of sweet incense rose to the sky. Lucia looked to silver-haired Tiberio, The Exalted, seated on the first row above her, next to his most powerful warpriests. She awaited the signal to begin. Tiberio brought his hands together in prayer.

Lucia tried to remember the words she wanted to speak. She tried to conceal her own tears, quickly wiping them away with her bare hands and forearms.

I'm tired of hiding.

She released her shoulders, dropped her chin to her chest, and raised her head again as she began to sob. She soon heard her people sobbing with her.

After a long silence, she began to speak.

"A sister should not have to bury her brother along with her father. Men should not die from pestilence. Parents should not lose their children to wars."

Tiberio trained his burning stare on her.

"So I believe. But our gods of Lux Lucis see things we do not. So I pray to them for grace, wisdom, and hope.

"My father believed in his war. My brother did not, not until the final days of his life.

377

"Yet the gods have taken them both."

She felt heat throughout her body. It was difficult to ignore Tiberio's penetrating glare.

"When Caio was himself, he wanted nothing to do with battles. He wanted to love and heal and uplift *all* the people of our world, light skins and dark. His death and my father's death have somehow brought peace back to our kingdom. I only hope the generations of Rezzia to come will remember their sacrifice.

"Perhaps they gave their lives to usher in a new world. It seems the gods did not want Rezzia to be left alone, without a Haizzem. After my brother and father died, the gods painted these markings on my arms."

She held up her red and black palms. Thorny vines worked their way around her forearms, down to her elbows. She grew uncomfortable as the markings began to itch and burn.

Tiberio gritted his teeth as his eyes pushed the heat of the sun into her body. Lucia tried to push herself to finish.

"I did not want this role. I wish my brother and father were still here. But I will fulfill the duty the gods of Lux Lucis have given me, with all the grace they can lend.

"I ask you humbly, to pray for the souls of the lost, the uncounted soldiers, the Strategos, the king, and the young Haizzem. Let us remember them."

She poured the remains of her father into the pit, and then Caio's ashes on top of his.

The Reveria resounded with the chant, "We love and adore Her."

'*'

Exhausted from the funeral, Lucia wrapped herself in white sheets and prayed to her goddess for a peaceful night's sleep. The warm black before her eyes felt soothing.

She dreamt of lying naked on a deserted beach, with her body roasting under the sun's rays and the chaos of the ocean a comforting noise inside her head. The azure sky stretched around the horizon, welcoming her mind's expansion.

The waves tumbled onto the shore, one after another, seeming to panic before crashing down against the sand and sea. The ocean reclaimed each reluctant wave.

She looked down at her normally olive skin and found only pink and red all over her body. She touched near her heart, between her breasts, and a searing burn pained her to her core.

She stood on the hot sands and ran down the slope, finally diving into the ocean.

"My Haizzema." A man's voice woke her.

"What is it?" she said, gathering the sheets about her in the dark. A thin line of candlelight stretched across the clay floor, through the barely open door.

"There is a family here. They claim Lord Danato sent them with something that must be done before the sun rises."

"I'll be right there."

She touched her skin to see if it was warm. It wasn't.

Lucia dressed herself in a presentable long robe and exited her chamber. Five guards stepped right and five stepped left, giving her a view of a tattered family of four, more sufferers of the new plague. The four of them sat with their legs folded and stared down shamefully at the elegant rug. The little boy and girl leaned against their mother, their bare feet twitching.

"My Haizzema, they assured us—"

"It's no problem. Don't worry," she said.

The father lifted his head slightly but kept his gaze downward. "Your Grace, we are dying. Can you grant us the gods' mercy? At least heal our children, if nothing more. Last night my son stopped breathing. We were sure he had died. He's still with us, but for how long? His episodes come at all times. Please."

"Our only son," the mother said with a whimper.

Lucia looked around to see if any tall figures hid among the shadows.

"Can you heal us, my Haizzema?"

The boy, no older than four, fell forward onto his stomach and began choking violently. He fought to suck in air, but his lungs wouldn't expand. His arms flailed as his parents fell to their knees and put their hands on his body.

Lucia ran to the boy and lifted him into her arms. His tiny face flushed with pain and begged her to save him.

Can I heal them?

"I can."

HERE ENDS BOOK I OF *SPLENDOR AND RUIN*
LOOK FOR BOOK II, *THE GODS DIVIDED*, COMING SOON

Afterword

Thanks very much for reading this story.

This is my first novel. It's the first piece of fiction I've written since high school, so I hope it didn't suck. I spent two years writing this one (I had a lot to learn, and still do), but I hope to put out at least a novel a year from now on—maybe three every two years (famous last words?).

I feel incredibly blessed to be following my dream. I want to thank my wife for her support. Believe me, she's tired of hearing me talk about this book. She's a saint. My amazing son, Athens, has been very patient with me, too.

In case you're wondering about the chapter titles, the more obscure titles are allusions to Homer's Iliad, the tale that this story was written in homage to. I also have also a shout-out to Robotech and The Decemberists among the chapter titles. The 85 chapters are there because of my childhood obsession, Robotech, a saga that was also split into three parts of 36, 24, and 25. You see, I'm a geek.

As an indie author, I don't have a publisher or a publicist or a marketing team. I've got me and my computer and a need to figure out how to write my next book (with a fried brain) while promoting this one ... with a second child on the way—which is another thing I'm thrilled about, by the way.

Whether I'll be able to write many more novels, as I'd like to, could depend on whether people enjoy my stories and tell their friends about this crazy Moses guy.

One powerful way to support *any* author is to write honest reviews of his or her books on Amazon, B&N, GoodReads, LibraryThing, Shelfari, etc. Reviews don't have to be long and thoughtful. Even just a couple sentences or a paragraph can do the trick. But if you write a review, please be honest. You don't have to use the kid gloves with me. Although, mean reviews will make me pee my pants.

Another amazing thing you can do is to drop me a line and let me know what you thought about this book. I'd love to hear what you liked about it and what you think I can do better in my next novel, which should be the next book in this series, *The Gods Divided* (Splendor and Ruin, Book II). If you'd like, I can also add you to my newsletter list, so that I can let you know about future releases. My email is MosesMerlin@hotmail.com. If you don't get a response within a few days, that probably means I didn't see your email, so feel free to write me again.

You can also follow my blog at www.ScienceFictionFantasyBooks.net and subscribe to email announcements of new blog posts, as well as my newsletter.

And if we never chat or meet in this lifetime, that's cool, too. My biggest goal as a writer is to inspire my readers to pursue their own passions, while pursuing my own. Now please, go forth and rock some worlds.

Speaking of rock, I don't think I could've written this book without loud music blaring in my face. Or if I could've, the journey wouldn't have been nearly as much fun. I'll mention some of the music I listened to in the Acknowledgements.

Thanks again. Reading this book was the greatest gift you could ever give me. From my heart, I appreciate it.

Acknowledgments

My three editors: D.P. (Derek) Prior (a.k.a. "the fount of knowledge") has probably done more to help me improve this book than anyone else; Joshua Essoe gave me some of the most brilliant suggestions I got about the novel, in addition to helping me with countless smaller issues; and Jillian Sheridan helped me tremendously with her incredible language skills. Anne "Arkali" Victory was an outstanding proofreader.

Brandon Sanderson read my first chapter in early 2010 and gave me some priceless advice. David Farland read my manuscript at one of his workshops and helped me tremendously. K.C. May and Penelope Schenk went above and beyond the call of duty as beta readers.

Here are some other people and websites I'd like to thank:

AbsoluteWrite, Authonomy, Chuck Taylor, Clancy Metzger, Colette Vernon, Colton Goodrich, Craig Saunders, Critters.org, D.T. Conklin, Damien Stolarz, David Anthony Durham, David Dalglish, David Kerschner, Debra L. Martin, Evan Braun, Grace Siregar, Jan Bird, J.A. Konrath, Jared Blando, Jessica Billings, Kevin J Anderson, Kylie Quillinan, Laura Resnick, Leah Petersen, Leigh Galbreath, Lenny Gredel, Libbie Mistretta, Lou Anders, Mark Phillips, Michael Tobias Herbert, Miranda Suri, Molly Siregar, Monique Martin, Nikki Neal, Rich W. Ware, Rinn Falconer, Scott Nicholson, Shaun Farrell, Steven Forrest, Tania Gilchrist, T.M. Roy, William Campbell, and Zoe Winters.

The writing of this story was powered by the album *The Hazards of Love* by The Decemberists. The editing was powered mainly by *Black Symphony* by Within Temptation. I also listened to this playlist a lot:

1. Lose Yourself, Eminem
2. Hurt, Johnny Cash
3. No Quarter (Live), Led Zeppelin
4. Grux, Dave Matthews Band
5. Shake Me Like a Monkey, Dave Matthews Band
6. Bard's Curse, Kit Soden
7. Won't Want for Love (Margaret in the Taiga), The Decemberists
8. Boy With a Coin, Iron & Wine
9. Catch and Release, Silversun Pickups
10. Joni(Stardust), Jozef Slanda
11. Different World, Iron Maiden
12. The Pilgrim, Iron Maiden
13. The Reincarnation of Benjamin Breeg, Iron Maiden

I want to say thank you to these musicians and to the muses who inspired them.

To make my playlist for book 2, I asked for song suggestions on my blog, on Twitter, and on Facebook. That effort turned up 20 amazing songs. If you want to see the playlist for book 2, see my blog post on 7/28/11:

http://sciencefictionfantasybooks.net/?p=1902

About the Author

When I was ten, I fell in love with an anime series: a space opera spanning three human generations, a saga that unfolded over 85 consecutive episodes and four months of after-school TV. Watching *Robotech* was a spiritual experience for me. I still remember how high I felt after watching the final episode for the first time. How many pleasures in life are better than a well-executed drama?

After that experience, I decided I wanted to be a storyteller when I grew up, hoping to someday inspire others as *Robotech* inspired me. Although I've written professionally and for pleasure over the years, it wasn't until recently that I got back to my heart's desire when I was a boy: telling the big story.

I've never had so much fun.